BLOODSTORM

TRICKED, POSSESSED AND manipulated by the foul daemon Tz'arkan, can things get any worse for the dark elf Malus Darkblade? However, when he returns to Hag Graef he discovers to his horror that he is homeless, penniless – and his father has become his most deadly enemy.

Barely escaping with his life, Malus must now seek the next artefact Tz'arkan requires – the Idol of Kolkuth. The sea voyage is perilous enough, but some of the most dangerous enemies Darkblade must deal with are his own family as he struggles to reach the sorcerous tower that holds the idol.

TOP-SELLING BLACK Library author Dan Abnett teams up with rising star Mike Lee to pen another tale of cruelty, battle and deception featuring the ultimate antihero, Malus Darkblade.

More Dan Abnett from the Black Library

A WARHAMMER NOVEL

BLOODSTORM

A Tale of Malus Darkblade

DAN ABNETT & MIKE LEE

A Black Library Publication

First published in Great Britain in 2005 by
BL Publishing,
Games Workshop Ltd.,
Willow Road, Nottingham,
NG7 2WS, UK

10 9 8 7 6 5 4 3 2 1

Cover illustration by Clint Langley.
Map by Nuala Kinrade.

A CIP record for this book is available from the British Library.

ISBN 13: 978 1 84416 192 8
ISBN 10: 1 84416 192 7

Distributed in the US by Simon & Schuster
1230 Avenue of the Americas, New York, NY 10020.

Printed and bound in Great Britain by
Bookmarque, Surrey, UK.

See the Black Library on the Internet at
www.blacklibrary.com

Find out more about Games Workshop
and the world of Warhammer at
www.games-workshop.com

THIS IS A DARK age, a bloody age, an age of daemons and of sorcery. It is an age of battle and death, and of the world's ending. Amidst all of the fire, flame and fury it is a time, too, of mighty heroes, of bold deeds and great courage.

AT THE HEART of the Old World sprawls the Empire, the largest and most powerful of the human realms. Known for its engineers, sorcerers, traders and soldiers, it is a land of great mountains, mighty rivers, dark forests and vast cities. And from his throne in Altdorf reigns the Emperor Karl-Franz, sacred descendant of the founder of these lands, Sigmar, and wielder of his magical warhammer.

BUT THESE ARE far from civilised times. Across the length and breadth of the Old World, from the knightly palaces of Bretonnia to ice-bound Kislev in the far north, come rumblings of war. In the towering World's Edge Mountains, the orc tribes are gathering for another assault. Bandits and renegades harry the wild southern lands of the Border Princes. There are rumours of rat-things, the skaven, emerging from the sewers and swamps across the land. And from the northern wildernesses there is the ever-present threat of Chaos, of daemons and beastmen corrupted by the foul powers of the Dark Gods. As the time of battle draws ever nearer, the Empire needs heroes like never before.

NAGGAROTH

Karond Kar

Sea of
Chill

The Monoliths

Granite Hills

Hotek's Column

Black Forests

Clar Karond

N

Vaul's Anvil

Doom
Glades

Sea of
Serpents

Grasslands

Arnheim

Chapter One
PRODIGAL

THE NAUGLIR LET out a hiss like hot steel quenched in blood, its muscular legs pumping furiously as the huge reptile scrambled around the narrow turn. Clots of snow and black cinders sprayed from beneath the cold one's claws and Malus Darkblade twisted in the saddle as he fought to keep his seat. Sibilant shouts echoed in the cold air behind Malus, rising over the thunder of hooves. A crossbow bolt buzzed past his ear like an angry hornet. The highborn bared his teeth in a feral grin as he regained his balance and put the spurs to Spite's flanks once more. Just ahead the Spear Road fell away into the dreadful Valley of Shadow and in the distance he could spy the knifelike towers of Hag Graef rising from the clinging tendrils of last night's fog.

Another bolt whipped a hand span from the highborn's face – then a third slammed like a hammer blow between Malus's shoulders. The broad, steel head of the crossbow bolt punched through the thick cloak of crudely stitched beastman hide Malus wore and slapped into the backplate of his armour with a flat *crack*. The silver steel plate and the thick leather kheitan beneath robbed the shot of much of its lethal force, but the bolt's tip tore into his back like a talon of ice. The highborn let out a wordless snarl of pain and bent as low as he could against Spite's heaving back. The gang of brigands galloping in Malus's wake let out a chorus of savage cries as they sensed the chase was nearly at an end.

It had been nearly three months since Malus and his retainers had slipped from Hag Graef and headed north, hunting a source of ancient power hidden in the Chaos Wastes. This was not the triumphant return he'd dreamt of all those months ago.

Countless leagues of snow and blood and starvation had left their mark on rider and mount. The cold one's scaly, armoured hide bore dozens of scars from sword, axe and claw, and Malus's saddle was cinched tightly over sharply etched ribs. The highborn's cloak of coarse, greasy black fur was tattered and rent and the silver steel armour beneath was tarnished and scarred from constant wear. His robes and kheitan were stiff with old sweat, blood and grime and his boots were patched with rags and scraps of deer hide. Malus's dark eyes were sunken and fever-bright, his cruel features paler and even more sharply defined. With hollow cheeks and thin, cracked lips, he seemed more wight than man.

Death had dogged his path from the moment his journey began. Every retainer who'd ridden from the Hag into the tainted north had died there, some by Malus's own hand. Yet he hadn't returned from the Wastes empty-handed: four large saddlebags bounced heavily on Spite's gaunt flanks, bulging with a Drachau's ransom in gold and gems.

Nor had he returned entirely alone.

Spite plunged down the long, steep slope toward the valley floor and for a moment the sounds of pursuit fell away on the far side of the ridge. Malus reached back and drew his crossbow from its saddle hook. His path back to Hag Graef had been fraught with peril: packs of fierce beastmen, twisted, Chaos-tainted monsters and gangs of druchii thieves had all sought to spill his blood, hungry for his flesh or the bags of treasure at his side. The highborn's sword was notched and pitted and his bolts were nearly spent. 'I didn't come all this way to die within sight of home,' Malus swore, calling on every blasphemous god he could name.

'Then kill them,' a cold voice replied, welling up in Malus's chest like blood from an old wound. 'There are but eight of them, little druchii. Let your cold one feast on their sallow flesh.'

Malus snarled, resisting an urge to pound at his breast with a gauntleted hand. 'Bold words from a daemon, who knows nothing of hunger or fatigue.'

'You have your hate, Malus,' the daemon Tz'arkan whispered, the words buzzing in his skull like flies. 'With hate, all things are possible.'

'If that were true I would have been rid of you long ago,' the highborn seethed, working the arming lever on the crossbow and readying it to fire. 'Now shut up and let me concentrate.'

He could feel the daemon's consciousness recede, his bones vibrating with Tz'arkan's mocking laughter. There were times, late in the night, when Malus would awaken and feel the daemon writhing within his chest like a clutch of vipers, slithering and tangling around his beating heart.

Desperation had driven him north, seeking power to use against his enemies. He sought the power to thwart the schemes of his father and his siblings, to bathe in their blood and drink deeply of their pain. And he'd found what he sought in a temple far to the north, standing before a great crystal surrounded by circle after circle of magical wards and the piled riches of a dozen kingdoms. Giddy with power-lust and ravenous greed, Malus had been oblivious to the cunning trap surrounding him. The highborn had plucked a single ring from the treasure heaped in the room – a perfect ruby cabochon, like a shimmering drop of blood – and had slipped it on his finger. And the terrible daemon bound within the crystal had claimed Darkblade's soul in return.

The steel bowstring locked into place and one of Malus's last bolts was levered into the firing channel. Spite had nearly reached the base of the slope as the first of the druchii brigands crested the ridgeline with a lupine howl. Malus twisted in the saddle and fired with an ease born from months of experience. The black-fletched bolt struck the brigand below the ribcage, piercing the rusted mail the druchii wore and tearing upwards through his vitals before lodging in the man's spine. The brigand's howl cut off with a choked cry and he toppled backwards out of the saddle.

Tall stands of darkpine and witchwood rose from the dark soil of the valley floor, their branches heavy with snow. Perpetual twilight reigned beneath the trees; in the narrow confines of the valley the sun's light reached the city and its surroundings for a few short hours each day. The Spear Road wound a sinuous course among the copses of trees, but Malus spurred his mount directly ahead, off the road and into the shadowy wood.

Malus bent low against Spite's neck as the nauglir crashed through low-hanging branches and leapt the rotting boles of fallen trees. Speed was of the essence. The thieves had been as patient as wolves, tracking him for days and gauging his strength. Now they knew he and his mount were almost spent and they knew that the safety of the city walls was less than a mile away. If they didn't pull him down in the next few minutes they would be cheated of their prize.

Sure enough, shouts and muffled hoof beats echoed across the snowy ground behind Malus. The highborn readied his crossbow and twisted at the waist, aiming backwards one-handed at the black shapes darting between the trees. He fired out of instinct and caught one of the brigands' horses in mid-turn – the animal lost its footing with a terrible shriek and crashed to the ground in a spray of dirt and snow, throwing its rider into a stand of fallen timber. Two of the bandits fired their weapons in response and a bolt struck a fan of bright sparks as it glanced from Malus's left pauldron. The blow knocked the highborn forwards – and his crossbow was smashed from his hands by a pine bough.

Pine needles lashed at the side of Malus's face and then suddenly the trees fell away on either side and Spite was lunging through drifts of piled snow. The cold one was losing speed rapidly. Ahead the black ribbon of the Spear Road crossed a narrow, snowy field and less than a quarter of a mile away loomed his home, the great City of Shadow. 'The race is nearly won, beast of the deep earth,' Malus rasped to his mount. 'A few more furlongs and then we will see how brave these dogs are.' As if understanding the highborn's words, Spite put on a final burst of speed, charging across the open ground for the basalt walls of the city ahead.

Malus drew his sword, holding it high in hopes of catching the attention of the men on the ramparts. The thunder of hoof beats brought his head around – the five remaining bandits had emerged from the woods and were lashing at their horses' flanks with whip and spur. Their pale faces stood out sharply against the dark background of the hooded cloaks they wore. Their eyes were intent, teeth bared against the icy wind.

The bandits were gaining ground, but slowly, too slowly. Malus was halfway to the city walls within moments and could spy the tall helmets of the city guard rising above the spiked battlements of the gatehouse. 'Open the gate!' he cried, with all the strength he could muster. If the guardsmen heard, they gave no sign.

Spite leapt onto the roadway, flat feet crunching across the pressed layer of cinders. Malus caught sight of several stubby poles with black fletching jutting at an angle from the frozen ground – the heavy bolts the city guard had fired at him months ago still lay where they had fallen, perhaps left as a warning to future travellers. He was less than a hundred paces from the tall city gates, yet the portal remained shut.

Malus hurled a torrent of curses at the guards on the battlements, hauling back on Spite's reins to stop the beast's headlong rush. The gate wasn't going to open in time – if at all.

The wounded nauglir stumbled to a halt right in front of the tall doors. Malus hauled on the reins and brought the beast sharply around, then lashed out at the dark iron with an armoured boot. 'Open the gates you low-born worms!' Malus roared.

Then the air around the highborn was filled with the angry buzz of man-made hornets. Three crossbow bolts shattered against the city's iron gates and two more struck Malus in the back. One bolt tore through his heavy cloak and skimmed the druchii's backplate with a harsh, clattering sound, while the second punched through his cloak, his left pauldron and part of the backplate it overlapped. Malus felt a stabbing pain in his shoulder and threw himself instinctively to the ground, taking shelter between Spite's bulk and the gate.

The sound of hooves had stopped. Spite turned his head to face his attackers, managing a weak hiss. Malus chanced a quick look over the nauglir's hindquarters. The bandits had reined in, right in the middle of the road, eyeing the city's gatehouse and debating their chances. The highborn could feel blood staining his robes and seeping down his back. 'Why aren't they opening the damned gate,' he muttered fiercely. 'Why aren't they shooting at these curs?'

'Biding their time, perhaps,' Tz'arkan said, faintly amused. 'The bandits kill you, they kill the bandits and then they have six bodies to loot.'

'I wouldn't sound so smug, daemon,' Darkblade said through gritted teeth. He planted the point of his sword in the ground and groped over his shoulder, trying to pull the crossbow bolts free from his back. 'There are five of them and I'm down to sword and knife. If they put a bolt through my eye, how will you ever escape that cursed temple?'

'Do not fear for me, Darkblade,' the daemon said. 'I have waited thousands of years in my prison and I can wait thousands more if I must. You should worry about the consequences if you fail me and I claim your soul for eternity. But that need not happen. These fools are fodder for your blade, if you allow me to lend you a little strength.'

Malus clenched his fists. The daemon had claimed him in the temple for one reason only – to be free from the prison he'd been bound into millennia ago. Darkblade was his agent in the world of mortals, seeking the keys that would unlock the magical wards trapping Tz'arkan in his crystal cell. And for all that the daemon threatened him with eternal torment, Tz'arkan was quick to lend the highborn a measure of his power when things took a turn for the worse.

There had been several times on the long journey home when Malus had been forced to accept Tz'arkan's gifts: knitting torn flesh and broken bone, staving off fever or frostbite or giving him unearthly speed and strength in battle. Each time, when the tide of unearthly power faded, it felt as though the daemon's taint had spread a little further through his body, strengthening Tz'arkan's hold over him.

And yet, Malus thought, did he dare refuse?

Suddenly the sound of hoof beats thundered through the air and Malus heard Spite utter a warning hiss. 'All right,' the highborn seethed. 'Lend me your strength one last time, daemon.'

'One last time,' the daemon answered mockingly. 'Of course.'

The power hit like a rush of black, icy water, racing through his body in a torrent that made every muscle strain at its fleshy bonds. Malus's head snapped back, his mouth dropping open in a wordless snarl. He could feel the veins on his face and neck writhe like serpents, pulsing with corruption. When his vision cleared, his senses were sharp and the world had slowed to a turgid crawl. The sound of the oncoming horses was like the slow, purposeful beat of a temple drum.

The bandits came forward in a rush, hoping to kill their prey swiftly and escape before the guards on the walls changed their mind. Malus heard two riders split off to the right, towards Spite's head, while the other three circled wide around the cold one's tail. Grinning like a wolf, Malus raced at the trio to his left.

Once again, the highborn was amazed at the way he raced across the ground, his steps so swift and light they didn't seem to actually touch the earth at all. He was on the brigands before they knew it, their attention focused on Spite and his deadly tail. The first horse caught wind of Malus and let out a terrified shriek, its eyes rolling back in its head with fear as it sensed the daemon inside him. It tossed its head and tried to back away, and Malus leapt in and sliced through its reins with a flick of his wrist. The animal reared and the rider lost his seat, tumbling backwards onto the road. Before he could recover, Malus buried his blade in the bandit's neck, spraying a jet of bright crimson across the churned snow.

A crossbow bolt droned lazily past his head. Malus turned in time to see the second bandit hurl the empty crossbow at his face. He batted the weapon aside with his sword and rushed forward, savouring the dawning horror in the bandit's eyes as the brigand tried to draw his sword in time. Malus's sword flashed, severing the bandit's right leg at the knee. Druchii and horse screamed alike and the bandit fell beneath the horse's hooves as the animal bolted, fleeing Malus's daemonic visage.

Malus heard another horse scream then saw the third bandit yank savagely on his reins and kick his lathered mount into a gallop, racing back down the road. The remaining two brigands joined him, frantically lashing at their horses' flanks.

They were about ten yards from the gate when the bolt throwers on top of the walls went into action. The metal strings snapped and sang and bolts three feet long streaked through the clear air piercing man and horse. As the bodies tumbled across the snowy ground Malus fell to his knees, guts heaving as the daemon's power leached from his body. He retched black bile onto the cinder-covered road and heard the sound of chains as the city guard began to winch open the great gates.

A small spark of something akin to panic welled up in Malus's brain. Control, he thought fiercely, trying to overcome his helpless nausea. Push back the daemon. Hide his traces…

There was no sin in Naggaroth save weakness: the Witch King commanded the fealty of conquerors and slave masters – anything less was prey. Malus well knew that if his people discovered Tz'arkan's hold over him they would slaughter him out of hand. It did not matter that the daemon's gifts made him the equal of any ten druchii – the fact that he'd allowed himself to fall into Tz'arkan's trap and become the daemon's slave made him unfit to live.

Over the long months in the wilderness Malus had struggled to master the telltale signs of daemonic influence that warped his thin frame. With an effort of extreme will, he slowed his racing heart, causing the black veins to recede from his neck and face. His skin, a chalky bluish-white, smoothed into a uniform alabaster tone. As the first of the guards charged out onto the road Malus wiped bile from his lips and forced himself to rise without the slightest sign of his exertions.

The armoured guardsmen of the city raced from the gateway, long knives gleaming in their hands. Spite raised his head from the carcass of one of the brigand's horses and roared a warning at the interlopers, his blocky snout smeared with blood and scraps of flesh. The warriors ignored both Malus and his mount, inspecting each of the brigands in turn and slitting their throats with quick, expert knife strokes, then searching the bodies for valuables. The highborn headed back towards Spite, keeping a wary distance until the nauglir had eaten his fill of horseflesh.

'Two dead and the rest put to flight in as much time as it takes to tell of it,' said a voice from the shadows of the city gate. 'A most impressive display, dread lord. Your time in the wilderness has suited you well, if I may be so bold.'

Malus turned at the sound of the voice, his fist clenching around the hilt of his sword. A guard captain stepped into the light, clad in fine armour and wearing a silver-chased sword at his hip. There was a wry look in the captain's dark eyes that Malus didn't care for one bit. There was something familiar about the man.

'Bold words from a craven captain,' Malus hissed, 'who hid behind stone walls while I fought alone. When the Vaulkhar hears of it you and your children's lives will be forfeit.'

Malus expected the man to quail at the words, but instead the captain smiled faintly and his dark eyes shone with cruel mirth. The highborn fought the urge to bury his knife in the man's mocking eyes – remembering who he was talking to. It was the same captain he'd bribed to escape the city months ago. His face had picked up a few new scars in the meantime, but judging by his new armour he'd clearly put Malus's gift to good use.

The captain stepped from beneath the gate arch and approached the highborn. 'You are of course free to make your complaint to your father the Vaulkhar,' he said calmly, 'but I don't think it would be a pleasant reunion, dread lord. In fact, it could be a fatal one.'

Malus studied the captain with narrowed eyes. 'And how would you know such a thing?'

'Because there is a standing order for the city guard – issued by both your father and the Drachau himself – that Malus, son of Lurhan, is to be arrested on sight and delivered to the Vaulkhar's tower.' The captain smiled. 'Does your father always treat his children like criminals, dread lord?'

The captain's audacity was breathtaking – but it was a carefully calculated ploy, Malus saw. The man was nothing if not ambitious.

Malus stepped closer to the captain. 'So you kept the gates closed as a favour to me, then?'

'Of course, dread lord. If I'd sounded the alarm and opened the gates, the commander of the watch would have to be informed and that would have necessitated your arrest.' The captain glanced around at his men. 'At the moment I'm just giving my men a break while I discuss business with a noble acquaintance.'

Malus grinned mirthlessly. 'Indeed?'

The captain nodded. 'Certainly. I know very well what your father and the Drachau are offering for your arrest. I'm curious to know what you'd offer to avoid that unfortunate fate.'

The highborn stared at the captain and began to laugh. It was a harsh, bloodless sound that drained the amusement from the captain's face. 'As I seem to recall I promised you a reward when I returned to Hag Graef,' Malus said. 'Allow me into the city, captain and I shall double it.'

'Is that so?' The captain considered Malus carefully, weighing the risks. Malus could see the avarice in the man's expression. 'I'll take the payment now if it please you, dread lord.'

'Are you certain that's wise, with all these men around? They'll want a cut, too and then where will you be?' The highborn took a step closer and spoke in a conspiratorial whisper. 'Do you know of a flesh house in the Corsairs' Quarter called the House of Brass?'

'I know of it,' the captain said warily.

'Then I have a favour to ask of you. Carry a message to Silar Thornblood – he is one of my sworn men – and tell him to meet me there this evening. You will find him at my tower in the Hag. Accompany him tonight and I will see you amply rewarded for your efforts.'

The captain cocked his head suspiciously. 'My dread lord is a cruel and canny man,' he said. 'So you understand if I have reason to believe this is some sort of deception.'

Malus grinned. It was hard not to admire such brazenness. 'Do I dare deceive you captain? If I do, you report me to my father and I can't have that.'

The captain thought it over for a moment, gauging the odds. 'Very well,' he said evenly. 'I will look forward to our rendezvous, then. What message shall I deliver?'

'Say that his lord is returned from the Wastes,' Malus said. 'That will tell him all he needs to know.'

THE HOUSE OF Brass was a den of pleasures that catered to highborn druchii in a seedier district of the city. Malus knew the proprietor well, having spent entire nights in one of the private suites entertaining disreputable guests and would-be allies. It was one of the first places the Vaulkhar's men would think to look if they knew he'd returned to the city, but he was certain that Mistress Nemeira knew him well enough that she'd never dare betray him. The House of Brass was a maze of chambers and narrow corridors – some hidden behind concealed doors and wall panels – that occupied half a city block at the border between the Corsairs' Quarter and the Slavers' Quarter. There were even secret escape routes from the building that supposedly led outside the city walls; Nemeira charged extra for their use.

Malus took another sip of wine and settled deeper into a mound of thick cushions. The room was decorated in the autarii style, with piles of thick rugs and pillows laid around braziers in a rough cloverleaf pattern around a circular hearth. His grimy, ragged clothes and kheitan had been taken away – to be burned immediately, Nemeira had said sternly – and his ravaged armour had been carried off to be mended by an armourer the proprietor knew well. After a long, scalding bath and vigorous scrubbing by two attendants, he'd changed into robes of rich silk and ordered the best wine the house could provide.

Weariness pulled at him with ever-strengthening fingers. Since the brigands had picked up his trail a few days before there had been precious few opportunities to sleep and no chance to forage for food. Exhaustion threatened to overwhelm him even as his mind roiled with suspicion.

There was a light scratching at the door. Malus set his wine aside, his right hand straying to the sword lying on the rug beside him. 'Enter,' he said.

The door opened silently and a human slave entered, head bowed and eyes downcast. 'Your guests have arrived and await your pleasure, dread lord,' she said softly. 'Will you see them?'

'Bring them in, then fetch wine and food from the kitchen,' Malus answered.

Now we'll have some answers, he thought. And a bit of pleasant diversion afterwards. He'd had hours to contemplate the long list of excruciations he would inflict on that upstart captain. It would be a fine way to celebrate his return to Hag Graef.

In moments the door opened again to admit three druchii. Silar Thornblood entered first, his tall frame slightly stooped due to the chamber's low ceiling. The young druchii wore full armour and his hand rested warily on the hilt of his sword. Behind him slipped a dark shadow wrapped in a heavy, hooded cloak. As the figure stepped into the light of the nearest brazier, Malus caught sight of Arleth Vann's pale, cadaverous face. His eyes glinted golden in the firelight, as cold and merciless as the stare of a hungry wolf. The last to enter was the guard captain, who eyed the room's luxurious furnishings with an equal mixture of suspicion and desire.

Silar caught sight of Malus and his expression changed from one of wariness to genuine surprise. 'When the captain sought me out I was sure this had to be some trick,' the young druchii said.

Malus rose, accepting Silar's formal bow. 'Well met, Silar – and you, Arleth Vann,' the highborn said, nodding his head to the hooded druchii. 'Though I'm curious why both of you elected to come.'

'I had to be certain we weren't followed,' Silar replied, his expression turning grim. 'Obviously you've heard about the warrant for your arrest. The Vaulkhar has his eye on us night and day, hoping we will lead him to you.'

Before Malus could reply, the guard captain took a step forward. 'Forgive me, dread lord, but I have no wish to intrude on you further. If we could conclude our business now, I'll be on my way.'

'Intrusion? There is no intrusion, captain,' Malus said easily. 'You have done me a great favour and you are my guest this evening.' He gestured at the cushions. 'Sit. We have much to discuss and I've been without stimulating company for quite some time.' He fixed the druchii with a hard stare. 'I insist.'

Malus's two retainers turned to regard the captain and the enterprising druchii's face went pale as he realised the snare he'd stepped in. 'I… yes… of course,' he said uneasily.

'Excellent,' the highborn said. 'I regret that I can't share the hospitality of my own apartments, captain, but I expect that my half-brother Urial has taken out his frustrations on them in my absence, eh, Silar?'

Silar turned to Malus, his brow furrowing in concern. 'You mean you haven't heard?'

Malus's good humour faded. 'Heard what?'

Without a word, Silar pointed to the hadrilkar around his neck. It was not the silver steel that Malus was familiar with, but pure silver, worked in the sigil of the Vaulkhar himself.

'Your tower has been confiscated by your father, along with all the property within,' Silar said, his voice grave. 'He has claimed your retainers, your slaves – everything. You've been disowned, cast out of the Vaulkhar's household.'

Chapter Two
THE FORSWORN

'DISOWNED?' MALUS'S MIND reeled at the thought. 'Why would my father do such a thing?'

'It's your own fault,' Silar replied flatly.

The guard captain's eyes went wide at Silar's thoughtless honestly and from his expression it was clear he expected Silar's head to go bouncing across the carpets at any moment. 'I told you that torturing the Naggorite hostage was reckless.'

'Fuerlan?' Malus spat. 'What does that toad have to do with any of this? He laid hands on me – *me* – in the Court of Thorns and dared to presume my acquaintance. I was well within my rights to *kill* him for such an affront.' The highborn folded his arms and glared at Silar. 'His excruciations were complex and intricate. They were a gift. If the fool had any sense of honour he would thank me for what I did.'

'Except that Fuerlan is a hostage. He's the Drachau's property and the Drachau is the one responsible for his punishment.' Silar spread his hands. 'Can you not see the political implications? It is an affront to Naggor at the very least.'

Malus shot Silar a venomous glare. 'So the Drachau reacted poorly to Fuerlan's torture.'

'He ordered your father to kill you with his own hands,' Silar replied. 'I expect it was the best way he could think of to avoid the threat of the Witch King's wrath. Balneth Bale couldn't very well demand justice if his most bitter foe had already taken steps to deal with the matter.'

Malus considered the problem. 'So when the Vaulkhar couldn't find me in the city, he confiscated my property?'

Silar smiled ruefully. 'Remember the nobles who invested in your slave raid? The ones who lost a sizeable fortune when your stock were slaughtered outside Clar Karond? They all got together and called their debts due a few days after you left. And since you were gone, they were able to petition your father instead. He settled your debt and disowned you by claiming your property to cover his loss. Now do you see what one reckless act has caused?'

'I do, indeed,' Malus answered coldly, his patience at an end. 'And I would do it again under the same circumstances. That's my privilege as a highborn, Silar. Do not forget that.'

Silar bowed his head. 'Of course, dread lord. I only wish to show you the depth of the problem you've returned to.'

The highborn laughed bitterly. 'It is more tangled than you know, Silar Thornblood. At least now I don't have to worry about assassins from the Temple of Khaine since my father has covered my debt.'

'Not so, my lord,' Arleth Vann spoke, the thin whisper rising from the shadows at the far end of the room. The former temple assassin sought out the shadows instinctively, like cleaving to like. 'The debt of blood still stands between you and the Lord of Murder.'

'But that makes no sense!' Malus shouted, his temper rising. 'My former allies have been repaid – why would they continue to keep Khaine's worshippers hounding my trail?'

'When our slave stock was wiped out several months ago, we assumed that your former backers hired the services of the temple to punish you for your failure,' Arleth Vann continued. 'I think perhaps we were too hasty in making that assumption. The nobles you chose to back your slave raid were picked specifically because they had little influence but moderate fortunes and ambition. And you ensured that each of these nobles invested the vast majority of their influence and funds in your enterprise to guarantee their continued support.'

Malus felt the slither of invisible snakes across his heart. 'What a tangled web you've woven, Darkblade,' the daemon chuckled. 'I've never seen a spider ensnare itself so tightly. Perhaps I made a mistake when I chose you as my saviour.'

'If you doubt my abilities then leave me and let the Outer Darkness take you!' Malus hissed – then stiffened, realising he had spoken aloud. Silar bristled, his eyes shining with suppressed anger, while Arleth Vann's face remained a pale, implacable mask. The highborn strode swiftly to where his wine cup sat and took a long swallow.

'So now you believe these nobles didn't approach the temple after all?' Malus said sharply.

'No, my lord,' Arleth Vann replied. 'I made a number of enquiries after you left for the Wastes and it appears that you chose your backers very well indeed – several of them invested more than they could truly afford and were on the verge of ruin when our enterprise failed. Even if they had combined whatever coin they had left, it would not have been enough to secure the temple's assistance. Someone else is responsible for the blood debt – and continues to maintain it even now.'

Malus went to take another drink from his cup and discovered that he'd already drained it dry. With a supreme effort he controlled the urge to hurl the cup across the room. 'So,' he said, setting the cup carefully on the floor, 'after three months travelling to the Chaos Wastes and back, I've returned home to find that I'm an outcast, the city guard has orders to arrest me on sight and the Drachau, my father the Vaulkhar *and* the Temple of Khaine are all actively trying to kill me.'

For a long moment, no one spoke. The guard captain glanced longingly at the door, suddenly very uncomfortable. Silar and Arleth Vann exchanged looks. 'That… would be an accurate assessment,' Silar said hesitantly. 'I trust the expedition to the Wastes went well?'

'Dead, my lord? *All* of them?' Silar regarded Malus with a look of shock and horror combined.

The house servants had come and gone, leaving plates of spiced foods and fresh bottles of wine. Malus was already on his third cup. The warmth of the wine seemed to fill the empty feeling in his chest and still the shifting coils of the daemon within. 'We knew when we set out that the journey was not without risk,' the high-born said grimly, his mind filled with disquieting images of the fight outside the temple.

'What was in the temple, lord?' Arleth Vann inquired. He sat cross-legged to Malus's left, his hands resting easily on his knees. The former acolyte had touched neither food nor wine. 'Did you find the source of power you sought?'

Dimly, Malus could feel Tz'arkan stirring in his breast. The highborn leaned back, bringing the bottle to his lips. 'Another piece of the puzzle,' he replied. 'There was power there, but I haven't the means to unlock it yet. I lack the keys, which brings me back to Hag Graef.'

'The keys are here?' Silar said, frowning.

'It is possible they no longer exist at all,' Malus said darkly. 'But then we thought the same thing about the temple itself. There are four arcane relics I must unearth before I can unlock the power in the temple and I have less than a year to find them.'

'Less than a year?' The guard captain asked, intrigued in spite of himself. He had appropriated a bottle of his own when the servants arrived, but had otherwise laboured to avoid catching anyone's notice.

'Yes,' Malus answered, biting back a surge of irritation. 'If I cannot unlock the wards in the temple within the space of a year, my... claim is forfeit.'

The highborn heard the daemon's voice whisper mockingly, but the sound was too faint to hear over the buzzing in his head. Malus chuckled. 'If this keeps up I may stay drunk for the next nine months!'

Silence fell over the druchii. Malus caught Silar and Arleth Vann's worried glances and realised he'd thought aloud once more. 'Think nothing of my mutterings,' the highborn said with a casual wave of his hand. 'I spent one too many months alone in the Wastes with nothing but my own voice for company.'

Malus took another drink, then straightened and set the bottle carefully on the carpet. 'Time is of the essence. I must gain access to an arcane library and begin searching for references to these relics, which means that I need to contact my sister Nagaira. This also means I will require trusted agents to be my hands and eyes in the Hag and elsewhere in the city.'

Silar nodded, looking at the floor. 'We have not forgotten our oaths to you, my lord,' he answered. 'But we must now answer to the Vaulkhar as well.'

'Not so,' the guard captain said.

Malus raised an eyebrow. 'And how is that?'

The guard captain paused a moment, collecting his thoughts and drawing a little more courage from the bottle clasped in his hands. 'Oaths of fealty are paramount,' he began. 'Not even the Witch King himself can usurp a druchii's oath of service to another. So long as you live and your retainers haven't forsworn their oaths, the Vaulkhar can't claim them as his own. He *can* claim to command them in your absence, since you owe fealty to him as father and Vaulkhar and aren't here to contest ownership.'

'And that isn't likely to change, so long as I want to keep my head attached to my neck,' Malus growled.

'True – but you can designate a representative to act as your executor,' the captain said, offering a faint smile. 'A signed writ presented to the Vaulkhar would free your retainers from his control.'

Malus regarded the man with narrowed eyes. Was there no end to his temerity? 'And who would you suggest assume this role?'

The captain smiled. 'I would consider it an honour to serve, dread lord.'

'Despite the fact that the two most powerful highborn in Hag Graef want me dead and the Temple of Khaine besides? Despite the fact that I've just returned from a journey that cost the lives of each and every one of my retainers?'

'Even so, dread lord. Honestly, it's a much better reward than a bag of gold or a handful of gems. There are far better chances for advancement serving a highborn than commanding a barracks of guardsmen.' The captain winked knowingly. 'I have a feeling there will be plenty more opportunities for coin serving in your household anyway.'

Malus shook his head. He had no reason to trust the conniving druchii whatsoever. But for the moment he could be useful, he thought. 'Your ambition is going to get you killed, captain…?'

'Hauclir,' the druchii answered, bowing his head.

'Hauclir? Like the famous general?'

'The one the Witch King later executed for treason, yes. My father had poor judgement when it came to choosing patrons, it seems.'

'Indeed,' Malus said. 'I'd venture to say you suffer from the same affliction. But nevertheless,' the highborn said wearily, reaching over and drawing his sword, 'I have a need and you will fulfil it.' He rose and Hauclir followed suit.

'The Dark Mother watches and knows what lies in our hearts,' Malus intoned, placing the tip of his blade in the hollow of Hauclir's throat. 'This steel is sworn in her service. Do you swear to pledge your life to mine, to serve as I command and to die at my call?'

'Before the Mother of Night, I swear it,' Hauclir answered. 'Let her steel strike me down if I am false. I shall wear your collar until you release me from it, in death or in reward.'

Malus nodded. 'Very well, then, Hauclir. You are mine now. May you live long enough to regret it.' He tossed the naked blade on the carpet. 'Tomorrow, you and I will create this writ you spoke of. 'For now,' the highborn said, sinking back onto the rugs, 'I intend to drink every last drop of wine in the room and sleep like the dead. Get out.'

The retainers bowed as one and slipped quietly from the room. Malus reached for his bottle and drained it dry, savouring the silence.

A WHISPER OF sound brought Malus out of dreamless slumber. Weeks of travelling alone in the Wastes had honed his senses to a razor's edge and conditioned his reflexes for instant action. At first the highborn held perfectly still, listening intently for the sound to repeat itself. When he heard it again – the faintest brush of a bare foot across the piled rugs – he opened his eyes ever so slightly, focusing on its source.

The braziers had burned low, filling the centre of the room with a faint reddish glow and leaving the walls in impenetrable shadow. Malus lay against a mound of cushions, bare feet pointed at the nearest brazier and empty wine bottles strewn around his legs. Another empty bottle was still clutched in his right hand. After his erstwhile retainers had left, Malus had drunk himself into a stupor. Now, only a few hours later, the highborn was faintly surprised at how little of the alcoholic fog remained.

Across the room a druchii servant cleared upended cups and plates with swift, silent movements. The slave worked his way quickly through the detritus. Within moments he was carefully pulling away the bottles around Malus's knees.

The highborn suppressed a flash of annoyance at his own paranoia, forcing his eyes to shut and trying to sink back into sleep. It's going to take some effort to start ignoring the servants again, Malus thought sourly.

He sank back into slumber. Then suddenly he remembered: *Mistress Nemeira didn't keep druchii slaves.*

Malus bolted from the cushions just as the assassin's dagger struck home, its keen blade sliding through the silk robe and sinking into his shoulder instead of opening his throat. It felt like a shard of ice – suddenly the highborn's left hand went numb. The assassin loomed over Malus, his eyes shining like molten brass. An acolyte of the temple, Malus thought furiously, fighting a surge of panic.

The assassin jerked his dagger free – Malus felt the hot flow of blood stain the fine robe and plaster it to his chest – and the highborn caught the man's wrist. Malus lashed at the man's head with the wine bottle in his other hand, but the assassin grabbed the highborn's wrist with effortless speed and then they were rolling across the rugs in a flurry of kicks, bites and head-butts.

Teeth sank into Malus's right forearm. He drove his knee into the assassin's groin and bashed his forehead into the man's temple until he felt the killer's jaws loosen. Malus jerked his weapon-arm away, hoping to pull free and land a blow, but the assassin responded by biting at the highborn's throat. Malus twisted, trying to use his weight to turn the assassin's dagger towards its wielder and drive it into the man's chest, but the numbness in his hand was intensifying and he could feel his grip start to weaken.

The acolyte twisted sharply at the waist and they rolled again. Malus's right shoulder struck something hard and unyielding and waves of heat beat at his face and arm. With a cold grin the assassin loomed above him, drawing his knife blade inexorably higher, the light from the brazier painting the acolyte's face with a daemonic leer. The blood on the knife-blade seemed to glow in the sullen light and Malus could feel his grip starting to give way.

Roaring with desperate fury Malus twisted his body with all his strength and threw the acolyte against the iron brazier, knocking it over in a shower of angry sparks. Caught off-balance, the assassin rolled onto the hot coals and Malus let go of his bottle to grab the man's chin and hold his head to the fire. The assassin stiffened and smoke curled around his shoulders. His black hair blazed into bluish flame, but still he struggled to pull his knife-arm free and plunge the blade into Malus's chest. Malus felt his strength fading with every moment, but the assassin's eyes remained fever-bright and focused on his destruction. Then without warning the acolyte let out a tortured scream and dropped his knife, his hands groping for the flames searing his skull.

Malus let go and rolled away, his eyes darting about the room for his sword. The rugs had started to burn and the air was full of acrid smoke. The highborn's left arm hung uselessly at his side. Where did I put that damned blade, he thought furiously, trying to cudgel his wine-fogged memory into focus.

Three sharp, stabbing pains in his right shoulder tore a shout from the highborn's throat. At once, searing pain blossomed at each of the tiny wounds, blazing like a fire wasp's sting. Malus staggered, his right hand groping at his back and pulled three slim, brass needles from his shoulder. He heard the crackle of burnt leather and turned to see the assassin rolling to his feet. The acolyte's hair was gone, his scalp blackened and his face grey with pain, but his pale eyes shone with murderous intent.

Malus leapt for the door, shouldering the thick oak aside with a hiss of pain and raced down the dimly lit corridor. There were no guards or servants about; few guests stayed overnight at the flesh house and the highborn reckoned it was close to dawn. The muscles in his chest spasmed as the needles' venom spread – it was difficult enough to breathe, let alone sound an alarm. Even if he could, he found himself wondering who, if anyone, might respond. Had Nemeira betrayed him after all? Had the acolyte followed Silar and Arleth Vann?

It won't matter if I'm dead in the next few minutes, he thought angrily. Revenge is the luxury of the living.

The highborn couldn't hear the assassin behind him, but Malus knew that didn't mean anything and he wasn't about to waste energy looking over his shoulder. He plunged on down the corridor, fighting for each ragged breath. For a moment he was tempted to call out to Tz'arkan, willing to beggar another piece of himself if the daemon could burn the poison from his body, but for once he found that he couldn't focus on Tz'arkan's presence. Damn that wine, he thought angrily.

Within moments the corridor began to turn to the right and angle slightly upwards. Malus turned the first corner and stumbled over the body of a naked slave. The human's face was turned to the ceiling, staring sightlessly with one blue eye – the other was a red ruin, pierced by the single thrust of a dagger. Malus fell headlong, scraping his forehead on the stone floor, but got his feet back underneath him and lurched on, fearing the bite of that selfsame dagger in his back.

He followed the curve of the corridor until it emptied into the main room of the flesh house, a circular chamber offset with dozens of veiled niches and set with plush divans that surrounded raised daises or delicately-wrought cages. Witchfire globes burned dimly around the perimeter of the empty room, shedding a pale greenish glow. At once, Malus caught sight of two druchii sprawled on the floor, both wearing the dark leather kheitans of Nemeira's guards. Both lay on their stomachs and judging by the huge pools of blood their throats had been expertly slit.

The highborn saw the curved swords at their hips and for a moment was tempted to grab one, but he knew that in his present state he couldn't possibly survive another fight with the acolyte. At the far end of the chamber the house's double doors stood open to the night air and the caustic yellow nightfog spilled across the threshold, filling the house's vestibule.

Gritting his teeth, Malus charged for the doorway. The fog would burn in his open wounds, but the assassin would be hard-pressed to find him in Hag Graef's twisting, shadowy streets.

Just as Malus crossed the threshold something buzzed past his ear and two more of the acolyte's brass needles struck the wooden doorjamb to his right. The highborn risked a quick look over his shoulder and saw the burned man at the far end of the room, leaning against the wall for support. Without hesitation he charged out into the fog-shrouded street, trying to remember if there was a connecting lane or alley mouth on the opposite side.

He reached the opposite side of the street and immediately saw the shadow of an alley mouth just a few yards away. Without skipping a beat Malus angled from the opening – and failed to notice the robed shapes rising from the shadows of a nearby shop front until it was too late.

There was a hissing sound in the air and a fine net of steel wire wrapped around Malus's torso. Fine hooks sank into his skin, binding the net to his body and then the acolyte jerked back on the thin chain attached to the net and pulled Malus off his feet. He roared in pain as he hit the slick cobblestones, the hooks sinking deeper into his flesh. The highborn tried to roll to his feet, but the acolyte pulled him onto his back with a flick of the wrist.

The second robed acolyte rushed forward, grabbing Malus's ankles and pressing them to the cobbles with all his weight. The druchii looked surprisingly young – little more than a child really – evidently an initiate accompanying the assassin and providing assistance where required. They had him trussed like a blood moon sacrifice and Malus watched helplessly as the burned acolyte staggered from the fog, his dagger held high.

There was a sharp *pop pop pop* as three crossbow bolts punched through the brittle leather kheitan the assassin wore and dug deep into his vitals. The killer looked down uncomprehendingly at the black fletching sprouting from his chest and then toppled onto his side.

Cloaked shapes rushed out of the fog like nighthawks, glittering steel clenched in their hands. The acolyte at Malus's feet started to rise, his hand going for his dagger, but a curved sword sliced into his neck and the boy's severed head bounced into the highborn's lap. The shapes rushed past and then Malus heard a brief struggle behind him. Steel clashed on steel and for a moment the chain attached to the net pulled painfully tight. Then came the sound of a keen edge biting into flesh and the tether went slack.

Malus couldn't move. He wasn't sure if it was the tension of the net, or the fact that his muscles were frozen by the assassin's poison. The highborn fought for every searing breath, his eyes searching the fog for signs of his rescuers. Then the cloaked figures returned, their silver nightmasks gleaming beneath the shadows of their black hoods.

'The Dark Mother smiles upon us tonight, brothers,' one of the figures said, his deep voice rumbling from behind the mask of a leering daemon's face. 'A moment later and our lord would have been very wroth indeed. Instead the temple has flushed our prey for us and wrapped him in silver for the Vaulkhar's pleasure.' The daemon's face lowered until it was inches from Malus's own. He could see the druchii's black eyes behind the silver eye sockets and hear the man's breath whistling through the slits carved between the daemon's fangs. Then darkness crowded at the edges of his vision, rising like a black tide and Malus knew nothing more.

Chapter Three
DREAMS OF BLOOD AND MADNESS

It seemed as though he fought on a raging sea of blood, beneath a sky that writhed and thundered and rained bone and ash.

He stumbled and lurched across the twisted landscape and a horde of angry ghosts clawed and gibbered at him every step of the way.

They reached for him with their misshapen hands and howled in tongues of fire, their eyes nothing but orbs of nacreous light. A withered elven sorceress leapt upon his back, sinking her cracked nails into his chest and tearing at the side of his face with her jagged teeth. A hulking, slithering creature formed of naked, roiling muscle undulated across the ground and lashed him with saw-edged tendrils of ropy flesh. A pack of hounds circled him hungrily, their gaping mandibles dripping green threads of venom.

He roared his fury at the storm and lashed at the ghosts with his blade, but their bodies parted like jelly beneath each stroke and flowed back together again.

THE MAELSTROM DISSOLVED in a blaze of pale light. Dark clouds coalesced out of the haze, taking the shape of faces. A woman bent over him, propping one eyelid open.

'His wounds are mending, dread lord.' The woman's lips were moving, but her voice didn't quite match their movements.

A man regarded him from an impossible distance, his face cruel and cold. 'More hushalta then,' the man said, harshly. 'I tire of waiting.'

Cold fingers pried open his lips and a thick fluid tasting of burnt copper poured down his throat. He choked, his body spasming, but strong hands pinned him in place.

The light dimmed, the faces receding into a reddening mist. Red faded to black and a familiar voice spoke in the darkness.

'You fool,' Tz'arkan said.

HE LAY UPON a bed of writhing bodies. Pale hands bore him up, caressing his body, clutching him in their hungry embrace. Lips pressed against his skin, tasting him, worshipping him. The air hung heavy and still, fragrant with incense and trembling with the moans and sighs of a hundred rapturous voices.

Faces rose around him, haunting sirens with hungry looks in their depthless eyes. They reached for him, running their hands across his bare chest, each delicate fingertip leaving a trail of heat across his flesh.

One siren climbed languidly onto him, her dark hair seeming to float around her fine-boned face. She stretched across him like a cat, long fingers reaching for his face. Her red lips twisted in a sensual smile as she laid her long nails against his cheeks and sank them deep into his skin.

Blood ran cold and thin down the sides of his face. She dug deeper, taking handfuls of flesh and pulling downwards, like skinning the hide from a hare. Flesh, muscle and tendons pulled away in a glistening mat, exposing his neck and the upper part of his chest.

He writhed in the grip of the sirens, but they held him fast. Now they tore at him as well, pulling away hunks of bloody skin. He felt the flesh of his entire left arm slough away like a soggy sleeve and when he wrenched it away he saw that the limb beneath was corded with muscle and wrapped in a pebbly, greenish-black hide. Then the pebbles ruptured into hundreds of tiny mouths, lapping at the streaks of blood running from wrist to elbow–

SOMETHING WAS DRAGGING at his feet. Malus opened gummy eyes and saw his toes scuffing along smooth flooring stones. Two druchii held him by his arms, dragging him easily along a passage lit by witchlights.

It was a struggle to raise his head and take in his surroundings. His mouth felt like dried leather. Hushalta, he remembered. They had been feeding him hushalta for days. His skin felt taut and slightly feverish, but whole. It's a wonder my mind is still intact, he thought dimly.

'That remains to be seen,' a faint voice echoed in his head.

Cool wind played across his face, stirring his lank hair. Chains clinked softly; pure crystal tones that made his blood run cold. Then the strong hands holding his arms released him and Malus fell to his knees on the slate tiles of a large, circular chamber. Globes of witchlight gleamed from ornately worked iron sconces around the perimeter of the room, illuminating bas-reliefs worked into the stone walls depicting a series of famous massacres from the long wars against the elves of Ulthuan. A mass of chains tipped with cruel hooks depended from the high ceiling in the centre of the chamber. The metal links clinked softly together in the cool air.

He could feel the eyes of others upon him. The highborn drew a shuddering breath and straightened, meeting the reptilian stares of the druchii who awaited him.

Lurhan Fellblade, Vaulkhar of Hag Graef, stood bare-chested before his son, his powerfully muscled upper body marked with dozens of scars from his service to the Witch King. His black hair was pulled back from his face, accentuating his fierce eyes and prominent, aquiline nose. The warlord's sheer presence filled the chamber, eclipsing every other person in the room.

Two broken men stood in Lurhan's shadow, their eyes gleaming with hate. One was tall, nearly as imposing as the Vaulkhar himself, though the druchii's right arm was hidden beneath layers of black robes. Urial had the same sharp, angry features as his father, but his face was gaunt and his pale skin had an unhealthy, bluish cast. His thick hair had been almost completely white since returning from his years in the Temple of Khaine and his eyes were the colour of molten brass.

The second druchii was bent and trembling, his sunken eyes like dark pits in a bloodless face lined with a network of fine scars. A thin, black beard shadowed his narrow chin and his hair was shaved but for a long corsair's topknot. The wretch wore a provincial-looking kheitan of red leather worked with the sigil of a mountain peak. Silver rings glittered from the scarred ruin of his ears. Fuerlan, hostage to the court of the Drachau, glared at Malus with a look of fear and rage combined.

Behind Lurhan and his companions a trio of druchii slaves worked with a cluster of silver chains that hung from the centre of the room's ceiling. Large, sharp hooks were attached to the chains at different heights. Small tables stood nearby, holding arrangements of gleaming tools laid out on silk cloths.

The two retainers backed away from Malus, retreating to the shadows by the doorway. The highborn returned his gaze to Lurhan and made an ostentatious bow. 'Well met, father and Vaulkhar,' Malus rasped. 'It's an honour to be invited into your tower at long last. Though considering your choice of company, perhaps it's not the privilege I thought it to be.'

Lurhan let out an angry hiss. 'Insolent churl! Do not presume to speak to me as an equal. You have been a stain upon the honour of this house from the moment of your birth! Would that I could have given you to the cauldron when you were but a babe.' Beside the Vaulkhar, Urial stiffened slightly, but his cold expression betrayed nothing of his thoughts. Unlike Malus, he had been thrown into the Lord of Murder's cauldron, his malformed body offered as a sacrifice – and emerged unscathed as one of Khaine's chosen.

'Speak to you as an *equal*, dread Lurhan? I think it is you who are presuming here,' Malus said slowly, trying to keep his speech from slurring. The sound of his words reverberated through him as though he was speaking underwater – doubtless a lingering effect of the restorative drugs. 'We could never be equals. I could never even rise to the level of the rest of your misbegotten brood. *You* saw to that. You gave me just barely enough support to survive, just enough to fulfil your obligations to my mother and then left me to wither.'

'You are not here to speak, you misbegotten bastard, but to suffer,' the Vaulkhar said. 'It was not enough for you to indebt yourself to a handful of petty nobles – a debt that I was forced to pay when you could not – no, you also stained the honour of the Drachau himself by laying hands on his hostage and jeopardising the truce with Naggor.'

'A truce to a feud *you* started,' Malus shot back. 'The Witch King himself ordered you to raid Naggor and take Eldire from her brother, but it was you who claimed conqueror's privilege and brought her back to the Hag instead of sending her to Naggarond.' Malus staggered back upright, fixing his father with a glare of pure hatred. 'Has she served you well, father? Has she shown you the future and steered you down the path of glory? Or did you find, too late, that she shares only what she chooses and then only when it suits her arcane schemes? But are you bold enough to cross her even now, with the Drachau ordering my death?' He grinned wolfishly. 'Do you dare tempt her wrath by killing me?'

Lurhan gestured and the druchii slaves approached, their robes whispering around their bare feet. 'I will not kill you,' the Vaulkhar said. 'I will *hurt* you. You will suffer agonies for days on end, until you beg me for release. Yet I will do everything in my power to help you cling to life, each and every day. I will salve your exposed nerves and lave your raw flesh and turn a deaf ear to your pleas for mercy. If you die it will be because *you* wish it. You can chew off your own tongue and choke on your blood, or simply will your heart to stop beating – I have seen it happen to far stronger druchii than yourself. No, I will not kill you. That is your own choice to make.' He studied his son critically as the slaves dragged Malus to his feet. 'No druchii has ever survived my attentions for more than five days. I think you will be dead within three and Eldire will have no one to blame but her own weak-willed son.'

The slaves dragged the highborn towards the waiting chains. Malus glared over his shoulder at the Vaulkhar. 'I have never failed to disappoint you, father,' he snarled. 'Mark my words, I will do so again and you will live to regret it.'

Lurhan chuckled cruelly and went to inspect his instruments. The highborn tried to struggle, but his limbs were leaden and useless.

Bestir yourself, daemon, Malus thought fiercely. I need no persuading now. Lend me your power!

The daemon uncoiled itself in the highborn's breast. 'Very well, you shall have it,' the daemon answered. 'When the time is right.'

Malus was forced once more to his knees. Hands pulled the tattered robe from his back. One of the slaves studied the chains thoughtfully and reached for a gleaming hook, oblivious to the highborn's cry of rage.

* * *

THERE WAS NO end to the pain.

Malus hung from the silver chains, twisting slowly in an agonising breeze. Even when the Vaulkhar put down his spattered tools, the air alone was enough to torture his exposed nerves and muscle.

He felt shrivelled and hard, like petrified wood. His wounds no longer bled. For a while he was able to measure time by the steady drip of blood upon the tile, but now there was no procession of minutes and hours. There were only periods of agony that gave way to irregular stretches of unrelieved suffering. As he hung from the chains and waited for the Vaulkhar's return, he could feel his life slipping away, receding like a tide. Yet every time his spirit ebbed, something dark and vital flowed into the space it left behind and lent him a small measure of strength. Sometimes the daemon whispered to him in a language whose words Malus could not understand, yet etched themselves deeply into his bones.

Each time Lurhan was done with him the Vaulkhar's slaves would carefully tend his ravaged body with sophisticated salves and potions. A foul mixture of wine and hushalta was poured past his torn lips using a thin metal tube. It was not enough to allow him to sleep, but it did cause him to dream.

THE TILES BENEATH him groaned.

He looked down, feeling the hooks pull painfully at the muscles of his shoulders. The slate was buckling, becoming concave; there was another long moan, then with a sharp crack the tile shattered, falling in upon itself. Below was absolute darkness, like the heart of the Dark Mother herself.

Such darkness, he thought. Such power. Take me from this place and loose me like a thunderbolt upon those I despise.

Something moved within the blackness. It seemed to shift and settle, though he could not say how he knew this; he simply felt the movement, as though the ancient blackness pressed against his ruined skin.

An armoured gauntlet rose from the darkness, its steel fingertips shaped into curved claws. The long fingers, almost delicate in their craftsmanship, unfolded with slow, malevolent grace.

The hand closed on his right foot and pulled.

He screamed in agony as the hooks in his back, arms and legs all pulled cruelly taut. Pierced muscles pulled away from his bones until the tendons creaked.

A second hand rose from the blackness and seized his other foot. Then, hand over hand, they began to climb upwards.

He felt his muscles began to tear. His skin trembled in waves of bright, burning pain. His throat seized, but the screams continued to come, making ragged, gasping noises each time the hands moved a little higher.

A helmeted head emerged from the blackness: peaked and plumed in the manner of a druchii knight, faceless and menacing. Little by little the armoured figure rose from the darkness, tearing him into pieces with each slow, methodical movement.

One hand rose high enough to close around his throat. His body seemed to sag against the hooks as his bones hung free from its fleshy sheath. The thin screams were stifled by the steel fingers gripping his neck.

The helmet rose until the black eye sockets were level with his own. He could feel the knight's breath: it was cold and rank, like the air from a tomb.

Its free hand reached up and pulled the helmet off. A multitude of thin, black braids fell loose from the helm; spiders and centipedes scuttled among clots of loam crusted into the hair. The knight's skin was grey and shrunken with rot, the muscles long since turned to foul-smelling ichor. A single, deep gash ran from the top of the knight's head to just above the left brow and the eye beneath was a swollen, black orb, the pupil gleaming with grave mould.

Lhunara's blackened lips pulled back in a gruesome smile, revealing jagged yellow teeth.

THERE WAS NO sensation of regaining consciousness; no fumbling, dawning awareness as the drugs failed to overcome his pain. One moment there was darkness and fever-dreams and the next moment his eyes were open and she was standing before him.

She was a statuesque figure in black, robed in the severe habit of the convent. Her alabaster face, stern and composed, seemed to float like an apparition in the darkness of the chamber. Long, black hair was drawn back in a single, heavy braid wrapped with silver wire, and a silver circlet wrought with tiny, arcane runes adorned her forehead. Her slim hands held a chain of gold, shaped from large, flat links set with precious stones. Unknowable power stirred in the depths of her violet eyes. She was utterly perfect, an image of the Dark Mother herself made flesh and he desired her with every fibre of his being.

Malus was certain she was another apparition, until the woman glided soundlessly forward and slipped the heavy chain around his neck. The instant the cold metal touched his skin a jolt passed through him from head to toe. In its wake his terrible pain faded and the last vestiges of the drugs vanished like morning mist. He was clear-headed and alert and suddenly he realised who it was standing before him.

'Mother?' Malus said wearily.

Eldire's penetrating gaze surveyed the ruin of her son's naked body. 'Lurhan has outdone himself,' she said coldly. 'I doubt even the Drachau himself could have done better. This will be something to remember, years from now. You will wear these scars with pride.'

Malus attempted a weak smile that was little more than parchment lips pulling away from a yellowed skull. 'Will I be some wight, boasting of my scars in the barrow-field? I will stay here until I die, Mother. Lurhan made this clear.'

'He said no such thing, child. He said he would make you suffer until you were willing to kill yourself. A craven distinction, but it is the only stratagem the great warlord has at his disposal.' She laid a hand on his cheek, brushing away layers of dried blood. 'Yet you have lingered well beyond his expectations.'

Malus did not question how Eldire knew what had been said between him and his father. Druchii witches were kept mewed up in convents in each of the great cities, forbidden to walk among the citizens by decree of the Witch King – yet the strongest among them had their ways of reaching beyond the convent walls.

'How long?'

'Today is the fifth day,' Eldire said. 'Your father is furious. The Drachau has commanded him to kill you, but if he does he will face a reckoning with me. This was the best way he could attempt to appease both of us and now the gambit looks likely to fail.'

Malus took a deep breath and tried to focus his thoughts. 'I was right. Whatever agreement you forged with Lurhan included producing a child. If he kills me, then he loses your gifts.'

Eldire seized his chin with surprisingly strong fingers. 'Do not pry into affairs that are none of your concern, child,' the witch said sternly. 'It is enough for you to know that every day past today it will become increasingly obvious that Lurhan is intent on torturing you unto death. Then the Vaulkhar will have to decide whose displeasure he fears more. So you must endure a bit longer.' She leaned close, peering deeply into her son's eyes. 'You are stronger than even I expected, child.'

'Hate is a cure for all things, mother. You taught me that—'

'That is not what I mean,' she said sharply. 'Your body is stronger than I expected it to be after so much punishment. Something has changed about you... something that was not there when you went into the Wastes.'

Without warning, Malus felt a fist clench around his heart. The coils of the daemon tightened – or were they shrinking, fearful of attracting Eldire's notice?

'I—it was a difficult journey,' Malus gasped. 'I was forced to return to the Hag alone and the Wastes consume the weak-willed.' He managed a defiant grin. 'I suffered much worse than this for weeks at a time.'

Eldire frowned. 'And was your journey successful? Did you find what you sought?'

Malus stiffened. 'Yes... and no. I found power there, but not the sort that would serve one such as me.'

'Nonsense,' Eldire snapped. 'Are there swords you cannot wield, because they were not made for your hand? Are there towers you cannot shelter in, because they were not made with you in mind? Power is shaped by the wielder. It is made to serve, in the way a slave is bent to the master's will.'

Malus started to formulate an answer when a thought suddenly occurred to him. Now it was his turn to regard Eldire suspiciously. 'How did you know of my trip north? Who told you?'

The witch laughed mirthlessly. 'Am I not a seer, child? Do I not ride the winds of time and space?'

'Of course,' Malus agreed. 'But you haven't taken such interest in my doings before.'

'That is not true,' Eldire said, stepping close. 'You are mine, child. Born of my flesh and blood. My eyes are upon you always.' She reached up to stroke his matted hair. 'I know your ambitions, your secret hatreds and desires. And if you love me, I will give them all to you, in time. Do you love me, child?'

Malus stared deep into her violet eyes. 'As much as I have ever loved anyone, mother.'

The witch smiled and kissed him gently on the lips. 'Then you will survive, you will grow powerful and in time you will conquer, my beloved child. Do not forget.'

With that she drew away. Malus felt the chain lifted from his neck. He opened his mouth to reply, but the ocean of pain that the chain had held at bay fell upon him with crushing force. He was borne under and knew nothing more.

* * *

AFTER THAT THERE were no dreams.

They stopped giving him hushalta and only the barest taste of watered wine. He lost consciousness many times, but whenever he opened his eyes again Lurhan was there, his fine knives working at Malus's ravaged body.

'Why won't you *die*?' The Vaulkhar said it again and again. 'What is it that keeps you in this ruined husk? You're weak. I know it. Why won't you stop this?'

It took ages to remember how to speak. Drawing in a tendril of breath was a heroic effort.

'S… sss… spite,' he finally gasped, with a faint rattle of laughter.

As time passed, Lurhan's work became frenzied and crude. He turned to larger knives and cut deeper and deeper.

And yet the highborn lingered.

Malus could feel the black stain of the daemon's taint stretching throughout his body, like the roots of some enormous tree. Huge taproots and tiny, hair-like capillaries, reaching from his tortured brain to the tips of his toes. If he concentrated his attention he thought he could still perceive the difference between the two – the demarcation where he ended and Tz'arkan began – at least, for now.

He felt himself jerk against the chains. There was a pressure on his neck. He dimly realised Lurhan had grabbed him, but he couldn't feel anything clearly any more. Something bright flashed before his eyes. Another knife, he supposed. A large one.

'It's over, Malus,' Lurhan hissed. 'It must end now. It *must*! Beg me to end your life. I will make it quick and your agonies will end. It is no dishonour. No one will fault you.'

Again, Malus fought to draw breath. 'Do... one thing... for me...'

'Yes?' Lurhan leaned close, almost pressing his ear to his son's ravaged lips.

'Tell me... what... day... it is.'

Lurhan let out a savage cry of anger. The knife felt blessedly cool, like a soothing piece of ice, as it slid between his ribs. The slaves cried out in alarm, calling to the Vaulkhar, but Malus paid them no mind. It felt as though his consciousness was seeping away, draining like wine from a pierced skin. The coldness spread through his chest, taking away the pain and he surrendered gladly to it.

THERE WAS CLOTH against his face, light and cool. His arms were folded tightly against his chest and his legs were bound together. With effort, Malus opened his eyes and saw only a thin layer of fabric resting against his eyelids. There was a smell of unguents and spices in the air.

Am I in my barrow-shroud, he thought?

'But for me, it would have been,' a voice said in his mind. Malus paid it no heed.

'Much of his skin and the flesh beneath is gone, or carved into ruin,' a diffident voice said. 'My master preserved most of his face and his eyes. A great many of his nerves were separated and splayed as well. Truly, I have never seen a more extensive series of excruciations. How he survived for seven days is truly a mystery to us and his injuries are far beyond our power to heal.'

A shadow moved between Malus and the dim light. Delicate fingertips, light as wasp's wings, brushed across his face. Swift, precise movements peeled back the cloth covering his eyes. For a moment, even the witchlights were dazzling.

'I can help him,' a voice spoke from the brilliance. As Malus's eyes adjusted, he saw a blurry shape looming over him. Cool fingertips brushed his cheek and the figure leaned closer.

'There are powers beyond bandages and unguents that will make him whole again,' Nagaira said, her lips twisting into a smile. 'His mother has commanded the Vaulkhar to deliver him to me and I will show her that her faith in my power is not misplaced. It is the least I can do to have my beloved brother in my arms once more.'

Chapter Four
MASKS OF FLESH

VOICES CIRCLED MALUS for days; they chanted and whispered in words that sent shivers through the air around him. Blurred figures swayed and gestured before his shrouded eyes. Sometimes in the dead of night shapes swooped before his vision, chittering sounds that were almost recognisable and leaving his skin tingling painfully in their wake.

Attendants with soft, perfumed hands waited on him, peeling back the shroud one thin layer at a time. He emerged from his agony like a dragon from its egg, his shell wearing away inexorably as flesh and muscles knit and strength flowed back into his frame.

As time passed and he could perceive more and more of the world through his thinning shroud, he began to take in greater detail of the acolytes who performed the healing rituals over him. Though he could not grasp the arcane tongue they spoke, their voices became distinct and familiar. All highborn druchii, both women *and* men, always chanting in groups of six. Nagaira led them in every ritual, her voice commanding and the others answering in a discordant chorus. Each time the rites were performed, Malus felt Tz'arkan respond, slithering against his ribs and whispering in blasphemous pleasure.

There was a pattern to the rites that Malus eventually discerned – once at the hour before sunrise and once again at the hour before sunset, and two short rites at the rising and setting of the moon. By this he reckoned that he had been a guest of his sister for at least five days. The fact that she hadn't slipped a knife into his eye or turned his skull into a drinking cup vexed the highborn to no end.

It had been Nagaira who had tricked him into undertaking the deadly journey into the Wastes – embarking on an elaborate plot to pit him against his brother Urial over a trivial slight. Because he had left her without warning the previous summer in an audacious plan to further his fortunes with an impromptu slave raid, she had decided to retaliate. She had spurned the advances of her younger brother Urial and blamed it squarely on devotion to him. The result had been a cunning ambush just outside Clar Karond that had cost him all of the slaves he'd so painstakingly harvested over the summer and put him at knife points with his cabal of investors. With his enemies smelling blood and circling nearer and assassins from the Temple of Khaine sworn to kill him, it had been all too easy to seduce him with a story of a hidden temple and ancient power lost in the Wastes.

Nearly two score druchii – several of them Nagaira's own retainers – and more than ten times that number of slaves had perished over an imagined slight. Malus's relationship with his half-sister had never been more than a series of brief, often violent affairs, so he was hard-pressed to understand why she'd been so affronted. Not that a highborn ever needed a compelling reason to engage in a petty game of revenge. Druchii women were widely considered the deadlier of the sexes when it came to drawn-out contests of spite. With fewer options to exercise their lust for violence they had plenty of time to contemplate elaborate, bloody-minded intrigues.

On the sixth day the routine changed. He was awakened by the chanted cries of the morning ritual and again by the evening rite. By this time only a single, thin sheet of fabric wrapped his body, the material stiff with layers of dried body fluids and healing unguents. His eyes reacted well to the shifting glow of the witchlights and Malus could easily discern the figures that surrounded the bier upon which he lay. The acolytes all wore layered robes of ebon wool that were dense with painted symbols in a sharp, spiky script. Their heads were covered in voluminous hoods that sheltered their faces in concealing darkness. The highborn had no doubt it was more than mere affectation; any one of them caught practising sorcery by one of the Witch King's agents forfeited not just their rank and properties, but their very souls as well.

When the time came for the rite at moonrise, Malus watched five acolytes enter the room and surround his bier in a carefully proscribed circle. The highborn felt the daemon stir expectantly as the acolytes raised their arms and began to chant. It was an invocation of some kind; Malus had heard the general form many times now. The chant lasted for some time, much longer than Malus had been expecting. Then, at its zenith, another figure stepped into view.

It was an elven slave, clad only in a thin cotton shift. Her golden hair had been carefully cleaned and pulled back to reveal a graceful, swan-like neck. A circlet of steel gleamed dully from her brow and her perfect face was rapt with a kind of horrified ecstasy. Behind the slave came Nagaira, pacing silently in heavy robes and a breastplate of cured human hide set with precious stones. The sapphires caught the light and described a spiral pattern that plucked at Malus's eyes. Unlike her acolytes, Nagaira's face was uncovered, her eyes bright and her head held high.

The chanting of the acolytes altered, becoming a slow susurration of breath, like the flow of the sea or the hissing of blood through artery and vein. Moving as if in a trance, the elven slave mounted the bier and slowly, lightly climbed onto him. She weighed little more than a willow wand, and the stiff sheets crackled faintly like brittle ice as she straddled his body. Malus's eyes narrowed appraisingly – and then the slave raised a curved, sickle-like blade in her hand. Her eyes bulged with horror as she watched her own hand move slowly and deliberately, drawing the razor-sharp inner edge of the blade across her throat.

Fat drops of hot blood spattered against the sheet like drops of rain, spreading like constellations before the highborn's eyes. Slowly, then gathering speed, the crimson rain fell, soaking the fabric and plastering it like a caul against his skin. The sodden material shrank against the skin of his face, pulling taut over his mouth and nose. His nostrils filled with the bitter tang of blood and he began to struggle, forcing his arms to move and pull at the clinging material. For a heartbeat it resisted and then the shroud parted like rotten cheesecloth, pulling from his naked body with a wet ripping sound. There was a final, gurgling whisper and the slave pitched off the bier, her blade ringing against the stone tiles. With a groan of pain Malus pushed himself upright, his bare face and chest streaked with fresh gore.

'Rise, dreadful wyrm,' Nagaira said, her eyes glinting lasciviously. As one, the acolytes fell to their knees, shouting in their arcane tongue. 'Stretch your wings and slake your thirst with the blood of the innocent.'

The highborn found himself in a small, hexagonally shaped room. Witchlight glowed from hemispherical lamps set in a cluster directly overhead and the black marble walls of the chamber were carved with hundreds of arcane runes and dusted with ground silver so that they glowed a pale green. The floor surrounding the bier was likewise carved in an intricate pattern of lines and circles, their glittering lines obscured by spreading pools of blood. Malus wiped the elf's vital fluids from his face with the back of his hand. 'If there was magic in your sacrifice, sweet sister, I regret that it failed to touch me.'

The druchii witch laughed. 'Her death had nothing to do with the rite. That was completed at nightfall. But it's been almost a fortnight fretting over your torn little husk and I needed to spill some blood.' She leaned forward and touched a pale finger to a crimson drop on the bier, then placed it against her tongue. 'She was a maiden you know. A princess, supposedly, from Tor Yvresse. You have no idea how much she cost.'

Tz'arkan slithered beneath his ribs. 'Such a fine one, she is! If only she had come north instead of you, little Darkblade. What a savoury prize she would have been.'

Malus paid the daemon little heed. 'A fortnight? I reckoned I'd been here only six days.'

Nagaira shook her head. 'You lingered at the edge of death for many days, sweet brother. I confess there were moments when I wasn't sure that even my skill could bring you back. But that is past now.'

She stepped around the bier, a wolfish smile playing across her face. Nagaira was the shortest of Lurhan's six children, rising little higher than the level of Malus's eyes. Her figure was softer and curvier than the rest of the Vaulkhar's lean brood, but her face was every bit that of her fearsome father, with a sharp nose and a black stare that could cut like a knife when she wished. She stepped up to Malus and took the remnants of the bloodstained shroud in her small, strong hands. The cloth parted easily and she tossed it casually aside. 'I took great pains to restore your vitality, brother,' she said. 'I'm eager to see the results of my handiwork.' The witch stood on her tiptoes and kissed him lightly on the lips. 'Cold as ever,' she said with a grin. 'And tasting of the battlefield.'

Nagaira snapped her fingers and a slave materialised from the shadows near one of the chamber walls. The human carried a gleaming goblet with both hands and offered the brimming vessel to Malus. The goblet had a thick stem of wrought silver, shaped in the manner of a curling nauglir's tail. The skull that held the dark wine had been recently boiled and still carried its sheen of fine oil. The top of the head had been sawn cleanly away, leaving a smooth, rounded lip to drink from –

clearly a work of superior craftsmanship. 'What's this?' Malus asked.

'A gift from me to welcome you home. You drink from the skull of a temple acolyte who sought to kill you while you convalesced here. Such a fool he was, to think that stealth and silvered steel would be enough to prevail in *my* house.'

'Pray he did not have companions like the pack that brought me down in the Slavers' Quarter. If word of your sorcery gets back to the temple you will have the wrath of the Witch King to contend with.'

Nagaira shrugged. 'If he did not come alone, his companions remained beyond the wards of my tower. Had they trespassed, I or my companions,' she indicated the robed figures, 'would have known of it.'

Malus drank deeply of the wine. It was thick and sweet, fit for a merchant's table. The highborn grimaced. Nagaira had many terrible powers at her command, but she still had horrible taste in wine. 'You appear to have gone to great expense on my behalf,' he said at length. 'Such generosity is surprising – considering how you sent me and six of your own men to die in the far north.'

Nagaira's smile turned cold and an appraising look came into her eyes. 'Leave us,' she said in a tone of icy authority. The acolytes rose to their feet and glided soundlessly from the room, followed by the slave.

'So you have acolytes now, sister?' Malus said with a raised eyebrow. 'When did you abandon the pretence of scholarship and consider yourself a witch in deed and name? Father has turned a blind eye to your studies for too long and it's made you reckless.'

'Those fawning students are from some of the most powerful houses in Hag Graef,' she said simply. 'Do not

concern yourself about Lurhan, or even the Drachau –
my influence runs deeper in this city than you realise.
There are many more than those five, sweet brother, all
pursuing their devotions in secret. In fact, summoning
them here to assist in these rites is a greater honour than
you know.'

The highborn growled deep in his throat. 'An honour
that no doubt comes with a steep price.'

Tz'arkan chuckled, an oily resonance in his chest. 'You
are learning, Malus. That's good.'

'I think of it as an investment, brother. You and I have
unfinished business.'

'Oh? What business would that be?'

Nagaira laughed, though the sound held little mirth.
'Don't be stupid. We agreed to share in whatever you
brought with you out of the Wastes. Now you've
returned and I know you didn't come back empty-
handed, my agents have found your cold one being
tended to in the nauglir den beneath the House of Brass.
The great beast is standing watch over a fortune in coin
and gems, but I care little for those. What else did you
find in the hidden temple?'

Malus met her eyes and sought to plumb their depths.
Was she serious? Had there been more to her scheme
than simple revenge? *If so, then she put me on the trail
of the temple because she already had an inkling of
what was there,* Malus thought. *But how much did she
know and how much did she merely suspect?* But there
were no secrets waiting to be read in the witch's black
eyes – he could sooner sound the deeps of the Outer
Darkness itself.

'I found a daemon,' he said simply.

Nagaira's eyes widened. '*Tz'arkan,*' she breathed.

Malus felt the daemon surge inside him, pressing against the inside of his chest at the sound of its name. The highborn's fingers curled into claws. It had become difficult to breathe. 'So... you knew... all along,' he said haltingly. He wondered if his sister understood how close she was to dying just then.

'I... suspected,' she replied, wetting her lips. Suddenly her self-assurance was gone. 'After I had a close look at the skull inside Urial's tower, I was able to focus my research while you were away. There are numerous references to the daemon in my library, but I hardly dared hope that we had discovered his very prison!' Suddenly she grew still and studied his face with care. 'Did you look upon the great prince? Did he speak to you?'

Malus hesitated. Within, the daemon had fallen still. 'I saw the prison where he resides. It is a great crystal, larger than two men and wider than the bole of an elder oak. My sword made no mark on it, no matter how hard I struck it.'

'No, of course not,' Nagaira replied, a distant look coming over her face. Suddenly she was the arcane scholar once more. 'The Tome of Al'khasur says that the great prince was bound in a raw, black diamond birthed in the raw energies of Chaos itself. There are sorcerers who would spill the blood of entire nations just to possess a *fragment* of that stone, much less the great power trapped within. Nothing less could contain the Drinker of Worlds.'

Tz'arkan swelled and Malus suddenly felt his heart begin to labour fitfully. He leaned against the bier for support, gritting his teeth. 'Clever, clever druchii. I have not heard that name in a very long time. Oh, she is fine! How I would love to possess her.'

'Be… my… guest,' Malus gasped.

Nagaira misunderstood his meaning. 'The stone is priceless, true enough, but nothing compared to the power harnessed within. Did the great prince bless you with his favour? What did he say?'

'He wishes to be free,' Malus answered. 'What else?'

The witch leaned close. 'Did he say how?'

Suddenly the daemon receded, shrinking inside the highborn's chest to wrap tightly around his heart. 'Answer with care, Malus,' the daemon warned. 'Answer very carefully indeed.'

'There are a number of items the daemon wants me to find,' he said carefully. 'Together, they will unlock his prison and return him to the sea of souls.'

Nagaira snorted. 'Return? Set him loose across the face of Creation is more like,' she said. 'The Drinker of Worlds would love nothing better. Tell me: what are these items?'

The highborn smiled. 'Tut, tut, sweet sister. Haven't I given you enough already?'

'I brought you back from death's clutches, brother,' Nagaira warned. 'The way I see it, the balance of the debt is still yours to bear.'

Malus raised his hands. 'Truce, then. I will give you the name of one of the relics. Do you know of an object called the Idol of Kolkuth?'

Nagaira frowned, her dark brows furrowing with thought. 'I have seen that name… somewhere…'

'No games, sister,' Malus hissed.

'Have you any idea how many books I have in my sanctum?' Nagaira shot back. 'How many scrolls and carvings? I read the name *somewhere*, but I can't place it just yet.' She grinned. 'Give me time, though. I'll find it.'

'Time is not something I have in ample supply,' the highborn said. 'The daemon warned me that I had a single year to retrieve all the items, or else the effort would fail.'

The witch cocked her head quizzically. 'Why would he say that? What does a year have to do with anything?'

'Am I a sorcerer, sister? How should I know? The daemon said I had a year, no more. And I have already spent the better part of three months just getting back to Hag Graef. So you can see that time is of the essence.'

Nagaira sighed. 'Well, if time is so short it would make much more sense to research all of the items at once.'

'Am I mistaken, or do you not wish to share in this power? If I can't gain it neither will you and you only get the name of one relic at a time. Don't try to barter with me like some fishwife.'

The witch's voice went cold. 'I could simply wring it out of you like a blood-soaked rag.'

The highborn smiled. 'After all the work you just went through to restore me, sweet sister? What a waste.'

She glowered at him a moment – then threw back her head and laughed. 'Oh, how I've missed you, dear brother,' she said. 'No one else vexes me as sweetly as you. In fact, you will be pleased to know that I have prepared a great celebration in your honour.'

'A celebration?' Malus said, as though unfamiliar with the word.

'Oh, yes! A grand feast of wine and flesh, of powders and spices and sweet blood. You will get to see just how deep my connections run – many of my allies are eager to meet you and there is much you could reap from such acquaintances. I daresay you would taste a bit of the power I know you've coveted your entire life.'

'And how many of the temple's devoted will find their way into the celebration and try to plunge their knives in my throat?'

'Let them come,' the witch smirked, tapping the edge of Malus's goblet with a long fingernail. 'I could use a few more goblets for my guests.' Her eyes widened. 'And speaking of the fete, I have another gift for you.'

She reached into the sleeve of her robe and produced a carefully wrapped bundle a bit larger than her hand.

'I should be scandalised at the way I lavish you with costly things,' she said, setting the parcel on the bier and carefully unwrapping it. 'All of the guests at the fete must wear one of these,' she said, holding the object up to the witchlight. 'I think this one will suit you well.'

Malus reached out and took the object from her hand. A skilled craftsman had used very keen knives to remove the top part of a druchii's face, peeling away the flesh down to the muscle. The hide had then been mounted on a mould and carefully cured back into its former shape, then painted with what appeared to be intricate tattoos. It was an exquisite mask, the tattoos forming the image of a dragon's eyes and snout.

'Masks on top of masks,' the highborn said, pressing the cured skin to his face. It fitted perfectly.

Chapter Five
RAIMENT OF BLOOD

IT WAS ANOTHER two nights before the grand revel began. At Nagaira's command, Malus was installed in one of the tower's apartments and afforded every luxury. A steady procession of slaves presented themselves before him, bearing new clothes, weapons and armour. There were black robes of watered silk to caress his skin and fine outer robes of indigo-dyed wool and a kheitan of the toughest, most supple dwarf hide he had ever seen. An armourer from the Princes' Quarter delivered a hauberk of fine mail and a fearsome harness of articulated plate that fitted over it. A weapon smith from the famous Sa'hreich forges appeared with an exquisite set of vraith and a human slave to test them upon. The sleek blades were forged with runes that kept the edges razor-keen and able to turn aside all but the most terrible sorcerous weapons without harm. Gifts fit for a prince and accompanied by every form of luxury he could imagine, from wine to flesh to exotic spices and vapours.

Yet for all that, Malus understood that he was a captive.

His every request to return to his own tower was met with a cunning denial. Nagaira claimed that he wasn't yet fully recovered from the healing rites and needed to regain his strength. Then it was because his tower had lain unused for more than two months and needed to be prepared for his arrival. Then it was because the grand revel was imminent and the slaves couldn't be spared to move his possessions until afterwards. Several times he lost patience with Nagaira's calm protests, but each time he found himself quickly drained by any heated exchange of words. After a while he began to hope that it was because he was still recovering – the thought that she might have somehow magically rendered him unable to resist her suggestions was too awful a fate to contemplate.

He had at least been permitted to meet with his retainers the day after the completion of the rites. From Silar he learned that they had been returned to Malus's service the day that he had been given into Nagaira's keeping and they had tried to take charge of him immediately thereafter. Nagaira had refused every attempt and there had in fact been points where Silar had considered bloodshed in order to rescue his lord. It was only after the failed assassination attempt in the witch's tower that the retainer grudgingly admitted that he was better protected under Nagaira's care than he would be in his own tower and further plans to retrieve him were abandoned.

Unfortunately, their presence was intermittent at best. There was a palpable tension between Malus's men and

Nagaira's; evidently word had spread about the deaths of Nagaira's retainers in the north and somehow that translated into antagonism towards his own. Malus had too few retainers to countenance a violent rivalry between the two camps, so he was ultimately forced to dismiss Silar and the rest to his tower. Had Nagaira wished him ill she'd had plenty of opportunity to harm him already, though it was clear that she had embarked on a comprehensive campaign to keep him isolated from the outside world. For the moment, he was willing to bide his time and wait to see what her next move would be.

'AND WHAT AM I to wear to this… revel?' Malus frowned at Nagaira from a high-backed chair near one of the tower windows, sipping wine from his attempted killer's skull. He looked out over the sharp spires of the city, wreathed in sickly nightfog. It struck him as odd that he felt his confinement more keenly in Nagaira's possession than he ever did hanging from chains in the Vaulkhar's tower.

'Do as you will,' Nagaira answered with a fleeting smile. She stood before a tall mirror, attended by a pair of druchii slaves. Her hair was pulled back in a thick braid and bound in wire; tiny barbed blades glittered evilly from the rope of black hair. The witch's naked body was covered in a spiralling tattoo she'd taken all day to paint; it reminded him of the marks she'd laid on her body before the raid on Urial's tower, twisting and pulling at his eyes. This time, however, it seemed to shroud her in a dark allure and his blood raced with each passing glance. 'Just leave that cold armour here – I think you'll find it inconvenient before too long.' As the spoke the slaves slipped a silken robe over their mistress, binding it loosely with a belt formed of silver skulls.

Grunting, Malus rose from the chair and pulled his kheitan from a dressing-chest. He could countenance leaving the plate and mail behind, but he wanted some measure of protection, even at a revel in his honour. By the time he was done buckling the light armour around his chest, Nagaira was regarding him from behind her own mask. It looked to be druchii hide like Malus's, pale and fine, with long strips of flayed skin around the temples that hung down past the witch's shoulders. More tattoos traced arcane patterns across the mask's cheeks, but these were more for ornamentation, Malus sensed, than any sorcerous purpose. 'Ready?' she asked, her voice breathy behind her mask.

'I've *been* ready, woman,' the highborn growled. 'Didn't this revel start an hour ago?'

Nagaira laughed. 'Of course. But you must be the last to arrive. Did your mother teach you nothing of society as a child?'

'My mother was locked in the convent almost from the moment she arrived in Hag Graef. She had little time for revels.'

His half-sister gave him a languid smile. 'Then this will be an education for you,' she said, beckoning to Malus. 'Come.'

She led the way from her apartments, down the long, curving stair from her quarters near the top of her tower. The two highborn passed numerous armed retainers on the stairs, accoutred in full armour and holding naked steel in their gauntleted hands. For all her pride in her magic, Malus noted that Nagaira was leaving nothing to chance. If the temple sent their acolytes into the tower tonight they would pay a very heavy price.

Other than the guards, the halls and stairways were deserted. Before, they had buzzed with activity as Nagaira prepared for the revel – the highborn hadn't realised how many slaves his half-sister had owned until she'd set them scurrying to work like a swarm of ants. Now the silence and stillness of the tower was unsettling by comparison.

The descent lasted several minutes, ending at last on the tower's ground floor. The large, circular room was empty, save for a handful of guards standing watch over the spire's ground floor entrance. The tall, double doors were the way in which most of the tower's visitors came and went – everyone from slaves to traders and guests from the city. Now the doors were securely barred with lengths of cold iron set securely into heavy brackets on either side of the doorframe. The centre of the chamber was dominated by a tall, imposing statue of a druchii maiden and a crouching manticore, worked in imposing black marble. The expression on the maiden's face seemed both inviting and menacing all at the same time – not that there were any guests to admire it.

Malus cast a sidelong glance at Nagaira. 'A fair turnout. I can't say I was expecting any differently for a revel held in *my* honour.'

Nagaira grinned, her eyes glinting with mischief. 'Stupid boy. When will you learn that nothing in my demesne is what it appears to be?'

With that she stepped forward swiftly, marching up to the towering statue – and disappearing inside it.

Tz'arkan stirred. 'A passable illusion,' the daemon observed. 'It would appear that your sweet sister has a great many talents – sorcerously and otherwise. I wonder where she learned them all?'

'Perhaps she has a daemon of her own to torment her,' Malus growled under his breath, then steeled himself to follow.

There was nothing more than a slight tingle as he passed through the illusory image – he had to close his eyes at the last moment because he couldn't quite convince himself that he wasn't about to walk face-first into a massive piece of carved marble.

A small hand on his chest brought him up short. When he opened his eyes he found that he was standing next to Nagaira at the top of a narrow, curving stair that disappeared below the floor. A circle of magical symbols enclosed the stairway landing and the air had a dusky shimmer to it. From the corner of his eye Malus could almost make out the lines of the statue, seen from the inside out, but the illusion vanished the instant he tried to view it directly.

'Well,' the highborn responded. 'What else haven't you been telling me, dear sister?'

'Come and find out,' she said, taking his arm.

They descended into darkness, Malus's booted feet echoing soft in the confined space. A faint smell rose up the stairwell, tickling his nose with its spicy odour. Just as he was about to ask where the stairs were leading, he turned another tight corner and found himself looking out over a large, subterranean chamber suffused with pale green witchlight.

Figures awaited them, all concealed behind masks of flesh. These druchii stood in concentric rings surrounding the spiral stairs – six in the first ring, twelve in the next, eighteen in the one beyond that – all facing him and all raising their arms in a gesture of supplication as he appeared. They cried out as he approached, filling the chamber with an exultant chant in a language he could not comprehend.

Beyond the masked circles lay a sea of writhing flesh.

Scores and scores of slaves filled the rest of the chamber, sprawled on the stone in a drugged delirium or climbing over one another in the throes of desire. Braziers situated around the room filled the air with incense and mind-altering herbs. Malus's heart quickened to see such a tempting feast laid before him. His skin tingled with each breath and for once even the daemon seemed to echo his kindled desire.

The chants of the supplicants washed over him and trembled in his bones. It was like nothing he had ever felt before and it left him intoxicated. Is this what it is like to be worshipped, Malus thought?

It was something he could grow to like.

Nagaira continued down the stairs, drawing Malus along with her. At the bottom another figure waited – a druchii in robes of newly-skinned human hide, still glistening with blood. The surface of the robe was tattooed with intricate runes and spiral patterns and a censer steaming with a pungent kind of musk hung on a golden chain from the figure's neck. Instead of a mask, the figure wore the skull of a great mountain ram, its bony snout hanging well below shoulder height and its long, curved horns gleaming like polished teak in the artificial light. The skull was painted with symbols and the figure's tattooed hands held a goblet brimming with thick, red fluid that steamed in the air.

The figure radiated a palpable aura of power and authority, one to which even Nagaira seemed to defer. Malus eyed the figure warily. This is no mere wine-soaked orgy, he thought. What have you drawn me into now, sister?

As they approached, the figure raised the goblet, offering it to Malus. Nagaira led him to the cup and spoke, her voice pitched to carry across the cavern. 'The Prince of the Revel is come! The cup is placed before him!' She turned to Malus, her voice still clear and carrying, but her words were focused directly to him. 'Anoint yourself with the nectar of desire and inflame the hunger of your heart. Drink deep!'

'*Drink deep!*' The masked figures intoned, their voices trembling with anticipation.

'Yes. Drink.' Tz'arkan whispered. Did the daemon's voice tremble as well?

Moving slowly, as if in a dream, Malus reached out and took the goblet from the figure's hands. It was heavier than he imagined and he raised it carefully; for some reason he feared to spill the thick, sloshing liquid. He raised the cup to his lips and drank.

Hot blood filled his mouth, bitter and salty. It slid like oil over his tongue and down his throat and it filled him with *hunger*. Not just his desires, but the appetites of each and every supplicant who had poured some of his or her blood into the cup. If he closed his eyes he could almost see them in his mind, tasting their pleasure as they slaked their terrible hunger.

Flesh. Food. Wine. Murder. Every appetite, every scintillating taste, reverberated through him in waves of heat and cold. His body shook and the supplicants roared.

'*Slaanesh! He is come! The Prince of Pleasure is come!*'

His consciousness tumbled like a leaf in the maelstrom of desire. Slaanesh! Malus's mind reeled. Nagaira, you foolish girl, what have you done?

Nagaira reached up and pried the cup from his grasp. He was surprised to discover that once he'd begun drinking, he hadn't paused until the cup was dry. Streamers of anointed blood ran down his chin and stained the front of his kheitan. She raised it high and the exultation of the supplicants fell silent.

'The Prince of the Revel has drunk deep and accepted the blessing of Slaanesh! Offer yourselves to him! Drink deeply of your desires and praise the Prince of Pleasure! Worship before the throne of flesh!'

The supplicants roared with a single voice. '*Slaanesh!*' The name of the Ruinous God reverberated through the cavern until the air itself seemed to curdle with an unholy presence.

Within Malus, the daemon seemed to swell until it filled him from head to toe, wearing him like an ill-fitting skin. It drew strength from the supplicants' ecstatic cries, as though it claimed some of the worshippers' devotion for itself.

In that moment, Malus Darkblade felt like a god.

Nagaira pressed against him, the heat of her nearly naked body radiating through Malus's silken robes. She pointed to the glistening bodies beyond the circle of supplicants. 'There lies your feast,' she whispered huskily. 'All of it has been prepared in your honour, you who have stood before the Drinker of Worlds. And that is but a foretaste of the gifts that await you.'

She reached out and propelled him forward. The ram-headed figure stepped aside and the rings of supplicants parted before him. He walked alone and as he passed each ring of worshippers he felt their hands caress him, strike him, claw at him with desire. Malus walked among them as a king, a god and he could feel their devotion to him surrounding him like a silken cloak.

All his life he had known nothing but hate and it had sustained him like bitter wine. Now he tasted absolute power and he knew that he would do *anything* to keep it.

It would not be enough to see his siblings destroyed and his father broken beneath his hand. It would not be enough to wear the armour of the Vaulkhar and go to war in the Witch King's name. No amount of gold or slaves, no lofty title or terrible authority would ever be enough for him. The entire world might not be enough to slake the hunger that now seethed inside him.

But he would feast upon it nonetheless.

Thunderous laughter filled his ears – drunken, lustful and triumphant. He could not be sure if it was his or the daemon's, but it mattered not one whit as Malus revelled in the delicacies that the Prince of Pleasure laid before him.

MALUS LAY UPON a bed of moaning bodies, his naked skin hot and streaked with sweat and blood. His dark hair was matted with wine and other fluids and his nerves sang with the effects of the drugged smoke and whetted desires. The air shuddered with release: whispers, moans, screams and cruel laughter, all mingled in a storm of sybaritic devotion. Every breath filled his lungs with a thick musk of drugs, blood, sex and wine. It was the taste of ecstasy and the highborn was surprised to find that it sharpened his mind like nothing ever had before.

He understood, among other things, why the Witch King had outlawed the Cult of Slaanesh among the druchii. The cold doctrine of Khaine was one thing – hate shaped the soul and sharpened it like a sword and like a sword it could be wielded against the enemies of the state. But desire was something else altogether. It had no limits, nor could it be shaped to suit the whims of a king. Hunger had no respect for states or boundaries – it existed to consume all in its path. Such hunger, when directed at the king on his throne, was a dangerous thing indeed.

Though legends claimed that the Prince of Pleasure was once the centre of worship for the peoples of lost Nagarythe, when the druchii made their way to Naggaroth the Witch King murdered the priests and priestesses of Slaanesh and elevated the Lord of Murder instead. Though cults of Slaanesh were said to linger amid the great cities of the Land of Chill, the Witch King's agents ruthlessly persecuted them, executing any worshipper they could find and enslaving their families as well. The thought that such a cancer lay unseen in the Vaulkhar's household brought a cruel smile to Malus's lips.

Of course, Nagaira had only trusted him with this knowledge because now he was tainted as well. Malekith would make no distinction between family members if the cult was uncovered, from Lurhan the Vaulkhar on down. The question was *why*. Clearly his half-sister had been part of the cult for some time; indeed she appeared to enjoy considerable rank among its members. Yet she had been utterly circumspect prior to this. If she'd wanted to initiate him into the cult it would have been easy to do so – he was brutally honest with himself and recognised that the taste of desire he'd felt tonight would mark him forever. In fact, if it weren't for the daemon's damned hold on him he had little doubt that he would have joined the cult gladly and then worked to manipulate it to his ends.

Ironically, he was certain that Tz'arkan was the reason that the cult wanted him in the first place.

Dimly Malus sensed the presence of other druchii surrounding him. He stirred slightly, glancing about with half-lidded eyes. Half a dozen supplicants approached him with a mixture of deference and fear. Malus remembered little of the last few hours – it had been a tempest of gluttony, rapine and slaughter. As prodigious as his own magically fuelled appetites had turned out to be, he had also been aware that the daemon had driven him to even deeper depths of depravity. The supplicants behaved as though he were Slaanesh incarnate and he allowed that he had probably come as close to the Prince of Pleasure as any of the cultists had witnessed before.

One of the supplicants bowed low before him. She was entirely naked save for her mask, her pale skin dappled with patches of dried blood and vomit. Like Malus, her black hair was matted with the fruits of her excess. 'Is the wine sweet, my prince? Is the flesh tender and delectable? Are the screams melodious? Are your desires sated by this grand feast?

He looked at her and smiled. Part of him wanted to reach for her, but his body refused to move. 'No,' he said at last. 'I still hunger.'

A ripple of reverent approval ran through the supplicants. Another of the masked druchii, male by the sound of his voice, said 'Truly you are blessed above all others, great prince. All have marvelled at your hunger,

the sublime rapaciousness of your fleshly desires. Truly
you are marked by the Drinker of Worlds and we are
blessed by your presence.'

A third supplicant, a man covered in scores of bleeding cuts, opened his crimson-stained hands in a gesture
of deprecation. 'We regret that our offering is so meagre,
great prince,' he said. 'There are even fewer initiates in
the city than elsewhere in the land. Well, enough to say
that there are few of us here, but those of us who do
honour the ancient beliefs are powerful indeed.'

Malus considered the man thoughtfully. They all
spoke with highborn accents and though the masks
muffled their voices somewhat, he fancied that some of
their voices were familiar to him. He had no doubt that
many of the supplicants were scions of the highest-
ranking households in the city. Nagaira received a
generous allowance from Lurhan, himself the second
most powerful man in Hag Graef, but not even she
could have afforded the enormous expense this revel
would have demanded. 'Only the most ancient and
proudest households in the city would dare uphold the
ways of lost Nagarythe,' he said carefully. 'It is an honour to have been a guest among such exalted company.'

The bleeding druchii bowed his head politely. 'You
must not think of yourself as a guest, great prince. Your
journey north has transformed you. We have all seen
with our own eyes how you have been marked by the
Drinker of Worlds. Indeed, you would hold a place of
great prominence among us – if you were to assume a
role in our meagre cult.'

'It is no small thing to set oneself against the laws of
the Witch King,' Malus replied. To the highborn's surprise, the man nodded readily.

'The power of Malekith is great and terrible,' the supplicant agreed. 'And his will is the law of our land. But we serve a power far greater, do we not? Does Malekith not defer to the priests of the Temple of Khaine?'

Yes, Malus thought, but they serve his interests. This cult is a threat. 'Of course you are correct,' he answered smoothly. 'But that does not lessen the risk.'

The female druchii knelt at his feet. 'We have worshipped the Prince of Pleasure in secret for centuries,' she said proudly. 'While we are few in number, we protect our own.'

'Indeed,' the male supplicant agreed. 'And we take care of our fellow believers. All are one in the crucible of desire. It would be a great sin if we were to let a true believer's appetites go unfulfilled.'

The implication in the highborn's words stirred the ambition in Malus's heart. 'Be careful, brother,' he said companionably. 'You've seen for yourself that my appetites are considerable indeed.'

That drew a respectful chuckle from the supplicants. 'True enough, but we also expect that you could give us much in return.'

Ah, but what is it you want from me, Malus thought? What is Tz'arkan to you and how do you know about him? More to the point, what else do you know about the daemon that I don't?

For the first time it occurred to him that perhaps Nagaira's efforts were infinitely more cunning than he'd given her credit for. What were the odds that the hidden temple in the north just happened to hold a daemon held in high regard by her cult? Was it possible that everything that had happened to him since returning from his slave raid had been an elaborate plot to make contact with a patron of the cult?

Ah, sister, I continue to underestimate you, he thought. You are *far* more dangerous than I realised.

Yes, it did indeed make sense. The question was, how could he turn it to his advantage?

Chapter Six
LEGENDS AND LIES

MALUS CONSIDERED THE supplicants thoughtfully. 'How may a humble son of the Vaulkhar serve the Prince of Pleasure?'

The bloody druchii held out one crimson-stained hand. 'That is not for me to say, great prince. Such matters are for you and the Hierophant to discuss – and he awaits the pleasure of your company.'

Reluctantly, Malus took the man's hand and allowed himself to be pulled to his feet. His limbs trembled from the exertions of the night until he stilled them with an effort of will and then gestured for the supplicants to precede him with a wave of his hand.

They crossed back through a ruin of spent bodies – some living, others dead. Scores of slaves littered the cavern floor in twisted heaps, as gruesome as any battlefield Malus had ever seen. His bare feet padded through cooling puddles of congealing blood and sticky wine. The revel had run its course and now Nagaira's household slaves worked their way through the detritus left behind, inspecting the bodies and dispatching those who physically survived but whose spirit had been shattered by the rapacious supplicants. As Malus watched, one slave rolled a catatonic victim onto his back and began strangling him with a silken cord. The slave made no attempt to resist.

Once past the towering spiral staircase the group crossed to the opposite end of the chamber and passed through an oval archway into an adjoining space. The walls were raw stone and rough-hewn, more like a cave than a finished room and Malus suddenly realised that they were most likely in a sealed-off part of the Burrows, the twisting maze of tunnels and caverns hollowed out of the rock beneath Hag Graef. He wondered idly if Nagaira's slaves would bother hauling the bodies up to the surface, or simply open a concealed passage that connected the chamber with the rest of the tunnels and let the wild predators that roamed there come and eat their fill.

The space was small in comparison to the revel chamber, perhaps fifteen paces across at its widest point. The bodies of a dozen slaves hung from chains around the perimeter of the chamber, their vital fluids mingling on the rough stone floor. In the centre of the space sat the druchii wearing the ram's skull who had anointed him at the base of the curving stair. The Hierophant reclined on a throne formed of living bodies – naked slaves were contorted and clasped together to form the seat, sides and backrest to support the reclining druchii. The slaves had been paralysed with some kind of poison to lock their limbs together and a palpable sense of agony hung over the Hierophant's throne. Acrid, pale green smoke rose to the low ceiling from two small braziers set to either side of the living chair, sending a burning tingle through Malus's nostrils.

The Hierophant's sharp, lacquered nails sliced thin tracks along the pale skin of his armrests. His eyes were bright and hard within the dark oculars of the ram's skull, glaring a challenge at Malus as he approached. Nagaira stood to one side of the throne, her expression inscrutable.

'Your appetites are prodigious, great prince,' grated the voice within the skull. The bone made strange echoes, distorting the Hierophant's words. Still, Malus fought to keep his expression neutral. He knew that voice from somewhere…

'When a man is given food, he eats.' Malus bowed deeply before the leader of the cult. 'With such a great and wondrous feast set before me, how could I not revel in it?'

The supplicants looked to one another and nodded in approval, but the Hierophant seemed unmoved. He leaned forward in his seat, his long fingers twining restlessly together. 'It is said you are but recently returned from the north.'

'Indeed, Hierophant.'

'I have also been told that you discovered something there of great interest to us. Is that so?'

Of interest to whom, Malus wondered, and why? He could think of several reasons why a Slaanesh cult would take interest in a bound daemon – favours and patronage alone would lend them great power – but the highborn sensed that there was more at work here.

The Hierophant is cautious, distrustful, Malus reasoned. But if Nagaira had steered him into the Wastes for the express purpose of finding Tz'arkan, did that mean she had acted without the Hierophant's knowledge? Was she making a play for power within the cult?

Malus kept his expression carefully neutral. 'I found a great temple in the Wastes, hidden in a valley at the foot of a cleft mountain.'

'We know of this place,' the Hierophant said curtly. 'The Tome of Ak'zhaal speaks of it and the sacred power bound within. But the temple is warded by the most powerful of barriers, by the very warp itself–'

'It was,' Malus answered.

The suppliants bent their heads and murmured excitedly to one another. The Hierophant silenced them with an upraised finger. 'What of the priests within?'

'Long dead, Hierophant.'

'And you took the boat across the poison sea to reach the daemon's sanctum?'

'No, I climbed a stair of floating rocks over a sea of fire,' Malus said, allowing his irritation to show. 'Surely your tome speaks of this as well.'

The Hierophant leaned back, tapping a bloodstained nail against the bony ram's snout. 'Indeed. So you stood before the great crystal and beheld the power within?'

Malus nodded. 'In time, yes,' he answered slowly.

'And the Drinker of Worlds spared you. Why?'

The highborn smiled. 'You will have to go ask him yourself. I could draw you a map if you like.'

Malus sensed the suppliants stiffen in shock. For a moment, the Hierophant was utterly still – even his taloned hands were frozen in mid-gesture, a flourish of blood-stained points. A brief smile played across Nagaira's lips.

Is this what you were hoping for, Malus thought? Did you draw me into this web merely to cross swords with this high priest?

'It had been reported to me that you required our help, great prince,' the Hierophant replied acidly. 'You are seeking certain relics on the daemon's behalf, arcane objects lost to the mists of time. A great scholar with access to an exceptional library might be able to locate references to these lost artefacts, given time. You do not strike me as much of a page-turner, however.'

Malus glanced sidelong at Nagaira. 'Forgive me, Hierophant. You are better informed than I realised. I wasn't aware that you were offering me your help. What I heard moments ago sounded more like an interrogation than a meeting of allies.'

The highborn could hear the cold smile in the Hierophant's voice. 'That is because we are not allies, great prince. At least, not yet. The anointed of Slaanesh are all one and we act to protect one another against the persecutions of the unbelievers. But you surely understand the precariousness of our situation. We can only extend our aid to those who are truly worthy.'

'I have been touched by the Drinker of Worlds. Is that not enough?'

'No. We only have your word that such a thing occurred. Your knowledge of the temple is correct in every particular, but you could have read the Tome as easily as myself – or had the facts related to you by... a third party.'

Malus noticed Nagaira stiffen slightly at the thinly-veiled implication.

'On the other hand, we cannot dismiss an opportunity to spread the glory of the Prince of Pleasure, no matter how... unlikely... such an opportunity appears. So I shall offer you a proposition.'

'Tell me.'

'I will place all the power of our cult at your disposal – our riches, our influence, even our strength of arms if we must – but only on the condition that you consign your soul in service to Slaanesh with a holy initiation. As I said, we take care of our own. Join us and all that we have will be yours as well.'

Malus considered the Hierophant's words, his mind working furiously. 'I will think on it,' he said.

The Hierophant visibly recoiled, his nails sinking deep into the armrests. Runnels of blood streaked the pale flesh and pattered on the floor. 'What? What is there to consider? You have *no* chance of completing your quest without our help.'

'I serve at the whim of the Drinker of Worlds, great Hierophant,' Malus said coldly. 'And while you are especially well-informed as to my intentions, there is still much you do not know. I must now decide whether it is in the interests of my daemonic patron–' Malus couldn't bring himself to say *master* – 'to enmesh myself in the petty agendas of your cult and place myself under your authority, or to continue my quest alone.'

Now the Hierophant glared angrily, first at Nagaira and then at Malus. 'Such insolence! Have we not lavished you with gifts of flesh and wine? Have we not honoured you with a grand revel the likes of which Hag Graef has never before seen?'

'Indeed, indeed, Hierophant – and I thank you for your lavish entertainments. But the great daemons do not want gifts. They want only to be *obeyed*. Think on that, if you still crave the Drinker of Worlds as your patron. Meanwhile, I shall consider your proposition with great care.'

The Hierophant rose abruptly from the chair, his hands bright with fresh blood. 'Consider it well, great prince, but keep this in mind as well. The night of the new moon approaches, when the Prince of Pleasure accepts initiates into his service. You have until then to decide.'

And then what, Malus thought? Will you kill me to keep your secret cult safe? One look in the Hierophant's eyes stifled his sarcastic reply, however.

Ah. I see. That's *exactly* what you mean.

Malus bowed once more. 'Then may the Prince of Pleasure speed my thoughts, Hierophant, and I hope you will excuse me so that I may rest and begin my deliberations.'

The Hierophant made no reply, but it was clear the interview was over. Nagaira bowed deeply and led Malus from the room.

Nagaira took Malus by the arm as they crossed the carnage of the revelry floor, pointedly oblivious to the tension hardening every muscle of the highborn's body. 'What a wonderful night,' she whispered, stealing a glance back the way they'd come. 'I knew you'd find a way to liven up the festivities.'

HOURS LATER, THE highborn lay awake in his bedchamber, listening carefully as the bustling of the servants gradually dwindled away. Moving slowly and carefully, the highborn eased from his bed. From the darkness beyond the narrow windows, Malus estimated it was only a few hours before dawn. He slipped on his silk robes and belted a dagger around his waist, then crept from his apartment into the corridor beyond.

The halls were as silent as a tomb. Days of frenzied preparations, followed by the monumental task of cleaning up the remains of the great revel had taxed the capacity of Nagaira's household to the utmost. Malus expected that nearly all of the house servants were occupied with tasks or taking what opportunity they had to rest before their mistress summoned them again. He was certain that the same could be said for the guards – after days at a heightened state of readiness it was only natural that they would relax as soon as the revel was concluded.

It was perhaps the only opportunity he would get to work his way out of the snare his sister had laid for him.

The meeting with the Hierophant had not only confirmed his fears about Nagaira but expanded their dimensions in troubling ways. Not only did she know much more about Tz'arkan and the nature of his imprisonment, she had shared the knowledge of his predicament with the members of the cult. The witch was using him to usurp the role of the Hierophant and using the power of the cult to gain greater influence over him. No matter which way he turned, she was always one step ahead of him, drawing him deeper into her web.

His only alternative was to take matters into his own hands and quickly, before she left him with no room to manoeuvre.

Malus reached the tower's main stair and turned right, heading down. The next landing ended in a door; he pushed it open quickly and quietly, paying no heed to the guard standing watch on the other side. The guards were well used to his presence and he had the run of the tower except for Nagaira's topmost sanctum. Malus continued down the stairs without a backward glance and the guard made no attempt to challenge him before he disappeared around the curve of the staircase.

The next landing ended in yet another door, which Malus opened much more slowly and carefully. Beyond was a small room, lined with racks of long spears and heavy crossbows. A circular table occupied the centre of the guardroom and two of Nagaira's men were slumped in their seats, snoring softly. The highborn shut the door behind him as carefully as possible, then crept the rest of the way down the staircase past the room. To Malus's left a short corridor led to a heavy, iron-banded door. A single globe of witchlight cast long shadows from its sconce at the midpoint of the hall. Malus plucked the globe from its iron holder and moved quietly to a thin arrow-slit just to the right of the door.

Malus could see another black, needle-like tower rising against the night sky – *his* tower, one of several granted by the Drachau for Lurhan and his family. A narrow bridge connected Nagaira's tower with his own; it was a treacherous walk in high winds, but had Malus wished he could have been within the relative safety of his own quarters in moments.

To do so however would have also meant braving the intricate band of runes surrounding the tall, arched bridge door. Malus had no idea how Nagaira's sorcerous defences worked, but he reckoned that at the very least she would be instantly alerted if he tried to cross one of the tower's warded thresholds.

The highborn raised the witchlight globe to eye level, counted three heartbeats and then lowered it once more. After three more heartbeats he repeated the process and then paused, his eyes straining to pierce the predawn darkness.

One moment stretched into the next, until Malus felt his patience starting to fray. Then his eyes caught sight of faint movement on the narrow span. A swift shape was flowing like dark water across the bridge, keeping low so as to avoid silhouetting itself against the faint starlight.

Malus watched as the figure reached the near end of the bridge and straightened its hooded head to peer at the arrow-slit. He did not need to see the druchii's face to know it was Arleth Vann. The assassin's whisper carried easily despite the wind keening across the bridge. 'I have the parcel, my lord. All is in readiness.'

Once it had become clear that Malus was to remain in Nagaira's tower without the support of his retainers, he had gone to some pains during one of their infrequent meetings to establish a contingency plan in the event he needed to escape. 'Give it here,' he whispered to Arleth Vann, readying his hands.

The assassin's arm emerged from his cloak, holding a narrow, square bundle shaped like a book. With a sharp flick of his wrist, the retainer sent the package across the intervening space and through the arrow-slit like a hurled dagger. Even prepared, the speed of the throw took Malus by surprise, the package striking him sharply in the chest. He fumbled with the parcel for a heartbeat and then clasped his hands around it. It was dark cloth bound with cord and he cut the bindings free with his blade and then turned his attention back to Arleth Vann.

'I'm not coming out yet,' he whispered. 'But soon. How goes the restoration?'

'It goes well,' the retainer replied. 'Silar has everything well in hand. He and Dolthaic have hired mercenaries to defend the tower until you can choose new retainers. Your mount has been brought back to the stables and is almost completely mended.'

Malus nodded. 'Well done. Now go back across and get some sleep. Keep to the same vigil, though – when I come out, it will likely be within the next couple of days, at right around this time.'

The hooded head bobbed. 'Yes, my lord,' he whispered and then was gone, like a shadow passing over the moon.

Malus returned the witchlight to its sconce and tucked the parcel within the folds of his robe. The men in the guardroom snored on as he climbed back up the staircase and slipped through the door. At the next landing the guard there watched him calmly and admitted him into his mistress's apartments with a deferential nod of his head.

Once past the guard, Malus drew out the bundle and unwrapped it. A layer of black cloth enclosed a box made of thin wood. Inside was a small, disassembled hand crossbow with five poisoned bolts, a set of lock-picks that he barely knew how to use – and most importantly of all, a smaller wrapped bundle the size of his palm. He plucked the cloth bundle from the box and slipped the rest back into his robe, then unwrapped the one key he truly needed to escape Nagaira's grasp.

The cloth contained a heavy, octagonal brass amulet fitted to a long chain. The amulet's surface was covered with intricate runes that Malus would have been hard pressed to describe, much less understand. What he did know was that the Octagon of Praan was a potent magical relic, capable of absorbing any magic directed at the caster, no matter its power. Since he'd fled the camp of Kul Hadar's beastman herd the octagon had rested at the bottom of a saddlebag hung from Spite's saddle and so it had gone undetected by ally and rival alike until Malus had directed Arleth Vann to make it ready for his use.

Malus slipped the amulet's chain over his head, letting the cold weight of the octagon rest against his chest. He was certain that it would defeat any magical defence in the tower that was aimed at him – but what about simple alarms triggered by his mere presence? He had no answer for that and the notion set his teeth on edge.

Only one way to know for certain, he thought grimly and started up the stairs.

There had been guards outside the entrance to Nagaira's sanctum the last time he'd visited. He hoped that with the mistress in bed the guards would be elsewhere. Malus rounded the corner of the spiral stairs, ready with a half-hearted excuse in case he was challenged – and found the small landing deserted. A pair of tall double doors stood closed, their surface gleaming with patterns of glowing green runes. Further runes etched the arched doorframe, rising to a stylised etching of a manticore leering down from the keystone of the doorway.

Malus swallowed nervously, pleased that there was no one about to witness his apprehension. After the sights he'd seen while raiding his half-brother Urial's tower – himself a sorcerer of sorts – he had some small idea of the kind of power those protective runes held. Yet they can't touch me, he told himself. The medallion will protect me. It *will* protect me.

He laid a hand on the door's latch. The metal felt cold and there was a strange ripple that disturbed the surface of the gleaming runes – as though he'd dipped his hand in a reflecting pool.

Steeling himself, Malus tripped the latch and pulled the door open, then stepped swiftly inside. There was a faint, oily sensation as he crossed the threshold, but nothing more. Breathing a quick sigh of relief, the high-born eased the door shut.

The sanctum was dimly lit by banked witchlights, plunging much of the room into deep shadow. The sanctum occupied the highest rooms in Nagaira's tower, making them consequently the smallest. A circular stone hearth – now cold – occupied the centre of the chamber, surrounded by two plush divans and a number of low tables. The tables, as well as every other bench, shelf, niche and pedestal, were covered with stacks of scrolls, books and other paraphernalia. Tall bookshelves lined every wall, groaning with the weight of grimoires and dusty tomes. At the far end of the room Malus saw a short ladder rising up to the floor above. He'd never gone up there, but now that he thought about it, he remembered that Nagaira had mentioned once that there was nothing up there but more stacks of books and scrolls.

For the first time Malus surveyed the room and took in the sheer vastness of the knowledge contained therein. Hundreds, perhaps *thousands* of works and not one of them kept in anything like a logical order.

He'd had it all wrong. Getting past the deadly wards wasn't the hardest part of his plan. Finding the one book he needed in this scrivener's maze was. And he had only a few hours before dawn, when the household slaves would start roaming the halls again.

The Hierophant had let slip the name of a book: the Tome of Ak'zhaal. If the high priest hadn't merely been making empty boasts, the tome contained details about Tz'arkan. Somewhere within its pages might also lie the resting place of the Idol of Kolkuth. And outside of the city convent, he could think of no better library.

'But where does the Tome of Ak'zhaal lie?' Malus muttered to himself. 'Blessed Mother, what if it isn't even written in druchast at all?' The highborn bared his teeth at the thought that the knowledge he sought could be under his very nose, concealed behind the illegible scrawls of some demented mage.

The daemon stirred, its chuckle rumbling through Malus's skull. Tz'arkan had lain quiescent since the mad feasting of the revel and the sudden voice caused the highborn to jump. 'Impetuous druchii! Only now do you think of these things? Did you imagine the sorcerers of old would write their secrets in your childlike alphabet?'

'How should I know? One set of scratchings are as good as another, are they not?'

'No. They are not.'

'You sound like you know many languages, daemon.'

'Of course. I know every spoken and written tongue this pitiful world has produced. In fact, I had a hand in creating–'

'Excellent. Then you can translate these writings for me, can't you?'

For a moment, the daemon made no response. 'Yes. I suppose,' it said peevishly.

'Good,' Malus said, eyeing the nearest bookshelf. 'Because we have precious little time to do our reading.'

Chapter Seven
THE ALTAR OF THE LOST

IT HAD TAKEN nearly two hours to cover a third of the books contained within the main room, to say nothing of the stacks of volumes kept in the room above. He had fought to keep his frustration in check – if he and Tz'arkan were truly integral to Nagaira's schemes then the books she had been consulting would be close by, not gathering dust in some far corner of her sanctum. Dawn was close at hand when Malus almost literally stumbled over the Tome of Ak'zhaal. As he had rushed to the next bookshelf in line he spied a large leather-bound book on the floor near one of the divans, hidden underneath a platter littered with bits of old cheese and breadcrumbs. The runes on the book's spine meant nothing to him – and yet when he looked at them it felt like a film of oil slid over his eyes and he instinctively knew what the ancient writing meant.

Even then, much of the text was indecipherable to him. Parts of it were history, parts of it references to sorcerous arts that completely escaped him. Malus scanned page after page, hungry for references to Tz'arkan and coming up wanting again and again. His attention wandered, after another half an hour he found himself listening for the sound of a hand on the door-latch and wondering what he would say to the slave – or worse, his sister – when he was discovered.

Then, two-thirds of the way into the book the references began. Initially, the comments were things he already knew: Tz'arkan was a mighty daemon that had once walked the earth during the First War, many thousands of years ago, but he had been tricked and bound into the service of five powerful Chaos sorcerers. With the daemon's power and knowledge at their disposal the sorcerers became fearsome conquerors, driving their foes before them. In the end, however, the daemon's diabolical gifts proved to be the sorcerers' undoing – one by one they were torn apart by rivals, driven mad by greed and bloodlust or consumed in sorcerous conflagrations too powerful for them to contain.

According to the book, the sorcerer Eradorius was the master of the enigmatic Idol of Kolkuth, a relic of a lost age even in those ancient times. Eradorius was the first to realise the peril of the daemon's gifts – and as a result he was the first of the five sorcerers to die. Beset by treacherous lieutenants who hungered for his power and fearful that his fellow sorcerers were scheming to assassinate him, Eradorius fled his enormous palace and his legion of retainers and sought refuge on a tiny island in the storm-wracked northern seas. There, he hoped to cheat the daemon's revenge by fleeing to a sanctuary that no enemy – mortal or daemon – could breach.

The highborn took a deep breath and returned his attention to the great book lying open on the low table by the divan. He carefully turned the page with the tips of two fingers, noting with alarm how the aged vellum crackled beneath his touch.

In the Time of Ash and Crimson the sorcerer Eradorius, known to the sons of Aenarion as one of the terrible Lords of the Black Stone, did leave the fastness of his citadel at Harash-Karn and rode the ash-laden winds like a great wyrm. Darkness and terror followed in his wake and the lesser minions of the Ruinous Powers quailed and cursed at his passing.

The sorcerer rode the heavens for seven days and nights, until the slate-coloured seas of the north stretched below him as far as his eyes could see. He soared above those cold and hungry waters until at last he spied a gnarled finger of stone rising from the icy mists – the isle called Morhaut, which in the tongue of the First Men means the altar of the lost.

Upon this haunted stone the dread mage alighted and stretched forth his claw-like hand to bend the cursed isle to his will. He used the secrets the Cursed One had given him and tunnelled deep into rock and air and the passage of years. A tower was built by Eradorius, raised with power and madness, reaching to the sky and sinking into worlds beyond, to a place without walls or passageways or doors. He dug into the bedrock of the world, seeking the empty place beyond, where the earthbound daemon could not find him. And there he passed from the ken of his fellows and from the talons of the Cursed One and was lost for all time.

'Morhaut,' Malus growled, his face grim. 'Of course. I should have known.'

The highborn felt the daemon stir within his breast. 'Oh? Why is that?'

Malus fought the urge to throw the old book across the room. 'Because it's little more than a legend and every druchii who's gone searching for it has never been seen again.'

He leapt to his feet and went to a large map that hung in a wooden frame against one of the sanctum's walls. 'I heard several versions of the story on the slaving cruise last summer,' he said, his eyes roving over the huge expanse of yellowed parchment. 'It's an isle of lost ships going back to the First War, surrounded by deadly reefs and impenetrable mists.'

The highborn traced a finger along Naggaroth's rough eastern coast, then north-east from the straits near Karond Kar. North and east, over a wide swath of hungry grey sea. 'Mother of Night,' he cursed softly. 'I'll need a whole *fleet*. Raiding ships and fighting men and damnable sorcery as well.'

'How grandiose,' the daemon sneered. 'You let that little taste of adoration go to your head, or you're simply looking for a reason to squander more of my treasure.'

'Would that were the truth,' Malus snarled. 'I'd throw every bit of your gold to the slaves in the Market Quarter if it meant an easy path to your damnable relics. No, the waters in the north are teeming with marauders. A single ship wouldn't last a week on those seas.'

'Marauders?'

Malus nodded. 'Norscan raiders claim the north seas as their own and there are marauder strongholds on nearly every island. They come south in the summer and make coastal raids against Ulthuan and the human lands, much as we do. Some of the more foolhardy bands even raid Naggaroth from time to time, or harry our raiding ships as they return home laden with plunder.'

'Indeed? I can see why you care little for them. They sound much like druchii.'

'They are *nothing* like us,' Malus snapped. 'We raid other lands for the gold and flesh to sustain our kingdom. The weak suffer so the strong may survive – that is the way of the world and we are its finest predators. These marauders exist only to destroy. They burn and slaughter without reason, without purpose. They are wasteful and ignorant, like animals.' The highborn's scowl deepened. 'Worst among them are the Skinriders.'

'You seem quite the expert on these marauding humans,' the daemon sneered. 'For a scholar, you have strange interests.'

'The Skinriders have been a thorn in Naggaroth's side for years, preying on our raiders as they return home loaded with flesh for our markets,' Malus replied acidly. 'They take the skin of others to cover their own raw, suppurating bodies. They worship a daemon god of pestilence and are rewarded with terrible strength and vitality. But the skin sloughs from their diseased bodies like putrid wax and they suffer constant agony unless they can clothe their raw flesh with untainted hide. Such are the rewards for placing faith in the words of daemons.'

'You insult me, little Darkblade. I am among the most honourable of beings. I have obeyed your every request to the letter, have I not? Do not blame me for your own lack of imagination or wit. Are not these Skinriders mighty warriors, blessed by their patron?'

'They are. In fact, they infest the northern sea like a plague – even the other raiders pay them tribute in fresh skins and sacrificial victims. In fact, legend has it their strength is so great and their sorcery so potent that they have claimed the most dangerous island in the region as their stronghold.'

'The Isle of Morhaut.'

'Now you begin to see the scope of the challenge set before me,' Malus answered grimly. 'Thus: a fleet, soldiers and a sorcerer. And soon. Damnably soon. The spring thaws begin in little more than a week and the corsairs at Clar Karond will be putting to sea as soon as they are able.'

'Ah, yes. The sands are trickling from the hourglass. You must find another way, Malus. There is no time for such elaborate schemes.'

Remembering where he was, Malus glanced at the nearest window and saw that the sky had nearly paled to the grey gloom of morning. The slaves were doubtless already stirring in the lower levels of the tower, preparing for the day. 'I have little choice, daemon,' Malus growled, dashing back to the divan and returning the tome to its place on the floor. 'If I can't raise such a force on my own I'll have to convince someone else to give me one.'

'The revels have left you unhinged, little druchii. Who would give you such power? The Drachau? The Witch King himself?' Tz'arkan laughed mockingly.

'I'd have better luck with my own father,' Malus said bitterly. Suddenly he straightened, his dark brows furrowing. 'On the other hand…'

The daemon squirmed beneath his ribs. 'Yes?'

Malus grinned like a wolf. 'I'm a fool. All the pieces are right in front of me. I just need to begin pulling some strings. It's *perfect*.'

The highborn could feel the weight of the daemon's attention settle on him like a mantle of ice. 'What lunacy are you contemplating now? Tell me!'

Malus raced for the door, his mind hard at work as the pieces of his plan came together. Tired as he was, there would be no sleep for him today. 'First things first,' he said, as much to the daemon as to himself. 'If I don't get back to my bed before the tower slaves awaken things could become awkward indeed.'

DOWN ON THE arena floor a slave screamed in terror, kicking up a spray of red-stained sand as he threw himself to one side before the cold one's charge. The young human almost made it, but he timed his leap a fraction of a second too late and the nauglir's jaws closed on the man's scabby legs. Razor-sharp fangs as long as knives snipped off both limbs just below the knee, sending the human tumbling in a bright fountain of blood. The cold one's black-armoured rider hauled at the reins, trying to check his mount's headlong rush and circle back to the slave while the highborn in the stands hissed in derision or shouted words of support.

The small arena shook beneath the combined weight of a dozen cold ones as the swirling game of shakhtila neared its end. Of the three score slaves who began the game less than a third still survived and they were scattered all over the playing field. Most of the survivors still clutched their flimsy spears or hefted short blades, their faces pale and heads turning wildly as they tried to keep all of the cold ones in sight. As Malus watched, the legless slave tried to drag himself by his hands across the arena floor, but two red-armoured riders from the opposing team caught sight of the man and spurred their mounts towards him. The druchii in the lead brandished a bloody sabre, while his team-mate hefted a long, slim spear. The riders expertly controlled the speed of their beasts, racing in a line as straight as an arrow right at the hapless man. Before the slave could register his peril the sabre flashed down, severing the man's head and the spearman following close behind caught it on the sleek steel point while the grisly trophy was still spinning in the air. The black rider howled in impotent fury as the red spearman raised his trophy to the small audience watching from above.

The arena was one of the most luxurious in the city, catering solely to the wealthiest households in Hag Graef. The lavishly-appointed viewing boxes surrounding the arena could normally hold little more than two hundred druchii and their retinues, but today the riders performed for fewer than two dozen nobles, all dressed in gleaming armour and chains of silver and gold. Many of them raised jewelled goblets in salute to the red team's point, while others picked at delicacies proffered on silver trays or argued with one another over the merits of the different riders. They were all young, rich men who wore their two swords with ostentatious pride and carried themselves with the reckless assurance of the all-powerful. Yet the highborn could not help but notice that each and every man, regardless of what they were doing, had positioned themselves so that they could watch every move by the statuesque woman who reclined in their midst.

Malus stood at the top of a marble stairway leading down to the viewing boxes from the lesser galleries above. With a start of surprise he caught himself checking the state of his own attire, adjusting the position of the enamelled plate armour and the arrangement of the paired swords given to him by his sister. With the octagon in his possession it had been a relatively simple matter to bypass Nagaira's wards and escape without raising an alarm. Silar and his men had been surprised at his sudden arrival in his refurbished tower, but a few sharp commands had set them scurrying to enquire about the location of the person he wished to meet.

Silar and Arleth Vann had tried to insist on sending him with a proper retinue, but once again, Malus was forced to order them to remain behind. His instincts told him that their presence would have only complicated things further; the last thing he needed was for an overheated noble to misconstrue a word or gesture that would lead to bloodshed. He had enough feuds to contend with as it was.

Malus took a deep breath, collecting his wits and started down the stairs. No less than three of the nobles leapt to bar his entrance to the viewing box, their hands straying to the hilts of their swords. So many young fools with so much to prove, he thought, careful to keep his disdain from showing on his face.

For a fleeting instant Malus wasn't sure how to address the men. It was a complicated tangle of etiquette: on the one hand each one of them clearly outranked him in terms of personal wealth and prestige, on the other hand they were also retainers and he had a blood-tie to the woman they served. There was also the fact that he'd likely killed more men in battle than all of the retainers combined and he wasn't in a mood to kowtow to anyone. 'Stand aside, hounds,' he said with an easy smile and a glitter of menace in his eyes. 'I'm here to speak to my sister.'

The leader of the trio, a sharp-featured man with finely-pointed teeth and a row of gold rings glinting in each ear, leaned forward and made to draw one of his elaborately ornamented swords. 'This is a private party, Darkblade. If you want the pleasure of my lady's company go make an appointment with her chamberlain, otherwise we'll chuck you into the arena for the nauglir to chew on.'

Malus met the highborn's stare. 'You're too close,' he said calmly.

'Am I?' The noble leaned in slightly closer, almost nose-to-nose with Malus. 'Do I make you uncomfortable?'

Malus grabbed the elbow of the noble's sword arm with his left hand and punched the druchii in the throat with his right. The retainer's eyes bulged and he doubled over, gagging and gasping for breath. With a shove Malus sent the man crashing into one of his fellows, sending both sprawling in a heap.

The third retainer's eyes went wide. Before he could more than half-draw his own blade Malus darted in until they stood almost nose-to-nose. The noble back-pedalled, trying to get enough room to finish drawing his sword and Malus helped him along with a hard shove in the middle of his chest. The retainer let out a yelp and tumbled backwards, falling over a pair of seated retainers and losing his grip on his blade.

Angry shouts filled the spectators' box and a dozen blades rasped from their scabbards, but over the din of the rising scuffle and the thunder of the combat below a woman's smooth voice cut through the tumult and stopped every man in his tracks.

'Enough. *Enough!* If my brother wishes to speak to me so badly he'd risk his own precious skin then I'll hear what he has to say.'

The retainers stopped cold. Even the man Malus had struck in the throat somehow stifled his hacking gasps for air. Her presence filled the spectators' box like a burst of cold winter sunlight and the nobles instantly subsided. They returned to what they'd been doing before the sudden interruption, making a path for Malus to approach the reclining form of his sister Yasmir.

She was watching him with an expression of mild curiosity and in spite of himself Malus felt as though he were being drawn into her large, violet eyes. He realised at that moment that the magical allure Nagaira used on him at the revel had been nothing more than a feeble imitation of Yasmir's personal glamour. She was every inch the ideal of druchii beauty: lithe and sensual, with perfect alabaster skin and a fine-boned face that seemed to glow against a backdrop of lustrous black hair. Not even Eldire's fearsome presence could compare; she had built a persona based on magic, vast influence and guile. With Yasmir, her glamour was effortless, like sunlight gleaming on the surface of a glacier. There was great danger there, of that he was certain, but he was nevertheless blind to it.

'Well met, sister,' he managed, struggling to regain his poise. It occurred to him that this was the first time in his life he had actually spoken to Yasmir; as the third oldest of Lurhan's six children, she had been nearing adulthood by the time Malus was born. Aside from mandatory observances like the annual Hanil Khar, they never saw one another. 'I... I had no idea you had an interest in sports.'

Yasmir smiled, the expression disturbingly unaffected and genuine. 'I would say it depends on the nature of the game,' she replied. Her voice was melodious and soft as sable fur. There was not a single rough edge to it and it made Malus wonder if she had ever had to raise her voice for anything in her entire life. 'Vaklyr and Lord Kurgal seek to prove whose fighting skills are superior, so they and their retainers are vying for heads in the arena. Lord Kurgal's red team appears to have the lead and Vaklyr's men are losing more than just the game.' There was an eerie gleam of mirth in her eyes. 'What do you think of their riding ability, Malus? Rumour has it you're quite the expert on cold ones.'

Malus shrugged. 'Lord Kurgal has served our father for many years as Master of Cavalry. He and his men are the true experts. I merely dabble in breeding nauglir when it amuses me.' He attempted to cover his unease by studying the movements of the riders in the arena. 'Vaklyr is too eager. Too aggressive. He's clearly trying to win more here than just a game.'

It was obvious that he'd walked in on the latest spat between Yasmir's ardent rivals. They were constantly vying with one another for her attentions and his sister always managed to give them just enough reason to hope to keep them coming back again and again. It was said that Yasmir had slain more of Hag Graef's knights than any enemy army. He had never really stopped to think how much craft such manipulations required, but now he was being shown a taste of it. *Lurhan should order you to choose a husband,* Malus thought, *or pack you off to the temple where you can do no more harm.*

Yasmir laughed, a clear, pure sound that sent shivers along Malus's skin. 'Vaklyr is an ardent one,' she agreed. 'So passionate and unbridled. I fear he won't ever amount to much, despite his family's connections, but right now his artless desire is entertaining.' She regarded

Malus almost languidly. 'What is it that you desire, brother? I must say, this visit comes as a great surprise.'

Again, Malus was taken aback by the sheer frankness of her question. Does she know nothing of guile, the highborn thought? And then it struck him: of course she did. She simply didn't feel the need for it. Yasmir was relaxed, open and genuine as a show of *strength*. Adored as she was by many of the most powerful nobles in Hag Graef, she had little reason to fear anyone, save perhaps the Drachau himself.

'I have come to enlist your aid, sister,' Malus said, summoning up a smile of his own. 'There is a matter I wish to propose to our elder brother once he returns to Clar Karond with his ships.'

To his surprise – and annoyance – Yasmir laughed again. 'Seeking another backer for a slave raid, Malus? I don't think you could win the support of a tavern full of drunken sailors, much less a corsair lord like my beloved brother.' At the mention of Bruglir, Lurhan's eldest son, a real look of hunger came over Yasmir's features. They saw one another for only a month or two at a time, just long enough to refit the raiding ships in Bruglir's fleet before he set out to hunt the seas once more. When he was at Hag Graef the two were inseparable. It was the one deterrent that had served to keep the nobles at the Hag from pressing a case for Yasmir's marriage. No one wished to cross the man who would be the next Vaulkhar – a man who was also reputed to be one of the finest swordsmen in Naggaroth and one of the most powerful corsairs in memory.

Malus felt his smile falter a bit and felt a flash of annoyance. Once again, he fought to regain his balance. 'Were I acting by myself, you would undoubtedly be correct, sister,' he said. 'But that's why I wish to enlist your help. Everyone knows that you alone have Bruglir's utter confidence. If you were to speak on my behalf, even the great corsair lord would have to listen.'

'Perhaps,' Yasmir said languidly. 'You're a bit better at flattery than I imagined, Malus. Have you been practising with Nagaira? You're quite the couple these days.'

'I... no,' he caught himself stammering. Once again, the irritation flared. He could hear the retainers chuckling quietly to themselves. 'I didn't think to win you over with mere flattery,' the highborn said. 'I plan to pay well for your aid, dear sister.'

For a moment, Yasmir was silent. Malus sensed a wave of tension ripple through the nobles. 'And what, pray tell, can you offer me that these worthies cannot?'

Malus turned back to Yasmir with a wolfish smile. 'Our brother Urial's head, of course.'

Yasmir sat bolt upright, her careless demeanour wiped away. Now her eyes were brilliant and intense. 'That's a fearful offer to make, brother.'

'I can think of no finer gift for you, dear sister,' Malus answered. He knew that was the one thing that she wanted nearly as much as Bruglir himself. Urial had made no secret of his infatuation for Yasmir, even though his twisted body and mind repulsed her. Yet he continued to pursue her affections and such were his ties to the temple and to the Drachau himself that no man dared raise a hand against him. 'As well-informed as you are, you are clearly aware of the... difficulties between Urial and myself. We are already at swords' points over other matters – I can either negotiate with him or end his threat to me in a more permanent fashion.'

'If you kill Urial, it will cost you. The temple will neither forgive nor forget.'

Malus shrugged. 'I am already at war with them, sister. So far I find it most agreeable. Regardless, that would not be your concern, would it? Urial would haunt you no more and I would face the consequences in your stead.'

Yasmir regarded him at length, her expression intent. 'Before you left for the north I would have thought you incapable of such daring,' she said. 'But now? I confess, it is a very tempting offer.' She leaned back against the divan and stretched out her hand. Instantly a young lord leapt to her side with a goblet of wine. Yasmir gave the man a brief, luminous smile and then turned her attention back to Malus. 'What do you wish of me?'

'Merely your support. I intend to speak to Bruglir in Clar Karond as soon as his fleet puts in. If you lend your aid and persuade him to join the expedition, then I will take care of Urial in turn.'

Yasmir smiled enticingly. 'Suppose I ask for payment in advance? A show of good faith?'

Now it was Malus's turn to laugh. 'You are wondrously beguiling sister, but please.'

'I was merely thinking of you, dear brother. Why, you could likely see to the problem right now. If you hurry, I expect you could catch him before he reaches the stables. I don't expect he can walk very fast with that twisted leg of his.'

Malus's smile faltered and no amount of willpower could bring it back. 'I beg your pardon, sister?'

Yasmir regarded him with a look of innocent surprise, though the look in her eyes belied the gesture. 'Why, he was just here, brother, pressing his nauseating case for my affections. When one of my men reported that you'd entered the arena he became very agitated and took his leave.'

'Did he? How interesting,' Malus replied. 'Perhaps he and I will have a conversation about you after all. Something to encourage him to seek his entertainment elsewhere.' The highborn's mind raced. How many retainers had Urial brought with him? How many more could he call on at short notice? *I have to get out of here.*

'Would you? That would please me very much,' Yasmir said.

Malus bowed deeply. 'Then may I count on your support with Bruglir?'

'For your efforts with Urial? Of course.'

'Excellent,' Malus answered. 'Then I will take my leave. I expect Urial and I will have much to discuss in the near future.' *Just not right here and now,* Malus hoped. He cursed himself for leaving his men at the tower.

He gave no time to Yasmir to respond. The nobles glared hatefully at him as he passed, but he gave the hounds little heed.

A roar went up from the arena floor as another man bled for Yasmir's pleasure. Malus had the feeling that he wouldn't be the last.

Chapter Eight
THE BLESSING OF STEEL

MALUS TOOK THE steps to the upper gallery two at a time, fighting the urge to draw his sword as he approached the dark portal leading to the spectator ramps beyond. Bad enough for Yasmir and her aides to see him run – he wasn't about to start jabbing his blades into every deep shadow he passed.

All was not entirely lost. He had no mount in the arena stables, having walked the short distance from the fortress. That worked to his advantage somewhat, it was likely that Urial would set up his ambush there. If he moved swiftly he could take a somewhat circuitous route down to the ground level, out through one of the arena's many open gates and onto the crowded city streets. It was late in the afternoon, when much of the city's business was conducted, so one more highborn walking the streets wouldn't attract too much attention.

His skin felt cold beneath the weight of his armour, black ice moved sluggishly through his veins. Malus thought about turning to Tz'arkan for aid. The daemon was strangely quiet, like a cat studying an unsuspecting mouse and the silence made the highborn uneasy. How deeply had Tz'arkan sunk his roots while Malus hung in the Vaulkhar's tower? How close was he to surrendering himself entirely to the daemon? Malus could no longer say for certain. And death brought no salvation either; if he died Tz'arkan would claim his soul 'til the end of time.

So I'd best survive then, Malus thought grimly, with nothing but my swords and my blessed hate. Just like old times.

The highborn plunged through the dark archway, his eyes momentarily blinded as he adjusted to the lack of light and that was the moment Urial's men made their move.

A sword struck his left pauldron, glancing off the curved metal and cutting a small notch in the highborn's ear. Another blade whispered through the air from his right, but Malus ducked instinctively and the keen edge missed his skull by less than a finger length. The highborn hurled himself forward with a shouted oath, crashing into yet another swordsman, whose blade clanged ineffectually from Malus's breastplate. The retainer, caught by surprise, tried to back-pedal out of the way, but Malus continued his rush, pushing the warrior off his feet.

Malus's sword flashed from its oiled scabbard as he fetched up against the far wall. His eyes were adjusting, the pain in his cut ear making his blood sing and lending a cold, clear focus to his surroundings. There were five men on the shadowy spectators' ramp, all of them in black robes and kheitans. They wore close-fitting hoods and silver caedlin, even in the light of day; the delicate masks were worked in the shape of skulls, their dark oculars devoid of interest or pity. They all held large, curved swords, wielding the great blades two-handed and moved with the speed and grace of skilled swordsmen. Fortunately for Malus, none of the retainers wore heavy armour – only hauberks of black mail that covered their torso and part of their upper arms. It lent him a distinct advantage, Malus thought, but how much? Urial, the highborn noted, was nowhere to be seen and he wasn't sure if that was a good sign or a bad one.

The man Malus had knocked down was already back on his feet and the five men rushed silently at him, instinctively forming a semicircle that sought to pin his back to the arena's outside wall. But Malus wasn't about to give them the advantage; with a snarl he rushed at the nearest man, swinging viciously. The retainer's blade was a blur of motion, flashing in the half-light. He blocked Malus's stroke easily and turned the move into a cut aimed for the highborn's skull, only realising too late that Malus's stroke was only a well-timed feint that reversed itself and swept low, slicing through the retainer's right leg. The sword had been forged by a master and its fearsome edge parted robes, skin and muscle with equal ease. Blood flowed in a torrent, splashing on the stone floor and the retainer collapsed with the faintest of groans. Malus had already leapt past the grievously wounded man and charged down the spectators' ramp, heading for the street.

Footsteps whispered along the stone in Malus's wake. Something hard rapped against his back, but the strong steel turned aside the hurled dagger and sent it ringing along the floor. The ramp curved and Malus raced around the corner, momentarily out of the line of fire.

The ramp switched back upon itself and now he was just one level above the street. Here the outer wall of the arena was pierced by tall windows that let in shafts of pale daylight to relieve the gloom. On impulse Malus leapt for the nearest window, turning as he jumped and tried to force his way through the tight space. He crashed through the thin glass, cold air rushing against his face as he plummeted to the street below.

Malus rolled slightly in mid air, taking the fall on his armoured back. The impact jarred him to the core and knocked the wind from his lungs, but the instant his vision cleared he was rolling on the paving stones, trying to regain his feet. There were shouts of surprise and muffled curses from passing druchii nearby, but Malus paid no heed, gasping for breath and groping about for his sword. Even now he could imagine Urial's retainers racing down the ramp to ground level, swords ready at their sides.

When the highborn staggered to his feet, however, it wasn't a skull-faced retainer standing in the arena's open gate, but Urial the Forsaken himself, his eyes burning like molten brass.

Like Malus, Urial wore full armour for his visit to Yasmir. Two short, slender swords were buckled to his waist, looking more like an adolescent's practice blades than true weapons of war. Sheathed in steel, his deformities were almost invisible unless one knew where to look. There was no one in between them; for a fleeting instant Malus was tempted to rush at his malformed half-brother and fulfil Yasmir's wish then and there. But then Urial raised his good arm and pointed at Malus and his thin lips moved in silent incantation.

The highborn turned, his mind driving him to panicked flight even though Malus knew that it was too little, too late. Pain flared along his body in a wave. Malus staggered, his mouth opening in a silent scream. Every nerve, every fibre hissed like red-hot iron.

Dimly he sensed a presence rushing at him. Finding his voice, he uttered a bestial snarl and lashed out with his blade. The retainer was caught by surprise, hurled backward with his throat gaping wide. The highborn turned and forced his limbs to work, stumbling, then lurching, then shambling down the paved street as fast as he could.

The streets of the Highborn Quarter teemed with groups of servants going about the business of their masters, their arms laden with parcels bought from the craftsmen's shops that filled the area. There were few highborn about; this late in the day many of the city's nobles had already retired to their towers, preparing themselves for whatever diversions the night promised. Small groups of druchii retainers and lesser nobles strolled along the narrow streets, busy on errands or scheming quietly to themselves.

The searing pain was fading. Malus gasped for air with lungs that seemed full of jagged glass. Druchii stepped from his path, many placing hands to sword hilts or spitting curses as he passed. Keep going, he thought. Keep going. Find a large retinue and mingle with them, turn a corner, find an alley. *Keep moving.*

Malus looked about wildly, trying to find his bearings. By sheer good fortune he'd gone the right way outside the arena; the Hag's towers loomed above him less than a quarter-mile distant. He continued to run, shoving through huddled clusters of slaves, weaving around groups of low-born druchii and looking for another group of highborn he could lose himself amongst. Just ahead was a corner and a large number of armoured druchii. He was almost upon them when they stepped left and right, clearing a path before him – and the knot of armed temple acolytes running towards him from farther up the street.

'Mother of Night,' Malus gasped, his eyes widening. He fumbled his second sword from its scabbard as well. It looked like close to a dozen holy warriors, wearing dark red robes and silver breastplates. Each one held a gleaming draich in their hands – the two-handed executioner's sword favoured by the warriors of Khaine and wielded with terrible skill. Their expressions were fierce in the fading light and Malus knew that his running was at an end.

'Damn you all!' Malus roared back, raising his blades defiantly. 'Come ahead then and pour out your blood upon my steel!'

The highborn readied his weapons as the acolytes came on and the highborn saw death glinting in their brass-coloured eyes. Then a sharp blow struck him at the base of his skull and the world dissolved in a flare of white light.

THE AIR SHOOK with the howls of the damned.

Once more he ran across a heaving plain of blood-red earth, while the sky churned and vomited ash and bone dust from its depths. Multitudes of ghosts surrounded him, reaching for him with gnarled hands and clashing jaws. Already his fine armour was rent and pierced in dozens of places, though no blood flowed from the cold wounds beneath.

His sword passed effortlessly through them. Gelid, pulpy bodies and misshapen skulls all turned to sickly vapour as his blade bisected them, only to coalesce once more in the wake of the blade's passing. At best, he could only clear a path before him with each stroke as he ran, pushing ahead towards a goal he only dimly understood.

The horizon before him was a flat, featureless line as dark as old brick, standing out sharply against the swirling grey sky. A single tower stood there, square and black, silhouetted against both earth and sky alike. It seemed impossibly far away and yet it radiated a solidity that the rest of the alien landscape did not. It was a source of sanity in a vast plain of madness and he fought his way toward it with the manic intensity of a drowning man. Yet no matter how hard he struggled or how many steps he took, the tower grew no closer.

'AWAKEN, DARKBLADE! THE sons of murder approach and the time of your death is at hand!'

Malus opened his eyes, yet for long moments he could not tell if he was indeed awake. There was a red haze to the air, a kind of indistinct shimmer that blurred the geometry of walls, doorways and ceilings. Even the solidity of objects seemed inconstant; one moment the dark stone surrounding him was dense and oppressive, then it became pale and translucent, lit from behind by an angry red light. There was a buzzing in the air, harsh and somehow metallic. If he focused on it he could make out the sound of voices: bloodthirsty, exultant, agonised.

There was pain. It came and went with the shifting solidity of his surroundings. Strangely, the less distinct things were, the sharper his pain became. He lay against a rack of brass needles of varying lengths, holding him nearly upright in the centre of a small, octagonal room. Each beat of his heart trembled through the scores of thin needles and reverberated back along his bones. When the walls faded to smoke, the agony was indescribable, leaving him gasping for breath when tangible reality wavered back into place. He could not move an inch; the needles were artfully placed to paralyse his muscles, pinning him like a living specimen in a display of grotesqueries.

He faced a set of double doors with iron hinges and brass facings. At the archway above the door were set a pair of faces worked in gleaming silver. The faces were exultant and bestial, their eyeholes were black voids; empty and yet somehow aware. He looked into those depthless pits and knew at once where he was.

'May the Outer Darkness take you, daemon!' Malus said, his words coming out in a hoarse whisper. 'You sat silent while Urial's men surrounded me!'

'This half-brother of yours is not like your zealous but self-absorbed sister,' Tz'arkan replied acidly. 'His sight is sharper than most. Had he sensed my presence he would have spared nothing to destroy you then and there and no aid I could have given you would have made any difference.'

'So you deliver me into his hands instead? You allow him and his damned temple lackeys to drag me to his tower? We stand at the gateway to the realm of murder! What would you have me do now?'

'I would have you save yourself, fool!' The daemon's voice was more agitated than Malus had ever heard it. Was there fear in the daemon's voice? 'Urial and his priests draw near, Malus. If they take you through the doorway standing before you, that will be the end. You will not emerge from the red place they will take you.'

Malus gritted his teeth and forced himself to move, pouring every ounce of his black will into drawing his right arm free from its bed of needles. Veins bulged from his temples and neck and his entire frame quivered with the strain, but his limbs would not budge. When the next wave of torment washed over him the sensation was so intense Malus was certain his heart would burst. The fact that it didn't was likely another testament to Urial's infernal skills.

'Spare me your insults and help me, cursed spirit! Lend me the strength to overcome these blasted needles, if nothing else! I can't get away if I can't move!'

'I cannot, Darkblade. Not here. It is too dangerous.'

Malus managed a bitter laugh. 'Too dangerous? For whom?'

But Tz'arkan did not reply. The doors swung open, the iron hinges groaning in torment. A group of blood-soaked druchii waited at the threshold, their hands bearing bowls and brass knives. Slowly and silently they filed into the room, half turning left, half turning right. As they surrounded him the room grew less and less distinct and a tide of irresistible pain swelled where each brass needle pierced his skin.

Urial was the last to enter the crowded room. Like the priests, he wore thin robes of white, soaked with blotches of fresh blood that somehow steamed in the thick air. Without the concealment of armour or heavy clothes there was no disguising Urial's gaunt physique. Muscles like thin steel cords stood out sharply across his narrow, bony chest and angular shoulders, lending his face an even more cadaverous cast than normal. His ruined sword arm was clutched tightly to his side. Even more shrunken than the rest of his body, Urial's right hand was twisted into a gnarled, paralysed claw, the palm turned upwards and the fingers curled inward as though shrivelled by an open flame.

The former acolyte of Khaine walked with a pronounced limp, dragging a crippled left foot, but his eyes were bright and he held himself proudly, like a king rather than a cursed cripple. Strange runes had been incised into the skin of his chest and arms. His white hair had been bound in a thick braid that lay over his right shoulder, hanging down almost as far as his waist. A third of its length was red with blood. In his left hand Urial held a long, broad-bladed dagger, its blade worked with fearsome sigils. There was a red haze around the weapon, as though blood coalesced from the very air around its sanctified edge. Heavy crimson drops fell from the blade's wicked point, spattering heavily on the stone tile below.

The tide of pain rose with every step Urial took. Once more focusing every iota of his will, Malus made his head bow in greeting. 'Well met, brother,' he wheezed through clenched teeth. 'It's... an honour to be invited into your sanctum, but you needn't put on such... a show for my sake.'

No emotion showed on Urial's face. His eyes regarded Malus with the same kind of dispassion as a priest inspecting a sacrificial slave. When he spoke his voice was resonant and harsh, like the penetrating note of a cymbal or bell. 'The honour is mine,' Urial said, without the slightest trace of modesty or compassion. 'There is no greater offering to the Lord of the Blade than to sacrifice one's own kin. I have been patient and dutiful in your pursuit and now Khaine has provided by placing you in my hands.'

'Blessed be the Murderer,' the priests intoned.

'I... I have wronged you, brother,' Malus said, his mind working furiously for a way to distract Urial from his deadly purpose. 'And the blood of your possessions lies on my hands. I wish to make amends.'

Urial paused, his brow furrowing ever so slightly. 'You will,' he replied, sounding faintly bemused. 'Your severed head will rest on a great pyramid of skulls, where you will gaze adoringly upon the glory of Khaine. I will see to it.'

'Blessed is he who slays in Khaine's name,' the priests intoned.

'But... is it not said that all warriors look upon the face of Khaine in the fullness of time?' Again, Urial paused. 'Yes. That is so.'

'Then what need is there to hurry things along?'

'You broke into my tower. You stole my possessions, killed my slaves and defiled my sanctum with your unclean presence,' Urial answered harshly. 'And there is the matter of the blood debt to the temple. An oath sworn before the Lord of Murder cannot be denied.'

'The call of blood is answered in sundered flesh,' said the priests.

'But it was a debt that you invoked against me,' Malus countered. 'And thus you could absolve it if you desired. I was deceived... '

Now Urial's expression became one of complete puzzlement. 'I did not invoke the blood debt,' Urial said. 'Nagaira did.'

For a moment, Malus couldn't speak. He struggled to accept what Urial had said and realised the full scope of the deception that had been built around him. 'Blessed Mother,' he said to himself, 'she played me at every turn. Everything she said was a lie.'

Urial nodded gravely. 'Such is the way of all flesh – a path of weakness and deception redeemed in the blood of the slain.' He stepped forward, raising the dagger. 'Soon you will know the truth, brother. The blessing of steel wipes all deception away.'

But Malus was no longer listening, caught up in a wave of cold, clear fury that washed his pain and fear away. 'Take this blessing from me and save it for one more deserving. It was Nagaira who made me her cat's paw, who told me of the skull in your keeping and who provided the means to violate your sanctum. She is the one who deserves your attention. I was merely the sword in her hand.' As he spoke, a plan took shape in his mind. 'I wish to atone for my crimes, brother. I wish to cleanse my soul with the blood of the unbeliever. If you will stay your hand, I will reward you and the temple with a rich gift of slaughter that will grant you the favour of Khaine.'

A stir went through the assembled priests, but Urial's expression was stern. 'You beg for *mercy* from a servant of Khaine?'

'No! I ask for the chance to serve his cause and provide a greater sacrifice in his name.' He looked his brother in the eye. 'What if I were to tell you that the Cult of Slaanesh is thriving within the very walls of the Hag itself?'

Urial's eyes narrowed suspiciously. 'The temple has long suspected this. Our agents search for signs of the apostates in the Hag and elsewhere.'

'The stain runs deeper than you know, brother. It reaches into the most powerful houses in the city,' Malus replied. 'Stay your hand and I can deliver them to you – our sister Nagaira stands high in their esteem. Think on that. Imagine the sacrifice *she* would make.' After a moment, he added, 'and there is more.'

Whispers filled the air as the priests reacted to the news. Urial silenced them with a look. 'More? What more can you offer?'

'Yasmir.'

Urial stiffened. He rushed at Malus, surprisingly swift for the deformities that warped his body. 'Do not dare impugn her honour, Darkblade! She who is pure and beloved before the god!'

'No! I did not mean that, brother – stay your hand!' Malus lowered his voice so only Urial could hear. 'I mean to say that I can bring her to you.'

Urial stared at Malus, his eyes wide and uncomprehending. 'Her thoughts are for Bruglir alone,' he said woodenly. 'And she refuses to give him up.'

'Of course,' Malus agreed. 'Of course. You know that as well as I. But all warriors see the face of Khaine in time, do they not?'

Urial stared hard into Malus's eyes, his expression unreadable. 'They do. They do indeed,' he whispered.

'This can be arranged, brother. I can see to it. But I would need your help. My plan requires a sorcerer of great skill.' He attempted a shrug but forgot the paralysing effect of the needles. 'I confess that I had planned to use Nagaira in my schemes, but this is so much more fitting. One might even see the hand of Khaine at work in this.'

After a long moment, Urial lowered his blade. Something glittered in his eyes, but whether it was desire or madness, Malus couldn't say. Perhaps there was little difference between the two.

'Perhaps,' Urial said at last. 'I cannot deny that your offer would make a glorious gift to Khaine. I also cannot deny that you have more twists in you than a viper. This could all be a lie.'

Once again, Malus bowed his head respectfully. 'That is so and I cannot convince you otherwise. So you must ask yourself: what have you to lose if I'm lying and what do you stand to gain if I'm telling you the truth?'

Urial's expression changed. It was not a smile, but rather a slight softening of his severe features. 'Well said, brother,' he replied, gesturing to the priests. 'I have little to lose by sparing you a little while longer. But tell me, how will you deliver the apostates into our hands?'

The priests of Khaine surrounded Malus, gripping him with their bloodstained hands and lifting him from his bed of pain. His cry of pain transmuted itself into a harsh laugh of triumph.

'Did I not mention it before, brother? I am to be initiated into their cult tomorrow.'

Chapter Nine
THE WITCH'S GIFT

MALUS WAITED IN shadow, preparing for the battle to come. Nagaira had been furious upon learning of his escape. It was well past nightfall by the time he had completed his plans with Urial and left his half-brother's tower. After that there had been nothing for it but to cross the grounds of the fortress and enter his own tower to inform his men of the part they would play in his upcoming initiation. The Octagon of Praan was left behind, locked in an ironwood chest within his own quarters, leaving the highborn to cross the narrow, windy bridge connecting his spire with his sister's. The guards were not surprised to hear his knock. They had been given orders to keep a watch for him the moment Nagaira realised he had gone.

Malus leaned back in his chair, his face twisting in a smile at the thought of his sister's wrath. He had never seen her so angry before – she hurled questions at him like thunderbolts, demanding he account for every step he'd taken upon leaving her tower. He'd mollified her somewhat when he told her that he was ready to undertake the initiation. For a moment she'd been pleased – and then her interest had become sharper than a razor as the witch demanded to know how he'd made his way from her demesne without her being any wiser. That had led to a string of threats and curses, both real and implied, that had lasted much of the night, until finally she summoned her retainers and banished him to his chambers, there to await his time before the anointed of Slaanesh.

The following evening a procession of servants swept through the room, bearing clothes, food and libations to prepare him for the ceremony. The slaves stripped away his armour, kheitan and robes, clothing him in a robe of expensive white Tilean linen and a belt of pebbled hide unlike anything he'd seen before. A circlet set with six precious stones was placed on his brow and braziers were lit in his room to fill the air with pungent incense. Then he was left to wait in silence, breathing the spiced air and feeling his skin tingle as the herbs did their work on body and mind.

Hours passed while Malus listened to the steady commotion of servants and guards outside as Nagaira made her preparations for the ritual. Then, as the hour drew close to midnight and the coals in the braziers had burned low, the door to the chamber swung wide and Nagaira swept in like a cold wind. Unlike the seductress of the previous revel she now carried herself as a priestess, clad in white robes and a breastplate of hammered gold worked with sorcerous runes. She wore another mask this time, a horned skull smaller but no less fearsome than the Hierophant's and like him she bore a brimming goblet in her hands.

'The hour is nigh, supplicant,' Nagaira said gravely. 'Drink with me as we await the Prince's pleasure.'

Malus considered his options carefully. The wine was likely drugged, but he could think of no plausible way to refuse. He took the goblet from her carefully and drank without a word. The wine was thick and sweet, with a resinous aftertaste. More traders' wine, he thought, suppressing a grimace. The highborn passed the wine back to the witch and was surprised to see her drink as well.

'We are all one in the crucible of desire,' she said, reading the expression on his face. 'After tonight we will be bound together more tightly than family, more intimate than lovers. As you dedicate yourself to the Prince, he shall dedicate himself to you and your devotion will be rewarded six-fold. Glory awaits, brother. Your every desire will be fulfilled.'

'I pray so, sister,' he said with a wolfish smile. 'With all my heart.'

A robed supplicant entered amongst whispers and bowed to Nagaira. Malus was startled to see that the druchii wore no mask and recognised the man as one of the Drachau's personal retainers. 'The Prince awaits,' he said, favouring Malus with a conspiratorial smile.

Nagaira stretched forth her hand. 'Come, brother. It is time to join the revel.'

Malus took her hand. As she turned to lead him from the room a quick pass of his free hand reassured him that the dagger within his robes was still securely in place.

They descended once more to the base of the tower, walking in silence and passing through shadow. The witchlights had all been dimmed and after a time Malus felt as though he were being drawn along through a sea of darkness, pulled by a hand of gleaming alabaster. The wine, he thought, trying to focus. The more he concentrated the more his focus broke into fragments, as though he were grasping at quicksilver. Not even his anger could avail him, it glowed like a dead coal, sullen and without heat.

Before he knew it they had reached the bottom of the long, curving stairs. The tall statue shed its own cold light in the darkened room, lit from within by its own sorcery. Its light shone dimly on helmets and breastplates, spear points and pauldrons. Rank after rank of Nagaira's warriors bore witness to their descent, their pale faces limned with pellucid fire.

They stepped slowly down the narrow, hidden stair. They sank downwards into air that was humid and sweet with the taste of incense and oiled flesh. A strange, piping music rose from the darkness. It was eerie and discordant, a song wrought for inhuman ears that set his teeth on edge and yet filled his heart with a terrible longing that was as alien as it was irresistible.

As they turned the final corner it seemed as though they looked down on starlight. Hands held aloft tiny globes of witchlight, throwing strange shadows and shifting currents of light across the assembled suppliants. None wore masks save the terrible Hierophant, who stood at the far end of the chamber across a sea of slowly undulating bodies. Naked, writhing slaves covered the stone floor of the room, lulled by the incense and stoked by the strange refrain of the unearthly flutes.

The moment the supplicants saw him they began to chant, filling the air with a husky litany in maddening counterpoint to the pipes. Malus felt the hairs on the back of his neck stand straight as a strange kind of tension crackled through the air of the chamber. There was a kind of pressure he could feel on his neck and shoulders, as though the blasphemous song had summoned the attention of a being that moved in a realm beyond mortal comprehension. A feeling of dread began to steal into Malus's heart. It swept away the lingering effects of the drugged wine, but left in its place an atavistic fear that threatened to rob his limbs of their strength.

The supplicants parted to let him and Nagaira pass. She drew him onward, towards the waiting Hierophant, who stood in the company of two attendants. One attendant bore a scourge of leather whose tails were studded with silver barbs; the other held a golden basin and a curved dagger made of bone. The Hierophant stood with his hands clasped before him. His long pale fingers waved languidly, like the legs of a hunting spider. Malus felt a sudden shock of recognition. Could it be?

Nagaira bowed before the Hierophant. 'I come bearing gifts for the Prince Who Waits,' she intoned. 'Will he come forth?'

The chanting and the piping flute stopped. Silence descended, heavy and oppressive. Malus felt the awful presence in the chamber increase. His sight seemed to waver at the edges as *something* pressed against the fabric of reality and the highborn felt his heart grow cold.

'The Prince will come forth!' intoned the Hierophant, raising his hands to the ceiling. The supplicants cried out in joy and terror combined and an awful groaning filled the darkness of the chamber. Then there came a tremendous crash of mortar and stone and the air shivered with rapturous war cries.

'The call of blood is answered in sundered flesh!'

The draichnyr na Khaine took the chamber by storm, pouring from breaches in the chamber walls with their curved draichs held high. The warriors were clad in heavy coats of mail reinforced with brass pauldrons, breastplate and helm. Their great swords flickered like willow wands, harvesting a bloody path through the scores of panicked slaves around the perimeter of the room.

Malus snatched his hand from Nagaira's and swung his fist at the side of her skull mask. The movement felt leaden and clumsy and the blow only glanced the goat skull's bony snout, knocking it askew. Cursed drugs, Malus thought. Nagaira recoiled from the blow, cursing herself and temporarily blinded by the skewed mask. As her hands clawed at the goat skull Malus tore the dagger free from his robes.

There was a great shout that ripped through the pandemonium, searing the air with is power. Malus turned to see the Hierophant brandishing a bottle of heavy, dark glass above his head. The highborn could feel the hatred from the high priest like a red-hot spear point pressed against his flesh. 'Mother of Night, what's he doing?'

'Sating his lust for vengeance,' Tz'arkan replied coldly. 'Did you expect the anointed of Slaanesh to be helpless?'

Before Malus could answer the Hierophant shrieked an invocation that smote his ears like a thunderclap, then saw the high priest dash the bottle against the stone floor. A roiling, purplish fog boiled up from the broken glass, expanding and gathering strength as it grew.

There were faces in the smoke – leering, obscene faces that made mockery of mortal senses. Malus snarled a bitter curse. The bottle had been a magic vessel containing the bound spirits of a horde of fearsome daemons.

The cloud of chittering, shrieking spirits enveloped the room, howling through the air like a chorus of the damned. More arcane commands reverberated through the chamber and the daemons descended on the panicked slaves. Malus saw one nearby human fall to the ground, choking and writhing as one of the spirits forced its way into the slave's nostrils and mouth. In moments the human began to change colour, the skin stretching as the muscles beneath swelled. Grasping hands twisted and deformed, the flesh splitting and falling away to reveal blood-streaked pincers formed of melted bone. With a shout, Malus leapt upon the possessed slave, plunging his dagger again and again into the creature's eyes and throat. One huge pincer smashed at the side of his head, sending him sprawling.

Malus rolled onto his back, blinking stars from his eyes as the possessed slave reared to its feet. Purple ichor poured from its ruined eyes and a terrible wound in its neck, but the daemon guided the slave's body unerringly as it advanced on the fallen highborn. The creature loomed over him, pincers snapping, then Malus caught a flash of brass above his head as an executioner swept past, swinging his bloody draich. The great sword sheared through the slave's bulbous torso, snapping ribs like dry twigs and lodging deep in the creature's spine. The possessed slave toppled, lashing out as it fell and catching the executioner's helmeted head in one oversized pincer. The creature's dying spasms ripped the executioner's head from his shoulders in a fountain of gore and both bodies fell onto the stunned highborn.

This is *not* going according to plan, Malus thought savagely, kicking himself free from the corpses. His robes were wet with gore and he'd lost track of his dagger. He kicked the body of the dead slave over onto its side and wrapped his hands around the hilt of the draich. With a curse and a heave the corpse's spine parted and the long blade pulled free.

The chamber echoed with the sounds of battle. Chaos reigned in the darkness as the executioners and possessed intermingled in a swirling, confused melee. Sorcerous bolts lashed at warriors and possessed slaves alike as the supplicants loosed their spells indiscriminately into the mass. There was no way to tell who had the upper hand, but Malus was certain that sheer numbers lay on the cultists' side.

A bolt of purple fire roared close by and in the flare of light Malus caught sight of the Hierophant, his hands working in a complicated series of gestures. The highborn couldn't guess at what the high priest was doing, but he knew that he didn't care to see its results.

Time to see who is really under that skull, Malus thought with a savage grin, and charged at the Hierophant over the heaped bodies of the dead.

The highborn stayed low, his great sword down and to one side to attract as little attention as possible. He expected one of the possessed slaves to leap upon his back at any moment, but their attention appeared entirely occupied by the remaining executioners. A fatal mistake, Malus thought, closing in for the kill.

He approached the Hierophant from his right side, his hands tensing on the hilt of the draich. Two steps short of striking range a blur of motion from Malus's left was all the warning he had as the Hierophant's dagger-wielding attendant leapt for his throat.

Instincts honed on a dozen battlefields caused Malus to plant his left foot and pivot, swinging his right leg around and reversing the stroke of his sword in a cut aimed for the attendant's midsection. The cultist's dagger flashed downwards, scoring a line across Malus's forehead as the draich opened the supplicant's belly. The attendant doubled up around the blade as he fell, nearly dragging Malus from his feet. The highborn planted a foot on the man's shoulder and hauled at the blade – and cords of raw fire raked across the side of his face as the second attendant lashed at him with his scourge.

Pain bloomed in Malus's right eye and he fell to his knees with a savage curse. The scourge fell again, the silver barbs shredding his right sleeve and biting deep into his shoulder. Another blow to the side of his head knocked the highborn to the ground, the hilt of the draich twisting from his grasp. Malus fell onto the disembowelled supplicant, smelling the stink of blood and spilt entrails as the man shuddered in the throes of death.

His left eye caught a gleam of metal on the floor and Malus threw himself upon it as the scourge clawed across his back. The highborn's hand closed on the hilt of the supplicant's sacrificial dagger and he rolled onto his back in time for the scourge-wielding cultist to aim another blow at his head.

Malus threw up his left hand and caught a handful of the scourge tails against his palm. Roaring with pain he grabbed hold of the leather thongs and pulled, dragging the supplicant off his feet and onto the highborn's up-thrust dagger. The curved blade punched through the man's breastbone and lodged against his spine, slicing his heart in two. Malus watched the hate fade from the druchii's dark eyes and threw the corpse to one side.

Not six feet away the Hierophant still performed his enigmatic ritual – too caught up in the intricacies of his spell to notice the life-and-death battle going on around him. Malus rubbed his right eye against the sleeve of his robe and was relieved to discover that he could still see through a thick film of blood. He grabbed the pommel of the draich and pulled the weapon free, then without a moment's hesitation he swung the gore-stained sword at the Hierophant's head.

At the last moment Malus realised his error. Without thinking he'd aimed the blow for the front of the Hiero-phant's neck instead of its unprotected rear. As it was, the blade bit into the ram's skull mask the high priest wore, shattering it and turning the blade slightly on impact. Rather than a decapitating blow, the sword tore a long, ragged gash across the Hierophant's throat and across his right shoulder, spinning him around in a spray of bright blood and fragments of yellowed bone.

The Hierophant fell to one knee, blood spilling from the shattered snout of his mask. Malus stepped in, bringing his sword back for a second stroke, when the high priest flung out a scarred hand and shrieked a bub-bling curse. Heat and thunder enveloped Malus and he felt himself thrown through the air. The impact knocked him senseless, sending the draich spinning from his hands.

It felt like an eternity before Malus's vision cleared. Much of his ceremonial robe had been burned away and the skin of his chest, arms and face stung from minor burns. Either he'd been hit with only a glancing blow or the high priest had failed to cast the spell properly. Malus sat up with a groan and saw the Hierophant staggering into the small chamber that had housed his throne of flesh not two nights past. Malus reclaimed his sword and lurched after the high priest, determined to finish what he'd begun.

When the highborn reached the entrance of the room he was prepared for another sorcerous barrage, but instead he discovered the Hierophant stepping through a narrow archway on the opposite side of the room – an escape route formerly concealed by some kind of embedded spell. Runes glistened along the doorway as the high priest stepped through. At once, the runes flared painfully bright and Malus sensed the danger burning within. He turned and flung himself back into the main chamber as the doorway erupted in a flare of purple fire, collapsing the small room in a shower of rock and earth.

A pall of dust and a thunderous concussion swept through the chamber, staggering the survivors still fighting around the curving stair. Malus regained his feet and saw that the cavern was lit again by young temple initiates bearing witchlight globes on slender poles. The slaves were collapsing, caught by the blades of the executioners or literally falling apart as the daemons possessing them lost strength and returned to their own blasted domain.

The supplicants were dead or dying, their bodies steaming from acids that burned from the depths of their ghastly wounds. Pale, blood-spattered sylphs glided among the cultists, fresh gore steaming upon their envenomed blades. Their long hair was unbound and flowed around their naked bodies like a mane. Malus felt his breath catch in his throat at the sight of the beautiful, unearthly women stalking silently among the carrion. The anwyr na Khaine were a rare sight outside the temple, called forth only in times of war or great need. Their poisoned blades and savage skill had clearly turned the tide and now they searched among the dead for more blood to shed in the name of the Lord of Murder.

Malus caught sight of Urial, attended by a bodyguard of executioners as he surveyed the bodies of the suppliants from a respectful distance. When the witch elves walked among the slain it was never wise to come between them and their prey. The highborn hastened to his side, slipping and sliding among the ruin of hacked and torn flesh littering the chamber floor.

'Where is Nagaira?' Malus called to him.

Urial shook his head, hefting a bloody axe with his one good hand. 'Our sister is not among the slain.'

Malus spat a savage curse. 'She must have slipped up the stairs during the battle! Hurry!'

The highborn raced for the stairs, darting among the witch elves and feeling the hairs on the back of his neck prickle as their attention turned his way. Carefully averting his eyes he leapt up the steps two and three at a time, wondering how much of a lead Nagaira had on him and whether her guards were still waiting on the floor above.

It was bad enough that the Hierophant had escaped, he thought. Now that she'd seen the depth of his treachery he didn't dare let Nagaira slip through his clutches as well.

He emerged from the illusory statue into the midst of a raging battle. Urial's plan of attack had been savage and thorough: even as he and the executioners struck the initiation chamber via the twisting passageways of the Burrows, his own personal retainers had hacked their way through the ground floor entrance and attacked the guards stationed there. As close as the battle had been down below, the fight at the base of the tower still hung in the balance, with Nagaira's rogues on their home ground and enjoying greater numbers than the invading druchii. The witch's retainers had rallied and had pushed Urial's men back towards the broken doorway, leaving a narrow path behind the defender's ranks that led to the main staircase. Without hesitation Malus ran for the stairs. The climb seemed to last forever. Distantly he thought he heard the rumble of thunder, but he knew that a storm this time of year was impossible. A few moments later he passed a burning slave running the opposite way, his agonised screams echoing up and down the stairway long after he'd disappeared from sight.

He reached the guardroom just below the sanctum without realising it at first, stumbling into a smoky chamber that reeked with the smell of burnt hair and charred flesh. Half a dozen bodies lay on the stone floor, tossed about like straw dolls by a sudden, violent explosion.

Armoured figures suddenly rushed at him through the smoke, bloodstained swords held ready. At the last moment the lead warrior checked his rush and raised his hand to the rest. 'Stop!' Arleth Vann ordered to his men. 'My lord! We nearly took you for one of the cultists.'

Malus paused, gasping for breath in the foetid air. 'Nagaira? Where is she?'

Arleth Vann nodded towards the ceiling. 'She tore through here like a storm, just as we were finishing off the last of the bridge guards,' he said. 'Killed two of ours and four of hers with some kind of thunderbolt and kept on going.'

'How long ago?'

The retainer shrugged. 'A few minutes, no more. Silar took the rest of the men after her.'

Malus nodded. He'd hoped his men would have been able to storm across the bridge and seize the sanctum during the chaos of the attack, but battle had a way of unravelling even the simplest of plans. 'Well done. Now take your men back across the bridge. Urial and his acolytes will be here any moment.'

Another thunderclap shook the air above the tower, this time sending drifts of dust raining from the ceiling. Fighting a strong sense of foreboding, Malus charged up the stairs.

The antechamber to the sanctum was full of smoke and swirling lights. The double doors leading to Nagaira's study were gone, leaving nothing but a jagged hole in the crumbling wall. Silar and his men lay on the floor, their armour smoking. Several were contorted in agony or lying motionless amid piles of jagged rubble.

A howling wind roared through the room, whistling through the ragged hole leading from the sanctum itself. A raging storm of multicoloured light blazed within.

'You are too late!' Tz'arkan cried. 'Leave this place before the spell she's cast consumes you!'

Yet Malus couldn't bring himself to give up, not within sight of his quarry. Seeing the power at work in the room beyond, he was certain that he didn't dare let his sister get away.

The highborn paused long enough to pull Silar upright and order the men out of the room, then he hurled himself through the jagged opening.

Within the confines of the sanctum the storm threatened to take his breath away. The light was blinding, a shifting pattern of sights and strange sounds that grew in strength with each passing moment.

The ceiling of the room was already gone, consumed by the ravening energies unleashed by the witch's spell. Her robed form hung in midair, surrounded by the vortex, her skin glowing with unearthly patterns of light. Nagaira saw Malus and her face lit with a triumphant smile. At that moment he knew that for once the daemon had spoken wisely. He'd made a terrible mistake.

'There you are, little brother,' Nagaira said, her voice one with the howling storm. 'I've been waiting for you. I have a gift to repay you for your treachery.'

The air curdled around the witch – and began to bleed. A nimbus of Chaotic energy took shape around her, split with jagged arcs of purple lightning.

Tz'arkan writhed inside Malus. 'Get out of here, you fool! She's calling down the storm of Chaos itself!'

Malus snarled, furious at the thought of retreat. As he turned to go, he caught sight of a leather-bound tome at the foot of a shattered divan. On impulse he leapt for it, just as a bolt of purple energy tore through the space where he'd stood. The arc of power played along the far wall, carving a path through the stone and leaving a wild pattern of flesh, scales and viscera etched in its wake.

The highborn's hands closed around the Tome of Ak'zhaal as another burst of lightning turned the remains of the divan into a puddle of stinking slime. The vortex surrounding Nagaira was swelling, increasing in velocity. Malus rose to his knees and flung the draich at her one-handed. It shattered into droplets of boiling steel before he'd reached his feet and started for the antechamber.

More lightning reached for him as he ran and the witch's voice rose in a shriek of thwarted anger. The air crackled and moaned around him. He felt his hair writhe and melt into the dried gore on his skin.

He did not stop upon reaching the antechamber; if anything, he spurred himself to greater speed, racing for the stairs. Nagaira's shriek rose to an unearthly wail – and then went silent.

The explosion that followed turned the world inside out.

A wave of energy washed over him as he tumbled down the stairs and he felt the fabric of the world come undone. For a single, endless heartbeat he hung from a precipice of sorts, dangling at the edge of infinity. Entire universes stretched before him, each one greater and less sane than the one before.

Worse still he glimpsed the impossible beings that crouched in the emptiness between the universes – and for a moment, *they* glimpsed *him*.

Malus screamed in pure, mindless terror – then the wave collapsed back in on itself and the entire top of Nagaira's tower exploded in a ball of unnatural light.

His head struck the edge of a stone step with a blinding flash of blessed pain, snapping his awareness back to the physical world. Malus rebounded off walls and staircases until he spilled out into the wrecked guard room below.

The pain was intense and sweet. It reminded him of his place in the world. For a long while, all he could do was clutch the great tome in his arms and laugh like a madman, grateful to be blinded once again to the awful expanse beyond the world of flesh.

Malus had no idea how much time had passed before he realised he wasn't alone. When the laughter finally died and he focused his eyes on the smoky room around him, he saw Urial looming over him. There was a strange look in his brass-coloured eyes.

'She is gone,' was all Malus could say.

Urial nodded. 'It is perhaps for the best. The question is: will she return?'

The thought chilled Malus to the bone. 'Mother of Night, I pray not.'

Once more, Urial stared intently at Malus, then surprised the highborn by bending over him and extending his good hand. His grip was surprisingly strong and he pulled Malus effortlessly to his feet. 'Best to save your prayers for later,' he said, his expression inscrutable. 'The Vaulkhar's troops have entered the tower to restore order and they have been commanded to escort us to the Drachau's tower. It would appear that we have some explaining to do.'

Chapter Ten
WRIT OF IRON

NAGAIRA'S TOWER CONTINUED to burn, its upper storeys wreathed in seething white flame that rose for more than a hundred feet into the night sky. The eerie glow of the burning tower shone like a white borealis through the crystal skylight set in the arched ceiling of the Drachau's inner court. It threw elaborate patterns of light and shadow across the tiled floor, writhing knots of white light and inky shadow that drew Malus's attention away from the undisputed lord of Hag Graef. Every time he bent himself to the task of focusing on the man presiding from the dais in the centre of the great chamber the shadows would twist and writhe at the edges of his vision. He caught the hint of patterns there, of meaning where none ought to be.

Malus and Urial had been brought into the Drachau's presence, only to be made to wait while he received reports from his lieutenants and the arrival of the Vaulkhar. It was all Malus could do to remain on his feet, his body was battered and torn and the cut across his scalp had bled so much he was dizzy and weak. But the Drachau offered him no comforts, nor would it have ever occurred to him to ask for any. Weakness was not tolerated in the presence of the Drachau, only the strong were fit to stand in his shadow and await his pleasure.

The highborn could not say how long he stood in silence, fighting a desperate battle to remain upright and conscious. At some point he heard the great double doors swing wide and the warlord of Hag Graef swept in like a storm, clad in his red-enamelled armour and wearing the ancient blade Render at his side. It was a testament to the majesty of the great court that Lurhan's fierce presence did not fill it like a turbulent sea. As it was, Malus could feel an electric tension in the air as his father approached and knew that the infamous Vaulkhar seethed.

Uthlan Tyr, the Drachau of Hag Graef, also wore a suit of fine plate armour – not the great relic armour worn at ceremonies like the Hanil Khar or on the field of war, but a mundane harness that was suitable for everyday use and worth a highborn's ransom. While the Vaulkhar carried his helmet tucked under one arm the Drachau disdained the great dragon helm of his station, his long, black hair pulled back from his face with a fine gold circlet and spilling down over his shoulders. He had a thin, almost boyish face despite being nearly eight hundred years of age and his small eyes glittered like chips of onyx beneath an imposing brow. He and Lurhan were distant cousins and both shared the sharp patrician nose of their ancestors and a defiant set to their pointed chins. Unlike the Vaulkhar, Tyr's hand rested on the pommel of a naked blade, its chisel point grounded on the wooden floor of the dais. It was a draich, similar to the weapon Malus had used at the tower, but the slender, curving sword had the hallmarks of a master craftsman and its blade was etched with runes of power that parted steel as easily as skin. It was said among the highborn houses of Hag Graef that Lurhan had fought in more battles than he had hairs on his head, but Uthlan Tyr had killed far more men than he. For the Drachau, spilling blood was as natural – and necessary – as breathing. Malus had little doubt that his life – and possibly even that of Urial as well – was balanced precariously on the keen edge of that blade.

The Vaulkhar climbed the steps of the dais and knelt before his lord. 'My men have secured the tower,' Lurhan said, his voice hoarse from shouting commands over the din of battle. 'Nagaira's retainers fought to the death rather than surrender. There were only a handful of slaves left alive in the tower and they have been taken by my men for questioning. The... chamber... beneath the tower is a charnel pit. It would appear that no less than two hundred slave stock were butchered there, many of them clearly twisted by the effects of powerful sorcery. Worse yet, there were three score highborn found below, slain by poisoned blades or the draichs of the temple executioners.' Lurhan turned to regard Urial coldly. 'When we arrived the bodies were being mutilated by a band of temple brides.'

Urial met his father's eyes with his own impassive stare. After a moment, the Vaulkhar glanced back to his lord.

'These were no mere highborn, dread one. They were the sons and daughters of some of your most powerful allies. When news reaches their kin the gutters will run with blood, mark my words.'

The Drachau's eyes swept contemptuously over Malus and settled on Urial. 'Explain yourself,' he commanded.

A lesser noble would have quailed beneath Tyr's murderous glare, but Urial was undaunted. 'I stand before you not as your vassal but as an agent of the Temple of Khaine,' he answered. 'This is a temple matter: you trifle with it at your peril.'

Lurhan's face went white with rage, but Malus was shocked to see the Vaulkhar hold his fury in check. The only sign of tension in the Drachau himself was a slight tightening of his hand on the pommel of his sword. His tone remained even as he said, 'Go on.'

'The Temple of Khaine has excised a canker growing in the very heart of this city. The Cult of Slaanesh had spread its rot through the highest orders of Hag Graef's nobility — including the Vaulkhar's daughter, Nagaira.'

'Have a care, Urial! Now it is you who dance the razor's edge,' Lurhan said, his voice full of quiet menace.

Does he fear that he will be implicated as well, Malus thought? Or does he know that the taint of the cult runs even deeper in his house and fears what the Drachau will say? He had been so focused on his own schemes that he'd failed to appreciate how politically damaging the events of the evening could be. A few carefully chosen words from Urial and the Vaulkhar could find himself kneeling before an executioner in the temple courtyard. The Drachau would have no choice but to order Lurhan's death, if for no other reason than to avoid the same fate should word reach the Witch King.

The notion restored a bit of the fire in Malus's veins. Lurhan and the Drachau had reason to be afraid and that gave Malus a small amount of power over them.

'These are grave accusations,' Tyr said carefully. 'Where is your proof?'

Urial scowled at the Drachau? 'Proof? We are the anointed of Khaine. We need provide no proof.' The former acolyte raised his hand to forestall the Drachau's angry protest. 'That said, I realise that these events have placed you in a precarious position, so I will provide you with some amount of detail.'

He indicated Malus with a nod of his head. 'This all began with your order to torture my brother to death for his recent indiscretions. After the Vaulkhar had tormented Malus beyond the endurance of the strongest druchii it was determined that he had fulfilled your wishes to the best of his ability and Malus was released into the care of his sister.'

The Drachau shot the warlord a stern glance, then returned his attention to Urial. 'This much I know,' Tyr said darkly.

Urial nodded absently, his expression vague as he focused on the chain of events laid out in his mind. 'While Malus was being treated by Nagaira – treated with both drugs and outlawed sorcery, I might add – she took advantage of his weakened state in an attempt to seduce him into her debased cult.' Urial's expression cleared and he eyed Malus coldly. 'Malus and Nagaira have been companions – some would say *more* than companions – for some time. She has used her forbidden knowledge to support him on more than one occasion. I believe she has been intent upon subverting him for some time now.' Tyr gave a snort of disgust. 'This libertine? What would be the point? He has nothing to offer!'

'So it would appear,' Urial said, his voice neutral. 'And yet it is a fact that the cult held a revel in his honour shortly after his recovery and that he was brought before their Hierophant and invited to join their ranks.'

Urial turned towards Malus, his pronounced limp the only outward sign of the exhaustion the crippled druchii felt. 'As soon as he was able, Malus came to me with this information, as was proper. He put forth a plan to use his proposed initiation as a trap to eliminate the heart of the cult here in the city.'

'By rights he should have come to me, first!' Lurhan growled. 'The honour of our house–'

'The honour of your house or any other comes second to the affairs of the temple,' Urial said flatly. 'It is our duty to keep the souls of the druchii pure, free from the weakness of our traitorous kin in Ulthuan. This is not merely the commandment of Khaine, but the wish of Malekith himself. Do you care to dispute this?'

'You have made your point, Urial,' the Drachau interjected. 'Continue.'

'Malus gave us the location of the initiation chamber, suggesting it was part of the tunnels burrowed beneath the city. I despatched scouts into the Burrows and located passages that had been walled off to isolate the chamber from the rest of the network.' Urial shrugged. 'After that it was a matter of alerting the temple and rousing its holy warriors to do Khaine's sacred work. We burst through the walls just before the culmination of the ceremony and attempted to capture the apostates.' The former acolyte gave a wintry smile. 'Fortunately, they chose to resist.'

Suddenly the white glow in the night sky flickered and went out. The Drachau glanced at the skylight above with evident relief, then returned his attention to Malus. 'What of this Hierophant Urial spoke of?'

'I fought the Hierophant in the initiation chamber,' Malus said hoarsely. 'Though I gravely wounded the high priest, he managed to escape. I believe that he would be easy to locate, however. Like his supplicants, he must be a high-ranking noble – someone close to the most powerful leaders in the city.'

Malus looked squarely at his father. 'I would suggest a search of all the spires in the Hag, my lords. Find the noble with the ruined throat and you will have your chief apostate. I expect you will not have to look very far.'

'What are you implying, you misbegotten churl?' Lurhan took a step towards Malus, his hand going to the long hilt of bone rising above his left hip. 'Bad enough that first you and then your sister defile our honour – now you try to heap more disgrace upon us?'

'I imply nothing,' Malus shot back. 'If you are so covetous of your house's honour then send your troops to my brother Isilvar's tower. Drag him here from his dens of flesh and ask him what he knows of this damnable cult. I warn you, though – he might not be fit to say much.'

'Be silent!' Lurhan roared, descending the steps like a thunderbolt as his hand tightened on the hilt of his blade.

'*No further!*' The Drachau leapt to his feet, pointing at Lurhan with the point of his own blade. 'Restrain yourself, Vaulkhar. Methinks your children are right: you place the honour of your house above the security of the state and that is a grave mistake. This high priest must be rooted out and the sooner the better. We will search the Hag, as Malus has suggested, because it serves our interests. Now,' he commanded, 'tell me of Nagaira.'

Malus made as if to reply, but Urial answered first. 'She is no more,' he said.

The Drachau nodded. 'And the fire?'

'Born of a Chaos storm, dread lord. Nagaira unleashed a powerful spell in an attempt to escape and to destroy evidence that might have led us to her patron.'

'Patron?' The Drachau frowned. 'You mean the Hierophant?'

'Not at all, dread lord. I mean the person responsible for teaching her the forbidden arts of sorcery and supplying her with the extensive library that filled the upper portion of her tower. It has long been an open secret that she flouted the Witch King's laws,' Urial glared accusingly at Lurhan, 'but no one chose to act upon it. Possibly because no one realised she'd become much more than a mere scholar of the arcane... or possibly because of the identity of the patron involved.'

'And tell me Urial, who would that patron be?'

Heads turned at the sound of the cold, powerful voice. Eldire seemed to coalesce from the shadows themselves, gliding soundlessly across the tiled floor towards the dais. No one had heard the tall doors part to admit her. Malus frankly wasn't certain that they had. The Vaulkhar's fierce expression disappeared, his previous fury suddenly forgotten. The Drachau eyed Eldire warily but held his tongue in the face of the seer's unexpected arrival.

Urial faced the sorceress, his face hard and expressionless. 'I... have my theories, but no evidence as yet. Still, there cannot be but a handful of people in the city who could possess such knowledge... and the majority of those reside in the witch's convent.'

'I imagine so,' Eldire replied coolly. 'The rest would be criminals against the state, after all, teaching the arcane arts to those with no right to possess it. Men like yourself, for example.'

Malus bit his tongue, careful to keep his face neutral as the air grew thick with tension. Urial stiffened, his expression growing strained, but he made no reply.

'You come into my court unannounced, Yrila,' the Drachau hissed.

'I am here to report that the city's coven has extinguished the fire at the tower,' Eldire said dryly. 'I had thought you would be pleased to hear it. Shall I tell my sisters to re-ignite the blaze and wait until you are ready to summon us?'

'You are too impertinent by half, Eldire,' the Drachau said querulously. 'Tell me of the damage.'

'The energies released by the spell consumed almost half of the tower – had it gone unchecked it would have continued to burn so long as there was stone to feed it. The entire city could have been lost.' Eldire glared at Urial. 'If Nagaira did indeed have a patron then he greatly underestimated her power. The spell she unleashed was beyond the power of a single sorcerer to control. As it is, the rest of the tower will have to be demolished, as the taint of the Chaos magic has seeped through it to the very foundation. Left unchecked that taint will spread throughout the entire city.'

He, Malus wondered, or *she*? The highborn eyed his mother with newfound respect... and uncertainty. Were you mentoring Nagaira? If so, why – and what do I have to do with it?

Tyr considered the news and nodded gravely. 'Then you have done your duty well, Yrila. Now, what of the bodies of the highborn in the initiation chamber?'

Eldire smiled. 'The bodies of the cultists were given to the fire, my lord. It seemed like the appropriate thing to do.'

'You *burned* them? All of them?' The Drachau was incredulous. 'It's monstrous! Their kin will be up in arms when they hear of this!'

'As of this moment these cultists are *missing*, not dead.' Eldire said sharply. 'The Chaos magic consumed them entirely – what little was left was not even recognisable as druchii, much less who they really were. Tomorrow the story will spread through the Hag that Nagaira and her household were consumed in a sorcerous conflagration, one that no doubt my husband and the Temple alike – ' Eldire glared forcefully at both Lurhan and Urial in turn – 'will decry as the just fate of all those who would dabble in the forbidden arts. An investigation will be promised and punishments threatened for any other unlawful sorcerers found in the city. If your allies wish to come forward at that point and publicly proclaim that their sons or daughters were present in the witch's tower when it burned then I should be greatly surprised.'

The Drachau sat back upon his throne, rubbing his chin thoughtfully. 'What of the presence of the executioners, to say nothing of the Brides of Khaine that were there?'

Urial shrugged. 'They entered by way of the Burrows and left in the same manner. Only my retainers and the Vaulkhar's troops were seen entering the tower and it can be truthfully said that they were there to put an end to Nagaira's sorcery.'

Tyr nodded, a sly smile spreading across his narrow face. 'Then that is the story we shall tell,' he declared. 'Doubtless there will be private complaints, but that can be mended with time and favours. That only leaves one last matter.'

'What is that, dread lord?' Malus asked. He had his own matters to discuss, if the opportunity presented itself.

The Drachau's expression turned cold. 'Whether to kill you now or execute you publicly as a cultist of Slaanesh.'

'*Execute* me? This cult was uprooted thanks to me–' Malus looked to Urial for support. The former acolyte said nothing, eyeing the Drachau warily.

Uthlan Tyr smiled cruelly. 'You know the law, Malus. Any druchii that tastes of the forbidden fruit of Slaanesh must die. By your own admission you have done so, have you not?'

'But you cannot execute me without admitting that the cult was here, hiding under your very nose,' Malus shot back. 'And then your allies will call for your hide, dread lord.'

Tyr rose from his chair. 'Then we shall slay you now, far from prying eyes.' The Drachau ignored Eldire's murderous look, turning instead to Lurhan and Urial. 'Have you any objection to this?'

Lurhan looked to Eldire, then to his lord. 'It is my duty to serve,' he said, a little nervously. 'Do as you will, dread lord.'

The Drachau acknowledged his warlord with a nod. 'Urial?'

Urial stared hard at Malus. Anger, desire and frustration alike warred behind his eyes. Finally he turned to the Drachau and shook his head. 'No. For now he is an agent of the temple and beyond your grasp, Uthlan Tyr.'

Tyr recoiled, his eyes widening in surprise. 'Are you mad? Have you not been baying for his blood all winter?' The Drachau held out his sword to Urial. 'Here. Strike off his head yourself. Bathe in his tainted blood! Is that not what you want?'

Urial's jaw clenched. A bitter smile twisted his lips. 'What I do, I do for the good of the temple,' he said. 'There is a task he must do for me. Until then, no man shall threaten him while I live.'

The Drachau shook his head. 'You are a fool, Urial!' He lowered his sword. 'I am no oracle, but I warrant you'll never have another chance like this again.' Tyr glared at Malus. 'This is twice now you've escaped death at my hands, Darkblade. Your luck cannot last forever.'

Malus smiled, sensing an opportunity. 'Doubtless you are correct, dread lord. Thus, I must press my advantage while I'm able. I demand you present me with a writ of iron.'

Uthlan Tyr laughed. 'Shall I give you my concubines and my tower as well?'

'No, that won't be necessary,' Malus answered, his tone calm and even. 'The writ alone will suffice.'

'Enough with your impertinence,' Lurhan growled, raising his fist. 'The Drachau must heed the wishes of the temple, but not I!'

'No, you have other oaths to consider,' Eldire said. 'And the consequences of breaking them would be far more terrible.'

Lurhan stopped in his tracks, his face turning pale. Tyr's alarm grew as he watched the exchange. He turned to Malus, all trace of humour gone. 'What makes you think I would give a man such as you so much power?'

'For all the proper reasons: I seek to serve the state in a great endeavour and to bring honour and glory to you and the city,' Malus replied. 'And to ensure my silence over what really happened within the tower, of course.'

'Just what endeavour do you speak of? Do you plan to drink the city dry, or exhaust all the flesh houses in the Corsairs' Quarter?'

Malus surprised Tyr with a hearty laugh. 'Will you give a writ for such a thing? If so I would be glad to have it. No, I need your authority to form an expedition. I will need ships, sailors and skilled raiders and time is short.'

'For what purpose?'

The highborn considered his response carefully. 'I have recently discovered the lost Isle of Morhaut,' he said. 'And I intend to drive the Skinriders from the northern sea.'

Uthlan Tyr shook his head, his expression incredulous. 'That's impossible. Where did you learn such a thing?'

'How I did so is unimportant,' Malus said. 'Consider what I am offering instead. The Skinriders have harassed our raiding ships and competed with us for plunder. If I am successful we will double our harvest for years to come. Not to mention the fact that the island is legendary for the ships and treasures lost on its shores. As author of the writ you would not only share in the glory, but the plunder as well. The fortunes of our city have suffered greatly in the long feud with Naggor – that can change in the space of just a few months. All I need is the writ.'

The Drachau started to protest, but Malus could see a spark of interest in the ruler's eyes. 'You wouldn't stand a chance. The Skinriders would kill you before you got within a mile of the island.'

'For a man who was about to have me executed, your sudden concern for my welfare comes as a bit of a surprise.'

The Drachau looked to Urial. 'What does the Temple say about this fool's errand? Did you not just say you have a task for him to perform?'

Urial sighed. 'Issue the writ, Uthlan Tyr. I like it no better than you, but in this he also serves the temple's interests.'

The Drachau's hand tightened on his sword. 'I am beset from all sides then,' he said in quiet exasperation. 'Very well Malus, you will have your writ of iron,' Tyr said. 'May it bring you a bounty of blood and fire.'

'Of that I have little doubt, dread lord,' Malus replied, a steely look of triumph on his face. 'And I swear you will share the fruits of it in the fullness of time.'

Chapter Eleven
DOORWAYS OF THE DEAD

HE WAS LOST.

There was a door in front of him, black wood with a silver knob worked in the shape of a leering daemon's face. He pushed it open and saw a hexagonal room beyond. Four staircases rose from the centre of the room, climbing into thin air in four different directions.

The same it's all the same it's all the same… his voice echoed in his head. He pulled the door shut.

A roar echoed behind him. Closer now than it had been before.

Before? When?

The roar echoed again, much closer now. He yanked the door open and found a staircase descending into darkness.

Now he could hear footsteps. Heavy, ponderous footfalls drumming like the beating of a bestial heart. Thud-*thud*, thud-*thud*, thud-*thud*–

He ran down the stairs, fleeing the sound of the footsteps.

The staircase curved abruptly, straightened, then curved back the other way. He raced through an arch – and found himself descending a staircase surrounded by open air, leading to a hexagonal room. Three more staircases rose up from the room, heading in three different directions.

There was a door of black wood set into one of the walls. As he reached the bottom of the stairs it shook on its hinges beneath a powerful blow. A roar thundered on the other side of the splintering wood.

MALUS AWOKE WITH a shout, sitting bolt upright amid a tangle of bed sheets and groping in the darkness for a weapon. By the time his hand closed on the hilt of the sword leaning beside his bed he realised that he had been dreaming and fell back against the mattress with a shuddering sigh. The cut on his forehead throbbed in time with his racing heart and the ragged scabs on the right side of his face stung as his cheek stretched into a weary grimace.

Pale moonlight slanted silver-blue through the windowpanes of his sleeping chamber. The night sky was unnaturally clear, with not a shred of cloud in the sky. Malus couldn't recall the last time he'd seen such a thing – clouds always hung heavy over the Land of Chill, especially during the late winter months. He wondered if it had anything to do with the fire the previous night, or the sorceries used to extinguish it. Everything felt strange, somehow unsettled.

With a groan Malus pushed himself back upright and rose shakily from the bed. He moved haltingly, the muscles in his back, shoulders and hips singing painfully with each shuffling step. In truth, he felt better than he'd been when he first stumbled back to his tower after the meeting with the Drachau. Delirious with fatigue and loss of blood he'd wandered the fortress for more than an hour before finally fetching up against the black oak doors at the base of his spire. Thinking back now, he couldn't remember how he'd got inside – an image stuck in his mind of falling inwards as one of the doors was pulled open and hearing Silar's surprised shout, but little else.

Malus staggered to the large, circular table that dominated a corner of the sleeping chamber. Among the piles of clutter was a tray with a wine bottle and a goblet. Next to the tray sat the Tome of Ak'zhaal. The highborn snatched up the bottle and pulled the cork with his teeth, spitting it into the nearest corner. He took a deep drink, barely tasting the vintage and opened the book at a random page.

…Stone he built upon stone, raised with sorcery and madness, as Eradorius built a tower beyond the reach of years…

A soft knock sounded at the door. Malus frowned, thinking again of the sword beside the bed. He reminded himself that with Nagaira gone, the blood debt to the temple had lapsed and forced himself to relax. 'Enter,' he said.

The door creaked open – few highborn cared for oiled hinges in places where they slept – and one of his retainers stepped into the room. It took a moment before Malus recognised Hauclir's scarred face. The former guard captain was sporting a few new cuts on his face from the recent battle, including a dramatic wound that ran at an angle from his forehead, across his nose and down to his chin.

'Do you typically block your opponent's blade with your face, Hauclir?' Malus said by way of greeting.

'If the tactic's good enough for my lord and master it's good enough for me,' Hauclir deadpanned. 'Forgive the interruption, my lord, but your brother Urial is here. He insisted on speaking to you at once, despite the unholy hour.'

'What time is it?'

'The hour of the wolf, my lord.'

'Mother of Night,' Malus cursed, taking another drink to fortify himself. 'The man is indeed a monster. Bring me a robe, then send him in.'

Hauclir scanned the room quickly, went and snatched up a discarded sleeping robe from the end of the bed and tossed it to Malus. The highborn let the bunched-up cloth bounce off his chest and hit the floor. He stared pointedly at the garment and then looked archly at his new retainer.

'I've already worn that.'

'Excellent,' the former captain answered. 'Then we're sure it fits.'

'I see,' Malus answered. 'Any other night I'd have your backside hung from a meat hook, but I'm too tired to bother just now. Go and get my brother and bring him here.'

Hauclir bowed. 'At once, my lord,' he replied and slipped quietly from the room.

Malus shrugged the silk robe over his shoulders, careful of the cuts and gouges across his upper back and right arm. No sooner had he cinched up his belt than the bedroom door groaned wide and Urial walked slowly into the room with Hauclir in his wake. The retainer made a clumsy attempt at presenting Urial after the fact, then sketched an awkward bow and retreated from sight.

'You keep the hours of a bat, dear brother,' Malus said around a swig of wine. He offered the bottle to Urial, who eyed it with disdain.

'Sleep is for the weak, brother,' Urial replied. 'The state never rests, nor does its true servants.'

'I was saying something very similar just a moment ago,' the highborn said, setting the bottle carefully on its tray. 'Why are you here?'

Urial scowled at his brother, drawing an object from his belt. It was a plaque of dark metal set in a frame of yellowed bone, about a foot long and four inches wide.

For all his fatigue and his numerous minor hurts, Malus's heart skipped a beat upon seeing the Drachau's writ. 'What are you doing with that?'

'By law and custom the Drachau presents his writ to the temple, who then delivers it to his chosen agent. We do this to bear witness that the delegation of power falls into the proper hands and to act as a guarantor of its temporary nature.' Urial held the plaque before him, his expression strained. He took a deep breath and spoke the necessary words:

'Malus, son of Lurhan, the Drachau Uthlan Tyr of Hag Graef desires you to perform an extraordinary endeavour in the service of the state and invests in you all the similar authority and power of his station, that you may accomplish the task set before you with honour and dispatch. He binds you with this writ of iron. Bear it before you and no druchii in the land will bar your way.'

All of a sudden Malus was glad for the wine warming his insides and steadying his nerves. Without preamble he reached out and plucked the writ from Urial's stiff fingers. The iron plates were thin and surprisingly light; they opened on tiny, oiled hinges to reveal the lettered parchment and elaborate seals protected in the shallow space within. 'It's smaller than I imagined. Is it true that if you fail they melt down the iron plates and pour them down your throat?'

'I certainly hope so,' Urial muttered. 'If my researches are correct you are only the eighth highborn in the history of the city to receive one.' He shook his head incredulously. 'And got it by blackmailing the Drachau, no less. The very idea is appalling.'

'Did your researches mention how the other seven acquired theirs? I expect it was exactly the same way,' Malus said absently, inspecting the parchment with a growing sense of wonder. Within the scope of the writ he effectively had the power of the Drachau himself.

'Be that as it may, this authority does not extend to the temple or its agents,' Urial said archly. 'Let us be clear on this from the start. Now perhaps you will explain to me how this will deliver Yasmir from her wanton existence and into the sacred bounds of the temple?'

Malus closed the covers of the writ and suppressed a frown. He'd hoped to put this conversation off for a while longer. 'Very well,' he said with a sigh. 'For years our sister has lived like a princess of lost Nagarythe, using her beauty and her wiles to drink the lifeblood of every enterprising nobleman in the upper reaches of the city's court. They surround her with riches and influence out of proportion to her station, each one hoping to convince her to ask for their hand in marriage. Not one of them has the courage to ask her themselves. And why is that?'

'Because she is the focus of our elder brother's affections,' Urial growled, his good hand clenching into a fist.

'Indeed and Bruglir is a very powerful, very jealous and extraordinarily murderous man,' Malus said. 'He fights duels just to test the sharpness of his swords. Any man who presses his case for Yasmir's hand must answer to Bruglir and so far our father has shown no interest in restraining him.' He gave Urial a curious look. 'I've always wondered why he never raised a hand to you. It's not as though you made any secret of your desire for her.'

Urial's expression hardened. 'Isn't it obvious? Because he knows without doubt that I'm no threat to him.' The former acolyte abruptly turned and plucked the bottle from the tray. No emotion showed on his face as he carefully filled the goblet, but the bitterness in his voice was evident. 'Yasmir told me once that she complained to him about me and he laughed at her. It was the first and only time he'd ever done such a thing, or so she claimed. It made her very angry for a time.'

'The point, however, is that the cornerstone of Yasmir's existence is Bruglir. Without him she becomes… vulnerable.'

Urial nodded thoughtfully, taking a cautious sip of the wine. 'So you plan to kill him.'

'Better to say that I intend to put him into a position that is very likely to end his life,' Malus said carefully. 'I don't dare try to kill him myself. In the first place I don't want to risk Yasmir's wrath if I'm caught and in the second place I'm not sure I'd succeed if I tried.' Malus smiled. 'No, he will meet a glorious death driving the

Skinriders from the north seas and then Yasmir will have to decide where her best interests lie.'

'An intriguing plan,' Urial said, swirling the wine in his cup. 'But where do I fit into this? You mentioned that you needed a sorcerer.'

Malus nodded. 'Yes, indeed.' He pointed to the Tome of Ak'zhaal. 'If my researches are correct, the Isle of Morhaut is protected by powerful sorceries. I will need a magic-wielder of great skill to penetrate them so we can reach the island.'

Urial eyed the book quizzically, as though noticing it for the first time. 'Never in my life would I have imagined such a thing.'

'What? That I need your help?'

'No, that you can actually read.' Urial stepped forward, setting the goblet down and turning the pages of the tome gingerly with his gloved hand. 'So you actually intend to fight the Skinriders?'

Malus shrugged. 'Only so far as I must. What I'm really after lies within a tower on the island – a sanctuary built by a sorcerer named Eradorius during the First War.'

'The First War? That was thousands of years ago! What makes you think such a place still exists?'

The highborn didn't answer for a moment. 'Call it intuition,' he said. 'I saw things in the Wastes that were even older than Eradorius's legendary tower, so I know that it's at least possible.'

Urial looked up from the book, his brass-coloured eyes boring into Malus's own. 'Does this have anything to do with the skull you took from my tower?'

Malus met Urial's stare unflinchingly. 'It was Nagaira who suggested robbing you of that skull. I suspect it had something to do with her plans for the cult.'

'That doesn't answer my question.'

'It's as much of an answer as you're going to get,' Malus said flatly. 'Does it matter, so long as Yasmir is yours in the end?'

Urial glanced one last time at the yellowed pages of the tome, then slowly and deliberately closed the cover. 'No. I suppose not.'

Inwardly the highborn breathed a sigh of relief. 'Excellent. Now the three of us need only prepare for a trip to Clar Karond in the coming weeks. I want to be there the moment Bruglir and his fleet puts in for supplies. With luck I can use the writ to hurry the process along and we can be on our way north within a month.'

'The three of us?' Urial inquired.

'We need Yasmir to accompany us on the voyage,' Malus said. 'While I may have a writ from the Drachau, neither you nor I are well-loved by our brother and we will be hundreds of leagues from civilisation and surrounded by his army of cut-throats. I intend to use Yasmir to keep Bruglir under control.'

'Ah, I see. And who will control Yasmir?'

The highborn chuckled. 'I will, of course.' And you will be the rod I will hold over her, Malus thought.

Urial nodded thoughtfully, his finger tracing the runes inscribed in the cover of the tome. 'An interesting plan, brother. But I am concerned about the lengthy delay. Many things can go awry in a month's time. The Drachau could even grow impatient and rescind the writ if he wished.'

Malus spread his hands. 'I can't make the winds blow any faster brother. I expect Bruglir hasn't even begun the voyage home yet. The straits around Karond Kar will be frozen for another couple of weeks at least.'

Urial gave Malus a wintry smile. 'Forgive my ignorance. Unlike the rest of you I was never allowed a hakseer-cruise of my own. Father wouldn't risk the embarrassment of being unable to hire a crew to go to sea under the command of a cripple. Still,' he added, his smile turning conspiratorial, 'what if I said that it was possible to go to Bruglir now? To meet him while his ships are still at sea and begin your expedition immediately?'

Malus's eyes narrowed. 'So magic is only heretical when it's being performed by someone outside the temple?'

'Do not seek to confuse the debased rituals of a cultist with the blessings of the Lord of Murder,' Urial growled.

Malus's first instinct was to dismiss the offer. He didn't care for the notion of being dropped into the middle of Bruglir's fleet with no warning or preparation, no time to sound out members of his brother's crew and perhaps test their loyalties with a little gold coin. On the other hand, time was the one commodity he needed most but had the least to spare. I need every day I can get, he thought ruefully. Then a sudden realisation made his heart skip a beat. Does he know? He had the skull of Ehrenlish in his possession for many months – does he know about Tz'arkan and the five relics? Does he suspect what I'm after?

'Does it matter?' Tz'arkan said. 'Does it change the fact that you must reach the island and recover the idol and that you need his sorceries to succeed?'

'No,' Malus muttered, half to himself. 'No, of course not.'

Urial nodded brusquely. 'Then deliver the news to Yasmir and prepare for the journey. You and she may bring one member of your retinue each if you wish – more than that would be too dangerous to risk.'

'What?' Malus stirred from his internal reverie with a start. 'I mean – yes, of course. When will you be ready?'

'We can depart this evening,' Urial replied, almost enthusiastic at the prospect. 'The moon and tides will be propitious. Come to my tower at nightfall, just before the rising of the fog and we will be on our way.'

Before Malus could think of a response, Urial turned on his heel and limped from the room, leaving the highborn to wonder just what he'd got himself into.

He held up the writ and considered its iron cover, shaking his head ruefully. Absolute power indeed, he thought.

THE FIGURINE WAS little more than one foot tall; formed from a single piece of obsidian, it depicted a priestess of the temple drinking the brains from the skull of a defeated foe. It was more than a hundred years old, carved by the infamous artist Luclayr before his spectacular suicide. Easily worth more than a highborn's ransom, the figurine made a sharp whirring sound as it spun through the air and exploded into razor-edged shards inches from Malus's head. The highborn ducked instinctively, grimacing at the shower of razor-sharp splinters.

'A sea voyage? With *him*?' Yasmir's violet eyes glowed with hatred. She stalked through the shadows at the far end of her sleeping chamber, her half-open silk robe trailing in her wake like the shroud of a wight. Her skin was luminous where the weak daylight touched it – she was the classic druchii beauty, at her most alluring when moved to anger. Even Malus had to admit that she was breathtaking, but as he plucked splinters of black glass from his cheek he also mused that the lovelier she became, the more attention he had to devote to staying alive.

'This was not our bargain,' Yasmir hissed. Another object – a wine goblet – struck the wall near the high-born with a hollow clang. 'You asked for my help convincing Bruglir to back your expedition. *Nothing* more. In return you promised to kill Urial, not put us at the mercy of his blood magic!'

'Plans change, dear sister,' Malus said, readying himself to dodge another missile. 'The Drachau took a keen interest in my plan and gave me his unstinting support, as you have seen,' he pointed to the writ, lying open on a small table near the centre of the room. 'With the writ in hand I was able to command Urial to transport us directly to Bruglir's ship rather than wait so many weeks for his fleet to make port. Time is of the essence, Yasmir and so I must regretfully insist that you accompany me.'

'*Insist!*' The word came out in a hissing screech. A barrage of shoes flew across the room, then another small piece of statuary moving too fast to identify before it shattered against Malus's breastplate. The rest of her furious reply tapered off into a wordless screech of frustration; she had read the writ with exacting care and knew that she had no real power to resist his summons.

Malus watched Yasmir's fit with considerable interest, wondering when the last time was that she'd been dictated to about anything. He'd first called upon her early in the day, only to be told by her slaves that she was indisposed. Hours passed, morning to noon and then well into the afternoon and after being rebuffed for a third time Malus had produced the writ and shoved the frightened slaves out of the way. Her retainers had rushed at him like angry cadaver bees, but for once their highborn upbringing proved useful, as one glimpse of the iron plaque had been enough to stop them in their tracks. And so he'd barged into her bedroom just behind a cloud of stammering slaves and sent Yasmir's rich and powerful bed partners scrambling for their robes.

At first she'd reacted to his intrusion with the same languid calm she'd displayed at the arena – until she saw the writ. Then her composure gave way to anger. She's grown too accustomed to being in a position of control, he thought. Take that away and she becomes fearful. And dangerous, he reminded himself.

'Our bargain still stands, dear sister. It is merely the circumstances that have changed,' he said, trying to sound conciliatory. 'I still need your help to encourage Bruglir's co-operation and I need Urial's magic to penetrate the sorcerous defences surrounding the island. Once that's done we can dispatch him at our leisure. In the meantime, you will be able to enjoy the company of your beloved Bruglir for weeks more than you normally would. Haven't you always wished to sail with him on his long sea raids, taking part in the bloody battles and choosing the choicest baubles from the treasure trove as befits a corsair queen?'

Yasmir paused. 'There is something in what you say, I suppose. It's not as though I wouldn't have Bruglir and his crew to keep that vile temple-worm away from me.' Malus heard her take a deep breath and then she stepped back into the light, drawing her robe securely about her graceful body. 'Very well,' she said, attempting a small measure of her former composure. 'Just one companion, you said? And we are to leave in…?'

Malus considered the light outside. 'In just a few hours, sister: just before the fog rises. I tried to tell you earlier, but–'

'Yes, yes, I know.' She drew herself up to her full, regal height. 'I shall be ready at the appointed time. Let it not be said that I do not honour my bargains to the letter, Malus. See to it that you do the same.' Yasmir scooped the iron plaque from the table and held it out to Malus. 'This writ won't count for much a thousand leagues from the Hag. On the seas the only law will be our dear brother the sea captain.' Her full lips quirked in a cruel smile. 'Disappoint me and it might be your head rolling along the deck beside Urial's.'

Malus took the plaque from her hand. 'I expect nothing less,' he said.

'WHY ME? WHY not Silar Thornblood, or Arleth Vann?' Hauclir looked up at the ominous bulk of Urial's spire from the barren courtyard outside its iron-banded doors. The former guard captain's face was faintly green in the early evening light; like almost everyone else in Hag Graef, he'd heard legends about the dread tower of the Forsaken One. Malus eyed him with some amusement and wondered what the man would think if he told him that all of the stories were true.

'Because Silar runs my household and is still in the process of rebuilding it. And Arleth Vann doesn't mix well with members of the temple,' the highborn said. 'You, on the other hand–'

'I'm expendable,' Hauclir answered, his face grim. The retainer wore full armour over his kheitan and robes and carried a single sword at his hip. A large pack hung from one shoulder, carrying clothes and supplies for both him and his lord.

Malus clapped Hauclir on the back. 'Come now, Hauclir, it's not like that. *All* of my retainers are expendable. You're just more expendable than the others at the moment.'

'And to think, I *asked* for this,' Hauclir grumbled, shifting the pack on his shoulder.

'Indeed you did,' Malus nodded. 'Delightful, is it not?'

Just then Malus caught sight of a group of druchii entering the courtyard from the opposite side. Yasmir walked amid a group of mournful retainers, several holding witchlight globes aloft on long poles to light their path. A slave walked several paces behind the party, almost doubled over with a huge pack on her shoulders.

Malus bowed as she approached. 'Well met, sister. Are you looking forward to being reunited with our noble brother?' The highborn savoured the stricken looks on Yasmir's entourage as she nodded.

'Indeed I am. It's the one part of this cursed voyage that I expect to enjoy at all.'

Yasmir was dressed all in black, with fine woollen robes and a long shirt of fine black mail that covered her arms and hung to just above her knees. A wide belt of nauglir hide circled her narrow waist and she wore two long daggers, one at each hip. Though the fog hadn't yet risen she wore her silver caedlin. Unlike many highborn who wore nightmasks worked in the shape of monsters or daemons, Yasmir's mask eerily mirrored her own features, almost like a death mask. Malus imagined the shock strangers must have upon seeing that ethereal mask – and then have it pulled away to reveal the startling reality beneath.

'Then send your hounds away, dear Yasmir. The moons have risen and Urial awaits.'

To her credit, Yasmir offered no melodramatic farewells – she simply beckoned to her slave and walked away from the noblemen without a single word. Malus felt the heat of their stares on his neck as he led Yasmir to the tower's tall doorway. As he raised his fist to strike the aged wood, the portal swung soundlessly open, spilling a wash of crimson light onto the cobblestones outside.

One of Urial's skull-faced retainers silently beckoned the highborn and their retainers to come inside. Malus found himself entering the tower with some trepidation. He could not help but feel a chill upon seeing the ranks of silver masks lining the walls of the circular room, all too aware of the malevolent beings that watched from behind the masks' sightless eyes.

Urial waited in the centre of the room, standing before a large brass cauldron brimming with blood. Beyond the cauldron rose what appeared to be a very tall mirror-frame of etched brass. The glass within the frame was missing and Malus saw that a small set of steps had been set before the empty brass oval. Half a dozen of Urial's retainers stood at a discrete distance from their master, along with a handful of robed acolytes, their heads bowed in concentration. Malus could hear them chanting in a language that set his hair on end.

'Your timing is good,' Urial said. 'The moon is in the proper alignment. Once the doorway is open you will have to move quickly, however – we will have little time.'

With that, he turned to the cauldron and spread his arms wide.

A sonorous chant rose from Urial's lips, echoed by the acolytes nearby. Yasmir looked to Malus; the highborn shrugged and walked towards the cauldron.

Within the brass vessel the blood was beginning to stir, as though churned from within by invisible hands. Steam rose from its surface, forming a reddish haze before the mirror frame. The chanting increased in volume and Malus saw a thick tendril of steam begin to twist like the funnel of a whirlpool, extending inexorably towards the empty brass frame.

The churning mist reached for the space within the wire oval and flattened as though it touched an invisible plane suspended within the wire. Blood radiated across this plane in concentric ripples, shimmering with unnatural power, until they reached the wire rim and rebounded back towards the centre. Malus could now hear a faint howling sound coming from the crimson mirror – was it the souls of the damned? No, he realised. It was the wind off the sea, cold and unbound.

Suddenly the funnel dissipated. The cauldron was empty and a sheen of bright blood, like a bubble formed in a pool of gore, glistened and trembled within the wire. 'Quickly now,' Urial said, his voice strained. 'Step through! It will not last more than a few moments.'

Once again, Yasmir looked to Malus – she had plucked her mask away and he could see the fear deep in her eyes. He gave her a mocking smile and stepped lightly up to the wire, gritting his teeth against his own palpable unease. This close to the portal Malus could hear other sounds above the wind: the creaking of wood and rope and the groan of a ship's hull as it surged through the waves. He hesitated only a moment, then with a deep breath he stepped into the swirling pattern of blood.

Chapter Twelve
THE SEA RAVENS

FOR THE SPACE of a single heartbeat it felt as though Malus hung above an impossibly vast space, filled with howling wind and the rushing presence of a multitude of angry ghosts. Then an icy shock washed over him, like a torrent of freezing water and he fell.

He felt no rush of air against his body, only the unmoored feeling in his guts as he plummeted through darkness. The further he fell the faster he went, until it seemed as though he were coming apart from within, unravelling like a tumbling skein of muscle, flesh and veins. Malus focussed his terrible will to hold the screams at bay. Then without warning his foot struck solid wood and a harsh slap of cold sea air struck his face as he staggered across the heeling deck of a druchii ship under weigh.

Unearthly darkness still clung to Malus's eyes as he lurched drunkenly across the deck. He blinked furiously, trying to see past the viscous blackness. Sights swam in and out of his vision, curious double-images that showed two or even three different versions of the scene around him. Malus saw the dark, polished deck of the ship gleaming in the early moonlight, then the image blurred and he saw the main mast cracked through and the debris of battle littering the blood-stained planks in the full light of day. He blinked and shook his head fiercely and when he opened his eyes again there were black-robed shapes rushing across the deck with naked steel in their hands. The shapes blurred, becoming bloody and torn, then resolved themselves once more.

The highborn clenched his jaw against a stream of curses and closed his eyes, focusing on steadying his feet against the rolling of the ship. What sorcery is this, he thought? Did the hushalta forever twist my body and mind, or is this something else entirely?

'Whatever it is,' he whispered to himself. 'It stops, here and now.'

The words stirred the daemon, provoking it to slow laughter. 'Here and now? There is no such thing, little druchii. If you cannot understand this then you are truly lost.'

Before Malus could reply, however, the thudding of boots across the wooden deck reminded him of more immediate concerns. The highborn opened his eyes and saw a score of druchii corsairs, armed with swords, bill-hooks and axes rushing towards him. Their faces were covered in heavy scarves rimed with frost, but there was no mistaking the anger and alarm in their dark eyes. The highborn raised his hands, showing open palms, only realising then as they continued to rush towards him that the crew had no interest in talking to him whatsoever.

The highborn's first instinct was to reach for his swords, but he knew that if he did it would only confirm the crew's worst suspicions. His disoriented mind raced furiously, trying to think of a proper response, but before he could speak the air crackled with electricity and a body thumped onto the deck behind Malus. The sailors recoiled and the highborn turned to see Hauclir on one knee before an oval-shaped crimson haze that waxed and waned in density just a foot above the deck. The retainer stared wildly about at his surroundings, his face a mask of pure terror.

'What manner of madness is this?' said one of the sailors, his eyes darting warily from Malus to Hauclir and back again. The air crackled with invisible lightning once more and the corsairs shrank back a step. The sailor glared sharply at the men to either side of him. 'Stand fast, you black birds!' he commanded in a leathery voice and the corsairs regained a measure of resolve.

Yasmir and her slave stepped through next. The highborn staggered slightly under the burden of Urial's spell, but with a blistering curse she banished the strange effects and straightened imperiously before the gawking sailors. Her slave, a pale human woman with bright red hair and vivid blue eyes, took one step and collapsed to the deck, convulsing uncontrollably.

'I am Yasmir, daughter of Lurhan the Vaulkhar of Hag Graef,' the druchii woman declared angrily, as though the band of armed corsairs facing her were more of an insult than a deadly threat. 'And I wish to see my brother at once.'

The leader of the corsairs stepped forward, riding the heaving deck with the ease of a veteran sailor. 'The captain has no interest in seeing you,' the man said with a harsh laugh. 'I've the watch while he is below so you'll be speaking to me, sea-witch, or I'll have the lads see you off with kisses of steel.'

Yasmir drew back, her face luminous with rage as she reached for the long knives at her belt. Malus stepped forward, drawing the plaque from his belt. 'I am Malus, son of Lurhan the Vaulkhar and I bear a writ of iron compelling your service in the name of the Drachau of Hag Graef! Put away your blades, or your lives are forfeit!'

The gruff-voiced sailor rounded on Malus. 'You're eight weeks' sail from the harbour of Clar Karond and the only law on this deck is the captain's.' Despite his bluster, the sailor's eyes were growing wider by the moment as he struggled to understand what was happening. Malus knew that the man could just as easily give in to his growing unease and order his men to attack if something didn't happen to change his mind.

That was when the air trembled with a hideous ripping sound, like a giant being torn in two, followed by a sharp thunderclap that sent nearly everyone on deck reeling. There was a bright flash of red light in the place where the shimmering crimson fog had hung, leaving Urial and six of his retainers standing in a tight circle on the pitching deck. If the former acolyte and his skull-faced men felt any distress at the effects of the spell, they gave no outward sign.

Several of the sailors fell to their knees, stunned by the blast of noise. Malus struggled to keep his expression neutral, even as his mind raged. *Six* men and every one a deadly warrior. Urial had lied to him!

Yet this was not the time for recriminations. Malus mastered his anger and moved quickly, taking advantage of the sailors' stunned reactions. He rushed to the side of the corsair officer, speaking in low, insistent tones. 'We've come a long way in an unpleasantly short amount of time on an important mission of state,' he said. 'If you deny the power of the writ in favour of the captain's law, then it is for the captain to decide what to do with us, not you.' Malus gestured sharply at the reeling corsairs. 'Send these sea ravens back to their roosts and call out your captain. Believe me when I say he'll speak with us once he realises who has come aboard.'

For a moment, no one spoke as the sailors picked themselves up off the deck and their officer struggled with the decisions laid before him. The only sounds were the cold wind whistling through the rigging and the groan of the masts under minimal sail in the face of the rough weather. The two moons broached like whales through the silver clouds scudding overhead, painting the ship in silver light.

The corsair shook himself out of his dreadful reverie and waved back his men with a curt gesture. He turned to Malus. 'The captain is not to be disturbed,' he said, a little shakily. 'He is below with his sea mistress.'

Yasmir's slave let out a strangled cry, then went silent. Malus turned to see his half-sister standing over the human, her boot across the slave's throat. The slave pawed weakly at her mistress's leg, her body writhing as she struggled for air. Yasmir's expression was beautiful and terrible to behold. '*What* did you say, seabird?' Her voice was cold as steel.

The officer's eyes widened further and his shoulders hunched, as though realising for the first time who it was he was addressing. 'Dragons Below take me,' he cursed softly to himself – or given whom he faced, perhaps it was a prayer. 'I… I meant to say he is below with the first officer, dread lady,' he said to Yasmir. 'Deep in their plans, belike, charting our course for the coming week.'

'Where?' Yasmir demanded. Small white fists pounded desperately at her lower leg. The slave's face was bright purple, her eyes bulging in their sockets.

'In… in the captain's cabin, dread lady,' the officer replied dully. 'But when he's in his cabin the crew is not to disturb him–'

'Except for his first mate, evidently,' Yasmir said venomously. 'Fortunately, we aren't part of Bruglir's crew, but his *beloved kin*.' Abruptly she took her foot from her slave's throat. The human rolled onto her side retching and gasping for air. Swift as an adder, Yasmir drew one of her long blades from its scabbard and took the slave by her hair. With a single, smooth stroke and the sound of a razor parting flesh the slave's forehead thumped back to the deck. Blood poured from the human's slashed throat in a swiftly spreading pool.

Yasmir straightened, bloody knife scattering red droplets across the lower half of her robes. 'Take me to my darling brother,' she said with a terrifying smile. 'Whatever the captain's plans, I assure you they are about to change.'

As the procession filed swiftly through the shadowy central passageway of Bruglir's ship, Malus had a moment to reflect that this made the second time in less than a day that he had barged into the bedchamber of a powerful and murderous druchii noble. It seemed an odd way to conduct affairs of state, but he had to admit it opened up interesting possibilities for the future.

While women marched to war alongside men they were expected to put down their weapons in time of peace and pursue other interests appropriate to their gender, like managing households or finding ways to murder their husband's enemies. Notable exceptions to this rule were the priestesses of the temple and sailors on the black-hulled druchii corsairs. The call of the sea was a sacred thing to most druchii. They regarded the black waters with equal measures of reverence and fear, for it was the raging ocean that drowned their ancestral home of Nagarythe, ages ago and thus it was the only link they had to the glories of their past. As the ocean claimed their birthright, the druchii claimed the ocean itself in return, riding its waves to gather the plunder and the glory that kept their people alive. Though the druchii called upon their women to give up their swords in times of hateful peace, they would never ask them to give up the sea.

It had never occurred to Malus that Bruglir would keep a sea mistress. Many captains did, Malus knew, but he'd always assumed that Bruglir was as devoted to Yasmir as she was to him. All at once his tangled web of deception took on a wholly different dimension and his mind raced as he considered the many possibilities.

The pirate officer led the way, moving with the reluctant step of a condemned man with Yasmir looming over him like a thundercloud. Malus followed close behind, with Urial bringing up the rear. He hadn't stopped staring at Yasmir since she'd taken her knife to her maddened slave and the expression on Urial's face was one of almost rapturous desire. The sight was both pathetic and deeply disturbing all at the same time.

There was no guard at the captain's door – for a man like Bruglir, it was a show of his own prowess that he needed no protection from daggers in the night. Eyeing the bloody knife still gripped in Yasmir's hand, Malus wondered if that policy might be changing in the very near future.

The druchii officer stopped at the door, bracing himself and preparing to knock, but Yasmir put a hand to the side of the sailor's head and pushed him aside with a startling show of strength. For a moment Malus thought she was going to put a boot to the thin panel door, but she turned the doorknob with fluid speed and stood in the doorway like one of Khaine's ecstatic brides, arms spread and bloody knife held high.

'Hello, beloved brother,' Yasmir said in a cool and sultry voice. 'Have you missed me?'

The captain's quarters lay in darkness, illuminated by squares of moonlight that waxed and waned with the whim of the clouds. Two figures clutched one another on the broad bed, their naked skin limned with lambent silver. At the sound of Yasmir's voice they leapt apart, one with a startled curse and the other with a yowl like a scalded Lustrian tiger. There was a rasp of steel and a woman stepped into the moonlight, naked as the blade in her hand. She was lean and hard as whipcord, her pale skin a dusky white from endless days at sea. Her body was made of hard muscle and scar tissue, a grizzled veteran's share of desperate battles and bloodletting. Bruglir's first mate had a striking, if severe face, marred by a long scar that ran from above her left temple down to her upper lip. The sword stroke had blinded her left eye and pulled her lip upwards in a permanent snarl. Her one good eye was black as jet and bright with fury.

'Begone, jhindara!' The corsair commanded, brandishing her sword. It was a short, heavy blade, broad and single-edged like a cleaver and nicked from hard use. 'Try to take him and I'll leave you squirming in your own guts!'

Yasmir's laugh was easy and light. 'Who is the witch and who the saviour, you scarred little churl?' She drew her second knife and seemed to float towards the corsair, her expression soulless and intent as a hunting hawk. 'Dance with me and we will see who the Lord of Murder favours more!'

'Stand fast!' roared a commanding voice that brought both women up short. A tall, powerfully-built figure leapt between the two. Bruglir had his father's height, standing half a head taller than Yasmir and had an unusually broad-shouldered frame that added to his imposing stature. The corsair lord very much resembled the Vaulkhar in his youth, with a chiselled brow and a hawk-like nose that lent him a ferocious presence even in repose. A long, black moustache hung down to his pointed chin, adding to his already fierce demeanour. 'She is mine, Yasmir, part of my crew by oath and by blood and you cannot have her.'

Yasmir regarded her beloved with dreadful intensity. 'She is yours, but are you not *mine*, beloved brother? Was that not the promise you made to me, the oath you renew again and again each time you return to the Hag?' Her voice rose in pitch and intensity, like a raging wind. 'And if this... this deformed wretch is yours, then by rights she is mine as well, to do with as I please. Is she not?' She leaned close to Bruglir, her lips nearly brushing his, her knives quivering in her hands. 'Answer me,' she whispered. *'Answer me.'*

The room was about to erupt into bloodshed. It was a particular kind of tension that Malus could almost taste, like the charged air that heralded a sudden storm. Thinking quickly, the highborn stepped into the room, brandishing the plaque. 'Actually, as of now all of you belong to *me*,' he loudly declared. 'And until I no longer have need of you, you will stay your hand or answer to the Drachau *and* our father upon our return to the Hag.'

Bruglir turned at the sound of Malus's voice, his natural scowl deepening as he saw first Malus, then his brother Urial. 'What's this? The Darkblade and the temple worm both fouling the deck of my ship? He glared at Yasmir. 'You brought them here?'

'No, brother,' Malus answered. 'More the other way around. I'd thought you would be pleased to see your beloved sister, but it appears I stand corrected.' He eyed Yasmir carefully. 'A druchii woman may take as many lovers as she pleases, but when a druchii man commits himself, he is expected to remain faithful as a measure of his strength. Honestly, brother, I expected better of you.'

Bruglir's expression turned incredulous, then pale with anger. 'I don't know how you managed this, Darkblade, but–'

Malus stepped forward and held the plaque under Bruglir's nose. 'You haven't been paying attention, brother. Listen carefully. I bear a writ of iron from the Drachau of Hag Graef, placing you and your fleet under my command for a campaign against the Skinriders. I act with the Drachau's will in this and any man who bars my path will answer for it with his life.'

'The only law at sea is the captain's law,' the first officer spat, her eyes still boring into Yasmir's.

'But if the captain ever wishes to set foot in his home again – and still claim the mighty fortune he's amassed there over the years – he'll see the wisdom in making his law *my* law as well.'

Bruglir snatched the plaque from Malus's hand, flipping open the cover as though he expected to find nothing there. His brow furrowed as he read the writing on the parchment inside and examined the seals thereon.

'There are ten of us, all told,' Malus continued. 'I'll require a cabin for myself and I assume Urial will require one as well. Sister?'

Yasmir still glared murderously at the first mate. She bit out her reply as though snipping veins between her teeth. 'I'll take her cabin,' she said. 'It's clear that she isn't using it.'

'Do you take us for fools?' the first officer snapped. 'You didn't come by boat, but by sorcery. So there's no one back home to know what actually happened to you. We can toss your innards to the sea dragons and sail for home–'

'Tani, *enough*,' Bruglir ordered wearily. The first officer glared hotly at her captain, but fell silent. 'Get dressed and go topside.'

Tani nodded curtly. 'Your will, sir.' She snatched a salt-stained sea robe from the deck by the bed and shrugged into it, never taking her eye off Yasmir and switching her heavy cleaver from hand to hand as she dressed. For a moment it seemed as though another confrontation loomed as Yasmir blocked the first officer's path to the door, but at the last moment the knife-wielding druchii stepped aside.

Bruglir followed her to the door, then closed it in Urial's face. He turned to Yasmir, holding up the plaque. 'Is this some kind of forgery?'

Radiant and hateful, Yasmir shook her head.

'Then it appears my worst nightmare has come true,' the captain said sourly, throwing the plaque onto the disordered bed. He turned to Malus. 'For the moment, you have me,' he said, his voice devoid of any emotion, though his eyes were pools of malevolence. 'But this remit has its limits. Sooner or later, the Drachau will rescind it and then I will destroy you.'

Malus managed a smile. 'I might have feared you more had we not also met your sea mistress,' he replied. 'If I were you, I'd be more worried about your own odds of survival once the writ runs its course.'

Bruglir looked to Yasmir and found himself staring into eyes as flat and cold as the blades in her hands. 'Damn you, Darkblade,' he hissed. 'If I do nothing else, I swear before the Dragons Below that I will ruin you. But until then,' he snarled, 'I and my fleet are at your command.'

THE WRIT OF iron evidently carried little weight with Urial's skull-faced retainers; they formed a wall of flesh and steel between Malus and their lord as he approached Urial by the port rail. His head hung low and he managed another aching dry heave as his stomach continued to rebel against the motion of ship and sea.

Malus threw back his head and laughed, savouring his half-brother's suffering. 'Now this is rich irony,' he said aloud. 'A gift from the Dark Mother herself.'

Urial turned until his back was to the rail. Dried vomit dotted his cheeks and chin and a thin stream of bile hung from his slack lips and twisted stubbornly in the cold wind. 'Hateful thing,' he grunted, sliding to the deck. 'I've slain men for less.'

Malus grinned cruelly. 'Would you care to see my hot blood roll across this pitching deck?'

'By the Bloody-Handed God, *shut up!*' Urial groaned, his eyes rolling in their sockets like a pair of thrown dice. The highborn pushed past the retainers and leaned against the rail, drinking deep of the salt air. It surprised him how much he'd missed the sea once he'd returned to the Hag. 'You know, in the old times, a druchii who couldn't get his sea legs was believed to be bad luck and thrown overboard to the Dragons Below.'

'If the sea is steady down in the depths, then throw me in,' Urial moaned. 'They can have me and may they choke on my bones.'

Malus looked out into the darkness. Before his recent slaving cruise he would have been utterly blind, staring out into the inky night, but his experienced eye could discern subtle shades among the blackness, revealing a long coastline of craggy cliffs less than ten miles off the beam. The wind was blowing westerly off the port bow as Bruglir's flagship tacked northward, her sleek hull slicing through the sullen waves.

'You lied to me,' the highborn said, his voice level.

'I did not.'

'You said more than one retainer each would be too risky.'

Urial nodded. 'Indeed – because I planned on bringing six men of my own. You didn't expect me to trust your word that Bruglir and Yasmir would honour the writ, did you?'

Malus shrugged, concealing his anger. 'No, I suppose not.'

'What did our illustrious brother have to say?'

'His fleet is scattered along the coast, looking for the last pickings before heading home,' the highborn said. 'We'll be turning soon, riding south before the wind as he seeks them out. He thinks it will be three or four days before he's got them all together and we can make our way north.'

With a heartfelt groan Urial gripped the rail with his good hand and pulled himself upright. 'What coast is that, yonder?'

Malus gave Urial a sidelong look. 'That's Bretonnia. We're close to Lyonnesse, I think.'

'Ah,' Urial nodded, sounding relieved. 'That's good.'

'Why?'

'Because I feared it might be Ulthuan, in which case I would be greatly disappointed,' Urial answered. 'I hope to see the home of our kin some day. I expect it's grand and mountainous, rising from the sea like a crown.' He grinned in the darkness. 'I dream of going there and watching those white cities burn.' Suddenly he turned to Malus. 'There's something I've been meaning to ask you.'

'You may ask,' Malus said, his voice promising nothing.

'Back at the Hag, you told the Drachau you'd found the Isle of Morhaut,' Urial said. 'How? The location's been lost for at least two hundred years. Even the temple's vast library holds no mention of it.'

'Oh. That.' Malus looked at Urial and grinned. 'That was all a lie. I haven't the slightest idea where the forsaken island is.'

Chapter Thirteen
PROMISES OF DEATH

'You lied to the Drachau,' Yasmir said, her voice chillingly pleasant. 'By all rights, that writ of iron you hold isn't worth the metal holding it together.'

Malus folded his arms and frowned at his half sister, trying to adjust his back into a more comfortable position without giving her the impression he was squirming. With Yasmir in the first officer's cabin there were precious few berthing spaces left for the unexpected arrivals short of sleeping with the regular crew. Urial was one deck below with the ship's chirurgeon, consigned to share a dank, lightless cell packed with jars of unguents, salves and animal parts. After some negotiation, Malus had managed to secure the ship's chart room for himself; it was a musty alcove that smelled of rot and old paper, crammed with boxes of rolled-up maps and one long chart table that ran the length of the outside bulkhead. The table was currently acting as his bed, supporting a thin bedroll of straw ticking and a pillow made from a spare cloak. Malus attempted to recline on his makeshift divan, back propped against his poor excuse for a pillow and craning his head a little awkwardly due to the curvature of the bulkhead behind him.

'I was right there when you stood in Bruglir's cabin and told him that our first task was to uncover the location of the lost island,' Yasmir continued. Only her pointed chin and her sensual smile could be seen beneath a black half-veil of Tilean lace that concealed the rest of her features. Malus couldn't imagine what had possessed her to bring such a thing on the voyage, but now she wore it whenever she left her cabin. It was the sort of thing a wife wore while keeping a death vigil over her husband – yet no matter what she was doing, Yasmir's lips were always smiling, as though she were tickled by some secret amusement. It had only been a day since their arrival on Bruglir's ship, but Malus was starting to wonder if perhaps the recent upheavals she'd suffered had pushed his radiant, pampered sister close to the edge of madness.

'You led the Drachau to believe you already knew where the Isle of Morhaut was – if Bruglir had spent more time reading what the writ actually said rather than checking its authenticity, he would have found you out and you would be hanging by your neck from the mast right now.'

'Fortunately he was somewhat distracted,' Malus answered calmly, his expression implacable. 'I hadn't realised you were so punctilious on matters of legality, dear sister.'

'Only where my freedom is concerned. You used that writ to try and make a slave of me! You have no idea how abhorrent such a thing feels!'

'Indeed, sister. You're quite right. I never stopped to imagine what it might be like,' Malus replied coldly. He spread his hands. 'Very well. You're free. What will you do now? Spread the news to your beloved?'

Yasmir laughed, a bubbling sound of artless joy that set Malus's teeth on edge. 'By the Mother, of course not! Let him toil in chains for as long as you'll have him.' She bent over him, her face inches from his. Malus could smell her sweetened breath and almost feel the silken brush of her lips and it disturbed him how much his body seemed drawn to hers, like iron to a lodestone. She whispered, 'There is a price for my silence, Malus. Will you pay it?'

'You know I will,' he said, squirming against the bulkhead now for entirely different reasons. Damned confined spaces! He should have guessed she'd been up to something when she'd barged into the chartroom unannounced. Now she was using every method at her disposal to keep him off-balance and he couldn't do a single thing about it.

'I want that scarred sea whore dead,' she said, the words spilling like pure venom from her smiling lips. 'I don't care how, but she must die and the sooner the better.' Malus attempted a laugh. 'I've already promised you Urial's head, sister! Is there no end to your greed?' But the false mirth died beneath Yasmir's implacable will.

'It is the price of your continued survival, brother,' Yasmir whispered. 'For now, you and I are partners, because I have an interest in seeing Bruglir suffer. He must atone for what he has done to me and the humiliation he

endures from serving you is sweet. So I have no problem
letting this campaign of yours continue. I'll even support
it so long as it suits my needs. But the woman must die.
Only then can I make Bruglir devote himself entirely to
me. Do you understand?'

'If you want her dead why not kill her yourself?'

For just a moment Yasmir's zealous smile faltered.
'Don't be a fool, Malus,' she hissed. '*Of course* I can kill
her, but that would gain me nothing. If she dies by my
hand then Bruglir becomes my enemy and makes my
plan that much harder.'

'So you would rather I make an enemy of him
instead?'

'Of course, if that's what it takes,' Yasmir replied. 'But
you are the leader of this expedition. I'm certain you can
find some crafty means of sending the vile woman to
her death that still keeps your own hands clean. Think
on it, brother. Think carefully. The sooner the better, or
I may lose my patience and tell Bruglir the truth.' Her
dazzling smile glowed beneath the blackness of the veil.
'It's possible that he might be so grateful at escaping the
writ that he'd kill the whore just to please me, but I
don't want to take that chance unless I feel I must.' With
that she turned on her heel and opened the door into
the shadowy passageway, slipping gracefully from sight.

Before Malus could slide his feet off the table Hauclir
ducked into the cramped room, gnawing on a chunk of
bread and holding a wooden platter of cheese, sausage
and apple slices in his hand. He held the food out to
Malus. 'It appears our timing was good; they raided a
human village not two days ago and were able to refill
their stores. Before that they were down to eating rats
while dodging Bretonnian coastal patrols. Your brother

is a madman for staying out as long as he does.' The guardsman pointed at the cheese, a small half-round the size of his palm. 'I think that's from a goat. You should try it.'

Malus took the proffered plate with a glare for his retainer. He pressed his fingertips to the platter and studied the number of cheese crumbs they picked up. 'Hauclir,' he said sourly, 'while it is your duty to test my food for poison, you don't have to eat half the cheese to do it.'

Hauclir paused in mid-chew. 'Test for poison, my lord?'

BRUGLIR'S FLAGSHIP WAS a long, ebon sea-blade named *Harrier*, built by the shipwrights in Clar Karond and wrought with the best craft and sorcery that the captain's ample fortune could buy. With three stepped masts and a long, narrow hull she could fly along the water with all her sails set and her crew knew the dance of wind and wave as well as they knew the lands of their birth. For some, the sea was the only homeland they'd ever known and all that they ever longed for when tied up in port.

But the qualities that made *Harrier* sleek and swift also made her difficult to handle in heavy weather; her tall masts and narrow beam made her prone to rolling dangerously in rough seas, which was what the nimble corsair faced now. Winter still stubbornly refused to yield to spring along the Bretonnian coast and a sharp wind still blew westerly from the open sea before a wall of heavy grey clouds. The ocean was the colour of unpolished steel, surging and crashing against the hull of the raider as she worked her way southwards into the areas where the remaining ships of the fleet were hunting for

prey. For the last three days Bruglir had collected his
scattered ships, using prearranged rendezvous points
and surreptitious signals made in the dead of night.
Eight other raiders now trailed along in the *Harrier's*
wake, their captains growing more nervous by the hour
as a fleet of black ships was bound to attract the attention of watchers along the coast.

Muffled shouts and pounding feet had brought Malus
topside with Hauclir in tow. There was a subtle change
in the atmosphere, an undercurrent of tension that he
recognised from his raiding cruise the previous year and
had learned to pay attention to. Something was happening and the crew was on edge.

A cold, salty wind slapped at the highborn's face as he
emerged on deck, prompting him to reach back for the
woollen hood hanging at his shoulders. He'd changed
into his armour and wore a cloak of raw wool to keep
the water from the expensive steel. The *Harrier* rolled
drunkenly as it staggered against another hissing wave
and the sailors up in the rigging relayed instructions to
one another from the woman standing at the ship's
wheel below. Malus caught sight of Tanithra, the first
officer, casting a weather eye on the storm front standing
out to the west as she led the ship a merry dance along
the sullen sea. Off to port, between *Harrier* and the
coast, Malus saw two new corsairs, their raked prows
pointing north as they tacked against the wind.

Hauclir staggered as the ship reeled in the opposite
direction as the wave surged past. The former captain
had yet to find his sea legs, though his stomach had
apparently adjusted easily enough. 'Looks like two of
our scattered sea birds came and found us for a change,'
he shouted over the waves and the rushing wind.

'So it would appear,' Malus answered, scanning the deck. Other than the day watch, the rest of the crew were below, knowing that they would have to suffer their turn in the freezing wind and spray soon enough. 'The question is why.'

The highborn turned and headed aft, towards the citadel. From the citadel the captain would command the ship in battle, able to look down on the main deck and across to the raised deck of the redoubt at the bow of the ship. The ship's wheel stood upon the citadel, just forward of a pair of powerful bolt throwers that could fire massive steel-headed bolts at enemy ships approaching the *Harrier* from the aft quarter or stern. Two short stairways led up from the main deck, one to port and one to starboard. On impulse, Malus crossed to the starboard stair. As he did, another wave surged against the hull and the corsair heeled over like a bottle bobbing in the surf. Hauclir staggered with a sharp curse, inadvertently bumping into Malus and sending him reeling towards the side of the staircase.

The highborn flung out a hand to steady himself and suddenly a powerful wave of vertigo seized him. His vision swam and a cacophony of sound waxed and waned in his ears – discordant, clashing noises and cries of anger and pain. Wetness, warm and thick, soaked across his palm. Malus reeled, holding up his hand to see a stain of deep red in his wavering sight. *Here is where I died*, a thought echoed crazily in his mind.

Then strong hands seized him by the shoulders and held him fast. Malus shook his head fiercely and the world seemed to snap back onto its moorings once more. He looked over his shoulder to see Hauclir bracing him with both hands.

'My apologies, my lord,' Hauclir said, somewhat sheepishly. 'How does anyone get used to this incessant tumbling?'

Malus shook himself free of Hauclir's grip. 'Perhaps I should have you walk the deck all night tonight until you learn.'

'Will that be before or after you've ripped out my fingernails and gouged out my eyes with a fish bone?'

'Eh?'

'So far you've promised to rip out my nails for being late with breakfast and then said you'd gouge out my eyes for airing out your good cloak and getting it soaked with salt water.'

Malus frowned. 'All that since we came aboard?'

'All that since this morning. Yesterday, you said–'

'Never mind,' the highborn muttered, grinding his teeth. 'When we get back home I'll have you fed to the cold ones and we'll leave it at that.'

Hauclir nodded, his face impassive. 'Very well, my lord. I'll make a note of it.'

'Are you *mocking* me now, you impertinent wretch?'

'Just trying to help you keep track of things, my lord. I'm here to be of service.'

'Indeed? Feel free to begin at any time.'

Malus worked his way around to the bottom of the staircase and made for the citadel deck, his retainer trailing obediently in his wake. 'Your pardon, my lord,' he said stiffly. 'I know I'm no good with clothes and meals and such. Perhaps if you gave me some task that suited my skills?'

'Extortion, you mean? I can manage that myself,' Malus growled. 'Though I confess you show a particular kind of artistry in that sort of thing.'

'Ambition is a virtue, my lord,' Hauclir said archly. 'As to my professional skills, I'm swift with a knife or a cudgel, I know how to deal with inconvenient bodies and I've got a good sense of what's going on behind a person's eyes, if you take my meaning.'

'Were you a guard in the Drachau's service, or a thug?' Malus asked, climbing the stair.

'Is there a difference, my lord?'

'No, I suppose not. All right, then. What do you make of our current situation?'

'Thrown to the cold ones my lord, with a steak round our necks.'

The image brought a sharp bark of laughter from the highborn. 'That good, eh?'

Hauclir shrugged. 'The crew is wagering which of your siblings will slip you the knife first. Every one of them – even that flat-eyed cripple Urial – all study you like a strange kind of insect. Right now they're more interested in what you are and what you're about, but sooner or later you can see in their eyes that they're going to crush you and move on.'

'None of this comes as much of a surprise,' Malus said. 'So you're well acquainted with the crew now, are you?'

Hauclir shrugged. 'They're a clannish lot, like most sea ravens, but they gamble and drink and complain like guardsmen, so I've had a chance to chew the fat with a few of them.'

Malus paused at the top of the stairs, tapping his chin thoughtfully. 'All right then, here's a task for you. I want you to find out how the loyalties of these sea birds lie. How well-loved are Bruglir and his first officer? If the illustrious captain were to die, who would they follow?' The retainer considered the command, then nodded.

'Easy enough to do, my lord.' He eyed his master and chuckled. 'You've promised each one of your siblings the other's head, it appears. Have you decided which one you're going to kill?'

Malus looked back at Hauclir, his smile cold and his black eyes glittering. 'I'm going to see them all dead or broken in the end, Hauclir. Who lives or dies by the end of this cruise depends on who remains useful to me for the future. Including you.'

Hauclir straightened, his eyes widening at the highborn's menacing tone, then collected himself. 'As you command, my lord,' he said stiffly, then turned and headed below.

The citadel deck was more than sixty paces long and twenty in width and with only the day watch topside it was sparsely manned. Four lookouts, two to a side, stood at the ship's rails, scanning the grey horizon and the rocky cliffs of Bretonnia with long spyglasses. A tall sailor with a heavy boarding pike stood guard at the head of each of the stair rails and the first officer performed a solitary dance with rudder and sail, her fingers light on the polished teak wheel. A junior officer paced the perimeter of the entire deck, keeping an eye on every member of the crew and seeing that each one kept to his task with eagle eyes. The guard at the top of the starboard rail, a scarred veteran of many cruises, eyed Malus with the wary belligerence of an old watchdog but stepped aside to let the highborn pass.

Malus paced slowly across the deck, sidling close to the first officer. The corsair's scarred face was intent, her good eye distant as she gauged forces described by the trembling of the hull and the warp of the sails overhead. Yet he could sense that she was also aware of him, keeping close track of his movements with the same intensity as she measured wind, tide and the positions of the ships around the *Harrier*.

The highborn walked to within an arm's length of the wheel and stood to one side of the first officer, staying upwind so his words would carry easily to her. 'What news? I didn't think we were due to meet any more of our companions until well after dark.'

'There's a Bretonnian coastal squadron hunting south of us,' the first officer rasped, her rough voice carrying easily over the wind and waves. 'Drove *Bloodied Knife* and *Sea Witch* off their patrol and pushed them towards us. Their captains came aboard a short while ago and are talking in Bruglir's cabin.'

Malus frowned, looking out at the churning, slate-coloured waves. They came across in this? 'Is there a problem?'

She shrugged. 'It could be part of a snare, working with another squadron further north to drive us together and bottle us up against the coast.' The first officer spared a moment's vigilance to throw Malus a vicious glare. 'I don't doubt every coast watcher from Lyonesse to Broadhead is calling for the coastal guard, watching us lumber along together like this. Probably think we're an invasion fleet.'

'Can the Bretonnians catch us?'

Again, the corsair shrugged, scrutinising the storm front bulking along the western horizon. 'The Bretonnians can read the weather as well as we,' she said, 'and their fat old scows can handle these seas a little better than we can. It's possible, if their captains are hungry enough and bold enough.'

'They can't be bolder than Bruglir and his captains,' Malus said confidently. He eyed the first officer appraisingly. 'Tanithra Bael,' he said slowly, using the officer's full name. 'You're an officer of no small repute yourself. I heard your name spoken more than once when I was rounding up my own crew at Clar Karond last year. Yet you're serving as second to Bruglir. I would have thought you'd be captaining your own ship.'

Bael's expression didn't change, but Malus saw her spine stiffen slightly. 'All things in their time,' she growled. 'Women can sail with the corsairs, but female captains are still rare. If I struck out on my own I'd have a hard time raising a crew, even with my reputation. Bruglir has promised me the next ship that comes available and we'll handpick the crew from all over the fleet.' She smiled then, imagining a vessel that sailed every night in her deepest dreams. 'Then the great captain and I will turn the seas red!'

The highborn nodded thoughtfully. 'But you've been serving as his lieutenant for more than seven years. That's a long time to wait for a ship, isn't it?'

Tanithra's smile faded. 'Fine ships take time to build,' she replied. '*Harrier* here sat in her cradle for almost ten years while the shipwrights laid on their sorceries. My time will come.'

'Of course, of course,' Malus agreed. 'But now there is the matter of his sister–'

'What of her?' Tanithra said hotly, this time turning to face him with both hands still clutching the wheel. 'He dallies with her a few weeks each year while I stay with the ship for her fitting-out. It makes no difference to me what he does on dry land. At sea, he's mine. If Yasmir had tried to drive me from his bed instead of taking my quarters, you would have seen then where Bruglir's real affections lie.'

Malus nodded. In truth, he'd been a little surprised that Yasmir hadn't tried to press that very point. Perhaps she'd sensed the truth as well and refused to acknowledge it? Something to consider, he thought. 'Still,' he continued, 'now *she* knows of *you*. You can't expect a proud and pampered highborn like her to let such an insult go unanswered. And she has the ear of many powerful nobles back at the Hag. She could make Bruglir's ambitions to succeed his father very difficult indeed.'

Tanithra glanced at him warily, her expression troubled. 'Perhaps,' she said, then gave a shrug. 'But that's years in the future. By then I'll have my ship and the rest will see to itself.'

The highborn nodded, though inwardly he smiled cunningly. 'I'm certain you're right,' he said. 'So long as Yasmir does nothing to poison Bruglir's mind against you, or find a way to murder you, or affect changes at home that force her beloved to give up the sea between now and then your position is perfectly safe.'

The first officer nodded, then Malus watched her expression darken as the full weight of his words made themselves felt. She turned back to the wheel, her face intent. Malus allowed himself a brief, outward smile, watching his seed take root.

Just then came a faint cry from the bow, the words tattered by the rushing wind. Tanithra became alert at once, her worries forgotten. After a moment a sailor at mid-deck repeated the cry, relaying the message to the stern.

Malus leaned forward, trying to catch the words. 'What's he talking about?'

'Maiden's favours,' Tanithra snapped, muttering a sharp curse. 'Square sheets – Bretonnian sails sighted ahead.' She sought out the junior officer of the deck and called out to him in a clear, piercing voice. 'Sound the call to battle! Topmen aloft and stand ready to unfurl sail!'

The junior officer stopped in mid-stride at the sound of Tanithra's voice and without hesitation put a silver horn to his lips and winded a skirling, moaning note that shivered along Malus's bones. Almost immediately the deck beneath his feet shivered as the crew of the corsair leapt to action, bounding for their positions on or below deck. Within moments Malus heard eerie echoes of the horn's cry riding the wind – the other ships of the fleet had heard the *Harrier's* war-horn or had seen the danger for themselves and were readying themselves for action.

Dark-robed figures boiled from the hatches like angry birds, some heading aloft on frost-rimed rigging while others stood ready with spear and shield or pulled oilskin covers off the menacing bolt throwers fore and aft. Tanithra glanced over at Malus, her one eye cold and hard like a stormcrow's.

'Here's where we see what those Bretonnians are made of,' she said, showing a wolf's hungry smile.

Chapter Fourteen
KNIVES IN THE DARK

'HERE COMES ANOTHER one!' one of the druchii lookouts yelled, pointing aft at one of the Bretonnian ships. Few of the veteran sailors on the citadel deck even turned their heads, but Malus couldn't help but watch in horrified fascination as a black dot arced skyward from the bow of the lead human ship and seemed to climb lazily into the air.

The dot was a sphere of polished granite, lobbed from a siege catapult mounted in the Bretonnian warship's bow – they were so large that only one could fit per ship, or so the corsairs claimed and dominated the bows of the broad-bellied coastal ships. They were a recent innovation of the coastal guard and if the corsairs had little regard for the Bretonnians' seamanship, they had a grudging respect for their marksmanship. The aft lookouts marked the flight of the stone with dreadful intent

and as Malus watched, the dot seemed to freeze its
motion for a single heartbeat, then swell with terrifying
speed. It seemed to be aimed right for him, a ball of
stone the size of his chest and heavy as three men and
Malus found his mouth go dry. Then at the last moment
he saw that the shot would fall short and the stone
whizzed into the ship's wake less than ten paces from
the hull, striking the water with a sharp *slap* and a high,
narrow plume of white.

'That's the closest one yet,' Hauclir said, standing just
behind Malus's left shoulder. He'd raced topside with the
sound of the horn, fully armoured in the space of five
minutes and ready to fight. The guard at the top of the
citadel stair had tried to block the former captain's way,
but Hauclir had frozen the man in his place with an officer's baleful stare and joined his lord for the long sea chase
that had transpired over the course of the afternoon.

Bruglir had reached the citadel within minutes of
hearing the horn, dismissing his visiting captains to
their ships and sizing up the lookout's reports. As
soon as the captains had pulled away in their long
boats he'd ordered flags set to turn the fleet northward, away from the approaching human squadron.
The Bretonnians looked to number no more than five
ships – twin-masted vessels with square sails of sap-
phire or crimson, arrayed in an echelon trailing off to
port – but it appeared Bruglir had no intention of
offering battle and risking damage to his fleet, not
with the closest friendly port hundreds of leagues west
and no chance of heading there any time soon. The
corsair captain hoped to stay ahead of the Bretonnians
until nightfall, when the black ships could easily
shake their pursuers in the darkness. Unfortunately,

tacking against a strong wind and fighting a heavy sea, the druchii ships could make little headway. The waves slapped at the flat of the blade-like corsair hulls and slowed their advance, while the broad-bellied coastal guard ships waddled like fat old ducks over the swells and pressed doggedly ahead, closing the distance slowly but steadily. Malus looked to the cloudy sky. It was little more than two hours until nightfall. With their course reversed, *Harrier* and her sister ships *Sea Witch* and *Bloodied Knife* were strung out at the rear of the corsair fleet, closest to the approaching Bretonnian ships. The highborn tried to gauge the rate of the human ships' advance against the passage of hours and found he couldn't be certain who was going to win the race.

'They are hoping to hit one of our masts or our rudder,' Bruglir said, glancing back to eye the Bretonnian ships' progress. The captain stood close by the wheel while a junior officer tended the helm. Tanithra had gone forward to the fortress deck, her appointed station during battle. 'The Bretonnians have the range – now it's just a matter of gaining a few more yards and letting fate take its course.'

Malus frowned. 'And if they don't hit us in our vitals – can we keep our distance until nightfall?'

The captain frowned, his long moustache nearly touching his enamelled breastplate. 'No. Not likely.' With a pained look Bruglir turned to Urial, who stood close by his men, axe in hand. 'Have you some sorcery that could lend us speed?'

Urial regarded the captain inscrutably. 'No,' he said. 'The ways of the Lord of Murder do not lend themselves to flight.'

'Of course not,' Bruglir said with a derisive snort. 'Dark Mother forbid the temple contribute anything but mayhem,' he grumbled.

Not even Malus could keep a look of surprise from his face at the naked scorn in Bruglir's voice. *I fear your years at sea may have kept you out of the petty feuds at home, but it's poorly prepared you for political realities at the Hag,* Malus thought. *You'll be a short-lived Vaulkhar indeed if you alienate the Temple of Khaine.* 'Why don't we shoot back?' he said, pointing to the bolt throwers standing ready at the stern.

Bruglir shook his head. 'The winds are too high and a bolt wouldn't do much to slow those big sea-cows anyway,' he said.

'Have you no dragon's fire aboard?'

The captain scowled at him. 'We've a few, yes, but I'll not fire them off unless I must. Each shot is like firing a bag of gold into the sea and I have a feeling we'll need them much more where we're going,' he said darkly. 'No, there's another option open to us.' He pointed to the storm front to the west, now much closer as the fleet had been tacking slowly but steadily away from the coast. 'We head into the squall line and lose them in the storm.'

'Won't that be dangerous?'

Bruglir shrugged. 'Some. As dangerous to them as to us, certainly and they won't be able to see more than a dozen yards in any direction. The fleet will be scattered, but that's not much of a concern. So long as we don't bump into someone in the storm, we should escape with no trouble.'

Malus didn't want to think about the consequences of a collision in the middle of a raging winter storm. 'When will you decide to head into the storm?'

One of the lookouts cried out, then a flat, droning sound filled the air a split-second before a dark stone struck the *Harrier's* stern. Sailors dived for cover as the round stone shattered a section of the stern rail just to the left of the portside bolt thrower and ploughed through one of its crew. The hapless sailor literally flew apart in a welter of blood and viscera and the stone rebounded from the deck's teak planking, racing in a black streak across the citadel and striking the sentry at the top of the starboard stair. Malus watched as the stone shattered the man's steel armour and flung his dead body into the air, carrying him over the side and into the embrace of the sea.

Malus straightened, only then realising he'd crouched to the deck instinctively from the first impact. 'Clear the deck!' Bruglir roared, even as unhurt sailors leapt to drag their wounded fellows below decks to the chirurgeon and the bolt thrower's crew tossed the pieces of their mate into the sea with a hurried prayer to the Dragons Below. The captain turned to his signal man. 'Flags aloft,' he ordered. 'Signal the fleet to turn three points west by north. If scattered, rendezvous at the Pearl Sack.' The officer repeated the message and headed to the rail, readying his flags of red and black.

'Come about three points to port,' Bruglir ordered, his voice carrying easily to mid-deck and the topmen aloft in the shrouds. 'Loose the topgallants and the stays! We'll see how stiff their spines are with ice rattling along their decks!'

Malus watched as the corsairs put on more sail and the ship responded, surging like a game horse into the heaving waves. Ahead, the other ships of the fleet were beginning their own course changes. A motion out of the corner of his eye caught his attention – Urial was beckoning to him with a nod of his head.

'Stay here,' Malus told Hauclir, then crossed the tilting deck as the corsair came about. Urial, he noticed, appeared to have finally found his sea legs, leaning unconsciously with the change in attitude of the wooden deck.

'What's happening?' Urial asked as Malus drew near. There was a subtle tension in the former acolyte's pale face. Was he anticipating battle, Malus thought, or something else?

'We're turning into that storm yonder,' Malus said. 'Bruglir hopes to evade the Bretonnians in the squall.'

Urial frowned. 'The famous sea captain won't offer battle?'

'He's taking the long view,' the highborn replied. 'There will be major battles aplenty where we're headed and he must conserve his force. I would do the same in his position.'

'But if the Bretonnians find us in the storm?'

'Then it will be a fight indeed,' Malus said. 'Close and brutal. Men are apt to die.'

Urial's eyes shone at the prospect. 'Indeed,' he said eagerly. 'Even a great sea captain could find a knife in his side from an unknown quarter, if an attacker were bold enough.'

Malus's eyes widened. He leaned close, his voice dropping to a harsh whisper. 'I haven't forgotten my promise, brother,' he said. 'But now is no time for assassins' knives. We need Bruglir to command his fleet. If he dies, the captains will look to their own, either fighting to control the fleet or turning for home. I can't have that. Not yet.'

Urial's face twisted into a grimace. 'So long as you remember your vow, Malus,' he hissed, 'you have my support. But my patience has its limits.'

'Of course, brother,' Malus said tightly, trying to conceal his irritation. 'Tell me, have you seen our sister since the horn was sounded?'

'No. She remains below, I think,' Urial said. 'I'm a trifle disappointed. I'd hoped that the prospect of battle would draw her from her cabin.'

Or she could be down on the mid-deck, stalking among the crew and waiting for a chance to get close to Tanithra, Malus thought. He wasn't sure how Bruglir would react if his first officer wound up dead with a knife in her back. Would he retaliate against Yasmir? There was no way to tell. For a moment Malus contemplated sending Hauclir forward to keep an eye on Tanithra, but he dismissed the notion almost as quickly. What could the retainer do? Come between the first officer and a murderous highborn lady? What would that achieve besides his death?

The wind picked up across the deck, buffeting Malus's hood and blowing a spray of fine ice crystals into his face. The sky was darkening as the *Harrier* crossed the squall line, plunging into the winter storm. Soon it would be hard to see more than a few feet in any direction and danger could fall upon them with little warning, striking from almost any quarter.

Even within, Malus thought, his eyes scanning the crew. An old proverb came to mind as the storm swept over them.

When darkness falls, the knives come out.

* * *

THE STORM LASHED at them like a tremendous serpent, battering hull, mast and sail with invisible coils of blustering, icy wind and hissing across the deck and rigging in a spray of ice and freezing rain. The teak planks and thick, hempen ropes were coated with a thin film of ice in moments, making every step treacherous and potentially fatal as the *Harrier* pitched and rolled in the fury of the storm.

It had been nearly an hour and a half since the ships disappeared into the grey haze. The deck crew crowded along the railings, peering into the formless gloom in search of dark shapes that could prove to be another ship. There were no friendly vessels in a storm like this; a collision with another corsair would be just as deadly as one with a Bretonnian and equally sudden.

Malus shivered beneath the heavy weight of his cloak. Despite layers of protection the icy wind found its way to his bare skin, soaking him to the bone in moments. Ice rimed the edge of his hood and crackled across his shoulders. He stood clutching the starboard rail not far from Urial, peering into the haze like everyone else. The highborn could tell the difference between sea and sky only in subtle gradations of grey. Everyone was tense, many fingering the hilts of their swords and dreading the sight of a dark shape looming from the haze in front of them.

Gritting his teeth, Malus turned away from the grey murk and cast his eyes over the crew instead. Bruglir still stood by the helm, ramrod straight in the face of the wind. White ice crusted the front of his cloak and the toes of his boots, but for all that he seemed unfazed by the howling fury of the wind. The helmsman beside him clutched the wheel in a death grip, trying to emulate the example of the captain. Urial stood with his retainers just a few feet further down the starboard rail, partially shielded from the icy wind by the tall robed figures of his warriors.

Hauclir stood at Malus's shoulder as ever, one hand steadying himself on the rail. The former guardsman had his hood back and stared bare-headed and slit-eyed into the storm. Malus leaned towards him. 'Do you want to lose your nose and ears to frostbite, you fool?'

The retainer shook his head. 'I've had frostbite more times than I can count, my lord. A bit of my mother's blackroot poultice and the skin's as good as new. No, I can't stand not being able to see all the way around me in a situation like this.' He hunched his shoulders. 'The hair on my neck is standing straight up, like there's someone out there pointing a crossbow at me. How long are we going to stay in this?'

Malus shrugged. 'Until the captain is satisfied we've slipped past the enemy. It will be dark soon, so I expect he'll try to head out to calmer waters then.' Though I have no idea how he'll manage it, the highborn thought. 'We're through the worst of it,' he continued, trying to reassure himself more than Hauclir. 'Every moment likely carries us further away from the Bretonnians–'

Just then a splintering crash echoed distantly over the howling wind to starboard, turning into a long, grinding crunch of breaking wood. 'A collision!' one of the sailors shouted, pointing uselessly off into the haze. 'Something's hit the *Bloodied Knife*!'

'Or two fat Bretonnian scows kissed hulls in the mist,' another sailor offered weakly.

'Silence on the rail!' Bruglir hissed like a rasping blade. The men fell silent. Malus looked back at his older brother – and saw the great, dark shape coalescing out of the murk on the opposite side of the ship, bearing down like a thunderbolt on the unsuspecting corsair.

Every man on the port rail seemed to cry out at once and Bruglir leapt into action without thought. 'Hard to starboard!' he roared at the helmsman, adding his own hands to the wheel and spinning it for all it was worth. The ship began to heel over, but slowly, too slowly. Malus watched men flock from the port rail like a flight of black birds startled from a bough. 'Hang on!' he bellowed, reaching for the rail and then the *Harrier* bucked like a bitten mare as the Bretonnian ship crashed alongside.

Wood splintered and snapped in a long, rending groan as the two ships met and the deck of the *Harrier* pitched further and further towards the heaving sea as the heavier human ship pushed her over. Black-clad sailors clung desperately to the icy rigging as the spars of the ship's three masts sank closer and closer towards the hungry sea. Malus held to the starboard rail with both hands, feeling his guts shrivel as it seemed as though the ship would be borne over and capsized. Then at the last moment the *Harrier* hit the bottom of a wave trough and started up the next and the hull heeled back to port, biting back at the flank of the human ship.

Bruglir's last-minute course change had saved them. Rather than be struck nearly amidships by the Bretonnian's prow the corsair had shied away and been scraped along her entire length instead. Yet now the two ships were stuck fast, their spars tangled together in one another's rigging and Malus watched as the human crew recovered quickly from the impact and flung boarding lines across the rail of the druchii ship.

Already the Bretonnians were rushing forward, axes and billhooks in their hands as they prepared to come to grips with their prey.

'Sa'an'ishar!' Bruglir roared into the howling wind, brandishing his sword in the air. 'All hands repel boarders!'

The Bretonnian ship was broader in the beam but lower to the water and so the corsair's citadel deck rose above the enemy's main deck. Sailors scrambled back to the port rail, hacking at boarding lines with short-hafted axes, but on the main deck below a wave of boarders surged over the rail and came to grips with the stunned druchii sailors. In the rigging above, topmen cut at the enemy's rigging and traded crossbow bolts with Bretonnians fighting to keep the two ships bound together.

Malus drew his sword, trying to work some feeling back into numbed fingers as he gripped the leather-wrapped hilt. He turned to Urial and the sailors standing around him. 'Down to the main deck! Keep the humans from the citadel stairs and drive them back to their own ship!'

Urial understood at once what Malus was saying. He raised his rune-inscribed axe high, its razor edges crackling with a nimbus of crimson energy. 'Blood and glory!' he cried and threw back his head to howl up at the storm. A jolt like lightning surged through the gathered corsairs, galvanising them to action. They took up Urial's cry and raced for the stairs, weapons held high. Malus pushed his way through the press, knowing that every moment that passed meant a dozen more boarders climbing aboard the embattled *Harrier*.

The surge of men for the stairs created a bottleneck at the top of the stairway. Malus beat at the backs of the

men with the flat of his blade, but they could move no
further or faster. Snarling, he pushed his way to the railing that looked out over the main deck and saw that the
humans had driven a broad wedge of men onto the corsair, almost completely isolating the fortress deck and
the citadel from one another. There were enemy boarders fighting at the base of both citadel stairways, keeping
reinforcements from reaching the embattled pockets of
corsairs surrounded on the deck below.

Hauclir pulled up short, peering over Malus's shoulder. 'They've almost got us,' he said. 'What now?'

'Follow me!' Malus cried. He leapt onto the rail and
hurled himself at the men below, screaming like a rak-
sha.

The humans barely had time to look up before Malus
crashed onto them, bearing down three men with his
own armoured body and splitting the skull of a fourth
with a downward sweep of his blade. They fell to the
deck in a welter of shouted curses and a tangle of thrashing limbs. A man's face bellowed at him and Malus
ground the pommel of his sword in the human's eye. A
hand tried to reach around and grab his throat. A blade
clattered off his right pauldron and someone kicked at
his hip. The highborn thrashed like a landed fish, slashing wildly in an attempt to clear a space where he could
stand. Then came another pounding impact as Hauclir
landed almost on top of him, laying about with his own
sword and a three-foot cudgel in his left hand. Men
cried out and scattered from the highborn as his retainer
killed or maimed every man he could reach, his face as
calm as a butcher's as he went about his work. The highborn rolled clear, pulling his feet up beneath him and
surging to his feet close by the staircase.

The din was incredible. Scores of humans and druchii shrieked their war cries and hammered at one another with furious abandon, the clamour blotting out even the howling wind and ringing in Malus's ears. His feet slipped and skidded in a slush of blood and ice as the enemy boarders recovered from his reckless attack and surged towards him, hacking with short, heavy cutlasses or trying to get a billhook around one of his legs. A gap-toothed human lunged at him with his cutlass and overextended, burying the point in the wood of the staircase. Malus opened his throat with a swipe of his blade and shoved the man backwards with the heel of his boot. Another boarder grabbed at his ankle and tried to pull him from his feet; Hauclir, to his left, spun on one heel and struck the man's hand from his wrist with a powerful stroke of his sword.

Crossbow bolts snapped through the air from all sides, fired from men in the shrouds or from the decks of both ships. A human in front of Malus coughed up a gout of dark blood and pitched over, a black druchii bolt jutting from his back. A boarder lunged for Hauclir, striking the retainer a glancing blow across his temple with a cutlass; Malus buried the point of his sword in the man's armpit, sliding past muscle and joint into the vital organs beyond.

The press of bodies was lessening. Malus found he had more room to swing before him and to his right more corsairs were forcing their way down the staircase and joining the battle. Then he saw a knot of black-cloaked figures surge from the base of the stair, their great draichs whirling in crimson arcs as Urial's men tore into the enemy. A great cry of despair went up among the human attackers and Malus responded with a bloodcurdling cry of his own as he surged forward, sword ready.

Suddenly Malus's vision blurred and his stomach heaved as a wave of vertigo crashed over him. The roar of battle echoed and re-echoed crazily in his ears, as if he were hearing not one but multiple versions of the same tumultuous din. The men before him doubled, trebled and quadrupled in his eyes. It was the same feeling he'd experienced earlier in the day, in the very same place by the starboard staircase.

All at once a premonition of doom swept over him. Without thinking, Malus dropped to one knee, bracing himself on the slick deck with an outflung hand. The highborn closed his eyes and shook his head savagely, the hairs on the back of his neck standing on end as he expected one of the boarders to try and take advantage of his confusion. But no blow fell and after a moment the world seemed to settle back onto its moorings. Malus surged to his feet and saw the boarders in headlong retreat, falling back to the portside rail as the two ships began to pull apart. As they did, they parted like water around a luminous figure in their midst, her naked body clothed in a raiment of steaming blood and Malus realised at once what had happened.

Yasmir had emerged onto the deck in the midst of the enemy, her twin knives in hand and heedless of her own life had danced among them like a temple priestess, taking a life with each sinuous stroke of her arm. Awed and terrified by the beautiful, deadly figure, they fell away from her on every side and that allowed more sailors to join the fight by rushing down the portside citadel stairway. These men had started hacking at the boarding lines connecting the two ships. Within moments the

Harrier had been cut free and the boarders, who moments before had thought themselves on the verge of triumph, now found themselves facing the dire fate of being trapped aboard a druchii raider. Already men were clambering onto the port rail and hurling themselves through the opening gap between the two ships, preferring to risk death in the deadly waters below than to be captured by the vengeful crew of the druchii ship. Yasmir stood amid heaps of the enemy dead, bathed in gore and laughing with sheer, mad joy at the slaughter she'd wrought. The attackers had laid not a single mark upon her.

Malus took a few more steps towards the routed enemy and stopped, suddenly weary. He lowered his bloody sword and gasped for breath in the freezing air, watching the Bretonnian ship heeling away to port. Someone on the citadel deck had trained the portside bolt thrower on the ship and had shot away her wheel, leaving the vessel at the mercy of the storm. A terrible wail went up from the survivors as the broad-beamed ship rolled helplessly in the waves and was swallowed by the swirling haze.

The highborn surveyed the scene upon the main deck. Bodies lay everywhere, steaming in the cold. Druchii sailors moved among them, dispatching the enemy wounded and throwing the bodies overboard. The corsairs moved hesitantly, almost reverentially, as they pulled at the corpses surrounding Yasmir. She watched them with something like a murderer's serenity as they worked. Urial and his men approached her and fell to their knees. The former acolyte's face was a mask of holy ecstasy.

Malus turned away in disgust. His left hand felt like ice. The highborn looked down at his blood-soaked palm and a shiver went through him. I've seen this before, he thought, feeling the cold hand of dread settle over him.

Like a man in a dream he walked back to the starboard stairway. Just short of the staircase he stumbled over the body of one of the enemy dead, catching himself with his left hand as he fell against the stair.

Next to his hand a black crossbow bolt jutted from the wood. It was at chest height, right where he'd been standing just minutes ago.

Here is where I died, he thought. Or would have died, but for the premonition I received. How was this possible?

The laughter of the daemon was his only answer.

Chapter Fifteen
THE BLACK SAIL

IT WAS ONLY an hour past dawn when the lashing storm lost its strength and the clouds gave way to early spring sunshine. They found themselves well out to sea, with no trace of land in sight, bearing north by north-west on a general course towards Ulthuan. Dark sails of human hide caught the freshening wind and soon the *Harrier* was flying across the waves like a bird on the wing.

Bruglir took the ship north and east, following the northern raiding route around the eastern coast of the elven homeland. They reached Ulthuan within several weeks, passing it late in the night; Urial stood a watch of his own then, peering into the darkness like a wolf, lost in private thoughts of fire and ruin.

Yasmir had retreated to her cabin once more after the last of the boarders had been slain. One moment she'd stood on the mid-deck among the piles of the dead, then the next she was gone. Her quarters were just down the passageway from the chart room where Malus tried to sleep; from time to time, always late at night, he heard faint whispers coming from that direction. Once, he'd risen from his makeshift bed and crept to the door. Peering into the dimly lit passage, he saw Urial kneeling outside her door, head bent as if in prayer and chanting softly under his breath, as though he knelt before a shrine to the Bloody-Handed God.

Amid the blood and mayhem of the confused battle in the storm it was a wonder that neither Tanithra nor Urial had been murdered, to say nothing of Bruglir himself. Of all the highborn on the ship, the only person to narrowly escape assassination that night had been himself.

And why not? They had little reason to fear him outside of the writ. Bruglir and Tanithra had a fleet of ships and men to avenge them. Yasmir had her suitors. Urial had the temple. He had nothing. The thought was enough to keep him in his own cabin after nightfall, drinking bottles of wine that Hauclir had pilfered from the galley.

He'd suffered no more dreams or waking visions since the battle in the storm. Malus suspected that the copious amount of wine he drank had something to do with it. It certainly seemed to keep the daemon quiescent, which made the effort worthwhile all by itself.

A week after breaking out of the Bretonnians' trap the *Harrier* reached the Pearl Sack, a secret meeting point among the tiny atolls where lost Nagarythe once lay. By the time Bruglir's ship arrived, the rest of the fleet lay waiting at anchor in the sheltered cove, riding indigo waters that threw back pearlescent reflections when the pale sun hung high overhead.

There were two ships missing. The *Bloodied Knife* was presumed lost, having collided with a Bretonnian ship in the storm. Another, the *Dragon's Claw*, had simply disappeared. She'd last been seen sailing with much of her sails set; possibly she'd been lost, or perhaps so damaged that she'd been forced to abandon the cruise and limp back to Clar Karond. The fleet waited three days in the hidden cove, lookouts scanning the seas for telltale signs of approaching ships, but finally Bruglir declared he could wait no more and ordered his remaining ships under weigh. The sooner they dealt with the Skinriders the sooner they could set course for home.

'THE PROBLEM,' BRUGLIR said, scowling at the chart spread on the table before him, 'is that the Skinrider ships don't carry maps.'

Sunlight slanted through the open windows in the captain's cabin, carrying with it the rushing sound of the *Harrier's* wake and the salty smell of the sea. They were four days north by north-west from Ulthuan, almost parallel with the straits leading to Karond Kar, some three hundred leagues due west. They were at the fringes of the wild northern sea; from this point forward, each day would carry them further into the realm of the Skinriders.

The chart spread across the pitted surface of the captain's table was the best reference any druchii sailor had of the seas north-east of Naggaroth and to Malus's eyes it said precious little of value. Lines depicting ocean currents made serpent trails across the open sea, weaving in and out among long chains of tiny islands without description or name. Coastal areas of the great continents were marked with the names of the twisted Chaos tribes that claimed them: Aghalls, Graelings, Vargs and others. The cartographer had drawn tiny depictions of tentacled things pulling ships apart or dragging them below the waves.

The highborn sat in a chair opposite the captain, drinking watered wine from a pewter cup. Since leaving Ulthuan most everything in the galley had begun to be rationed, as no one knew for certain how long the voyage would be. It was a prudent move, Malus knew, but terrible for the crew's morale. It certainly wasn't doing *his* mood any good.

'Come now, brother. I'm no sea bird like yourself, but even I know that's impossible,' he replied sourly. 'How do they navigate?'

Bruglir shrugged. 'They have small hideouts on many of the islands in the area,' he said, indicating the spray of tiny dots on the page with a sweep of his hand. 'I think they keep their charts locked away there. When their captains make port they study what they need to reach their next stop and press on. That's the only possible explanation I can think of.' The captain's moustaches twitched in an expression of distaste. 'The Skinriders are hideous, loathsome creatures, but they are clever in their own way.'

'What about torture?'

'How?' Bruglir snorted in disgust. 'Their skin turns to mush and slides from their bones. Their flesh seethes with pestilence and their veins are filled with corruption. Open them up with your knives and all you get are diseases raging like a fire through your crew.'

Malus scowled into the depths of his cup. 'Then we'll have to raid one of their hideouts.'

Bruglir nodded. 'My thoughts exactly. But such a thing is easier said than done.' He leaned back in his high-backed chair and folded his arms. 'You aren't the first highborn to try and exterminate these vermin. I even attempted it myself several years ago. No one has succeeded, for two reasons. Firstly, the whole area is like a hornet's nest – every little bolt-hole on these islands is within a day's sail of another, so word of an attack spreads very quickly. Each hideout keeps at least one vessel crewed and ready to sail at a moment's notice. At the first sign of trouble it will flee and spread the alarm and within two days the seas around the island will be full of Skinrider ships seeking vengeance. Secondly – and most importantly – there is the problem of plague. Their ships are bad enough, but their hideouts are cesspits, seething with every imaginable sickness. Bring a single scrap of parchment back aboard your ship and your crew would be decimated within days.'

'I spoke to Urial before leaving the Hag and he says he has a means of combatting the Skinriders' pestilence,' Malus said. 'Can you guarantee that you can keep any Skinrider ships from escaping during the raid?'

Bruglir pursed his lips thoughtfully. 'I have enough ships to cordon off a small island,' he said, 'and the Skinriders are indifferent sailors at best. Nothing is certain, but I believe our chances are good.'

'Very well,' Malus nodded, not entirely happy with the answer. 'Have you an island in mind?'

A scarred finger tapped a speck of ink on the chart. 'This one,' Bruglir said. 'The Skinriders may have a name for it, but it's just a knob of rock jutting from the sea, perhaps three miles across. They've kept a small way station there for years because it lies so close to our northern raiding route. We'll have to approach the island carefully – there will be scouts and regular patrols in the area, so I plan on separating the fleet into three small squadrons and disperse us on different courses. *Harrier*, *Sea Dragon* and *Black Razor* are the fastest, so we'll travel together. We can be there in two days' time.'

'And you're certain that there will be charts there?'

'Am I a Skinrider? Of course I'm not certain,' Bruglir growled. 'But it's the best place I can think of to look.'

'Then that will have to do,' Malus said, rising to his feet. He finished the wine and set the cup on the table. 'I'll inform Urial to begin his preparations.' Halfway to the cabin door the highborn paused, then looked back at the captain. 'You also might want to give your cross-bowmen some time to practise, as well. The man you ordered to murder me during the boarding action was a terrible shot.'

Bruglir's eyes widened slightly. 'Did someone try to murder you, brother? I had no idea. Perhaps it was Tanithra – she's talked of nothing but slitting your throat since you brought our dear sister on board.'

Malus smiled. 'That's an idle threat, brother. Your first officer may not like me, but she gains nothing from my death. She's more likely to try her hand at Yasmir than to attempt to kill me. You, on the other hand, have much to gain by my death, not least of which is freedom from the power of the writ.' The highborn chuckled. 'And as for Tanithra, I'd be more concerned for my own health were I you. She has to know that Yasmir is going to force the issue between the three of you sooner or later and she has a great deal riding on the choice you must make. Choose wisely. I daresay your life depends on it.'

Without waiting for a reply, Malus turned on his heel and left the cabin, his boots thudding softly on the creaking deck. Hauclir, who had been leaning against a bulkhead outside the cabin, rose from his reverie and trailed along in his master's wake.

'Did you tell him about the crossbow bolt?' Hauclir asked.

'Yes,' Malus said over his shoulder, making no effort to conceal his annoyance.

'What did he say?'

'He denied it, just as I expected he would. But it let me plant the seed I needed to about Tanithra. What have you learned from the crew?'

'Some interesting things, as a matter of fact,' Hauclir said, checking the passageway fore and aft for potential eavesdroppers. 'If you'd asked these birds three weeks ago whom they'd follow in place of Bruglir, they'd have said Tanithra, hands down.'

Malus paused. 'And now?'

'Now they don't much care for her feud with Yasmir. Seems these sea ravens have got it into their heads she's some kind of saint, what with her beauty and her strange airs and the way she cut through those Bretonnians back during the storm. Have you seen the door to her cabin lately? Sailors have taken to carving little prayers into the wood, asking for her protection on the voyage. '

'Indeed? That *is* interesting news.' Malus tapped his chin with a long forefinger. 'It appears she's enamoured more than just my brothers. And they don't care much for Tanithra's ire?'

'No, my lord. They think she's putting them all at risk by plotting against Yasmir.'

The highborn considered this and smiled. 'Excellent. Feed the fire, Hauclir. Spread the rumour that Urial fears if Yasmir were to be murdered that Khaine himself will take vengeance upon the crew.'

Hauclir eyed Malus warily. 'So you've settled on how you'll play your hand?'

'Nearly so,' the highborn responded. 'But don't worry, Hauclir,' he said, turning and clapping his retainer on the shoulder. 'You're still in the running. I may kill you yet before this whole thing is done.'

TWO MOONS SPREAD a blanket of silver across the restless sea. He breathed and the air stank of corruption, a foetid reek that sank into his lungs like a thick mist and festered there. His skin felt loose and greasy, sliding over flesh and bone.

In the distance he saw a tall mast and a black, triangular sail, rising like a dreadful banner on the horizon.

The air rippled like water, turning grey and cold and he couldn't breathe. There were bony hands wrapped around his throat, bending him backwards beneath the surface of a pool of slimy water. He thrashed and kicked, snarling and spitting filthy liquid from his mouth. He pushed back with all his strength, forcing himself upwards – and found himself face to face with a horrific creature, its rotten form swathed in drapes of pus-stained skin that hung from its frame like a poorly-stitched robe. He could feel the pulpy flesh of the creature's fingers weep rotten blood as they tightened around his throat. Its eyes were little more than grey-green orbs of mould, burning with hate from the depths of a faceless hood made of rotting human skin. He opened his mouth to speak, but his throat filled with the stink of rotting corpses, choking off his words in a surge of bitter bile.

Another sickened creature joined the first, grabbing him by the shoulders and forcing him back down towards the water. They were going to drown him in the bilges of the ship! More hands grabbed at his arm, waist and leg, lifting him off the ground. His head dipped back into the filthy, cold water. He writhed in their stinking grip, but they held him fast...

MALUS FELL FROM the chart table with a strangled cry, tangled in sweat-stained bed sheets. He hit the deck with a painful thud, rapping his elbow hard against the polished wood. But the bright flare of pain did little to dispel the waves of vertigo or the blurring vision that left him dizzy and confused.

'Damn this!' Malus rolled onto his back, screwing his eyes shut and gritting his teeth at the waves of dislocation that rippled through him. 'Bestir yourself, daemon! Help me!'

Tz'arkan slithered against his ribs. 'But Malus, I've already done all I can. You must find your own way out of this labyrinth.' The daemon chuckled cruelly to itself, as though amused by some private joke.

The highborn snarled, beating the back of his head against the deck until the pain forced the dizziness from his mind. After a moment he opened his eyes, teeth bared at the ache in his skull. It was late and the twin moons hung low in the sky, sending a shaft of silver-blue light slanting through the small porthole above his makeshift bed.

He studied the pale light and a powerful feeling of dread came over him. Malus levered himself to his feet, pulled on boots and sword-belt and headed topside.

The night was cool and windy and the deck of the ship was silent save for the rumble of sails and the creak of the hull as the *Harrier* sped north. Off to starboard Malus saw the rakish silhouette of one of the corsair's sister ships, her sleek bow slicing effortlessly through the steel-grey waters. The highborn stood at the rail for several long moments, his eyes straining to pierce the darkness along the horizon. Finally he gave up and made his way forward to the fortress deck.

The upper deck at the bow was twice the length of the citadel, mounting four bolt throwers instead of two and coiled boarding ropes with hooks stowed by the rail. Ruuvalk, the ship's second mate, stood nearby, smoking from a long-stemmed pipe and idly supervising the bow lookouts. The sailor gave Malus a suspicious stare. 'Come to stand the wolves' watch with us?'

'There's a ship out there,' Malus said. 'A tall mast with a triangular black sail.'

Ruuvalk stiffened, his expression suddenly alert. 'Where?'

'I… I don't know.' The highborn looked about, now cudgelling his brain to remember the image of the ship in his dream. He compared the image in his mind with the one before him, looking off the starboard bow. 'There,' he said, pointing. 'Somewhere out there.'

The lookouts on the starboard side turned in that direction, unable to resist the highborn's commanding tone. Ruuvalk stared at Malus, slowly shaking his head. 'Pardon, dread lord,' the corsair said carefully, 'but are you drunk?'

'Sail ho!' One of the lookouts flung out a hand, pointing to the north-east. 'Four points off the bow.'

Ruuvalk's eyes went wide. With a parting glance at Malus, he rushed to the rail, forcing himself in between the lookouts. 'Damn me, a black triangle,' he muttered, staring into the darkness. 'A Skinrider scout, I warrant. Have they seen us?'

'Most like,' the lookout said grimly. 'She's come about sharply. Looks like she's getting ready to make a run for it.'

'Damn! I thought we'd get closer than this before the alarm went out,' Ruuvalk muttered. 'We've got calm seas and a good wind, though. Those plague dogs haven't got away yet.' He leaned back from the rail and looked to the stern. 'Black sail off the starboard bow,' Ruuvalk bellowed to the junior officer of the deck. 'Sound the call to battle! Lay on full sail and come three points to starboard.'

As the first wailing notes of the war-horn echoed through the night air Ruuvalk turned back to Malus. 'If we hadn't known where to look, we'd have never seen her. She could have turned tail and slipped over the horizon with no one the wiser. How did you know she was out there?'

Malus met the sailor's stare, considering any number of possible answers. Finally he shrugged and settled on the truth.

'I saw it in a dream.'

THE SKINRIDERS' SHIP was once a Lustrian vagabond, or so the druchii sailors called her – low to the water and broad at the stern, long and twin-masted, but with sharp-edged triangular sails instead of a Bretonnian's squares. She was nimble enough, like a dancer in the face of the druchii corsairs, but she couldn't cut through the waves like the black hulls of her pursuers and little by little the druchii ships closed the distance, stalking the vagabond like a trio of hungry wolves.

Hauclir grunted softly as he tightened the last set of the buckles on Malus's armour. The highborn rotated his arms slowly, testing the way the harness fit, then nodded curtly to his retainer and returned to the group of druchii watching the pursuit from the bow. Bruglir and Tanithra stood side-by-side at the rail, occasionally sharing observations in low, professional tones a short distance from the starboard lookouts. The starboard bolt throwers had been uncovered and made ready, the crews idling near their mounts. As Malus walked to the rail his progress was momentarily checked by a trio of grunting sailors carrying an open-topped barrel full of water. Three long bolts jutted from the barrel, their steel heads wrapped in cotton and submerged in the dirty water. The sailors inched along the deck, mindful of the explosive dragon's breath bolts they carried. Even with the steel heads and their glass bulbs cushioned in layers of cotton batting, a greenish glow from the sorcerous compound turned the sloshing water bright emerald.

One of the lookouts suddenly pointed. 'Arrows!' he cried. Black-shafted arrows made a momentary flurry of splashes in the water between the two ships. After two and a half hours of pursuit, the corsairs were only just now coming into firing range. The moons had set and the pale glow of false dawn was lightening the sky to the east.

'How much longer?' Malus asked, leaning against the rail to the captain's right.

Bruglir turned away from Tanithra and eyed him with evident distaste, as though he'd barged his way into a private function. 'A few minutes more. We'll start by trying to cut their rigging and spill their sails, then pull alongside and set them afire.'

Malus grunted. 'I'm surprised they're not coming about and trying to put up a fight.'

The captain shrugged. 'Spreading the alarm is more important. Every minute they remain under weigh is another minute that might bring them closer to another Skinrider ship. If they can spread the word, they've won. Nothing else matters to them.' Bruglir turned to the bolt thrower crews. 'Try a ranging shot. Let's see how close we are.'

Malus watched absently as the crews ratcheted back the heavy steel cables and loaded standard bolts onto the long tracks. The Skinriders fired another volley of arrows, again falling short of the druchii ship. The bolt throwers banged on their mounts; two seconds later one of the six-foot bolts buried itself in the planks of the vagabond's stern with a splintering crash.

Bruglir nodded approvingly. 'Switch to mast cutters,' he ordered.

Suddenly, Malus stiffened. 'Alarm…' he muttered. Then the highborn turned and beckoned to Hauclir. 'Go and get Urial and bring him here.'

As the bolt thrower crews reloaded, Malus tapped Bruglir on the arm. 'We must capture the Skinriders' ship,' he said to his half-brother.

Bruglir looked at Malus as though he were mad. 'That leaky old scow? If you're hungry for prize money there's little to be had in that worm-ridden old hull.'

'Prize money be damned,' Malus hissed. 'That scout is our way into the Skinriders' hideout. We can sail in close and make our way into their camp without raising any alarms!'

The captain shook his head. 'That vessel is a plague den–'

'Their hideout will be even worse. You said so yourself. Better to see if Urial can combat their pestilence here than once we're ashore, don't you think? Send me over with a boarding party and cast off. If we can't protect ourselves from the sickness onboard, you've only lost a few dozen crew.' And the man holding a writ over your head, he thought, but didn't say so aloud.

Perhaps Bruglir read the unspoken thought in Malus's eyes, because his expression became pensive. 'Who will command the prize?'

Tanithra surprised them both. 'I'll do it. Let me pick my boarding party and we'll sail her right into the pirates' cove,' she said. The first officer glanced at her captain, then turned her gaze back to the vagabond with a frown. 'Probably the closest I'll get to a real command.'

If Bruglir caught the bitterness in Tanithra's voice, he gave no sign. 'Very well,' he said brusquely. 'Round up your men, Tani. I'll need to pass signals to *Black Razor* and *Sea Dragon*.' The captain headed aft to the citadel, where the signalman and his lanterns waited. Tanithra followed close behind, calling out the names of men who would seize the Skinrider ship.

The men at the bolt throwers finished winding their weapons and now the loaders were fitting special bolts into the firing tracks. Instead of a pointed steel head, these had large, crescent shapes like sickle blades. They were capable of inflicting horrific damage to a ship's crew, but their primary function was to sever rigging and split sails. At close range the curved blades could split masts like saplings. The bolt throwers banged and the mast cutters arced across the water. One landed somewhere on the deck and the other clipped the rearmost mast, scattering a fan of splinters from the blow and spinning away in a glinting pinwheel to crash into the water on the other side.

'You called for me?'

Malus turned to Urial. 'Back at the Hag you said you could counter the pestilence of the Skinriders. Well, your powers are about to be put to the test.' He nodded at the enemy ship. 'We're going over there in just a few minutes. Can you be ready by then?'

Urial nodded. 'I must pray. Summon me when it is time,' he said, limping away.

Malus turned his attention back to the developing battle, just in time to catch sight of another flight of arrows arcing from the stern of the enemy ship. This time the raiders were in range and black arrows drummed against deck and hull. A sailor staggered backward with a vicious curse, clawing at the shaft jutting from his shoulder.

They were close enough now that Malus could see the archers standing by the stern rail; broad, misshapen men wreathed in dirty grey vapours, fitting arrows to dark recurve bows made of sinew and horn. They looked like the hideous creatures of his dream, their bodies covered with ragged surcoats of crudely stitched hide that covered their arms, chest and much of their heads. His nostrils wrinkled as he caught a faint stench trailing from the fleeing scout; it was the sickly sweet smell of rotting meat, like a battlefield under a hot summer sun.

The bolt throwers fired again. Splinters flew from the scout's port quarter, then sprung rigging and shroud lines leapt into the air as the mast cutter slashed through the lower half of the aft sail. As Malus watched, the second bolt skimmed right over the stern rail and tore through the archers. Two men caught squarely by the curved blade simply exploded in a rain of green and yellow bile. What horrified Malus even more was another man who was struck a glancing blow that tore through his chest like a sword stroke. Thick fluid burst from the man's body in a putrid spray of bilious green. He staggered back a step – then bent to retrieve his dropped arrow as though nothing had happened. Malus felt his mouth go dry.

With half her sails gone, the scout lost speed quickly. 'Bolt throwers! Make ready to fire grappling lines,' Tanithra ordered as she strode purposefully across the fortress deck. Men streamed up the stairs in her wake, some carrying crossbows while others hefted spears, swords and shields. The shield men pushed their way up to the rail, while the crossbowmen crouched and began to load their weapons. An eager kind of tension began to spread among the men as the druchii looked forward to the prospect of battle.

More Skinriders took up position at the stern and began firing arrows as quickly as they could ready their bows. The druchii boarders crouched behind their shields as the arrows struck home. Minutes passed and the *Harrier* swept down on the vagabond like a hunting hawk. 'Get Urial,' Malus ordered Hauclir. 'It's nearly time.'

Tanithra crouched close by Malus's side. She wore a hauberk of light mail over a jerkin made of cork – steel armour was useful in a fight but a death sentence if one went over the side – and carried her cleaver-like sword unsheathed at her side. 'Will your bloody handed sister not be joining us?' she asked darkly.

Malus shrugged. 'She's not mine to command, Tanithra. Khaine alone knows her mind these days.'

A stir went among the crowded boarders. Malus looked over and saw Urial working his way through the group, touching each man on the head and muttering a short phrase as he went. Each man he touched shook himself like a dog, then watched the crippled man limp away with a look of mingled fear and awe.

Tanithra raised a little to peer over the shield wall. 'Bolt throwers ready! Take aim! Fire!' Both weapons fired as one, the heavy boarding ropes uncoiling with a frenetic hiss. Malus straightened as well. He could see the Skinriders clustering along the port side of the ship, brandishing rusty swords and axes and taunting the druchii in a harsh, croaking tongue. The grappling lines sped in a flat line for the hull of the enemy ship, the barbed heads biting deeply into the planks of the ship's port quarter.

The first officer turned to the boarders. 'Belay and haul!' Tanithra ordered. The men raced to a pair of great wooden windlasses set just aft of the bolt throwers and began to wind them as fast as they could. Within moments the boarding ropes grew taut and the two ships began to draw relentlessly together. On cue, the crossbowmen pushed their way to the rail, sniping at Skinriders who tried to dislodge the ropes or cut them with their blades.

Malus felt fingertips brush his forehead and a voice mutter words that crackled in the early morning air. At once a wave of heat washed through him; for a brief moment the cold touch of the daemon faded and he felt vibrant and powerful. I'm *invincible*, his body seemed to say, but then the cold tendrils of Tz'arkan coiled once more around Malus's heart and the fire Urial had kindled dwindled to a sullen coal.

'He cannot have you!' Tz'arkan said with surprising intensity. Whether the daemon meant Urial or perhaps Khaine himself, Malus wasn't certain.

A sickening miasma settled over the fortress deck, as though the ship were downwind of a charnel house. The smell of rotten blood, festering skin and spilled entrails made a stench that Malus could almost physically see. There was a discordant buzzing in the air. At first the highborn thought it was the sound of distant voices, but then he realised it came from swarms of huge black flies, hanging over the refuse that choked the deck of the Skinrider vessel.

At this range the exchange of missiles was fierce. One druchii swordsman fell limply to the deck with an arrow buried in his eye. Another let out a yell and staggered backwards, staring in shock and surprise at an arrow that had penetrated his shield and the arm beneath. Crossbow bolts were raining down on the enemy crew as well, striking bodies with a glutinous *slap!* that sparked gobbling cries of rage and pain. The image of the Skinrider shrugging off the blow of the mast cutter hung in his mind. What had he got himself into this time? Malus turned to Tanithra. 'If we kill their captain will they surrender?'

The druchii threw back her head and laughed. 'Skinriders don't surrender,' she said. 'The fight is over when the last of them is dead. And don't forget to make sure you've killed your man – crush his skull or sever his head. With these things, nothing else is certain.'

Just then the two ships met with a bone-jarring thud. Malus pitched forward, propping himself up with an outflung hand, but Tanithra leapt nimbly to her feet. 'Away boarders!' she cried and with a thunderous chorus of war screams the corsairs leapt to obey.

Chapter Sixteen
THE RAIDING PARTY

THE CROSSBOWMEN AT the rail let fly a ragged volley of bolts and then dropped to their knees. Tanithra and the first wave of boarders vaulted the rail and dropped onto the Skinrider ship, their weapons glinting in the weak morning light. Almost immediately the sounds of battle rose from the deck of the enemy ship. Malus surged forward with the second wave, checked his grip on his sword and leapt nimbly to the rail.

A desperate battle was raging less than twelve feet below. The volley of crossbow bolts had killed or wounded a handful of the Skinriders, but the rest had held their ground by the rail, awaiting the druchii onslaught with inhuman determination. Tanithra and her corsairs had literally fallen on them from above, slashing and stabbing, but the Skinriders had not retreated an inch. Tanithra fought against two of the corrupted raiders, warding off their blows with savage parries of her heavy sword as they pushed her step by step back towards the rail.

Roaring out a warcry of his own, Malus vaulted the rail and dropped onto the Skinrider ship, aiming to land beside one of the raiders hammering at Tanithra. As he fell, however, another Skinrider rushed at the female druchii, reaching for one of her legs with a short-hafted bill hook and stepped directly into Malus's path. The highborn's feet struck the Skinrider on his hooded head and both he and Malus collapsed to the noisome deck in a clatter of weapons and armoured limbs.

The deck planks stank of rot, covered in puddles of brown and yellow fluids and mounds of decaying refuse. Malus's furious snarl caught in his throat as he choked on the miasma rising from the corrupted ship. He slipped and slid in the greasy fluids, trying to get his feet as the Skinrider he'd landed on pulled a corroded dagger from his belt and leapt at him with a gurgling cry.

Malus checked the Skinrider's rush with a raised boot, planting his heel in the raider's shoulder. The Skinrider's knife jabbed against Malus's breastplate; the tip of the blade snapped, but the raider only stabbed all the harder, searching for a vulnerable point to sink the weapon into the highborn's chest.

Malus slid backwards along the slippery deck, unable to find purchase until his head and shoulders fetched up against the ship's port rail. The Skinrider loomed over him, dagger raised, but the highborn moved with the speed of a striking snake. He made a backhand slash with his sword, striking the raider at the base of his jaw and shearing through his skull from right to left. The Skinrider's head burst like an over-ripe melon, pouring out a stinking mush of rotting blood, brains and squirming maggots. Cursing viciously, Malus got his boot planted on the raider's chest and kicked the corpse away.

Roaring and spitting, Malus leapt to his feet, sparing a glance at Tanithra, who was still locked in combat with two raiders less than five feet away. Both of her foes were intent on battering through her defences and so Malus caught them unawares as he darted towards the nearest one and sliced the raider's head from his misshapen shoulders.

Tanithra despatched her opponent and added her own sword to the battle going on to her right. More boarders were coming across as the initial counterassault faltered and the druchii were widening their hold on the stern of the enemy ship. Malus looked aft and saw the ship's wheel, guarded by the ship's captain and a pair of Skinriders with spears. The highborn drew his second sword with his left hand and circled to starboard, hoping to catch the raiders unawares. He stepped around the raised coaming of the aft hold – a large square hatch fifteen feet across and a third again in length – and as he rounded the hatch's starboard quarter he ran headlong into a crouching group of Skinriders coming the opposite way.

There was but a moment to react and Malus threw himself at the enemy with a snarl of rage. The first raider tried to rise, bringing up a battered buckler to shield his head, but the highborn knocked it aside with his left-hand sword and beheaded the man with a sweeping stroke from his right. Malus kicked the raider's body backwards onto the next man in line and surged forwards, both blades singing through the air in a deadly, interlocking pattern.

The raiders fell back, more and more of them forced to their feet and exposed to the fire of the crossbowmen nearby. Bolts buzzed angrily through the air, tearing through bloated muscle and sacks of rotting viscera. A Skinrider suddenly leapt at Malus, stabbing for his belly with a broad-bladed spear. The highborn pivoted on the ball of his right foot and let the spear point slide past, then slashed open the raider's throat. The Skinrider staggered and Malus gave him a backhanded stroke that completed the job and sent the raider's head bouncing wetly across the deck. The highborn threw back his head and shouted in exultation, lost in the joy of the slaughter.

A Skinrider roared in response and charged at him, empty hands reaching for his throat. Acting instinctively, Malus levelled his sword and ran the man through, the steel blade sliding cleanly between the raider's ribs and bursting from the man's back. Too late, Malus realised that his blade was now trapped – and the Skinrider was still coming, his swollen lips twisted in a grimace of rage.

Another raider dashed around the first and came at Malus from the side, throwing himself on the highborn's sword arm. Malus barely had time to cry out before the Skinrider he'd impaled crashed against him, spattering the highborn with stinking fluids from the gaping wound in his chest. Malus staggered against the blow – then his boot stepped in something slick and went out from under him and he fell backwards, crashing against the aft hatch cover. The rotting wood gave way and the highborn and his foes were falling through cold, foetid darkness.

Malus felt a spine-jarring crash as they landed in the bottom of the aft hold below. Something like old bone crunched beneath his shoulders and the weight on his left arm fell away with a grunt, but then there was another grinding, splintering crunch of rotten wood and he was falling again, this time landing in a pool of reeking fluid that closed greasily over his head.

The bilges! They'd landed among the bones of the decrepit scout, thrashing about in the polluted water standing in the bottom of the hull. The image from Malus's dream returned with sickening force, just as the raider he'd stabbed tightened his rotting hands around the highborn's throat and forced him deeper into the filthy water.

Malus thrashed and heaved, trying to gain some kind of leverage, but his right arm was trapped underneath the weight of his attacker. His left hand was empty – at some point on the way down his off-hand sword had been torn from his grasp – and he beat uselessly at the rotting hood. Flailing desperately, the highborn grabbed hold of the hood, groping with his fingers for an eye socket. He found one and sank his thumb into it, feeling cold, thick liquid run down his wrist. The Skinrider thrashed and Malus pushed against him, managing to pull his head out of the foul water. He gasped for breath, gagging at the vile taste in his mouth and blinking furiously at the oily water stinging his eyes. All he could see was a ragged hole far above him and a patch of grey light – everything else was dark in the cavernous space below the hold. The raider was weakening. Malus remembered the dagger at his belt and fumbled for it – just as the Skinrider he'd shaken off in the hold above dropped down through the hole and threw himself against Malus's shoulders.

The highborn drew in a mouthful of air as his head was once more pushed beneath the water. It felt as though a wall had fallen on him – no matter how hard he fought against the weight of the two men he couldn't budge them an inch. There was a roaring in his ears and the skin on his cheeks began to tingle. He tried to speak, to call for the daemon's power, but his mouth filled with reeking water. Precious air burst from his throat in a cloud of bubbles. His chest began to ache and the need to breathe was like a fist twisting in his lungs.

Suddenly there was another heavy impact, strong enough to drive the back of Malus's head against the curved ribs of the ship – and then the weight on his chest was gone. The highborn flailed weakly, no longer certain if his hands were out of the water or not until a strong grip seized him and pulled him from the bilge.

'You shouldn't go running off on your own like that, my lord,' Hauclir said casually. 'It's hard enough work guarding your back without having to chase after you all the time.'

Malus managed to roll onto his knees in the stinking water, coughing and spitting as he tried to shake the oily liquid from his hair and ears. 'The damned Skinriders took me on a tour of their ship and I wasn't in a position to argue,' he gasped. 'How go things topside?'

'The last I saw, Tanithra had killed the Skinrider captain and was sending men forward to finish off the last of the crew,' the retainer said.

'And she's welcome to them,' the highborn said, rolling over the body of the raider that had trapped his blade and grabbing the long hilt with both hands. The sword came free with a sucking sound. 'Mother of Night, these Skinriders *stink*,' he said, feeling his gorge rise.

'Let's find the stairs and get back on deck and pray there's a stiff wind blowing.'

BY THE TIME Malus and his man had reached the open air the battle was finished. Tanithra's men had forced the surviving crewman into a tight knot at the far end of the bow and then methodically slaughtered them with crossbows and blades. The bodies were stripped of their hide surcoats and thrown over the side and the dead corsairs were wrapped in their cloaks and taken aboard the *Harrier* after one last benediction from Urial.

The next few hours were spent taking on supplies and tools from the *Harrier* to repair the damaged mast. The boarders bent to the task with a will, splicing severed ropes and hauling a spare hide sail from one of the holds below. By midmorning the vagabond's damage was repaired and the ship was ready to get under weigh.

'If the wind remains favourable you should reach the hideout by midnight,' Bruglir said, shouting at Malus and Tanithra from the fortress deck of the *Harrier*. 'We'll be just over the horizon to the south-west, waiting for your return. Remember to keep a sailing watch ready so that you can leave as soon as you've secured the charts.'

The highborn nodded. 'How many raiders are there likely to be on the island?' Malus asked, shading his eyes with his hand as he looked up at the captain.

Bruglir shrugged. 'There is no way to know. Maybe a couple of ships, plus a small garrison. Their numbers change with the season and the whims of the raiders. With luck, you'll have little problem slipping into the camp.'

'Just be where you say you'll be after midnight. I've no doubt the Skinriders will chase us to the Outer Darkness and back once they realise what we've taken.'

'Cast off!' Bruglir ordered his men. 'We'll be waiting, Malus,' he said, then raised his arm to Tanithra in salute. 'Good hunting, captain! Take good care of your new ship!'

The crew on the fortress deck laughed as the *Harrier* pulled apart from the rotting vagabond. Tanithra returned the salute, but only Malus could see the corsair's teeth clench at the hoots of derision thrown her way. 'I'm sure he's speaking in jest,' the highborn said.

Tanithra didn't reply, staring darkly at Bruglir's dwindling form. Inwardly, Malus smiled in satisfaction. Things were coming together nicely.

THEY'D OPENED EVERY hatch cover to let in the sea breeze, but it still did nothing to lessen the stench. Malus leaned against the bulkhead, staring up at the square of night sky overhead and listening to the hiss of the sea against the ship's hull. Things could be much worse, he reminded himself. The handful of sailors on deck had been forced to put on the hide surcoats they'd stripped from the bodies of the dead crew.

Two score druchii corsairs sat in the reeking hold, cleaning their weapons or gambling with one another in tense, whispered voices. They kept a respectful distance from Malus and Urial, giving up the aft part of the hold to the highborn. Hauclir rested his head against the bulkhead to Malus's right, snoring softly and rocking in time to the swaying of the ship. As tired as he was, Malus couldn't bring himself to sleep. The stench was terrible, but more than that he feared what terrible visions waited for him in his dreams.

Malus sought out his half-brother, who sat on the deck just a few feet away with his bad leg stretched out before him. 'I've a question for you, brother,' he said.

Those cold eyes turned his way, fixing him with an owl-like stare. 'You may ask,' Urial said, promising nothing.

The highborn grinned mirthlessly, hearing his words thrown back at him. 'How is it that seers can peer into the future?'

Urial blinked. 'Because there is no such thing.'

'None of your sorcerer's riddles, brother,' Malus growled. 'I'm tired and I smell like a midden heap and I'm in no mood for games.'

'Then listen and learn,' Urial said, leaning towards him. 'Imagine that you are standing in the middle of a river.'

Malus grunted. 'That's easy enough. I've been dreaming about a bath for hours now.'

'In the middle of a river, all you are aware of is the water rushing past your waist. Your only point of reference is the spot on the riverbed where you are standing. All else is in motion, changing from moment to moment before your very eyes. That is how most mortals perceive the flow of time.'

Malus considered this, frowning in thought. 'All right.'

'Now imagine stepping out of the river and standing on the bank. Your perspective has changed. You can look back at the river and see its course in both directions. If you want, you can catch a glimpse of a floating piece of wood and trace its course along the moving stream. You can see where it came from and where it will go, because you can see the totality of its course. That is how seers perceive the future – by altering their perspective and taking in the totality of existence.'

Malus thought about what the acolyte had said, formulating his response. 'Is… is it possible for someone who isn't a seer to alter their perspective in this way?'

For a long time Urial was silent. 'It is possible,' he said at last. 'If a man were to step outside the realm of the physical world he could look back at the river of life and view its course. Or he might receive visions if he were being possessed by a potent enough spirit.' The acolyte studied him intently. 'Why do you ask?'

Before Malus could reply, a hooded figure peered over the lip of the hatch, barely discernible in the abyssal darkness. 'We're sailing into the cove,' he whispered. 'Landing party topside.'

Glad for the interruption, Malus nudged Hauclir with his boot. The retainer was awake in an instant and rising silently to his feet. Malus, Hauclir and four corsairs, all hand-picked for their ability to move and kill silently, gathered together near the topside ladder.

Urial rose as well and limped forward. 'You are all still protected by the aegis of the Bloody-Handed God,' he said in a low voice. 'But the power of the enemy will be much stronger within the camp. Touch nothing save what you must, or even my power may not be enough to protect you.

'Next thing you'll say is that we can't kill anyone,' Hauclir said sourly.

Urial smiled coldly. 'Have no fear on that score. Spill blood in Khaine's name and his blessing will remain strong.'

'Then let's go do our holy duty,' Malus growled, nodding for the men to follow him as he started up the ladder.

The sea breeze was cool and brisk as Malus made his way onto the deck, but he had barely a moment to savour it. Tanithra was waiting for him at the top of the ladder, draped in one of the raiders' stinking hides. The lower part of her face was all the highborn could see from beneath the surcoat's crude hood, but he sensed that she was worried. 'We have a problem,' she hissed and pointed over his shoulder.

Malus turned. The island cove spread before him, the waters glittering in the pale moonlight. Six Skinrider ships lay in the anchorage, every one a seagoing raider twice the size of the little vagabond. It was almost midnight, yet Malus could see crewmen swarming over the big ships, clearly readying them for sea. Longboats scurried to and fro between the squadron and the shore, carrying supplies to the waiting ships. The highborn bit back a curse. 'Someone's planning a major raid,' he growled.

'And I'll wager this old boat was out scouting for them,' Tanithra said. 'We don't have much time before whoever's in charge realises we're not supposed to be here and sends someone to ask a lot of awkward questions.'

'Then we're going to have to hurry,' Malus said, forestalling the question he read in the corsair's eyes. 'I didn't come this far to leave empty-handed. Be ready to sail the instant we return.'

Malus scanned the rocky shoreline until he found the point where the Skinriders were loading the grounded longboats with supplies. From there, he gazed deeper inland, following the antlike procession of labourers until he spied a squat tower, almost invisible against the background of dark fir trees about half a mile from the shore. He pointed to the tower. 'That's where the charts will be kept,' he told the assembled druchii. 'We'll have to move overland – the shore is too exposed.'

Malus dashed silently to the starboard rail, where a group of sailors had lowered the ship's longboat into the placid waters of the cove. Without a backward glance Malus threw his leg over the rail and clambered down a rope ladder into the boat. He was no sooner settled in the bow when Hauclir landed in the boat behind him, holding a loaded crossbow. The retainer passed the weapon to Malus and settled down beside him. The remaining members of the landing party took their positions swiftly and silently. At a nod from Malus the portside oarsman pushed them away from the hull of the vagabond with his oar and within moments they were rowing towards the shoreline, their course largely concealed by the bulk of their anchored ship.

The trip to shore seemed to last forever. Malus listened to the faint sounds of the Skinriders at work on the distant ships, expecting to hear a thin cry of alarm at any moment. His attention was so fixed on the sounds carrying in the night air that the sudden grounding of the boat in the shallows took the highborn by surprise. Two sailors leapt from the boat, landing in the water with scarcely a splash as they stabilised the boat for the others to disembark. Malus stepped over the gunwale and stalked quietly into the shadows as the corsairs dragged the heavy boat onto the shore.

There was little light beneath the trees, but compared to the tangled woods of the far north the forest on the island was almost free of undergrowth. The landing party moved silently beneath the tall trees, drawn by the sounds of the loading crews. Malus was surprised to find no sentries or patrols keeping guard over the wooded approach – likely every man that could be spared had been dragooned into readying the ships for sea.

The Skinrider camp was actually a small fort, with a wooden tower three storeys high rising amid a cluster of wooden buildings surrounded by a wooden stockade. The corsairs crouched at the edge of the forest and watched a steady stream of men pushing wheelbarrows past the stockade's open gates. Tall torches had been driven into the ground at regular intervals along the route, providing ample light for the labourers – and the guards standing watch at the entrance.

Malus felt Hauclir crouch silently down beside him. 'All this hustle and bustle will serve us well,' the retainer said. 'The inside of that compound is likely to be busier than a beehive – one more group of labourers isn't likely to attract any unwanted attention. And the guards will all be focusing their efforts on the traffic moving through the gate.' He indicated the tower with a jerk of his head. 'Let's have a look on the back side of the stockade and see if it can be scaled.'

The corsairs rose silently and slipped like shadows beneath the towering fir trees, circling around the camp's perimeter until they stood by the wall directly opposite the gate. There they sank onto their bellies and crawled through the sparse scrub and fern until they had a clear view of the stockade and the square tower beyond. After several long minutes of study, Malus and Hauclir exchanged looks. There were no sentries to be seen. The appalling lack of defences made Malus's hair stand on end. There was something here that he wasn't seeing, but he couldn't imagine what it was and there was no time to waste puzzling it out. Finally he shrugged and waved two of the corsairs forward.

The men rose from cover and raced across the cleared area leading up to the wall. They disappeared in the shadow of the wall, then Malus heard a low whistle. The scouts had determined that the wall was scalable. The highborn rose to a crouch and the rest of the raiding party followed.

The logs were made from the local fir trees, broad and sturdy and pegged together by thick iron nails. White mould grew in the chinking between the logs and swarms of insects crawled along the wood's countless fissures. The highborn made a conscious effort to ignore the squirming carpet of life covering the palisade and focused on the faces of the scouts. 'Wall's not too high,' one of the men said. 'We can boost a man up and go over in relays.'

Malus nodded. 'All right. Hauclir, you first.'

Hauclir gave his lord an impertinent stare. 'I live to serve,' he whispered and put his boot into one of the scouts' interlaced hands. With a faint grunt the scout propelled Hauclir upwards and the retainer immediately found good handholds on the wall. He wedged his armoured form between the pointed ends of two of the logs and then bent down, reaching for the next man. Moments later a second man straddled the top of the wall and both men together began pulling the rest of the raiding party up and over as fast as they could grab them.

Malus was last to go. The two druchii took his hands and pulled him up to the top of the wall as though he were a straw doll. Without pausing he swung his legs over the palisade and dropped to the other side, drawing his crossbow as he landed. From his vantage point Malus could see that the square tower was built at the far end of a long feasting hall, similar to ones the autarii or even the barbarian norsemen liked to build. There were lights burning beyond narrow arrow slits set into the walls of the great hall and sickly-sweet smoke rose from the hall's two chimneys. Nearer to the wall were two square wooden buildings, their windows dark and shuttered. The raiding party was taking cover in the shadow of these buildings and Malus raced to join them. Within moments Hauclir and the remaining corsair were off the wall and ducking behind the building opposite the one where Malus crouched.

They watched and listened for several minutes. There was no sign of activity around the corsairs. Malus waited as long as he dared, then rounded the corner of the small building and led the raiding party to the tower.

The closer they came to the tower, the more Malus felt a kind of tension in the air, like the sky just before a summer storm. Sorcery, he thought bitterly. He was getting all too familiar with the sensation.

Up close to the tower, it looked as though there were plenty of footholds for a skilled climber. The walls were made of the same fir logs as the palisade, though some kind of glistening membrane had been stretched across their surface. Malus reached out a hand and touched it and it parted like rotting parchment, releasing a horrid stench like a ruptured bowel. Squirming insects poured from the hole and raced along the ground. Beneath the membrane the wall appeared chinked with some kind of moist red clay.

Malus eyed the tower with a grimace. 'No wonder they don't rely on guards,' he hissed. 'Who in their right mind would want to seize such a place?' He looked up, gauging the length of the climb. Finally he sighed and reached for a handhold, splitting the membrane further and filling the air with more noxious gas.

The corsairs, accustomed to scrambling up wet rigging day and night, scaled the tower with ease. Malus and Hauclir quickly fell behind, taking the climb one hand and foothold at a time. There was a narrow window frame inset at each storey and the raiders took special care to pass them with wide margins.

Malus and Hauclir were almost at the second storey when suddenly a silhouette leaned out of the open frame and looked left and right along the wall. The highborn froze, pressing himself against the insect-infested wood and praying to the Dark Mother that the diseased creature didn't think to look directly below him. The crossbow, still cocked and loaded, was slung on his back, for all intents and purposes a thousand miles away.

The highborn watched the hooded form of the pirate scan the walls of the tower one last time and then pause in thought. Was he trying to explain away the strange sounds he'd heard? After a moment the figure receded – then abruptly leaned back out and looked down. Malus found himself staring into a pair of sickly grey eyes only five feet from his own.

There was a rustle of fine metal, like the unravelling of a necklace, then Malus sensed Hauclir make a sudden, sweeping move off to his right. A fine length of chain lashed like a whip through the air and wrapped tightly around the Skinrider's throat. The hooded man barely had a moment to gasp for air before the retainer hauled backwards and pulled the man from the window. The body hurtled silently past them and hit the ground with a wet *smack*!

Malus glanced at Hauclir and gave him a nod of approval and the two resumed their climb. Minutes later they joined the rest of the raiding party.

The top of the tower was crenellated and afforded a commanding view of the entire camp. The four corsairs lay on their bellies in the middle of the floor, keeping out of sight. Malus crawled over to them. One of the druchii pointed towards one of the floor's corners. The highborn spied a trapdoor there, inset with a dark iron ring.

As Hauclir settled down beside the corsairs and gasped for breath, Malus crawled to the far side of the tower and rose up enough to peer over the battlements at the activity below. There was a large open field just past the main gate of the camp and it was packed with crates and barrels, many protected from the elements by large hide tarps. The torchlight field was swarming with Skinriders – possibly the entire camp and a sizeable portion of the crews of the anchored ships.

Movement near the gate caught Malus's attention. A Skinrider had run up empty-handed to the gate and was speaking excitedly to the sentries. After a moment the most senior of the guards appeared to reach a decision and pointed to the tower. Without hesitation the man ran on. Clearly he had news for someone.

Malus turned to his men. 'It looks like someone in the cove has noticed the ship,' he said in a low voice. 'We've run out of time.'

Chapter Seventeen
THE EMERALD FIRE

MALUS EDGED BACKWARDS from the battlements, his mind racing. Had the ships in the cove already attacked the vagabond and killed Tanithra and the rest of the crew, or were they asking for permission to challenge the new arrival? Worse still, what if some sharp-eyed lookout had spotted the longboat?

On the other hand, it could have nothing to do with us whatsoever, Malus the highborn thought angrily. There was no way to be certain, but it seemed wise to expect the worst.

He crawled to the trapdoor inset at the north-east corner of the floor, motioning for Hauclir and another druchii with a crossbow to join him. Malus pointed to Hauclir and then at the iron ring, then rose into a crouch, aiming his crossbow at the doorway. The second druchii mirrored his movements on the opposite side of the door.

The retainer took up the ring with both hands, took a deep breath and swung it open slowly and carefully. Reddish torchlight rose from the doorway and transformed the three druchii into hellish figures doused in crimson and orange. The stench of rot and rendered fat rose in a smoky cloud from the spaces below.

Below, Malus saw the top of a curving flight of stairs and a broad landing lit by torches fitted into sconces along the walls. Much of the landing lay in shadow, but he could clearly see a wooden door almost directly below. Malus passed the crossbow to Hauclir without a word and reached for the ladder waiting below the open door.

Descending into the tower was like sinking into a steam bath. The air was rank and humid and seemed to tremble with a life of its own. It pressed against Malus's exposed skin like oil, sliding greasily into every crevice and hollow and his flesh tingled sharply at the touch. He edged stealthily towards the door and drew one of his swords. There was an indistinct rumble of noise rising up the stairwell from the floors below – Malus imagined the long hall filled with Skinriders preparing for their voyage. By now they would be looking curiously at the messenger darting through their midst.

The highborn eyed the progress at the ladder – Hauclir was the last man to descend, already half way to the floor with the rest of the corsairs spread out around the stairs and looking to him for orders. Malus told two men with crossbows to cover the stairway and motioned the rest to accompany him. Then he turned and laid a hand on the door's iron ring. Moving cautiously, Malus eased the door open and peered through a narrow gap into the room beyond. The chamber was dimly lit; light from two banked braziers cast a faint glow across what looked to be a table of some kind. A figure struggled weakly on the platform, apparently bound there by rope. The stink of spilled blood hung heavy in the room, along with the familiar odour of decay.

Malus swung the door wide and rushed into the room, sword ready and peering into the dimly lit corners for waiting foes. But for the wretch twitching on the table in the centre of the room, there was no one there. The highborn looked about for a moment with a mixture of relief and consternation.

The room was like a rustic shrine to the Bloody-Handed God. The wooden table in the centre of the room was worn and stained with layer upon layer of dried gore and the wooden floor was tacky with pools of old blood. The shuddering figure bound spread-eagled to the tabletop was naked and had been – rather crudely, Malus noted in passing – skinned from the waist up. Maggots, flies and red wasps crawled over the glistening flesh. Yellowed teeth shone from the tortured gums and exposed musculature of the jaw; the mouth worked, but nothing more than a tortured whisper rose from the man's ravaged throat.

Hide curtains had been stretched across alcoves lining three of the room's walls. In the midst of the wall opposite the door stood a life-size statue of what appeared to be a broad-shouldered Skinrider, his hood decorated with a pair of massive, downward-curving horns and his right hand extended towards the skinning table as if demanding the portion of flesh that was due him. The Skinriders had laid voluminous hide robes on the armature of the statue, lending the figure a disturbing degree of life. The folds of the robe shifted slightly in the draft created by the open door.

Hauclir stood in the doorway, studying the room with a grimace of distaste. 'What is this place?' Malus shrugged. There was an undercurrent of tension in the air, ebbing and flowing like the slow beat of an unseen heart. More sorcery, he suspected. 'Some kind of shrine, perhaps,' he said, pointing at the statue with his sword. 'Whatever it is, it's important to the Skinriders. Search the alcoves.'

The corsairs went to work with their knives, slashing open the curtains and examining the items stacked behind them. There were dusty tomes and scrolls, jewelled skulls and gilded weapons, jars of arcane liquids and sealed boxes inscribed with curious runes and bound with silver wire.

'Looks like a treasure room,' Hauclir said, eyeing a matched pair of bejewelled swords with an avaricious grin.

'Remember what Urial said,' Malus warned. 'Touch only what you must, unless you want to end up watching your skin melt from your body.' The highborn studied the stacks of plunder carefully. 'Unusual treasures,' he muttered. 'Not a sack of coin among them, which means that the bulk of their treasure is stored somewhere else. So they're keeping only their most valuable items here.' He frowned, poking at one of the books with the point of his blade. 'If that's so, then the charts must be up here as well.'

His gaze ran along the alcoves, peering into their shadowy depths. There was something about the room that wasn't quite right, but he couldn't place what. He turned in a complete circle, studying the walls, until finally returning to the horned statue looming over the corsairs across the room. The robes shifted silently and then Malus realised what was missing.

'There was a window on this level,' he said as he stepped up to the statue. The highborn reached out with his sword and pushed the hanging robes aside. Behind the hanging cloth wasn't the body of a statue, but a narrow wooden door.

Grinning like a wolf, Malus grasped the door's iron ring and pushed. The door swung open, revealing a second room lit only by a narrow band of pale moonlight from the window opposite. From where he stood, Malus could see wooden bins filled with tall rolls of parchment and his heart quickened. Then, from the deep shadows in one of the room's far corners, he heard the faint rustle of chains.

'A torch,' Malus said, holding out his hand. 'Quickly!'

Hauclir was by his side in moments, having taken a torch from one of the sconces by the stairwell. Malus tore the robes from the wall, stirring up a cloud of iridescent flies as the stained cloth tumbled to the floor. Holding the torch high, he edged slowly inside.

The room was indeed a repository for the camp's sea charts, the bins arranged around a wooden table similar to the layout aboard the *Harrier*. There was a sharp rattle of chains as the torchlight spilled into the room; Malus oriented on the sound and walked forward, sword held ready.

Ruddy light pushed back the shadows, finally reaching the corner and revealing a huddled, emaciated figure shackled at wrists and ankles, its naked body covered in grime and weeping sores. The human raised thin arms as if to shield itself from the bright light, then suddenly it froze. Above the hissing of the torch, Malus heard furtive sniffing.

The human stiffened. His face, shadowed by a fall of greasy, black hair, turned towards the highborn. Malus saw that the slave's eyes had been put out, leaving raw, burnt holes where hot metal had cauterised the wounds. The human sniffed the air like a hunting hound and began to tremble. His toothless mouth gaped as the wretched creature pointed a crooked finger at Malus and unleashed a horrific, paralysing shriek.

It was no mere noise that erupted from the human's throat, but a sorcerous force that cut through the druchii like a freezing wind. The scream froze the corsairs in their tracks, their hands pressed to their ears in shock and pain. And the sound went on and on, long past the point when a mortal's lungs would have failed.

Teeth bared, Malus roared back at the slave, feeling the paralysis waver in against the heat of his rage and he ran across the room, his sword held high. The curved blade flashed downwards and sent the creature's head bouncing across the floor.

The sudden silence was deafening. Malus staggered, trying to clear his head, but the rising thunder of scores of feet pounding up the tower stairs quickly focused his thoughts. He rounded on his men. 'Take those braziers in the skinning room and anything else that will burn and empty them onto the stairs – throw the torches, the robes, everything! With luck this tower will burn like a candle wick.'

Hauclir leapt into action, snapping orders at the men with the forceful tone of a proven officer and the corsairs leapt to obey. Satisfied his orders were being carried out, Malus turned back to the wooden bins and pulled out the largest and thickest charts he could find, binding them in sheaves with twine he pulled from his belt. The sheaves then went out the narrow window as quickly as he could throw them.

There were screams from the stairwell behind him and the thump of crossbow strings. The braziers were tipped over with a loud crash and then a general commotion ensued, punctuated by the clash of steel. Malus grabbed the wrist of the slave and dragged the body into the centre of the room until the chain pulled taut. About eight feet each, he calculated and began hacking off hands and feet. Once the chains were free, he pulled at the iron staples holding the chains to the walls, but no amount of tugging would tear them free. He turned back to the doorway. 'Bring me an axe!'

One of the corsairs dashed into the room, bleeding from a cut to his forehead. 'The stairs are burning, lord,' he gasped. 'But the Skinriders keep charging through the flames. I don't know how long we can hold them.'

The highborn pointed at the wall. 'Get three of those chains loose – only three – and we won't have to hold them long at all.'

'Your will, my lord,' the druchii said and bent to the task. A few sharp strokes later and he was holding three chains in his free hand. Malus took them and rushed to the doorway. 'Fall back into the skinning room!' he called to the men defending the stairwell. 'And bar the door!'

As the corsairs retreated from the burning landing, Malus went to work on the chains. He threaded one chain through the closed manacle of the second, drawing them together until the two manacles met. Then he picked up one of the U-shaped staples from the floor and threaded it first through the closed manacle of the chain still stapled to the wall and then through the last link of one of the freed chains. Malus held out his hand for the axe and used its hammer-shaped back to beat the soft iron staple shut. With one quick check of his handiwork he tossed the now-elongated chain out the window. 'It won't reach all the way to the ground,' he said, passing back the axe, 'but it will be close enough. Now go!'

The corsair nodded and went out of the window without a word. Malus leaned out and watched the man scramble down the length of the chain and nimbly drop the last few feet onto the ground. Satisfied, he ran back into the skinning room. The corsairs had dragged the heavy skinning table and its tethered victim across the room and braced it against the door and now they watched the smoking portal with mounting dread.

'Everyone out of the window,' Malus ordered. 'Once you're on the ground grab as many charts as you can and then run for the wall!'

The corsairs leapt to obey. Hauclir retreated to stand by the highborn's side. 'Something's going on,' he said, eyeing the door warily. 'The shouting's stopped, but I think I can hear chanting over the sound of the fire.'

Tz'arkan stirred. 'I smell sorcery,' the daemon whispered. 'Potent sorcery. You've made someone very angry, Darkblade.'

'Out of the window,' Malus snarled. 'Hurry!'

'You first, my lord,' Hauclir insisted and then the door across the room exploded in a ball of greenish flame.

Shards of burning wood buzzed lethally across the room, trailing streamers of fire. The heavy skinning table flew over Malus and Hauclir and shattered against the head and shoulders of the horned Skinrider, showering both druchii with debris. There was a figure in the doorway, limned by firelight; Malus caught a passing glance of a naked, skinless form, the thick layers of muscle across his chest incised with complex magical runes and eyes that were globes of seething green fire. Everything else was a blur as he turned and ran for the open window as fast as his feet could carry him.

Malus leapt upon the chart table and snagged the chain with his free hand. There was the sound of steel striking flesh behind him, followed by a torrent of words that hissed venomously in the air. There was a flash of greenish light and a powerful blast smote Malus in the chest, hurling him through the window. He fell for almost twelve feet before his body slammed back against the wall of the tower, partially slowing his descent. Still half-blind with pain, he managed to get his legs around the chain and control the speed of his plunge the rest of the way down. When his feet hit the ground it surprised him so much his knees went out from under him and he collapsed on his side. Hauclir hit the ground beside him a heartbeat later, his robes smouldering and much of his short hair burned away.

Hands pulled at him, trying to draw him to his feet. Malus staggered upright, looking up at the tower. Green light seethed from the narrow window and the square tower top was haloed in angry flames. Malus glanced at his retainer. 'What did you *do?*'

The retainer rose shakily to his feet. 'I threw my knife at him. I didn't think he would be in much shape to cast his spells with a blade sticking out of his chest.' He ran a hand across his scalp, his palm coming away black with charred hair. 'Apparently that was a mistake.'

'Or perhaps it's the reason we're still alive.' The highborn said. 'Let's not push our luck any further. Grab some charts and let's get out of here.'

Despite his orders, none of the corsairs had fled for the wall. Any other time the gesture of loyalty would have pleased him, but now he jostled and shoved at the men to get them moving. Hauclir may have wounded the sorcerer, but Malus knew from experience how difficult such men were to kill.

He was just a few paces short of the wall when the wooden palisade was lit by a flare of greenish light. Energy sizzled through the air and Malus looked back to see a jagged bolt of emerald lightning arc from the top of the tower and play along the ground in the wake of the fleeing corsairs. Malus could see the dark form of the sorcerer silhouetted in the window frame. 'Hurry!' he cried to the laden druchii.

The first man reached him and leapt into Malus's waiting hands. The highborn caught the foot and propelled it upwards, hurling the corsair skyward. The man nimbly caught the top of the wall and swung one leg over, reaching down for the next man in line. Malus sent him upwards as well and the second corsair settled into place and reached down to help the others across.

Another arc of lightning crackled through the air, burning a jagged line across the ground and licking up the side of one of the camp's outbuildings. The log structure didn't explode so much as disintegrate, rotted into a steaming mush by the sorcerous bolt. Howls and angry cries echoed from the far side of the hall. Malus helped the third and fourth men up and over the palisade. Only Hauclir was left and this time he made no attempt to bring up the rear, his face sickly with fear as he put his foot in Malus's hands and leapt for the top of the wall.

A crowd of running Skinriders turned the corner of the outbuilding closest to the hall just as the sorcerer let loose another bolt. This time the lightning clipped the corner of a nearby building and then boiled across the ground to within a yard of where Malus stood. Shouting a startled curse, he leapt for the outstretched hands of the men on the wall. They grabbed him on the first attempt and all but hurled him over the row of sharpened logs.

Malus staggered as he hit the ground, turning back to yell for the men on the palisade when there was another flash of green light. The corsairs straddling the wall were blotted out in a blaze of emerald fire and the men below were caught in a shower of steaming flesh and bone. The highborn stumbled and fell backwards, staggered by the horrific effects of the blast. Not only the two druchii, but a sizeable portion of the wall they sat upon was simply gone. Through the wisps of steam rising from the ravaged logs, Malus saw a figure wreathed in green fire step lightly from the top of the tower and descend on a seething pillar of emerald light.

'Blessed Mother of Night,' Malus breathed, his eyes wide. He scrambled to his feet, turning to his stunned, gore-slicked men. 'Fly, you sea birds, fly!' he said, breaking into a run.

By the time the palisade dissolved under the sorcerer's magical bolts the druchii were gone, running for their lives through the shadowy depths of the forest.

Chapter Eighteen
THE DRAGON'S KISS

IT WAS AS if Malus was back in the Chaos Wastes again, hunted through the forests like an animal. The dark woods echoed with howls and cries of fury as the Skinriders poured from the camp into the shadows beneath the trees. To the highborn it sounded as though the raiders were fanning out in a wide circle, which told him that they were poor trackers to begin with and unsure of the direction he and his men had fled in. The surviving members of the landing party raced along in a ragged line behind Malus, leaving little trace of their passing. Every yard of distance they gained from the Skinrider camp made their trail that much harder to find.

Malus paused to gain his bearings. Off to the right he thought he could see the waters of the cove through the gaps between the trees. He reckoned that their longboat was two and a half miles from the camp and

273

they'd covered half that distance so far. The cries of the raiders were fainter now, but he knew from experience that sounds could be deceiving inside a thick wood. Hauclir and the surviving corsairs caught up to the highborn, their faces taut with fear. Malus jerked his head in the direction of the trail and ran on.

There was a loud shout in the distance, followed by a chorus of baying voices.

Several minutes later Malus veered off the path and headed towards the shore. There were no landmarks to point out his location but the terrain and the amount of time they'd been travelling felt right to him. He plunged from the trees onto the rocky shoreline and was relieved to see the longboat just a dozen yards away.

There were shouts from further up the shoreline. Malus turned to see a knot of Skinriders brandishing torches and charging across the rocks. 'Hurry!' he called to his men.

The corsairs were already at the longboat, pushing it into the cold water. Hauclir waited nearby, a crossbow in his hands. Malus raced like a madman over the treacherous shale. 'Get in the boat, damn you!' he roared.

Hauclir waited until the highborn ran past, firing a parting shot down the shoreline before wading out into the surf and clambering aboard the boat. The corsairs were already at the oars and as Malus grabbed his retainer by the collar and pulled him aboard they dipped the oak paddles into the water and accelerated into the bay. The Skinriders pulled up at the edge of the water, shouting and cursing. Arrows buzzed through the air and made thin splashes in the sea. One struck the hull of the longboat with a sharp *thunk*!, making Malus duck. The remaining arrows fell short as the longboat pulled steadily out of range. The highborn watched the crowd fire a few more arrows, then after a moment they turned and began lumbering down the shoreline towards the camp's landing area.

The sky above the camp roiled with black smoke and rising clouds of bright cinders. It appeared that the Skinriders were having little luck extinguishing the burning tower. A large mob had gathered at the landing and longboats were rowing furiously between the shore and the six raiders at anchor in the bay. Malus looked back over his shoulder at the vagabond, growing closer with every broad sweep of the oars. He saw pale-faced figures racing along the decks; Tanithra and the rest of the corsairs had cast off any pretence of deception and were readying the ship to sail as quickly as they could.

Minutes later the longboat pulled up alongside the reeking hull of the captured scout. Malus and Hauclir scrambled up the rope ladder onto the ship, clutching crumpled sheaves of stolen charts under their arms.

Tanithra was waiting for them on the main deck, her expression tense. 'So much for guile and secrecy,' she said.

'Sorcery makes a mockery of us all,' Malus growled. 'Where is my esteemed half-brother?'

'He went below as soon as the thunder started onshore.'

Malus grunted. 'Let's hope he's preparing a surprise for their sorcerer. How soon can we make sail?'

'We're taking in the anchor now.' She nodded at the crumpled charts. 'Did you find what you were after?'

'I have no idea,' Malus said with a shrug. 'The Skinriders weren't being very obliging.' He handed his load of charts over to Hauclir and went to the rail, looking out at the Skinrider ships. 'What do you think they're going to do?'

'Normally, I'd say they would scatter, spreading the alarm to the rest of the nearby hideouts. But if they know you've run off with their sea charts, I'd expect they'd chase us all the way to Clar Karond to get them back.' She pointed at the frantic efforts of the Skinrider longboats. 'The good news is that a lot of their crews were ashore and their ships aren't ready to sail. The captains over there will have a hard time sorting themselves out.'

At that moment the crowd on the shore scattered like rats as a figure wreathed in green fire moved in their midst. When the sorcerer reached the water's edge he raised his hand and rose on a crackling pillar of emerald lightning. Higher and higher the sorcerer rose, like a fiery arrow shot into the air over the bay, then he plunged slowly and steadily down onto the deck of one of the nearer enemy ships. Skinriders scrambled across the deck, backlit by the angry glow of the sorcerer's presence.

'I think the captains are going to be encouraged to hurry,' Malus said, his voice tinged with dread. 'Let's get out of here.'

DAWN FOUND THE vagabond well south of the Skinriders' island, racing along the waves with the wind strong and bearing on her starboard quarter. Tanithra had put on all the sail the little ship had and with her hands on the wheel the scout was as nimble as a race horse, plunging headlong for the horizon with a pack of sea wolves loping in her wake.

Two hours after leaving the bay the lookouts spotted the sails of the lead Skinrider pursuers. A mix of Tilean and Bretonnian ships, they were twin-masted like the vagabond, but could hang a greater weight of sail and thus gain more power from the steady wind. Druchii ships like the *Harrier* could have sailed effortlessly away from the broad-beamed raiders, but Tanithra and Malus could only look on with mounting unease as their pursuers slowly and steadily closed the gap between them.

As the sun was rising Urial came on deck, joining Malus and Hauclir at the stern, his expression troubled. The former acolyte carried his rune-inscribed axe, clutching it more like a talisman than a weapon of war. 'No sign of Bruglir yet?'

Malus shook his head. 'It shouldn't be long now, or so Tanithra says. An hour perhaps, or less.'

'We may not have even that much time,' Urial replied, glancing back at the Skinrider ships. 'I can feel the sorcerer on board the lead ship. He is summoning terrible power to unleash against us.'

'Isn't there something you can do to make us go any faster?' Malus said, a trace of exasperation slipping into his voice.

'My skills lie in different disciplines than wind and waves,' Urial said. 'I believe I can counter much of the Skinriders' spells, but I will be sorely tested in the process.'

Malus shook his head. 'The Skinriders won't need spells to finish us. Those big ships mount catapults, just like Bretonnian coastal ships. They can smash us to kindling or turn us into a flaming wreck and there's little we can do about it.'

'Then we'd best pray that Bruglir is where he said he would be.'

Before Malus could respond a lookout cried, 'They're shooting!'

A rough-hewn rock arced high into the air from the bow of the lead Skinrider vessel, speeding towards the vagabond. Malus watched its trajectory, feeling his throat go dry. The small boulder fell well short of the fleeing ship, striking the water with a tremendous splash.

'A ranging shot,' Malus said, his expression grim. 'We're still out of reach, but not for too much longer. If you've power of your own to summon, I suggest you get started now.'

The highborn left Urial at the stern and joined Tanithra at the wheel. Her one good eye flickered from sail to horizon to the nearby sea and back again as she constantly made small adjustments to the wheel. The expression on her face was strained, but Malus thought he saw a faint smile on her lips as she led the sea chase.

'I don't suppose we can go any faster?' Malus asked.

Tanithra gestured at the nearest mast. 'Why don't you climb up there and blow into the sail? Put that hot air to some good use.'

Malus grinned. He was growing to like the rough-edged corsair.

A cry echoed from the forward mast. 'Sails on the horizon!'

Malus bent, trying to see beneath the low booms of the sails and past the bow at the distant sky. He couldn't see a thing, but Tanithra let out a shout and pointed just slightly to starboard. 'There! Two points to starboard! But I only count three ships. Where are the other six?'

'Who knows?' Malus replied. 'Four against six is much better odds than we had a moment ago!'

Tanithra altered course to intercept the oncoming druchii ships, just as the Skinriders tried another shot. The boulder spun through the air and ploughed into the water close enough to douse the stern with spray. 'More like three against six,' Tanithra said angrily. 'There's nothing we can do against those ships.'

Malus managed a gallows laugh. 'Well, we're doing a pretty good job of drawing their fire.'

Two more boulders plunged into the sea around the vagabond, one ahead and the other behind the little ship. The Skinriders were redoubling their efforts to cripple or sink the fleeing ship. One of the corsairs at the stern shouted, pointing aft. Malus turned and saw a greenish-black nimbus surrounding the lead raider, the air curdling like a bruise as the enemy sorcerer mustered his strength.

The druchii ships had seen the vagabond and her pursuers and two of the ships turned to starboard, angling to intercept the captured scout while the third held its course and continued north. If the vagabond held its course it would pass between the druchii ships and lead the Skinriders into a crossfire. Malus watched the sleek corsairs slicing through the grey water like sharks, moving swiftly even with the wind on their bow. Looking aft, Malus saw the Skinrider formation spread out to meet the new threat. Two ships angled to the south-east and one ship angled to the south-west, heading right for the druchii ships. That left three raiders bearing down on the vagabond.

Malus saw a speck of green fire appear at the bow of the closest enemy ship. The sorcerer had revealed himself at last. Urial straightened, spotting the enemy sorcerer as well and raising the axe as if to ward off a blow.

A stone flew from the bow of the lead Skinrider ship. Malus watched its trajectory and saw that this time their luck had run out. 'Take cover!' he yelled to the men at the stern. The corsairs scattered left and right as the boulder struck the aft rail in an explosion of long, needle-like splinters. The rock crashed along the deck like the hammer blows of a god, making the ship buck and quiver with each blow. It missed the wheel by less than a yard, struck the aft mast a glancing blow and plunged through a hatch cover.

Tanithra spun the wheel hard to port. 'Lyrvan!' she called to one of the corsairs nearby. 'Get below and see if that rock went through the hull! If we're holed below the waterline we're finished!'

Wounded men writhed on the deck, clutching at splinters jutting from arms, legs and torsos. One corsair kicked in his death throes, his lifeblood spreading in a vast pool from the jagged piece of wood jutting from his throat. There was a dark blur as another boulder whipped through the air over Malus's head and punched a hole in the aft sail before plunging into the sea on the other side of the ship. The Skinriders were mediocre sailors, but their aim was another matter entirely. The three Skinrider ships pursuing them hadn't altered course at all and looked as though they would cut across the vagabond's stern, heading south as the scout moved to the south-west. For the moment they were closing the range rapidly. The highborn gritted his teeth in frustration, wishing for a way to pay the enemy back, blow for blow.

Then came an angry sizzling sound that cut through the air from farther south. Malus looked back in time to see a tongue of green flame streak through the sky and plunge onto the deck of one of the pursuing ships. The sphere of dragon's fire fixed to the bolt shattered and spread a sheet of all-consuming magical fire across the bow of the raider. Hooded figures fled from the hungry flames, many of them blazing like torches. The druchii cheered and Malus joined in.

With surprising agility, the other two pursuers came about, pointing their bows directly at the vagabond and trying to pull away from the corsairs further south. Malus saw the sorcerer clearly now and watched the blazing figure raise his hands into the air. The highborn felt his heart grow cold and cried out a warning just as the sorcerer unleashed a jagged arc of lightning. The green bolt seemed to reach directly for Malus – then diffused with a sharp thunderclap against a hemisphere of reddish light just a few feet from the ship's stern.

The air hissed and crackled to Malus's right. He turned and saw Urial staring defiantly at the enemy sorcerer, his axe held high. The runes inscribed in the weapon's twin blades glowed a fiery red and the air around them shimmered with heat. For a fleeting moment the highborn felt a surge of relief – then a stone from the second raider passed overhead and struck the aft mast with a splintering crash. Iron fittings flew across the deck and ropes parted with a sharp snapping sound as the mast toppled sternwards like a felled tree. Tanithra was forced to dive across the deck as the mast crashed against the wheel. The vagabond began to heel over into a port turn, heading back towards her pursuers.

Malus raced across the pitching deck, knowing even as he did so that his efforts were in vain. The wheel was buried beneath hundreds of pounds of oaken mast and tangled in a web of frayed rigging. He looked back over his shoulder and saw the bow of the Skinrider ship pointed at them like an axe blade and drawing closer with every passing second. There was no way they were going to avoid a collision.

'Ready boarding ropes!' Malus roared. 'Brace for impact!'

The Skinrider ship struck the vagabond amidships with a thunderous boom of broken timbers, stopping the smaller craft dead in the water. Malus was hurled from his feet as the deck canted sharply to starboard, throwing him against the fallen mast. For a moment it looked as though the vagabond wouldn't recover from the blow, but then she swung heavily back upright, grating against the prow of the enemy raider. The two ships were locked together and Malus saw that for the moment there was as much shock and confusion on the enemy ship as there was on his own. The enemy sorcerer was nowhere to be seen.

Men shouted in fear and rage and the highborn struggled free of the entangling ropes, drawing his sword and raising it into the air. 'At them, sea birds!' he cried. 'Away boarders!'

The corsairs responded with a savage yell, eager to repay the Skinriders for the punishment they'd endured. Boarding ropes were cast onto the raider and the druchii clambered aboard, striking savagely at the stunned raiders. Hauclir and Urial joined Malus by the wheel. Urial moved with a surprising degree of strength and agility and his eyes were fever-bright. The axe still glowed brightly in his hand. Malus eyed him appraisingly. 'Do you think you can make it onto the enemy ship?'

'It's either that or swim!' Tanithra interjected angrily, coming around the end of the fallen mast with her sword in hand. 'Between that first stone and the collision, this old tub has sprung her seams. She's sinking fast!'

There was a blaze of greenish light on the enemy ship and men shrieked in terror and pain. 'Hauclir, get below and grab the charts!' Malus commanded. 'Tanithra, take command of the boarders. Urial and I are going to kill that sorcerer!'

Malus ran to the port side of the sinking ship with Urial close on his heels. He leapt onto the splintered rail, grabbed a quivering boarding rope and nimbly scaled his way up onto the deck of the enemy raider.

The highborn landed amid a scene of carnage. Dead raiders lay everywhere, spilling corrupted blood and vile fluids onto the deck. Arrows and stones buzzed through the air, fired by Skinriders high in the ship's twin masts. Another flare of emerald caught Malus's eye and he saw the enemy sorcerer at the waist of the ship with his back to the main mast. Crossbow bolts and broken, rusting weapons protruded from his chest and in his rage he lashed out at every man within his reach, be they friend or foe. A bolt of jagged lightning played across a knot of Skinriders and corsairs locked in fierce melee, reducing all of them to blackened bones and stinking mush.

Urial pushed in front of Malus. 'Stay behind me,' he said, his mouth twisted into a fierce grin. He made for the sorcerer at a steady, deliberate pace, holding his axe at the ready with his one good hand. Malus drew his knife with his left hand and followed warily behind him.

The press of battle around the mast all but vanished as the combatants fled in every direction to escape the sorcerer's fury. Malus watched the Skinrider straighten painfully, his eyes and open mouth blazing with green fire as he spoke words of power and surrounded himself with a nimbus of energy. The weapons piercing his body disintegrated, decaying in an instant.

Two fleeing Skinriders stumbled across Urial's path. The axe flashed in a crimson arc and the two raiders fell to the deck, their bodies ruptured and steaming. The fiery light surrounding the axe seemed to glow slightly brighter as Urial spoke in a thunderous voice.

'Servant of Corruption! Slave to the Lord of Decay! The cleansing fire of the Bloody-Handed God is upon you! Redeem yourself upon the razor edge of his mercy or I will cast your soul into the Outer Darkness for all time!'

Druchii and Skinrider alike reeled from the unearthly power seething through Urial's voice. Even Malus, who had walked at the edges of the Realm of Murder and peered across the Abyss into undreamt-of worlds, heard the voice of Khaine resounding from his mouth and was amazed.

The sorcerer reeled back as though struck, his shoulders striking the main mast hard enough to send cracks shooting along its length – then he rebounded, opening his mouth wide and vomiting a torrent of black bile at the axe-wielding druchii.

The virulent gout of acidic slime washed over Urial's wards and burst into crimson flames, spattering the deck with burning globules that ate through the oak planking in an instant. Malus crouched low, bent slightly forward as though advancing against a storm wind and let the blazing mess fly over him. They advanced steadily upon the sorcerer and the axe in Urial's hand was glowing now like a desert sun.

Words of power burst from the sorcerer's drooling lips and every surviving Skinrider within thirty paces groaned in pain and terror. Arcs of greenish fire played across their bloated bodies and they staggered awkwardly, as though no longer in full control of their limbs. Then a single, despairing wail rose from a dozen cankered throats and the raiders hurled themselves at Urial.

The devoted servant of Khaine met their frenzied charge with a joyous laugh and the slaughter began in earnest. The Skinriders struck a ward made of enchanted, razor-edged steel; the axe whirled in a hungry blur, hurling the raiders back with shorn limbs and shattered torsos, their blood burning in an offering to the Lord of Murder. But such was the mindless fury of the raiders' charge that Urial's advance faltered. Swords clashed against his armour and gangrenous hands groped for his throat for fleeting moments, each blow slowing the druchii a bit more, until he was nearly at a standstill. The sorcerer gave Urial a mocking, fiery smile and then spread his hands, rising slowly on a crackling pillar of emerald lightning.

'Oh, no you don't,' Malus said coldly, stepping around from behind Urial and hurling his knife.

The keen blade flew straight and true for the sorcerer's heart. The Skinrider's blazing eyes widened and at the last moment he brought up his hand and took the silver steel dagger through his palm. The sorcerer snarled in pain and uttered a virulent curse as he clenched his fist and dissolved the knife in a rain of glittering rust. It was only a moment's distraction, but it caused the sorcerer's ascent to falter and in that instant of hesitation Malus hurled himself at the servant of decay.

He crashed into the sorcerer's chest, surprised to find rock-hard muscle instead of the bloated, bulbous flesh of the other raiders the highborn had fought. Malus rolled onto the sorcerer and raised his blade, but the Skinrider seized him by the throat and caught his sword wrist in an iron grip. And then he began to draw Malus downward, towards his blazing eyes and fiery lips.

Tz'arkan writhed and hammered beneath Malus's ribs and the highborn looked into the twin orbs of the sorcerer's eyes and saw the face of another daemon staring back at him.

Malus felt Urial's blessing begin to sputter, like a candle that had reached the end of its wick. The pure fire scouring his skin began to wane, leaving an unhealthy fever in its wake. Black smoke rose from the possessed sorcerer's hungry mouth and Malus could feel vermin writhing within it as the vapours slid down his throat. He could feel the corruption blooming in his lungs and taking root in his guts. Thick trails of pus leaked from his eyes, oozing down his cheeks.

The sorcerer drew Malus downwards until their faces were inches apart. The highborn could feel the presence of the pestilential spirit roiling within the Skinrider. The possessed man chuckled, his true voice bubbling up from corrupted lungs. 'Look into the face of a daemon and despair,' the sorcerer said.

Malus met the sorcerer's eyes and gave a cold laugh of his own. 'As you wish,' he said. 'Show him your face, o Drinker of Worlds.'

Black ice surged through his veins, freezing the pestilence in his flesh and swelling his limbs with inhuman power. The highborn's eyes were swallowed in utter blackness, the endless cold of eternal night. His fingernails stretched into talons and his teeth sharpened into terrible fangs. The sorcerer stiffened. The daemon inside him quailed before Tz'arkan's fury and the Skinrider screamed in terror.

Malus plunged his left hand into the sorcerer's belly, his razor-edged talons tearing out the man's guts. 'Slither, slither little worm,' Malus said in a voice not his own. 'Flee down your burrows of tumour and rot, but you'll not escape me.'

His sword tumbled to the deck. The sorcerer writhed and shrieked, begging for mercy and the highborn tore the man apart. He emptied the man's chest, split his ribs and reached up his throat and into the man's skull, until at last he pulled free a long, black worm that twisted madly in his dripping hands. Malus crushed it in his fist, sensing Tz'arkan's ecstasy as the lesser daemon was hurled screaming back into the nether realms.

It was long moments before Malus realised the daemon's presence had subsided. He was sitting on the deck and a roaring noise echoed in his ears. Tendrils of frozen mist rose from his gore-splashed armour. There was little left of the sorcerer that was still recognisable.

After a moment, the roaring resolved itself as the sounds of battle and Malus remembered where he was. A thrill of terror ran down his spine as he grasped the implications of what he'd done. He looked about wildly, expecting to find Urial standing above him, his fiery axe poised to strike.

Instead he had given in to his own unearthly master, transported by the ecstasy of battle. He'd slain every Skinrider the sorcerer had thrown at him and grown drunk on bloodshed, charging further aft where the fight for the ship still raged. He'd fallen upon the ship's defenders like a thunderbolt and the corsairs, recognising the touch of the divine, had taken heart and redoubled their efforts as well. There had been no one to witness Malus's transformation save the dead and for the moment he was alone among them.

The highborn rose to his feet, feeling weary to his bones. All around the ship, the sea was red with fire. Off to starboard, the last of the three ships that had chased after the vagabond now drifted with the wind, its deck a raging inferno. A trio of black ships slipped past the blazing hulk, gliding effortlessly south before turning back upwind. Farther off to starboard the *Harrier* cruised north, battered but unbowed. The raider that had turned her way at the start of the battle was now a blazing pyre sinking below the waves.

Off to port the battle had not gone so well. The *Black Razor* drifted in a burning embrace with a Skinrider ship – one vessel had boarded the other and in the furious battle that followed both ships had caught fire and no one had been able to extinguish the flames. The *Sea Dragon* was sinking slowly, the waves lapping over her rails as the sea poured through the jagged holes punched through her hull. But her killer had little time to savour her victory. The last Skinrider ship was now well to the south, trailing burning rigging and a broken mast and dogged by three more druchii corsairs that harried her like wolves.

Bruglir had never been outnumbered, Malus realised. He'd divided his force into three squadrons and sent two of them off to east and west, just over the horizon. When the battle had begun he'd signalled them and they'd swept down on the Skinriders' flanks, closing on them like a set of jaws.

The sounds of battle at the stern suddenly subsided. Malus turned and saw the Skinrider captain drop his sword and fall to his knees before Tanithra – evidently the blazing visage of Urial and his axe had been enough to force an uncharacteristic surrender. Tanithra let out a shout of joy and struck the man's head from his shoulders and the crew let out a long cry of victory.

The cries of celebration were so loud that Malus almost didn't hear the thin wail coming from the bow. The highborn frowned. That sounds strangely familiar, he thought. Then he remembered: Hauclir!

Malus rushed to the bow. The vagabond was gone, swallowed by the hungry waves. The highborn peered over the side and saw the retainer hanging from a boarding rope, clutching bundles of soggy charts. Malus let out a startled shout and hauled on the rope for all he was worth, wishing he still had a little of the daemon's strength left in him.

Long minutes later Hauclir rolled over the rail. Water ran from his pale face and hair and poured in a flood from beneath the weight of his heavy armour. He still held the charts in a death grip and the look he gave Malus was both insubordinate and horrified at the same time.

'The Dark Mother forbid,' Hauclir said shakily, 'but if we're ever on another sinking ship and something's been left below, you can damned well go get it yourself, my lord!'

Chapter Nineteen
ISLAND OF THE LOST

'THERE IT IS,' Bruglir declared, tapping a point on the yellowed parchment map with one gauntleted hand. 'That's the Isle of Morhaut.'

Malus folded his arms beneath the heavy cloak he wore, fighting against another bout of shivering. The icy touch of the daemon had yet to lapse, even though the battle on the Skinrider ship was more than four hours past. It was close to midday and the heaving northern sea gleamed like polished steel beneath diffuse, pale sunlight. The druchii corsairs were going about barefoot and shirtless, basking like lizards beneath the welcome heat, but Malus still felt frozen to the core. He'd told Tanithra and the rest that he'd been soaked fishing Hauclir from the water and the winter cloak had merited only passing interest from Bruglir and Urial. The highborn leaned over the captain's table, squinting at the mosaic of finely-scrawled lines and bizarre notations on the Skinriders' map. He'd seen sorcerer's tomes that were clearer and simpler to decipher. 'How can you be so certain? Everything is in some kind of pidgin language.'

'Actually it's Norse,' Bruglir answered, 'Look here.' His finger retreated from the tiny mark representing the island and pointed to eight larger islands scattered across the approaches to the northern sea. 'Three of these islands are well-known as being major Skinrider camps and we can assume that the other five are significant outposts as well. You'll notice that all of them have clearly defined courses laid out that connect them to one another.' His fingers traced the long, curving lines that ran from one rocky outline to the next, each one annotated in strange runic script. 'Now, what else do these islands all have in common?'

Malus studied the map. When Bruglir pointed it out, the answer leapt from the jumble of lines and runes. 'They all have a course plotted to a centrally-located island that's smaller than all the rest.'

The captain nodded. 'Exactly. This central island is their headquarters. Nothing else makes sense.' He reached over and leafed through a sheaf of druchii charts piled on a nearby desktop, finally settling on one and laying it out. The thin vellum rested on the Skinrider chart and showed the markings beneath, creating a composite picture of the same area. 'See how the island doesn't even appear on our charts?' Bruglir smiled cruelly. 'This is the secret they fought so hard to try and protect. Now we know where their heart lies – and we can tear it out and hold it up to their disbelieving faces!'

Malus gritted his teeth against another wave of trembling and surveyed the other druchii sharing the cabin. Tanithra nodded to herself as she studied the map, her expression thoughtful. Urial the Forsaken stood rigidly erect, his eyes bright and fierce. Clearly the ecstasy of battle still sang in his veins and the look he gave his older brother nearly amounted to an outright challenge. The highborn wondered if Urial had ever fought in a true battle before today. Clearly the taste was to his liking. Malus considered the changes that had come over Yasmir since their arrival on the *Harrier* and wondered what this would mean for his plans. Very soon now he was going to have to act and he couldn't afford to have Urial or anyone else doing something unpredictable.

The battle with the Skinriders had gone on for another hour after Tanithra and her men had captured the raider. Three of the enemy ships were totally destroyed, their hulls savaged by the sorcerous fire of the dragon flame bolts. Of the three remaining, two were stripped of everything useful and then set adrift with blazing pitch scattered across their decks, as there wasn't enough spare crew to man them. The *Bloodied Knife* was given to the flames as well – her captain and nearly all of the crew were dead and her rigging all but completely destroyed during the fight. The majority of the crew of the *Sea Dragon* had been lost as well, freezing to death in the cold waters before another ship could arrive to rescue them. That just left the ship Tanithra had taken – and clearly expected to keep, judging by her pointed requests to Bruglir for more crewmen and supplies.

Once the battle had concluded the *Harrier* had pulled alongside the captured raider. Malus and Urial had gone aboard with the charts and the highborn had sent

Hauclir to dry himself out and learn what had transpired in their absence. Now the remainder of the fleet was tacking northward, working slowly but surely towards the Island of Morhaut.

'All right,' Malus said. 'It appears that everyone agrees with your conclusions, captain. What next?'

Bruglir shrugged. 'Providing we encounter no other Skinriders on the way we'll reach the island within the week,' he said. 'After that, it's up to Urial to get us past the island's defences – if he's capable.'

Urial stiffened further, a flush rising on his pale cheeks. 'Oh, I'm capable of many things, brother,' he said with surprising venom. 'You're going to learn that very soon indeed.'

Malus cleared his throat in the sudden silence. 'What do you know of the island's defences, Urial?'

For a moment Urial and Bruglir continued to lock eyes over the spread charts. Finally Urial turned away. 'There are few concrete details, unfortunately,' he said to Malus. 'The libraries at Hag Graef contain few references to the island at all, but I was able to unearth some information about Eradorius, the sorcerer who resided there and supposedly created the defences thousands of years ago.' Urial's brass-coloured eyes shone like heated coins. 'It appears that Eradorius was a servant of Chaos during the years of the First War – a conqueror and a master of arcane lore who was a terrible foe of Aenarion and his twisted kin, until he fled from his castle of iron and bone and took refuge on a distant island in the northern sea.'

Malus felt his mouth go dry. 'Fled, you say?'

'So it would appear. Most likely his lieutenants turned on him, coveting his wealth and power,' Urial replied.

'Whatever it was that Eradorius feared, he devoted all his remaining power to try and escape it. According to legend he laid many sorcerous wards around the Isle of Morhaut, meant to destroy anyone foolish enough to approach it.'

Tanithra frowned. 'Wards?' she said with a grimace, as though disliking the taste of the word. 'Like what? Storms of blood and flocks of daemons?'

Urial chuckled. 'No. Such defences require great power to maintain and wouldn't have survived without regular infusions of power. No, these wards were more subtle, twisting an intruder's perceptions so that they more than likely wouldn't even notice the island at all.'

'And if they did?'

'Then they would become forever lost.'

Tanithra shook her head. 'I don't understand.'

The former acolyte spread his hands. 'That was all the legends said. I will know more once I've had a chance to study the wards first-hand.'

'We will use the captured raider,' Bruglir said. 'Once Urial has found his way through the defences we'll take the rest of the fleet in.'

'So does that mean I'll get the crewmen I need?' Tanithra asked.

Bruglir took a deep breath and straightened to his full height, his head brushing the beams overhead. 'After the last battle the fleet has few sailors to spare,' he said carefully. 'I don't want to leave our ships undermanned with another major battle looming.'

'You're leaving one dangerously undermanned right now,' Tanithra shot back.

'I have no intention of taking the raider into battle,' Bruglir replied. 'Once we've found the way past the island's wards and have a sense of what lies beyond, we'll scuttle the ship. It has no value to me as a prize.'

Tanithra's jaw dropped. Her dark eye flashed with anger. 'You're talking about *my ship*, captain. I won her with blood and steel and no one decides to scuttle her but me.'

'You had a ship, Tani and you lost her in the battle,' Bruglir answered coldly. 'And every captain on every ship in this fleet serves at my pleasure. I'll need you back here on the *Harrier* when the battle begins in earnest.'

Malus gauged the reactions of the two corsairs carefully. He cleared his throat. 'Brother, you are being unfair to your first officer. She handled the vagabond with great skill and she led her crew to victory over an enemy more than twice her size. Even I know that the law of the sea dictates her claim to the prize.' He paused for effect. 'If this is about Yasmir–'

'This is about my command of this fleet,' Bruglir snapped. 'Something that your precious writ has no influence on whatsoever. This meeting is concluded,' Bruglir said coldly, then bent to the charts before him. 'We will reach the Isle of Morhaut in six days. Now get out.'

Malus turned on his heel, concealing a fleeting look of amusement. He reached for the cabin door but Tanithra swept past like a fast-moving thunderhead, all but shouldering him aside as she stomped down the passageway. Hauclir, waiting just beyond the door, barely leapt out of her path in time.

Urial followed close on Malus's heels, pulling the door closed behind him. 'Is this your plan?' he asked the highborn in a harsh whisper. 'Provoke Tanithra to murder?'

Malus cast a glare at Urial over his shoulder. 'I'm sure I don't know what you're talking about, brother,' he hissed. 'After all, this is a ship under weigh and even *discussing* what you're talking about is grounds for public vivisection.'

But the former acolyte was unfazed by the thinly veiled warning. He stepped close to Malus, his voice dropping into a lower but no less intense register. 'She won't kill him,' Urial whispered. 'The other captains would tear her apart in an instant. I had expected you to take more of a direct hand in this.'

Malus turned until the two were practically nose to nose. 'Why, so the captains can tear me apart instead?' The highborn looked Urial up and down. 'You have grown a bit overbold since we took that raider, brother. If you're so keen for Bruglir's blood, why not challenge him yourself?' He nodded at the cabin door. 'You looked as though you were working up to it back there. What's preventing you?'

Urial stepped back, a snarl twisting his features, but if he'd intended an intemperate reply he appeared to master himself at the last moment and his face settled into a stolid mask. 'I merely wish to remind you of your obligation,' he said. 'I might decide to call your debt due before we reach the Isle.'

'Don't be stupid, brother,' Malus hissed. 'Like it or not, we will need Bruglir to defeat the Skinriders. You've suffered his existence your whole life; can you not wait a few days more?'

'My patience is limitless,' Urial said flatly. 'My trust, however, is not. Think on that, Malus,' he said, pushing past the highborn and continuing down the passageway.

The highborn watched his brother turn a corner and disappear from sight, shaking his head in disgust. 'And to think I feared them once upon a time,' he muttered. 'Such artless fools!'

Hauclir shrugged. 'On the other hand, even the wiliest rat dies if you stamp on him hard enough.'

'Are you calling me a rat?'

'Not at all sir,' the former guard captain deadpanned. 'Just saying there's a lot of big boots stamping around on this ship, that's all.'

'Have a care one doesn't land on your head.'

'It occupies much of my waking moments, my lord.'

The highborn failed to smother a sigh of exasperation. 'Tell me you've spent the remainder of your precious time serving my interests.'

'It wounds me to hear you say such a thing my lord,' Hauclir replied archly. 'Of course I have.'

'Then what transpired while we were away from the ship?'

The retainer fell in alongside Malus as they headed for the chart room. 'Yasmir never left her quarters, though there are rumours that she has collected the crew's offerings into a sort of shrine in her cabin. Urial's men watched her quarters day and night.'

Malus nodded. 'So that's why he left them behind. Interesting. What were their orders?'

Hauclir snorted. 'Who knows? Perhaps they were watching to see if she'd show herself. They didn't try to enter her room, nor did they interfere with the crew's offerings.' Hauclir glanced about, his voice dropping into a near-inaudible whisper. 'They also did nothing when Bruglir visited her in the dead of night.'

The highborn smiled. 'So the great captain is being cautious. And how did the visit go?'

The retainer shrugged. 'There weren't any loud shouts and Bruglir left with the same number of limbs he arrived with. Make of that what you will.'

'How do you know of this?'

'One of the hands caught sight of the captain leaving Yasmir's quarters shortly after midnight. Everyone down in the ship's mess is talking about it.'

Malus nodded thoughtfully. 'Then I believe an agreement has been reached. That's excellent news.'

Hauclir's brow furrowed in consternation. 'It is?'

'Oh, yes. That fits my plan perfectly.' They had reached the highborn's cramped quarters. Malus pushed the door open and paused in the doorway. 'Now all we must do is reach the island and penetrate its wards and everything will be in place.'

'I see, my lord,' though from the expression on Hauclir's face it was clear that he did not. 'What shall I do in the meantime?'

'Take a bath. You smell like dead fish,' Malus answered, closing the door in the retainer's face.

THE WIND WAS brisk off the port bow, whistling through the rigging and slowing the captured raider to a near crawl as she approached the spot where the Isle of Morhaut was believed to be. Malus stood close by the ship's wheel, dividing his attention between scanning the northern horizon and watching Urial's preparations just a few feet away.

Urial knelt close to the deck, a brass bowl in one hand and a rune-carved brush in the other. The wind blew thin streamers of congealing blood from the surface of the bowl, painting livid streaks in his hair, but Urial paid it no mind, absorbed in the task at hand. He had painted a small circle on the planks with his brush and now turned slowly in place, decorating the inner arc of the figure with complicated sigils. Tanithra stood at the wheel, her expression savage and brooding.

She had returned to the captured ship immediately after the conversation with Bruglir, now almost six days past and the great captain had not summoned her back since. In that time Hauclir reported that Bruglir had visited his sister twice more, both times in the dead of night. Once, there were sounds of what might have been a struggle, but what actually happened in the cabin was anyone's guess. Malus believed that Bruglir was trying to make amends, having offered to kill Tanithra at the earliest available moment in order to redeem himself. Urial haunted her quarters like a wraith, watching the comings and goings of Bruglir with something akin to righteous indignation but taking no action of his own. At this point Malus felt that the only reason Urial hadn't sent his men to murder Bruglir in his sleep was that he needed to pin the captain's death on Malus in order to gain Yasmir's affection. The highborn wondered how much longer Urial's patience would hold out.

Malus had busied himself in the intervening days by drinking up every bit of liquor to be had on Bruglir's ship. Despite Hauclir's protestations each and every night that he'd scrounged up the very last of the ship's spirits, somehow Malus's combination of wit and malicious threats brought the retainer to his door the following evening with a new bottle in hand. As much as the highborn hated to admit it, he was beginning to find the former guard captain indispensable.

He needed to drink to keep the dreadful chill of the daemon's influence at bay. Though not as strong as it had been in the wake of the sea battle a week ago, it was still painfully evident, enough for Malus to fear that he'd finally crossed some threshold into the daemon's clutches that there would be no coming back from. That thought was bad enough to keep him awake at night; worse still was the fact that he was having more and more strange dreams, each one more intense and terrifying than the one before.

There was no rhyme or reason to them, as though they were images painted on a hundred different cards and then tossed to the wind, fluttering and falling in chaotic patterns that hinted at meaning but ultimately revealed nothing.

Corridors and stairways, he thought. Doors opening onto the same rooms, over and over again. It was as though it was the same scene replaying itself endlessly in his mind. The only difference was the footfalls. Each night they seemed to get a little closer. Huge, thundering footfalls, like the tread of a giant. And he knew, with the omniscience of the dreamer, that when those footfalls finally reached him, he was going to die. It was only a matter of time.

'What if they are not dreams,' Tz'arkan said. 'What if you see the future, like drowning in the bilges on the pirate ship?'

'That cannot be,' he hissed. 'These sights are pure madness. Nothing in this world can be so twisted and malign.'

'Even so, little druchii. Even so.'

'Be silent! Do you hear me? Be silent!'

Malus felt eyes watching him. He looked up and saw Tanithra studying him warily.

The daemon chuckled. 'She thinks you mad, Darkblade.'

'And why not?' Malus muttered. 'She's probably right.'

His work complete, Urial set the brush aside and straightened, holding the bowl with both hands. 'Furl all the sail you can and still make headway,' he told Tanithra. 'Once we begin threading the maze we will need to move slowly and deliberately.'

'With this wind off the bow we'll have to struggle to make headway at all,' she said, never taking her eyes from the horizon.

But Urial shook his head. 'If my theories are correct, it won't be the wind propelling us inside the maze.'

At that, Tanithra turned, but if she was expecting a more detailed explanation, she was to be disappointed. Urial had already bowed his head over the bowl and was muttering a long, breathless chant. Once again, Malus looked to the north, but the horizon seemed like an empty plain of featureless slate. He looked back astern and in the far distance he could still spy the black sails of Bruglir's fleet. The corsairs would stand well out to sea while the captured ship attempted to penetrate the island's wards.

The chanting was growing louder. Or rather, it was making its presence felt more intensely – he couldn't hear an increase in volume, but the air was trembling with each syllable. He could feel each ripple against his skin, like tiny wavelets stirred by an invisible hand. They washed over him and radiated away from the ship in ever-widening circles, reaching to the horizon.

Something was happening ahead of them, perhaps a mile off the bow. There was a mist gathering in the air, slowly spreading to the east and west like an unfolding screen.

Urial straightened, raising the bowl to the sky as if making an offering to the divine. His head tilted back and he poured the bowl of blood onto his upturned face. Crimson soaked into his white hair and pooled in his open eyes and mouth. The blood steamed as though freshly spilled, rising in curling tendrils from his eye sockets. When he looked down and smiled, his eyes were orbs of purest red, shining with power.

'I can sense it out there,' he said, his voice sounding clear but somehow diminished, as though he spoke from a great distance. 'It is like an unravelling of the world. Tanithra, do exactly as I say, without the slightest hesitation and all will be well. Now, take in your sails. We will be at the threshold in just a few moments.'

'All hands! Furl sail!' Tanithra cried at the men in the rigging. 'Smartly now, sea birds, if you value your lives!'

The mist was thickening, filling the sky ahead of them. It had no discernible shape – just a vast, shifting mass of curdled air, blown by a wind not of this earth. The last sails were brought in and Malus could feel the ship slowing in the water as she came up against the windborne waves. She rose on the white-capped swell and then as she nosed over the crest Malus could feel the ship gather speed, as though she were a wagon at the top of a high hill. He felt his guts come unmoored as the ship plummeted down, down and down, falling forever and then the mist closed over them, blotting out the sun.

'Three points to starboard!' Urial cried. 'Steady! Steady! Now two points to port! Quickly now!'

Malus could see nothing. The air shrieked and whistled, but he felt no wind against his face. The ship twisted and yawned, first one way and then another, as though she were caught upon four different seas at once.

To the highborn's horror, the world began to waver about the edges, as though he stood upon the verge of another waking vision. He fought against it with all the rage that was left to him and prayed to the Dark Mother that it would be enough.

Someone screamed. Urial continued to shout course changes to Tanithra. Malus looked over and saw the hard-bitten corsair bent almost double, her one eye tightly shut even though they were wrapped in shadow. Yet her hands still plied the wheel, driving the ship through its countless gyrations as it fought a storm unlike any other.

Suddenly, the wind dropped to a muted growl and Malus heard the pure tone of a ship's bell echoing out of the mist. Through the swirling mists to port the highborn thought he saw the rough outline of a railing, then a ship's deck strewn with debris and stricken with age. Boards were warped and covered with mould and fittings were pitted with rust and grime. And yet Malus saw scrawny shapes scrambling along the deck, clad only in tattered rags and sniffing the air like animals. One turned towards the highborn and he saw the figure point and throw back his head to let loose a long, plaintive wail bereft of sanity or hope. Before he could see more the raider abruptly turned to starboard and the ragged figure was swallowed by the mist.

He could hear more cries now, coming from lookouts at the bow and high up in the masts – he shivered at the thought of men high above the deck, surrounded on all sides by the unearthly smoke.

'Ten points to port!' Urial said, his voice sounding even fainter than before. Something made Malus look in that direction – a premonition perhaps, or the unseen manipulations of another waking vision – and abruptly saw a wide-beamed shadow looming from the mist, heading directly at them! If they didn't turn the ship would strike them on the beam and break them in half.

'Hard to starboard!' Malus cried. 'Put her hard over or we're lost!'

'NO!' Urial roared. 'Steady as you go.'

The ship loomed before Malus, pointed at them like a dagger aimed for his heart. 'Brace for impact!' he cried, flinging up his hands in a vain attempt to ward off the blow he knew to be coming.

And yet, nothing happened.

Malus lowered his arms and his mouth gaped in horror. The ship was passing *through* them, like an apparition, yet it looked as solid as the one he was standing on.

Then Malus realised that he recognised the grim figures watching him as the ship passed by.

It was *their* ship.

Malus saw a pale, grim-faced Hauclir watching him stonily from the apparition's bow. Other crewmen became apparent, each one grim as death as the ships passed one another. He saw Tanithra, still bent before the wheel and blind to the madness surrounding her. When he saw the gaunt, pale-faced apparition at Tanithra's side, Malus started as though stung.

Is that what others see when they look at me, he thought? He watched the ghostly version of himself recede into the distance until the ship was once more swallowed by the mist. Then the deck he was on plummeted once more before coming to a bone-jarring halt. The highborn staggered, his heart in his throat at the fear that he would be thrown about like a cask of ale and tossed overboard into the ghostly storm. And then he realised that the moaning was gone and the mist receding like early morning fog.

They were sailing across dark water beneath a dark sky and before them an island reared up from the water like the ruins of a drowned kingdom. The isle's steep cliffs were piled with the broken debris of hundreds of years of lost ships. Directly ahead of the raider lay a sheltered cove with long stone sea walls like two curving arms, their surfaces studded with twin towers that jutted into the sky like broken teeth. The shoreline of the cove was piled with the jumbled detritus of countless shipwrecks and upon the dark and refuse-strewn waters rode almost a dozen ships at anchor – Skinrider ships, some larger and far more powerful than the captured vessel the druchii had arrived in. High on the cliffs overlooking the cove rose a ruined citadel, crumbled and broken by the weight of centuries and the ceaseless gnawing of the sea wind. Pale fires burned in the citadel's windows and the arrow slits of the malevolent towers on the sea walls. Everywhere lay the crushing pall of enormous age, as though this were a place the rest of the world had forgotten long, long ago.

They had reached the Isle of Morhaut.

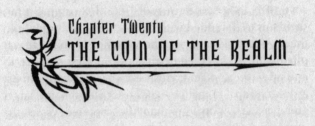

Chapter Twenty
THE COIN OF THE REALM

THE RAIDER DRIFTED from the bank of mist, riding uneasily on choppy grey waves. A breath of wind, reeking of rotting bone and wet mould, brushed Malus's face and pulled at the furled sails high above.

No one spoke. Even the sound of the water slapping at the hull was muted somehow – it was as though everything lay buried beneath an invisible mantle of incalculable age. Finally, it was Malus who broke the silence. 'We should lower some sail and learn what we can before returning to the fleet.'

Tanithra didn't seem to hear him at first. She turned to look at him, moving as though in a dream. 'Why is the sky dark? The sun was shining when we went into the fog.'

'It's this place,' Urial said. 'It… is elsewhere. A place that is no place, teased from the fabric of physicality like a thread pulled from a tapestry.'

The corsair shook her head savagely. 'Stop it! You're making no sense!'

Malus managed a quiet, bitter laugh. 'Such are the ways of sorcery, Tanithra. I like it no better than you. Focus instead on what you *do* understand. Like those towers yonder,' he pointed to the citadels rising from the sea walls, 'and the ships in the cove. What are we facing here?'

Tanithra gave him an uncertain look, but turned her attention to the island just a few miles away. 'We'll have to get closer,' she said after a moment. 'At least with all this darkness we should be able to make a fairly close run in towards the cove and then head back into the mist without raising any alarms.' She snapped out a series of orders to the men in the rigging. Moments later the mainsails were unfurled and the raider gathered headway, running before a mild wind that now blew from the south – if such a direction had any meaning in a place like this.

Malus turned to Urial. 'Can you sense any other wards between us and the island?'

Urial shook his head. His eyes still glistened red. 'No. But… it is difficult to be certain. The very air here seethes with power. A skilled sorcerer can conceal much beneath such a shroud.'

The highborn sighed. 'I shouldn't have asked.'

The former acolyte shrugged. 'For what it is worth, the sorcerer we fought on this very ship wasn't particularly skilled – merely a receptacle of a great deal of power. I don't think the Skinriders are any better sorcerers than they are sailors.' He turned about, taking in the dark vista around him. 'They are merely skulking in the ruins of a much greater power.'

'Eradorius, you mean.'

Urial nodded. 'He was one of the mightiest sorcerers in the time of Aenarion.' He paused as his eyes fell upon the ruined tower. 'I wonder what he was fleeing from?'

'That was millennia ago. Does it matter?'

Malus's half-brother fixed him with a bloody stare. 'Time is a river, Malus, remember that.'

'You highborn and your riddle games,' Tanithra growled, shaking her head. 'If I were you, I'd be more concerned about the twelve ships anchored in the cove.' She surveyed the distant hulls with an experienced eye. 'The smallest of them is as big as *Harrier*. Big Tilean and Empire warships, not the clapped-out scows we've been facing. I'd wager these are the Skinrider chieftain's prize ships, the fist he uses to keep his men – and the other North Sea raiders – in line.'

Malus frowned. 'Can we outrun them?'

Tanithra nodded. 'Oh, yes. We can sail circles around them, even in this awkward beast.' She patted the wheel almost affectionately. 'But we can't outfight them on the open sea.'

The highborn considered this and shrugged. 'Then we catch them at anchor and burn them. A swift raid into the anchorage with Bruglir's ships and a dozen dragon fire bolts and the Skinriders are broken.'

Tanithra chuckled coldly. 'A flawless strategy, Admiral – but they've anticipated this.' She pointed towards the towers rising from the sea walls. 'If you look closely you can see that those citadels have stone throwers situated to fire on the approaches to the anchorage, all the way up to the gap between the sea walls themselves. That's plunging fire, lobbing stones in an easy arc right down onto a ship's deck. A skilled crew could hole a ship in minutes and we know that the bastards are good shots, if nothing else.'

Malus shook his head in consternation. 'Then we put on all the sail we have and give them as little opportunity to fire at us as possible. We can be in and out of their reach again in minutes. You said yourself that stone throwers only cover up to the entrance of the cove.'

The corsair grinned mirthlessly. 'That's right. Now why do you suppose they would do that?'

The highborn considered the sea wall for a moment, trying to put himself in the minds of the raiders tasked with defending the cove. 'Because… they don't *need* to fire past that point.'

Her grin widened. 'Just so.' She pointed to the tower on the left. 'Look closely near the base of the tower.'

Malus did, but it was Urial who spotted it first. 'There's a chain leading from the tower into the water behind the sea wall.'

'That's right. A harbour chain, stretching across the mouth of the cove from one tower to another. If a ship hits that she'll be stopped dead in the water, helpless in the shadow of those two towers while the crew tries to turn her around and escape.' She looked back towards the stern. 'And with the wind coming up from the south, a ship would actually be *pushed* against the chain, making their job that much harder.' Tanithra nodded sagely. 'It's a tactic the Bretonnians perfected after they got tired of us raiding their seaports and the Skinriders have put it to good use here.'

'All right. How do we drop the chain?' Malus asked.

Tanithra shook her head. 'I expect the tower guards only allow in ships that they recognise. We can't break the chain from out here. We'd have to get into one of the citadels and lower it from there.'

Malus studied the towers at length, tapping meditatively at his chin. Plans swirled in his head as he considered the problem. He began to discern a way to thread them all together and a slow smile spread across his face as the pieces fell into place. 'Then that's exactly what we'll do,' he said. 'Turn us around. I think we've seen enough.'

Urial studied Malus warily. 'You have a plan, then?'

'Dear brother, I *always* have a plan.'

BRUGLIR FOLDED HIS arms and leaned back in his chair. 'That's the stupidest plan I've ever heard.'

Malus was unfazed. 'We don't have to fool them, brother. Just *tempt* them and even then only for a short time.'

The captain frowned. 'But Karond Kar?'

'Our ships fight the Skinriders every summer as they return to Naggaroth. They wait for us to head back with full holds and then try to steal our plunder. And what do they take? Gold? Gems? No. They take the slaves and as many of the crew as they can. Now think of Karond Kar and how many slaves pass through there every month. Thousands, all shackled and ready to transport.' Malus took a sip of wine from one of the captain's cups. 'The challenge will be in convincing them we aren't trying to attack them long enough for them to listen to our ruse.'

Bruglir's fierce glower swept over Malus, Urial and Tanithra in turn, as though he believed he was being made the victim of some kind of elaborate joke. 'So while we're talking to their leader, a landing party slips off the ship, somehow enters one of the sea wall towers and lowers the chain just in time for our fleet to attack the anchored ships.'

The captain thought it over once again and once again shook his head. 'A great deal can go wrong.'

'There is a certain element of risk in every daring plan,' Malus replied. 'Don't worry about what might go wrong – we'll be working to ensure that doesn't happen. Consider instead what will occur if things go *right*. The Skinriders will be broken, their treasure houses will be ours and you will return to Hag Graef as a hero. A *very wealthy* hero, I might add. You could buy a ship for each and every man in the fleet – every woman, too, for that matter,' he added, nodding towards Tanithra.

The druchii captain continued to brood, tapping at the table with a gloved finger. Finally he sighed. 'How would we co-ordinate our actions? The fleet will have to come in effectively blind.'

Malus looked to Tanithra. They had discussed this at length on the way back to the rendezvous. 'After we pass through the mist, the fleet waits two hours before starting its own passage. We will have men waiting in one of the towers by that point, ready to drop the chain.'

Bruglir thought it over. 'And if the Skinrider chieftain doesn't believe your story?'

The highborn shrugged. 'It doesn't matter, ultimately. By that point the fleet would be on the way and our men in place in the tower. Those of us brought before the chieftain will just have to put up a stiff fight and try to hold out until help arrives.'

'Your chances would be almost non-existent.'

Malus nodded. 'It's a risk I am willing to take.'

Bruglir rose to his feet, hands clasped behind his back. 'And it's a risk you've no compunction demanding of the rest of us, too.' He spread his hands. 'It ultimately doesn't matter what I think. Your writ trumps my authority in this case.' He sighed. 'Very well, Malus. We'll follow the plan. But the Dragons take you if it fails.'

Suddenly Tanithra shot to her feet. 'There's one more thing,' she said. 'If I lead the ship into the harbour and bring down that chain, I'll have something in return,' she said, the words coming out in a rush. 'I'll have command of the captured ship. I'll have bought it with blood twice over by that point. And I'll not ask for any extra hands. I'll sail her back to Clar Karond and hire my own sailors–'

Bruglir cut her off with a sweep of his hand. 'You won't be leading the raider in, Tani. You'll lead the landing party, but I'll have overall command.'

'*You?*' Tanithra exclaimed.

'Of course,' the captain snapped. 'The survival of the entire fleet will depend on the outcome of this raid. Did you think for a moment I wouldn't take a personal hand in its execution? You'll have the task of dropping the chain while Malus and I distract the pirate chieftain.'

Tanithra's face went pale. When she spoke, her voice trembled. 'You… you promised me a command. Years ago, during your hakseer-cruise. And I've served you faithfully. I let you dally onshore with that sister of yours and never said a thing–'

'The business of the highborn isn't of any concern to you,' Bruglir said coldly. 'And don't presume to remind me of my obligations. You'll get your command. Perhaps once we put in at Clar Karond. You heard Malus. There will be gold aplenty then.'

Tanithra started to reply, her eye glittering with rage, but abruptly she reined herself in. She took a deep breath and stilled her trembling hands. 'Yes, captain. Of course. A little longer then.' The corsair stood straight, her head high. 'Will that be all?'

Bruglir studied her for a moment, a flicker of concern in his eyes. 'Yes. I believe so. We will make preparations tonight, then I'll transfer to the raider at dawn and we will set the plan in motion.'

Malus rose to his feet. 'Of course, brother. Until then.'

They filed from the captain's cabin. Tanithra brought up the rear, walking slowly and carefully, as though she'd lost her sea legs since entering the room. Outside the cabin Urial turned and gave Malus a meaningful glance: the endgame approaches, his brass-coloured eyes said. Your move.

The highborn merely nodded and Urial walked away.

Hauclir straightened from his now-habitual spot against the bulkhead, his expression curious. Malus shook his head fractionally then walked away without a word, vanishing around a nearby corner. That left just Malus and Tanithra. When Malus turned to look at her, he was secretly delighted to see the stricken expression on her face.

'Are you about to return to the raider?' Malus asked, feigning casual interest.

Tanithra frowned, looking at Malus as though he'd suddenly grown out of the deck. Her expression hardened. 'What else? I have no intention of staying here.'

Malus smiled. 'Then I'll go over with you – if you'll allow me to get some things from my cabin first?'

A look of weary disgust played across her scarred features, but Tanithra managed a shrug. 'As you wish,' she said, motioning him to lead on.

Malus made his way down the cramped corridors to the chart room, offering no other comment until he'd pushed open the door and stepped inside. He reached deep inside a chart bin and held up the last bottle of rum. The highborn drew out the cork with his teeth and offered the bottle to Tanithra, who stood out in the corridor with her arms folded tightly against her chest. 'It would appear that Bruglir has decided to redeem himself in his sister's eyes,' he said quietly.

Tanithra shot Malus an angry glare, but after a moment she stepped inside and took the proffered bottle. 'He wouldn't have had to make the choice in the first place had you not brought her aboard. She'd *never* set foot on the *Harrier* before this.'

'How was I to know? It's not as though Bruglir spoke of you at the Hag. Believe me, had I known about you and my brother I would have left Yasmir at home.' He watched the corsair take a long pull of the fiery liquid and reached for the bottle himself. 'Of course, this also provides you with a unique opportunity.'

Tanithra snorted in disgust. 'Opportunity?'

'Oh, yes,' Malus assured her, taking a drink of his own. 'You now have a chance to split them apart for good.'

'I could split her easily enough on the edge of my sword, but that will just poison Bruglir against me,' she said bitterly.

'Then have Bruglir do the poisoning instead of you.'

Tanithra frowned. 'I'm not in the mood for more of your riddles, highborn.'

Malus passed back the bottle. 'Let me explain. What if we were to make Yasmir think that Bruglir was going to betray her?'

The corsair's eyebrow rose. 'We?'

Malus paused. 'Of course. I don't have any interest in seeing the two of them together any more than you do. So why not work together? Consider this,' he said, forestalling her reply. 'What if Yasmir was to believe that Bruglir was going to sacrifice her to the Skinriders?'

Tanithra paused, the bottle halfway to her lips. 'Why in the Dark Mother's name would she think such a thing?'

'Because we are going to seize her in the dead of night, smuggle her onto the raider and make her think it was Bruglir's idea,' he replied. 'We'll let her overhear that Bruglir plans to give her to the Skinriders in order to buy his way into their confidence.'

'What then?'

Malus shrugged. 'You'll be remaining behind with the landing party while the rest of us go and speak to the pirate chieftain. Turn her over to the pirates if you want. Once the attack begins, they'll throw her in a cell and she'll be rescued later, but by then the seeds of hatred will be sown in her heart.'

'She'll try to kill him.'

The highborn nodded. 'And Bruglir will be forced to slay her with his own hand. A rather neat conclusion and a fitting way to punish him for his fecklessness.'

Tanithra said nothing, her expression thoughtful. She took another drink from the bottle. 'Do you really think we could do such a thing?'

'Of course.' Malus stepped around her and closed the cabin door. 'Return to the raider. I'll stay behind and have my man keep watch on her cabin. Bruglir will likely visit her tonight, so return to the *Harrier* with a handful of trusted men just past the hour of the wolf. Once Bruglir's gone back to his quarters we'll make our move.'

Tanithra regarded him in silence. 'You know, I never spent much time in the Six Cities. I was born on a ship off the coast of Lustria and I can count on one hand the number of times I've spent more than a week ashore. My father was once a captain himself. He told me that betrayal is the coin of the realm in Naggaroth. Until just now I never knew what he was trying to tell me.'

She passed the bottle back to Malus. 'Tell me more.'

THE SHIP ROCKED gently in calm seas, silent at last after many hours of frenzied preparation. Malus reclined on his makeshift bed, the Tome of Ak'zhaal open in his lap. The hour of the wolf was close at hand; from where he sat he could glance through the tiny porthole and track the progress of the twin moons through the night sky. He was far too tense to sleep and thanked the Dark Mother for it.

Malus turned a page of the book with a gloved fingertip. He waited in black robes and an unadorned kheitan that belonged to Hauclir, as well as a shirt of fine mail of the type favoured by the corsairs aboard ship. A glass of watered wine rested on a sheaf of maps on a nearby shelf.

On a whim he'd taken the book from his bag as a way to pass the time. He turned the pages, puzzling over the strange diagrams and sketches, but after a few hours he found that he could understand the spidery script. He wondered if that was a reflection on how deep the daemon's taint ran in him, but feared to speculate further.

His finger traced the drawing of a square stone, its surface inscribed with a complicated sigil. The words beneath it were foreign to him, yet they gave up their secrets as his eyes passed over them.

Stone upon stone Eradorius built his tower, but its foundations he laid on darkness eternal, where there are no paths and no sun to mark the seasons. And there he laid passageways where there were none before, each to his own desire and not bound by the ways of the living world. The crooked passage he made straight and the straight he bent back upon itself so that no man knew the way into his sanctum save he.

Yet still Eradorius was afraid, knowing the fate that waited for him. So he made a guardian to watch over the twisting ways and commanded that it let no man pass into his sanctum, but that it should feast upon them and grow in strength. This it did, growing in strength and bestial cunning and its tread was like thunder in the twisting ways and its breath was like the desert wind.

Malus stopped. His heart went cold. 'Mother of Night,' he said softly. 'I haven't been dreaming at all.'

'Clever, clever little druchii,' the daemon purred. 'You aren't such a fool after all. That's reassuring.'

'Why didn't you tell me?' Malus cried. 'What profit did you gain by tormenting me?'

Tz'arkan laughed, a sound like rattling bones. 'That question answers itself, little druchii! Your fear is sweet. Your madness more so.'

'But how can this be? I saw corridors turn back upon themselves! Crossed the threshold from one room and entered it again on the other side! It's not possible!'

The daemon's laugh pealed inside his head. 'Foolish little ape! The answers are right in front of you, yet you refuse to see them! You refuse to *believe* in them, because you cannot see past the tree you shelter in. How pitiful you are, Darkblade. What am I to do with you?'

Malus fought with all his will to keep from hurling the ancient book across the small cabin. 'You may begin,' he said through clenched teeth, 'by giving me some answers!'

'Ask the questions,' Tz'arkan said with a sneer. 'I will answer them.'

'Did Eradorius come here to escape the fate of the other four sorcerers?'

'He did.'

'How?'

'By going where I could not.'

'But where?' Malus glowered at the tome. 'Wait – you were bound inside the crystal. You were trapped here, in the physical world.'

The daemon said nothing.

'Eradorius fled beyond the physical world to escape you, didn't he?'

'Yes.'

'But how?'

'I cannot explain it to you,' the daemon said. 'Your pitiful brain could not comprehend it. Suffice it to say that he used potent sorcery and leave it at that.'

Malus paused. 'Yet he also created this impossible labyrinth to protect him. He still needed to protect himself from intruders, so his tower must still somehow touch upon this world, correct?'

'Indeed,' Tz'arkan said. 'Physical form cannot exist in the realms of ether, little druchii. It must be… anchored, if you will, in order to retain its form. So the tower's foundations still touch upon the physical realm.'

'The tower still exists, then?'

'I do not know for certain,' the daemon replied. 'It has been many thousands of years. If the anchor was

destroyed the tower and everything inside it would be
lost within the ether.'

'Don't you know?'

'Did I not mention that he fled *where I cannot go?*' the
daemon replied archly.

Malus set the tome aside and swung his legs over the
edge of the table. 'You're still not telling me everything
you know.'

The highborn could feel the daemon's wicked smile.
'Of course not. You haven't asked the right questions
yet.'

'What do you want from me?' Malus cried angrily. 'You
lure me into your damnable trap and set my feet on this
impossible quest and then you keep me ignorant of the
challenges before me! What do you hope to achieve? Is
it not enough that you've taken my soul? Must you have
my sanity as well?' He grabbed the glass of wine and
hurled it against the wall. 'Answer me! ANSWER ME!'

Silence fell, broken only by the lapping of waves
against the hull. It took several moments before Malus
realised he wasn't alone.

He turned to find Hauclir standing in the doorway, his
expression impassive. Malus fought down a surge of
panic. He searched the retainer's eyes for signs of suspicion, but could find none. 'Yes?' he said at length.

'It's time, my lord,' Hauclir said, his expression
inscrutable.

Malus straightened, running a hand through his dark
hair. 'Very well,' he said, pulling up a voluminous hood
that swallowed his face in shadow. 'Let us begin.'

Chapter Twenty-One
THE HOUR OF THE WOLF

'CORRECT ME IF I'm wrong, my lord,' Hauclir grumbled as they made their way down the dark, narrow passageways of the *Harrier*, 'but I fail to see how this plan of yours will accomplish anything except getting the two of us killed.'

'Your boundless faith in my skills never ceases to amaze me,' Malus replied. With the hood concealing his face, he was a black-robed apparition, a patch of night gliding among lesser shadows. 'I should think it obvious; by the end of the day I intend to see Bruglir and his sea mistress dead and myself in command of the corsair fleet.'

'And you plan to accomplish this by kidnapping your sister?'

A faint chuckle escaped the darkness within the hood. 'It will be the spark to the tinder that's built up between her, Bruglir and Tanithra. Consider how... changed Yasmir has become since she discovered Bruglir's betrayal. Now imagine how she will react when she thinks he's betrayed her again – and worse, intends to give her as a gift to the Skinrider chieftain.'

'Except for the fact that she'll be trussed up like a festival pig and thrown in the bottom of our cargo hold by the time she realises any of this.'

Malus nodded. 'That's where you come in.'

'Ah, yes. I should have guessed.'

'When Bruglir and I go to speak to the Skinrider chieftain you will remain behind, ostensibly to join the landing party that will lower the chain. Before that happens, I want you to go below and free Yasmir. Tell her that Urial learned of her capture and you and I have been trying to find her ever since.'

Hauclir nodded, his expression thoughtful. 'She'll try to kill Tanithra. You know that.'

'I'm counting on it. She was always known as being skilled with those knives of hers, but after seeing the carnage she wrought when we were boarded weeks ago, there's something almost supernatural in her ability to kill.' The highborn paused, considering his words carefully. 'For the first time I'm starting to wonder if perhaps Urial's obsession with her is motivated more than by simple lust. She might actually possess the touch of the divine.'

'So that's why you decided to side with her?'

'I'm siding with her because Bruglir must die. Otherwise he'll certainly kill me as soon as we've beaten the Skinriders. And if he dies, Tanithra must die as well, because I can't afford anyone else vying with me for control of the fleet.'

'And Urial?'

'For the moment we still need one another.' Malus said. 'I need him to get inside Eradorius's tower and he will need me to intercede with Yasmir on his behalf.'

The former guard captain considered the scheme for several moments in silence. 'So instead of merely kidnapping the lover of the Vaulkhar's heir, you're actually setting a plan in motion that's guaranteed to unleash a storm of bloodshed on your own allies just hours before a major battle?'

'That's a rather superficial way of looking at it, but essentially correct.'

Hauclir sighed. 'Well, I suppose it could be worse. Though at the moment that's only a theory, mind.'

'Enough moaning,' Malus said. 'What of Urial? Are you certain he's stopped watching Yasmir?'

'He hasn't even visited her cabin door since his return and his retainers haven't been seen either. I expect he's been busy drafting the charts that will direct the rest of the fleet through that damnable mist.'

'And you gave him my message?'

'I told him just as you said: the time for paying debts is almost at hand. He gave me a nod and disappeared inside his cabin. That's the last I've seen of him.'

'Very well. Maybe that will be enough to keep him out of our way for the next few hours. After that he can do as he pleases.'

Before Hauclir could respond the two druchii turned the corner of an adjoining passage and came upon half a dozen corsairs waiting impatiently just a few feet from Yasmir's cabin. Like Malus, most of the corsairs were clothed in black and concealed their features with hoods or leather masks. Only Tanithra kept her face uncovered and her expression was nothing short of joyfully murderous. Two of the corsairs carried a rolled-up sheet of sail hide between them, while the rest held black-coloured coshes in their hands.

'You took your time getting here,' Tanithra hissed. 'I've got men topside loading supplies onto the longboat, but we've only got a few minutes before they're done.'

'Calm down,' Malus said smoothly. 'Yasmir is likely asleep by now. We'll knock her out, roll her up and be gone before anyone knows what's going on.' He nudged Hauclir, who nodded sheepishly and pulled a black sailor's scarf over his face. 'Do your men know the plan?'

'Aye.'

Malus nodded. 'Good. And remember: no one speaks until we're aboard the raider and *no one* mentions any names save Bruglir's in her presence.' He turned to the corsairs. 'Let's go.'

Without waiting for a response, Malus slipped quietly down the passage until he reached Yasmir's cabin door. The thin wood was literally covered with votive runes and the names of sailors asking for Khaine's blessing. Here and there the tracks of the carved symbols were coated with dried blood. Malus ran his fingertips over the symbols. A feeling of intense apprehension suddenly gripped his heart, but with an effort he pushed it aside.

He held out his hand. Hauclir laid the handle of the cosh against his palm. The highborn took a last moment to make sure the corsairs were in place. 'Remember,' he said in a barely audible whisper. 'Move fast. Don't give her any chance to react.'

Heads nodded. Malus took a deep breath, pushed the door open and rushed soundlessly into the dimly lit cabin beyond.

The air inside was hot and stuffy. The deck planks were
tacky with splashes and loops of spilled blood, sticking
noisily to the soles of his boots. Across the cabin six can-
dles had burned low, spilling long trails of wax over the
lip of a narrow shelf and extending gleaming pillars all
the way to the deck.

The cabin's single narrow bunk was empty, its blan-
kets neatly arranged. Yasmir knelt in the centre of the
room, her black hair unbound and spilling like a mantle across her naked shoulders. Her skin glowed in the
soft candlelight, showing the gleaming red trails of the
intricate patterns of cuts on her arms, legs and shoulders. Her back was to the corsairs as they swept into the
room, but Malus took one look at Yasmir and knew that
things had already gone terribly wrong.

He was halfway across the room when she rose to her
feet, turning with an almost languid grace at his
approach. Her face was beatific, unmarred by the razor
edges that had decorated much of her naked body; her
violet eyes were half-lidded and serene, as though she
moved in a dream. It was the serenity of the executioner,
the elegance of death incarnate.

Long, narrow-bladed knives made silver arcs in her
seemingly delicate hands as she rushed towards Malus
and instincts born of bloody-handed experience told
him that if he let her reach him he was dead. She smiled,
spreading her arms like a lover as she came to him and
Malus threw himself to the deck rather than fall into
that deadly embrace.

Malus rolled across the blood-spattered planks. He
piled into a table and chair, knocking empty bottles of
wine and a tray of breadcrumbs onto his head. Then
came the sound of razor-edged steel slicing leather and

skin and Malus heard a bubbling gasp where he'd stood only moments before.

Two bodies hit the deck with a single, muffled thud. Malus had ducked out of Yasmir's deadly rush and the two corsairs behind him had borne the brunt of her charge instead. Her knives had struck like adders, killing the men as they gaped at the unearthly vision before them.

Yasmir passed between the dead men as they fell and the corsairs beyond scattered like sheep before the wolf. One man who didn't move quite fast enough died with a knife through his temple and then there was no one between Yasmir and Tanithra. The female corsair snarled a wordless challenge and drew her heavy sword from its sheath. Malus scrambled to his feet, knowing that he would never reach the two women in time. For all her skill, Tanithra would be dead in moments and Malus was going to need an entirely new plan.

Suddenly there was the dry rustle of metal links and Yasmir fell forward. Hauclir pulled for all he was worth, dragging Yasmir backward by the chain he'd looped around her ankle.

Tanithra lunged for Yasmir and Malus leapt as well, determined to reach her first. His half-sister rolled onto her back as he loomed over her and her hands blurred in the air. Malus gritted his teeth and lashed out with the cosh, striking Yasmir squarely in the forehead. The back of her skull struck the deck with a sharp *thump* and she went limp. The highborn toppled to the deck beside her and Tanithra came up short, checking her sword stroke at the last moment.

Hauclir was beside Malus at once, standing between his lord and the female corsair. One of Yasmir's daggers jutted from the retainer's shoulder. 'Are you all right?' he whispered in a strained voice.

The highborn nodded, rolling onto his back. He gritted his teeth and reached down to his right thigh, his hand closing on the knife hilt and drawing the weapon from his leg. A hot rush of blood poured over his thigh, soaking into the woollen robes.

The retainer knelt, ignoring the blade in his own arm and probed Malus's leg through the hole in his breeches. 'Missed the artery by less than a finger's width,' he said grimly, then reached up and pulled Yasmir's other blade free. 'Let's hope she isn't the sort to poison her knives. I hear that's fashionable among the ladies this season.'

Malus ignored him, gritting his teeth against the swelling tide of pain as he glared up at Tanithra. 'I suppose you were planning to knock her out with the flat of your blade?'

'Of course not,' Tanithra spat. 'If she'd taken another step I'd have hacked her open like a sausage. You saw what she did to my men.'

'Then it's good for us that my man got to her first,' the highborn replied. Biting back a groan he pushed himself to his feet. 'Get her wrapped up. Now.'

'What about my men?' Tanithra exclaimed, pointing to the bodies in the middle of the room.

'Keep your damned voice down!' Malus hissed. 'Leave them. No one will come calling on Yasmir until the battle's done and by then it won't matter if they're found. Now get her tied up before she regains consciousness and we have to do this all over again!'

Tanithra snapped her fingers and the surviving corsairs leapt into action, binding Yasmir's hands and feet and gagging her with a strip of hide before rolling her up in the sail. With a grunt the two men levered the wrapped hide onto their shoulders and the female corsair ducked her head through the open door to make certain the coast was clear. Satisfied, she gestured to the men, who rushed from the cabin and down the passage.

Malus limped after Tanithra, wincing with every step. It surprised him how tempted he was to call upon the daemon to heal him, even in front of witnesses, but he steadfastly resisted the urge. 'Get back to the raider,' he told her, 'and see to it she suffers no accidents along the way. Remember, Bruglir must be made to kill her, or else you gain nothing by her death.'

Tanithra regarded him with an implacable stare. Saying nothing, she pushed past the wounded highborn and trailed after her men.

Once she was out of earshot, Malus turned to Hauclir. 'Do you have Yasmir's knives?'

The retainer nodded, pointing to where the hilts of the two weapons protruded from his belt. Hauclir's eyes never left Tanithra as she receded down the passageway. 'That one's not to be trusted, my lord,' he said, his voice tight with pain. 'She's too unpredictable.'

Malus shook his head. 'The die is already cast, Hauclir. She won't kill Yasmir now that I've reminded her of the consequences and she has no one else to turn to. We hold the upper hand.'

'For now, my lord,' Hauclir said darkly. 'For now.'

MALUS WALKED SLOWLY onto the deck of the captured raider, trying to conceal his limp as he climbed the narrow stairway. With great reluctance he'd allowed Hauclir to give him a small draught of hushalta and the stab wound ached fiercely as the drug did its work. The narcotic effects of the drink had kept him below as Bruglir and Urial had come aboard and the raider made its way once again through the mists surrounding the island. Already the sands were flowing through the glass; in less than two hours the rest of the fleet would follow Urial's charts and the attack would begin.

The highborn stepped onto the main deck under a dark sky, with the narrow towers guarding the island's sea wall looming ominously above the captured ship. They were less than half a mile from the opening to the cove and closing fast under a full spread of sail. Already Urial was moving among the crew, touching each man and imparting the blessing of Khaine to ward them from the corrupting touch of the Skinriders. Bruglir stood at the bow, studying the cove with a sharp eye. The highborn turned and caught sight of Tanithra at the helm, her expression grim. Hauclir was nowhere to be seen. Malus imagined that he was already below, waiting in the shadows near the cargo hold where Yasmir lay.

Malus worked his way forward, moving slowly and deliberately to the bow. He'd removed the light mail and now wore his customary full armour and the twin swords Nagaira had given him. Bruglir, by comparison, wore battered but functional plate armour and a single sword that had been well-cared for and obviously saw regular use. The highborn was irritated to see that his half-brother managed to arm himself like a knight of simple means and yet appear regal and heroic at the same time. Malus stood at the bow rail and squinted into the gloom. 'Any sign they've lowered the chain yet?'

'Not yet,' Bruglir answered. 'They'll likely wait until the last moment.' He pointed to the towers on the sea wall.

'Probably wondering what we're doing here and trying to find someone who recognises the ship.'

It hadn't occurred to Malus that the men standing watch at the tower might not be familiar with the captured raider and bar its entry on general principles. The thought was both absurd and terrifying all at the same time. 'You don't suppose they can tell we aren't Skinriders?'

Bruglir chuckled. 'Not unless they've stuck hawk's eyes in their skulls. They'll know us by the cut of our sails and the shape of our hull and that's all.' He nodded to the big ships anchored in the cove. 'Things will get interesting when we have to run *that* gauntlet, however.'

They were almost at the entrance to the cove. Malus eyed the tower to port. From this distance he could see how roughly it was made. Parts of the circular wall and the facings of the tower had fallen away and the top of the citadel was ragged and uneven. The firing positions near the top of the tower looked well-made, though and were perfectly sited to fire on ships approaching the cove. He couldn't see the squat stone-throwers or their piles of carefully hoarded stones, but he knew they were there. The windows of the citadel gleamed with pale light.

'There!' Bruglir pointed into the darkness ahead. Malus followed the gesture but all he saw were turgid waves and more shadow. 'Someone must have recognised us. They're lowering the chain.'

The captured ship sailed past the towers into the cove. Now that they were on the other side of the sea wall, Malus spied the huge links of the sea chain running from the portside tower, the greased links still playing out into the water as the barrier was lowered into the depths. Again, he was struck by the nature of the tower's construction. He supposed that the Skinriders had found their way to the island, saw the sea walls were undefended and did what they could to rectify the problem. It was crude but effective work, the highborn had to admit, but where did they get the materials?

Muted orders from the helm set the riggers to work overhead. Sails were brought in, slowing the ship. Bruglir placed a boot on the rail and leaned forward, resting his arms on his bent knee as he studied the distant coast. 'Those big ships draw too much water to move close to shore, but we should be able to tie up somewhere if we can find a pier.'

They were already coming up on the nearest Skinrider ships – two large Empire warships with old, wide mouthed brass culverins gaping like dragon's jaws both fore and aft. Malus wondered if the Skinriders still had powder for those huge cannon and if they could still fire without bursting apart. If they could the damage they would wreak would be appalling.

Hooded figures moved on the warship's main deck, shambling to the rail and looking down on the smaller raider as it sailed by. The druchii made no effort to conceal themselves and Malus fancied that he heard shouts of consternation on the deck of the towering warship as it receded into the distance.

The Skinrider armada was scattered across the breadth of the cove, maintaining enough distance from one another to allow them to get under weigh without risking a collision. Tanithra guided the ship past the two older Empire vessels and wove a seemingly meandering course past a Bretonnian guardship and two Tilean arrow-ships, their decks bristling with serried ranks of crude bolt throwers. Bruglir caught sight of a stone pier at the far end of the cove and barked orders to Tanithra. The clear, carrying orders, spoken in druhir, brought a chorus of startled shouts from the Skinrider ships nearby. Within moments a Norse horn winded an eerie, skirling note from the closest vessel, a sound soon taken up by every other ship in the cove, like the baying of a pack of wolves.

Shouts and gibbered cries echoed across the cove as the Skinrider crews boiled like ants from below decks and rushed to get a look at the interloper sailing past. Many carried lanterns gleaming with pale light and in their sickly glow Malus saw that these raiders were not merely skinless, but also hideously bloated and gangrenous, their bodies twisted by the corrupting power of the vile god they worshipped. Clouds of insects raged in the air above their putrefying bodies, stirred to frenetic activity by the Skinriders' distress. Officers – or what Malus presumed to be officers – bawled commands at the pestilent crew, ordering them back to work. Long-limbed, swollen figures climbed the rigging of the ships like gangly spiders, scrabbling for the stays binding up the tattered sails.

'Are they going to weigh anchor?' Malus mused aloud.

Bruglir shook his head. 'Unlikely. I expect they just want to be prepared in case they're called into action.'

'So they'll respond all the more quickly when your ships arrive,' the highborn said grimly and was surprised when Bruglir laughed.

'Believe me, once that chain falls it will be like wolves among the sheep. We could tell them right now that the fleet was coming and it wouldn't make any difference. In two hours this cove will be burning from end to end and we'll be hauling gold by the ton from their treasure houses.' The captain's dark eyes glittered with avarice and Malus smiled.

The captured raider came about slowly, aiming for the pier. It was made of cut stone, far better built than the ramshackle towers of the Skinriders and Malus wondered who might have made it. How many people had claimed this island in the thousands of years since Eradorius landed here? For the first time he felt a real tremor of doubt. What if the tower was no more and the idol long since taken by some enterprising sailor?

His dreadful reverie was broken by a roar that reverberated from the shoreline. A mob of Skinriders had rushed to the edge of the long pier, brandishing corroded weapons and thundering a challenge at the approaching corsairs. Lanterns bobbed on long poles above the mob, throwing their diseased faces into flickering relief.

Bruglir glanced at Malus and grinned. 'They've given us a welcome fit for a king,' he said dryly. 'I wonder if there will be slave girls and carafes of wine?'

Malus and the corsairs nearby laughed and everyone took heart from the sepulchral sound. Before, Bruglir seemed diffident about the plan, but now that the enemy was before him he had come alive, fearless in the face of peril and his men responded in kind. It was a revelation that filled Malus with surprise and bitter envy.

The raider pulled up alongside the pier. Bruglir turned to the men on deck. 'Cast away lines and make fast!' he ordered and the men leapt to obey. Heavy ropes went over the port side and men followed with nimble assurance, heedless of the raging mob howling at them only a few yards away. The captain smiled, pleased with his men's courage. 'Ready the gangplank!' he cried.

There was a groan of coiled ropes and the deck beneath Malus shifted as the big ship slowed against the pier. Almost immediately the raider's gangplank came down with a rattle and bang and Bruglir was on the move, forcing Malus to grit his teeth and lumber along painfully in his wake. Urial administered the last of his benedictions, hefted his axe and moved to join them, his masked retainers taking formation around him like a murder of brooding crows. Three heavily armed corsairs already waited at the gangplank, ready to provide escort for their captain.

'Tani, you have the ship,' Bruglir called. 'You know what you must do.'

Tanithra said nothing, watching the captain depart with a resentful scowl. Farewell, Tanithra, Malus thought. The Dark Mother grant we never meet again.

The highborn made his way carefully down the bouncing gangplank. Bruglir and his men were already halfway down the pier, forcing Malus to hobble along quickly to try and catch up.

Malus noted similar movement at the far end of the pier. Someone with rank had evidently asserted their control over the mob, because the shouts had fallen silent and the crowd was making way for a tall figure flanked by a handful of guards. As the figure approached the druchii on the pier, Bruglir started forward as well, intending to meet the Skinrider halfway. As soon as they were within shouting distance, Bruglir spoke something in a harsh, guttural language and Malus was surprised when the Skinrider answered in accented druhir.

'Don't humiliate yourself trying to speak our tongue,' the Skinrider said, his voice a harsh, bubbling rasp. The raider was clothed in thick hide that reminded Malus of a cold one's scales, crudely stitched together around his broad-shouldered, muscular form. Over the hide the Skinrider wore a Norscan's heavy chain hauberk that hung to his knees and his skinless hands gripped the haft of a huge, double-bitted axe. A black woollen mantle with a voluminous hood covered the raider's head, concealing most of it in shadow. When the Skinrider spoke, Malus could see gleaming muscles moving the raider's jaw and torn lips pulling back from pointed teeth. 'I can understand your pathetic mewlings well enough.'

Bruglir glared haughtily at the man. 'Do you speak for your chieftain, Skinrider? Because I did not sail for thousands of leagues to be met at the shore by a pack of his lapdogs.'

The Skinrider's jaw shifted in what Malus took for a smile. 'It is well that my men cannot understand your pulings. They would tear you to pieces for saying such things.'

'Then explain it to them, skinless one, or spare me your empty threats. I've come with a rich offer for your master.'

'Tell me what it is and I will decide if it is worth my master's attention.'

'Dogs have no place in their master's business,' Bruglir sneered. 'Take me to him and you will have served your purpose.'

'You think me a fool to allow you into my lord's presence? A pack of filthy, treacherous dark elves not worthy to lick the excretions from my master's feet?'

Bruglir laughed in the man's face. 'Does your great chieftain fear a dozen druchii that much?' The captain took a step forward. 'Are all the legends about the infamous Skinriders mere bedtime tales, meant to frighten soft human children?'

The Skinrider roared in anger, meaning to raise his heavy axe, but Bruglir fixed him in place with a single look. 'Raise a hand against me, you slug and it will be the last mistake you ever make,' the captain said.

A tense silence stretched between the two men. Finally the Skinrider lowered his axe. 'Follow me,' he growled.

The Skinrider turned, bellowing a command in Norse to the men at the end of the pier. Bruglir followed with a disdainful scowl, but to Malus there was no mistaking the cold glitter of triumph in his eyes.

Savour it while you can, the highborn thought. He followed along like a ghost in his brother's wake, smiling secretly to himself as he watched his scheme unfold.

You play your part well, brother, thought Malus as they began the long climb to the citadel on the cliff. But you forget that I am its author and this is a tale writ in blood.

Chapter Twenty-Two
DARKNESS FALLS

THE CITADEL WAS built upon the bones of the dead.

From the pier at the base of the cliff the Skinriders led the druchii through an empty village of stone houses, their walls covered in moss and their roofs rotted to dust many centuries past. They had the appearance of a cairn-yard, the stone outlines arrayed like barrows in orderly rows and left for the ravages of time. As they walked through the narrow lanes between the buildings Malus noticed how still and silent the air was; not a breath of wind or wild sound disturbed the funereal silence. Open doorways and empty windows seemed to tug at them as they passed by, tempting them with ancient mysteries hidden in their abyssal shadows. The highborn thought he could feel unseen stares scrutinising him from those ruined buildings – the flat, implacable gaze of restless ghosts, waiting in the darkness for the fleeting warmth of a mortal too curious for his own good.

Past the haunted village was a broad, slightly sloping field that had been cleared of trees at some time in the distant past – Malus could see dozens of mounds of very old tree stumps rising from the grass and low shrubs. A path worked its way across the field and forked on the other side. The left-hand path began to climb the cliff face in a long series of switchbacks that rose to the citadel, while the right hand path led to the wooden gates of a log stockade built against the base of the cliff itself. Vines climbed the logs of the palisade and green moss grew from the chinks between them. The narrow firing slits in the two corner towers and the windows of the stockade house that rose from behind the wall were black and empty as those in the village, but here the blackness exuded malignant, debased hatred. Even the Skinriders gave the abandoned structure a wide berth and Malus once more wondered how many other sea-farers had come to the island over the millennia, seeking fortune or safe haven but finding only madness and ruin instead.

It was a long and arduous climb up the cliff face. The paths were steep and narrow and the Skinriders set a relentless pace. About midway up the cliff they began to encounter gaping holes high in the cliff walls, often in groups of two or three set side by side and exuding thick streams of smoke or mist that reeked of decay. Once or twice he heard a high-pitched rumble, like the hiss of a hot spring reverberating through the stone.

After a time the highborn tried to distract himself by looking out over the cove and the surrounding shore. He saw more abandoned buildings, broken monuments and even the rotted hulls of ships, all piled on top of one another over the progression of years. The twin towers of the sea wall stood in stark relief against a wall of mist that rose into the dark sky in every direction. The highborn tried to work out how long it had been since they'd passed through that barrier themselves. Had it been an hour? An hour and a half? How close were the ships of the fleet and was the landing party in position to lower the chain? There was no way to tell, he finally admitted to himself. Time was slippery on this side of the mist. It wasn't long before he caught himself stealing glances out to sea, dreading the sight of tall masts and black sails that meant the fleet had somehow arrived early and was headed for disaster.

They had reached the top of the cliffs before Malus realised it. The path turned sharply and entered an arched alcove that ended in a crumbling, stone stairway. He could feel the weight of the citadel looming over them, a pile of old stone built by skinless, diseased hands and mortared with blood and bone.

The stink of rotting blood was thick in the air. Up close, Malus could see the crumbling, rust-coloured cement clinging to smooth, glassy bricks that could have been ten thousand years old. He ran his fingers over the surface of one brick and felt a tingle of power sink through his fingertips. Something nagged at the back of his mind; a sense of familiarity that he couldn't quite place. Before he could consider it further the stairway made a turn to the left and Malus rose into a realm of utter madness.

The stairway emerged into the base of the citadel – or so Malus suspected, since he could see no walls from where he stood. The air was thick and humid, suffused with a greenish glow that shone through narrow, stitched curtains of skin that hung from somewhere high above. Streaks of blood and bile ran across the surface of the glistening hides, the pulsing flow drawing Malus's attention. After a moment he squeezed his stinging eyes shut and turned away, unable to shake the sense that there were *patterns* in the flow of sickly fluid, promising knowledge and power if he would open his eyes to them.

Clouds of blue and black flies hung like smoke in the air, filling the space with a keening buzz that played counterpoint to a chorus of ragged screams that echoed from somewhere high above. Drops of blood spattered down from the heights, falling upon the druchii's head and shoulders in a warm, bitter rain.

The curtains of skin made close spaces and narrow lanes in the interior of the citadel; Malus wondered if the whole structure was in fact an empty shell, partitioned by tapestries of torture and disease. The flaps of skin swayed in a faint breeze, seeming to reach for the druchii as they followed the Skinriders through the stinking labyrinth.

He turned to Urial, who was marching stolidly along behind Malus with his axe held across his chest like a sceptre. 'Have you any idea how long it's been since we entered the mists?' Malus whispered.

Urial shook his head. 'I can't say for certain, but it feels as though our time is nearly up.'

Malus nodded, his head turning this way and that as he attempted to keep his bearings in the confusing maze of rotting skin. 'I feel the same way.' He shot the former acolyte a pointed look. 'We may have to find our own way out when things become heated.'

Urial shrugged. 'If we are in an audience with their chieftain when our friends arrive we might be able to turn the situation to our favour,' he whispered, 'but if we've been here as long as it seems then there should already be alarms sounding from one of the sea wall towers. We've heard nothing yet and that worries me.'

The highborn felt a chill run down his spine – the faintest, teasing caress of Fate. 'Tanithra is a seasoned raider,' he replied quickly. 'There's no telling how many times she's stolen upon a watchtower in the dead of night and cut the throats of the men inside.'

'Perhaps you are right,' Urial said, but his expression was grim. 'We will know soon enough.'

It seemed as though they walked for a long while down the green, fleshy corridors, turning this way and that without apparent rhyme or reason. The drippings from the ceiling stained their shoulders and the sleeves of their robes. One of Bruglir's retainers stumbled and doubled over, retching violently. The rest of the procession filed on by, saying nothing. As bad as it was, Malus expected it was going to get much worse.

At length the procession came to a halt, bunching up in a group at the top of another curving stairway. This one led down, following the rough-hewn wall of a circular shaft that sank down into the cliff. A pillar of mist like the ones in the cliff wall outside rose from the depths, filling the inside of the tower with the festering stink of corruption. As Malus sidled through the crowd to stand beside Bruglir he heard a clattering sound echo from overhead. Pieces of glossy black brick flashed in the green light as they tumbled into the pit, bouncing from one wall to the next.

The huge armoured Norscan stood to one side, his axe propped on one mailed shoulder. The raider's skinless

chin and white teeth gleamed eerily in the light as he
spoke. 'Our lord waits below,' he said, pointing with a
clawed finger. He made a rasping sound that might have
been a chuckle. 'Present your gifts to him, druchii and
he will make a place of honour for you at his side.'

A twinge of uneasiness passed through Malus, but
before he could consider the situation more carefully
Bruglir shot the Norscan a defiant look and started
downwards, moving quickly and purposefully along the
dripping stairs. Without hesitation Malus followed in
his wake, casting a quick glance over his shoulder to
check the progress of the rest of the party. Bruglir's
retainers were the next to move, casting angry glares at
the highborn for inadvertently shaming them. Urial
came next, his shoulder pressed to the rough wall as he
negotiated the steps with his twisted leg. His eyes were
fixed on the mist and the depths below, as though trying
to discern what lay at their source.

Just beyond Urial, Malus saw a Skinrider slide
between the fleshy curtains and bow his head before the
Norscan. The Skinrider's shoulders were heaving and he
spoke to the tall warrior in quick gasps. The highborn
felt his heart skip a beat as the Norscan stiffened and
shot Malus an accusing look. That's it then, Malus
thought. He's learned about the attack on the tower. But
just as Malus went for his sword the Norscan pushed the
messenger aside and rushed off the way he'd come, leaving the Skinrider loping along in the big warrior's wake.

Now what was all that about, Malus thought? Perhaps
the raiders had learned something was amiss at one of
the towers, but weren't certain exactly what. The
Norscan suspects, though, the highborn thought. Urial
caught his eye with an arched eyebrow and Malus

shrugged in reply, then turned and went down the stairs.

Bricks continued to fall in a steady trickle from the top of the crumbling tower, sometimes striking the rock wall close enough to shower the druchii with dust as the projectiles hurtled past. The further they descended the thicker the air seemed to become, until Malus fancied that the tendrils of mist had taken on a life of their own. They swirled about his head and plucked coyly at his lashes with sticky, ghostly fingers, pulled at his lips and reached down his throat. He could feel Tz'arkan stir angrily in his breast, like a bear cornered in its den. Every time the mist seemed to thicken in his lungs, he could feel the daemon swell, scattering the fog and pushing it from Malus's body.

The descent seemed to last an eternity. After a time the air quivered with a stentorian hissing, like a dragon's hot breath issuing from below. Malus was reminded of the hot geysers that blasted skyward on the Plain of Dragons in Naggaroth, but as they descended still further he could hear an undertone to the loud exhalation of steam. There was a curious, piping note that rose and fell in pitch, almost too faint to hear beneath the sharp blast of trapped air. The sound seemed to come from dozens of sources at once, rising and falling in perfect unison. Despite the close atmosphere the tremulous wail chilled him to the bone.

As they descended further the mist thickened, surrounding them and making their footing difficult. Malus stumbled ahead, barely able to see where to put one foot ahead of the other and trying to focus on the hazy outlines of Bruglir's shoulders and head. The highborn took another step – and came up short, realising

that their descent had ended at last. He walked forward
hesitantly, enveloped by stinking clouds of pestilence,
until Bruglir's tall form resolved itself out of the haze.
The captain had his hand on the hilt of his sword, peering warily into the mists around him. He caught sight of
Malus and for a moment he actually seemed relieved.
The hissing sound – and the chorus of cries that rose
beneath it – resounded thunderously from the rock
walls around them.

Then, without warning the mist billowed – and then
abruptly receded, retreating like an ebb tide towards an
irregular circle of grey light that grew in brightness and
definition as the fog thinned. After a moment Malus
realised that the circle was one of the rough openings
that decorated the side of the cliff. A stiff wind had
blown up, racing across the cliff face and drawing the
steam away for the moment.

Any sense of relief the highborn might have felt vanished
in a single instant as he saw what the mists were concealing. Beside Malus, Bruglir recoiled with a startled curse.

They stood in a natural hollow within the cliff, with a
rough but relatively level floor that stretched almost
eighty paces across. In the centre of the chamber lay a
circular pit approximately fifteen paces at its widest
point. Steam rose in gusts from a thick, heaving surface
of red and yellow. Arms, legs and hairless heads rolled
and bobbed in the horrific stew; lifeless fingers seemed
to wave as the hands rose and fell with the escape of
trapped gases. The gangrenous air over the mass seethed
with flies, their buzzing rasp lost in the reverberating
voice of the pit.

With growing revulsion Malus's shocked mind took in
every detail of the pit's hideous contents and a small

part of him realised that it was a stew of melting bodies, tossed in by the hundreds and left to ferment in the steam. The whole surface heaved with an eruption of stinking gas and as the highborn watched, the heads riding the surface of the mass rolled back on melting necks and *moaned*. Their voices were the source of that terrible symphony of pain that rose with the steam and the highborn was stunned in awe and horror at the sight.

'Mother of Night and the Dragons of the Deep Sea,' Bruglir whispered. 'What monsters are these?'

'Supplicants of the Ruinous Powers,' Malus said gravely. 'Worshippers of the god of pestilence and decay. You knew this from the beginning, Bruglir. You said it yourself.'

'Yes, but...' the captain's voice trailed away as he tried to grapple with the enormity of the scene before him. 'I never imagined...'

The surface of the pit heaved again, but this time it wasn't the roiling pressure of steam behind the motion; the fleshy skin of the human stew stretched like a caul as a powerful figure rose from the depths before the stunned druchii. Malus watched the clinging mass of skin and jellied bone drape like a cloak around a broad-shouldered, muscular figure. Yellow-green folds of soft skin stretched from the tips of huge, downward-sweeping horns and then parted, tearing a hole that settled around the top of the creature's head like one of the Skinriders' crude hoods. Two green points of light burned where the beast's eyes should be and the flesh of the hood ran down its dark cheeks in a mockery of tears.

The Skinrider chieftain raised his powerful arms, draped in sleeves of skin and bone and turned his blazing eyes upon the druchii. Malus met that baleful stare and understood that the creature before him might have been a man long ago, but now a fell daemon possessed the body standing before him. Tz'arkan noticed as well and this time Malus sensed the daemon recoil warily in the face of this new threat.

'Come forward.' The daemon's voice was like the death-rattle of a god, a sound like pooled blood and pus bubbling from a diseased wound. Malus's guts shrivelled at the sound and he heard Bruglir groan in dismay as the captain took a lurching step forward and then another. Malus felt the pull as well, though it seemed distant and dreadful rather than an iron fist that defied resistance. He could hear the rest of the party take halting steps toward the daemon and the highborn joined in rather than reveal his advantage to the chieftain.

'Ah,' the daemon sighed, 'the flesh of Naggaroth. The sweet blood of the lost elves. Bones like fine, cool ice. You are welcome here. I will savour you in my embrace and you will entertain me with song.'

The daemon spread his powerful arms in welcome. Malus saw the molten heads in the chieftain's raiment shudder, the mouths working in a chorus of madness and horror. Milky eyes rolled in their sockets, focusing on the druchii lumbering helplessly to their doom.

'You will not defile the chosen sons of Khaine!'

The words cut through the air like the shriek of a red-hot iron against skin. Urial the Forsaken limped fearlessly towards the daemon, his axe held high. His pale cheeks were deeply slashed and his own blood burned like a fiery brand from the razor edges of the arcane weapon. Urial's voice thundered in the cavernous space. 'The chosen of Khaine are not for you or your master to touch! They are marked for fields of gore, not the stinking pit of human mud!'

Bubbling laughter echoed from the towering figure. 'And what will you do, poor cripple, if I choose to take them anyway? Will the Bloody-Handed God make his presence known through a flawed vessel such as yours?'

Urial met the daemon's blazing eyes and smiled. 'My body is weak, yes, but my faith is like shining gold. Go ahead, daemon. Tempt the wrath of the Lord of Murder and feel the full measure of his terrible vengeance.'

The chieftain started to reach for Urial with one taloned hand – and then hesitated. The former acolyte faced him with the fiery zeal of the true believer and in that moment Malus saw the faintest tinge of doubt creep into the daemon's eyes. 'Very well,' the chieftain said at length and the highborn felt the being's terrible presence lift from him like a collar of iron. 'Say what you have come to say and I will decide if it is worth your lives.'

Bruglir took a silent breath, composing himself and then took a measured step forward. There was no mistaking the terror in his eyes, but the captain's voice was steady and sure. 'I and my men wish to join your ranks, terrible one. We wish to become Skinriders ourselves.'

Another croaking chuckle. 'Indeed? You chosen sons of Khaine would abandon your god and your precious white skin and serve me like dogs? Why?'

Malus swallowed. Think quickly brother, he prayed. He couldn't say a word to prod Bruglir, or else the daemon would know he was being fed a lie.

To Malus's great relief, the captain barely skipped a beat. 'Why, revenge, of course,' he said. 'My father is dead and my brother Isilvar has betrayed me. He has

taken my home and slaughtered or enslaved every
member of my household. I am an exile, hunted by the
best assassins my brother can buy. Where else can I find
sanctuary? Where else can I ally myself with a force
powerful enough to make my brother – and all Hag
Graef – pay for the way they betrayed me?'

The daemon studied Bruglir in silence, folding his
clawed hands over one another like a fearsome mantis.
'Tell me. What form would this vengeance take?'

'With your leave, I would command a raiding fleet that
would sack the slave tower of Karond Kar, then cross the
inner seas and strike Hag Graef itself. There are hidden
tunnels that lead into the city – we could strike swiftly,
in the dead of night and put half the city to the torch
before anyone realised their peril! Think of it – we could
return with holds full of every kind of flesh to fill your
great cauldron and entertain you for *years*. We would
return with enough wealth to make you the undisputed
lord of the northern seas for a very long time to come.'

The daemon leaned towards Bruglir. 'And what do you
stand to gain from all this?'

Bruglir shrugged. 'The best is reserved for me, of
course. I see my enemies broken and driven before me.
I burn everything they hold dear and paint them with
the ashes. I hear their cries of anguish as I feed them into
your stew pot one by one. And I get to continue terror-
ising them for decades, taking what I will and destroying
that which does not please me. What man could wish
for more?'

'Indeed.' There was a wet, slithering sound as the chieftain rubbed his greasy hands together. 'And how will
you lead my fleet down the deadly straits and assault the
tower of Karond Kar?'

To Malus's surprise, Bruglir rose to his full height and drew a deep breath, evidently ready to launch into a long-winded plan that the captain must have been rehearsing for several days. He'd planned for everything, Malus saw with a touch of admiration. *I'd thought to kill you last of all*, the highborn thought ruefully. *Now, you may have to be the first, brother. My congratulations.*

Just as the captain began to speak however there was a commotion on the stairs. Malus turned to see the Norscan warrior advancing across the chamber at the head of a large band of Skinriders wielding swords and spears.

The alarm has sounded at last, Malus thought, reaching slowly for his sword.

'What is the meaning of this?' said the daemon, anger bubbling in his voice.

'A runner has arrived bearing news,' the Norscan said.

'And it is worthy enough to trouble me?'

'It is,' said a voice from within the mass of Skinriders. 'There is a druchii fleet approaching, aiming to catch your ships at anchor and burn them, then sack your tower and stake you out to die in the sun.'

A shock ran through Malus's body. Bruglir and Urial turned at the sound of the voice, their eyes widening in recognition.

'What of the great chain protecting the cove?'

'They meant for it to fall,' said the voice. The raiders parted as the speaker worked her way towards Malus and the rest. 'While you wasted your time talking to these liars, a landing party was to slip into one of the sea wall towers and lower the barrier.

'I should know,' Tanithra said with a cold smile. 'It was a task they entrusted to me.'

Chapter Twenty-Three
BLOODSTORM

TANITHRA STEPPED FROM the crowd of Skinriders, one hand resting on the hilt of her sword and the other dragging a naked figure by her long, raven-black hair. Yasmir was still gagged, bound at the wrists and hobbled by ropes around her ankles. Her lithe body was scraped and bruised from head to toe, but her violet eyes blazed fever-bright, tinged with fury – and a kind of fearlessness – that made Malus wonder how much of her sanity still remained. The female corsair was flanked by almost a dozen members of the captured ship's crew, their faces and arms stained with spatters of blood. Hauclir, Malus noted, was nowhere to be seen. Had he escaped the bloody mutiny or died with the rest of the crew?

'The Dragons Below take you, damned mutineers!' Bruglir took a step towards Tanithra, his sword glittering in his hand. The big Norscan and six Skinriders moved to meet the captain, ringing him in a half-circle just beyond sword reach. Malus turned slowly in place, sizing up the situation as the rest of the Skinriders fanned out around the rest of the druchii with swords and axes held ready. He bit back a curse, thinking furiously. The sea chain was still in place and time was rapidly running out.

Bruglir barely took notice of the huge Norscan and the Skinriders. His face was an alabaster mask of rage. 'I gave you a place on my ships and a life on the red tides! And this is how you repay your oaths to me?'

'You speak to *me* of betrayals?' Tanithra shrieked, her face contorting into a mask of near-bestial hate. 'I kept my oaths to you for *years*, commanding the crew of the *Harrier* better than any of your other captains. I tolerated your dalliances with this pampered witch–' she hauled Yasmir nearly upright with a savage jerk of her hair, 'and I waited for you to make me a captain, as was my right. That ship down at the pier was mine by right of blood, but you took it from me. You convinced me then and there that you weren't going to keep your oaths to me, o great and mighty captain. So it is *you* who are forsworn, not I.' She looked to the daemon towering from the charnel pit and nodded in salute. 'So I will seek a ship of my own with another great leader and buy it with your blood.'

Bruglir snarled like a wounded wolf and took another step towards his sea mistress, his sword trembling in his hand. The Skinriders growled in response and Bruglir's retainers took their place beside their captain with naked steel in their hands.

Malus hissed in frustration, casting about for some way to salvage the situation before everything spun out of control. He looked to Urial, but he had forgotten everyone else save for the pale figure in Tanithra's grip. Urial clutched his axe, his face stricken with fear and rage. His six retainers held their greatswords in their hands, waiting on their master's command. One wrong move, one hasty word and a storm of bloodshed would erupt. The highborn turned to the Skinrider chieftain. 'She lies, great one,' Malus said hastily. 'We've long suspected she might be an agent for the Witch King and now she reveals herself in an attempt to protect Naggaroth from your fleet.'

Tanithra threw back her head and laughed with bitter fury. 'You are slick as an eel, Malus Darkblade!' she cried. 'You've poured your poison in our ears all along, twisting our minds with your lies! But I was not the fool you took me to be.' Once more she tightened her fist in Yasmir's hair and gave her a rough shake. 'Did you really think I wouldn't see through your scheme to kidnap this wretch from her cabin? You thought to provoke Bruglir to kill Yasmir *and* me while you lurked like a rat in the shadows!'

Malus felt the hairs on the back of his neck prickle as both Bruglir and Urial rounded on him. 'Viper!' Bruglir hissed. 'Would that you'd died in that winter squall. You've brought me nothing but ruin since you stepped aboard my ship!' He levelled his blade at Malus's throat. 'The Darkness take your damned writ! After I've killed every last one of these mutineers I'll hold your beating heart in my hands!'

'*Silence!*' the chieftain thundered and Malus once again felt the daemon's will settle on him like a heavy cloak. Bruglir groaned, swaying on his feet and his sword fell slowly to his side.

Slowly, ponderously, the chieftain stepped from the pit, his raiment of soft, living skin trailing behind him like a noble's gown. He towered head and shoulders above every other person in the room, even the huge, axe-wielding Norscan. 'I see the truth of things now,' the daemon said. He pointed to Tanithra with a taloned finger. 'And I accept your service. Already you have served me well, druchii and soon you will enjoy the blessings of the Great Father. Name your reward.'

Tanithra smiled in triumph. 'There are seven ships and more than three hundred souls sailing into your clutches, great chieftain. Leave me just one of those ships – just one – and I will be content.'

The daemon hissed in pleasure. 'And you will accept the benedictions of the Great Father Nurgle?'

'Oh, yes,' the corsair said. 'Melt this scarred hide from my body, great chieftain.' She pulled Yasmir to her feet, glaring into the highborn's violet eyes. 'I'll wear this one's perfumed skin instead.'

'No!' Bruglir cried, his eyes wide with desperation. 'Spare *me*, great chieftain! Slay the rest – take all the ships and the men. I ask nothing from you and I can still deliver Naggaroth into your hands!' With an effort he turned his head to indicate Yasmir. 'She will be a sweet sacrifice indeed, great chieftain! A highborn woman, worshipped like a saint by my crew! Take her into your embrace!'

The daemon moved in a blur, lashing out at the druchii captain with a backhanded blow that flayed the skin from the right side of his face. Bruglir fell with a shriek of terror and pain and his retainers cried out in frustration and despair.

'Fear not, druchii. You will indeed deliver Naggaroth to me. You will sing to me its secrets as you melt within my grasp.' The daemon stepped past the stricken captain, its eyes focused on Yasmir. 'But you are right. I can smell the musk of divinity rising from her tender skin. I will save her for last and let you watch as she submits to my will.'

It was all spinning out of control. Malus watched Bruglir roll to his feet, skin hanging in wet, grey strips from his cheek and the bone beneath already rotting from the daemon's touch. His retainers struggled to draw their blades, their faces contorted with hatred even as the Skinriders standing nearby moved to strike them down. The highborn started to speak, thinking to seduce the great chieftain with promises of hidden treasure in the tower of Eradorius. But his voice was lost in beneath a wild roar as Urial the Forsaken hurled himself at the Skinrider chieftain and the killing storm broke in all its fury.

Urial slashed one-handed at the chieftain, but the axe blade had tasted little in the way of blood or magic so the attack was awkward and weak. The chieftain recoiled from the gleaming blade nonetheless and the Skinriders responded with shouts of rage. They rushed at Urial in a shambling tide, only to be met by the whirling draichs of his silver-masked retainers. The daemon hissed and spat words of fell power, causing Urial's axe to blaze like a brand and Malus felt the chieftain's oppressive will vanish in the battle.

Malus drew his sword with an ululating war scream and spun on his heel, slashing at the pair of Skinriders who were charging at his back. He caught the first man across the eyes, dropping him to his knees and knocked aside the downward-sweeping blade of the second raider. Knocked off-balance, the man stumbled forward and Malus's backhanded return stroke sent the Skin-rider's bulbous head bouncing across the cavern floor. The highborn stepped past the toppling, headless body and thrust his sword through the blinded raider's throat. The keen edge parted the spine and burst through the back of the man's neck, pushing him over backwards.

As Malus put his boot on the raider's chest and made ready to tear his trapped blade free a powerful sense of vertigo washed over him. His knees trembled and the walls seemed to blur. He heard footsteps behind him and the sound of steel slicing flesh and watched the ghostly image of his own head tumbling through the air.

Without hesitation the highborn ducked – and the world snapped back into focus as Bruglir's sword hissed through the air where his neck had been a heartbeat before.

Malus aimed a savage cut at the captain's knees, but Bruglir deftly parried the stroke and responded with a lightning-fast cut at the highborn's head. Malus blocked the stroke, just barely and threw himself into a powerful thrust at Bruglir's eyes. The captain batted the sword aside but gave ground, allowing Malus to rise to his feet and press his attack, aiming a vicious series of cuts at Bruglir's head and neck.

The captain's face was a creeping horror; as Malus fought he could see black rot blooming across the muscle and bone of Bruglir's flayed cheek. Already the captain's right eye was turning milky-white and the veins of his neck blackening with corruption. He responded with a feint to Bruglir's throat and a sudden chopping stroke at the captain's right knee, but the bent joint brought the blow up short and a sudden stab of pain from his wounded leg caused him to stumble. The blow glanced from Bruglir's armour and Malus was left unbalanced and off-guard, his neck exposed to the captain's sword. A chill raced down his spine as Malus waited for the blow to fall, but a thunderous clash of steel caused the highborn to look up just as the Norscan's heavy axe crashed into the back of the druchii captain's shoulder. The blow spun Bruglir half around, tearing through the straps of his left pauldron and causing the armour plate to flap loose like a broken hinge.

Bruglir roared in pain – a cry tinged with madness and fear and aimed a backhanded stroke for the Norscan's neck. The warrior caught the blade on the haft of his axe and pressed downwards, forcing the blade to the floor. His left hand shot out and closed around Bruglir's throat, the muscles on the back of his skinless hand standing out like steel cords as he squeezed the life from the wounded captain. One of Bruglir's retainers leapt at the Skinrider, stabbing into his shirt of heavy mail, but the huge warrior slashed upwards with his axe and smashed the blade into the retainer's face. Blood and bone splattered in all directions and the druchii fell with a strangled cry.

Malus lunged forward with a shout, swinging his sword in a short arc that severed the Norscan's hand at the wrist. Dark blood sprayed over Bruglir and Malus both and the Skinrider reeled backwards with an anguished roar. The Norscan swung his axe one-handed at Malus, forcing him to dodge backwards, then the highborn twisted to parry a thrust from Bruglir that narrowly missed his throat. Malus stabbed once again at Bruglir's ruined face and was surprised when the point scored muscle and bone just beneath the captain's milky eye. The captain screamed in shock and pain and fell back and the highborn slashed wildly at the Norscan, raking his blade across the warrior's mail shirt.

Despite his terrible injuries, Bruglir's ferocity and skill were barely diminished. He pivoted slightly until he could see Malus with his left eye and aimed a series of punishing blows at the highborn, battering aside his guard and making a ragged cut across Malus's neck. Before Malus could respond the Norscan lunged at him from the right with an overhead blow that the highborn barely knocked aside.

Thinking quickly, Malus feinted with a thrust to the Norscan's eyes, then lunged between the two attackers and towards Bruglir, aiming a blow at the captain's left side. Bruglir pivoted to keep his good eye on Malus, his breath coming now in wheezing gasps – and the Norscan's axe blow, aimed at Malus, struck the captain in the back of the head instead. Bruglir stiffened, his head haloed for a single moment in a corona of bright red, then collapsed to the ground.

The Skinrider cursed, trying to pull the axe free one-handed and Malus turned and swung his sword down in a single motion, cutting off the warrior's axe arm at the elbow. The Norscan roared in fear and pain – until the highborn's next stroke split his skull from crown to chin. Malus pulled the pus-streaked sword free as the body crashed to the ground and swayed on unsteady feet, trying to look in every direction at once. Only a dozen feet away Bruglir's last retainer fought a desperate battle against two Skinriders; a rusty spear jutted from the man's shoulder and his left arm dripped long streamers of blood, but he fought the pair of raiders with berserk ferocity.

Urial and the daemon still fought, the former acolyte's axe leaving trails of molten light in its wake as it slashed at the chieftain. For all Urial's fury, however, the daemon's speed was fearsome – though its robe of flesh was tattered and rent, the deadly axe had yet to bite into the chieftain's rotting body. Urial's retainers had leapt into battle with the Skinriders and reaped a terrible harvest of ruptured bodies and severed heads. Now they fought a two-way battle between the surviving raiders and Tanithra and her mutineers. Two of the silver-masked warriors were already dead, pierced and hacked into torn mounds of flesh.

As Malus watched, Tanithra traded blows with one of Urial's retainers, her heavy sword almost a match for the fearsome draich the retainer wielded. The warrior stepped forward, bringing his blade down in a diagonal slash that meant to split the corsair in two. At the last moment however, she ducked and leapt inside the blow, letting it pass harmlessly to her right, then brought her sword up in a disembowelling cut. The retainer collapsed, clutching vainly at his spilled guts and Tanithra charged headlong at Urial, leaving Yasmir bound like a sacrificial goat on the cavern floor.

Malus bared his teeth in a predatory snarl and swung wide of the daemon and Urial, circling around to where Yasmir lay. He watched Tanithra descend on Urial like a hawk, but before the highborn could shout a warning Urial seemed to sense the corsair's presence and he turned with surprising speed, knocking her blade aside but then finding himself forced back on the defensive as Tanithra pressed her advantage, hammering at him with a non-stop rain of punishing blows. One of the silver-masked retainers abandoned the melee and ran to his master's aid – only to be seized by the possessed chieftain. The daemon's hand closed about the retainer's sword wrist and Malus watched with horror as the limb melted like a candle held to the flame.

The highborn fell to his knees beside Yasmir, gently rolling his half-sister onto her side. 'I'm going to set you free, sister,' he hissed into her ear as he worked at the knot securing her gag. In a moment the greasy rag was pulled free and Malus drew his knife, turning to the ropes binding her ankles. He could feel her eyes upon him, though she said not a word. There was a serene, passionless cast to her face amid the chaos and slaughter that Malus found both seductive and deeply disturbing. 'Tanithra's lies have doomed us all,' he continued, sawing carefully at the ropes. 'Bruglir is dead at the enemy's hands and the daemon rages unchecked.'

There was another terrible, bubbling shriek. Malus stole a frantic look over his shoulder and saw another of Urial's retainers dissolving in the daemon's hands. A draich protruded from the chieftain's skull; the daemon reached up with one hand and crumbled it in a rain of blood-red rust. Then Malus locked eyes with the chieftain and the daemon snarled a challenge, tossing the melted warrior aside and striding purposefully towards him.

Malus sliced through the ropes around Yasmir's ankles. He reached for her wrists. 'Sister, we're going to have to run,' he began and then a shadow fell over him.

He looked up. A Skinrider loomed over him, a bloody axe dangling in one gloved hand. The highborn's eyes went wide and he tensed himself to leap – until the raider dropped the axe and reached for the drooping hood. With one hand he pulled the slimy surcoat free and Malus stared in shock at the stained face of Hauclir.

The retainer hefted a stitched leather bag, like a wineskin, its rough seams dripping water. 'You're going to want to duck, my lord,' Hauclir said and flung the bag at the daemon.

Malus looked back at the chieftain. The daemon saw the ungainly projectile lobbed at him and caught it deftly with one hand. Smiling, the creature closed its fist, crushing the bag in a spray of water – and smashing the globe containing the dragon's fire hidden within.

In the blink of an eye the daemon was engulfed in a cloud of ravenous green fire. The sorcerous compound seethed across the chieftain's body, eating through muscle and bone as though they were old parchment. The daemon whirled, shrieking and beating at the hungry flames, but the dragon's fire was not to be denied. The surviving Skinriders fell back, crying in dismay as the possessed man let out a long, tormented scream and ran, leaving pools of burning fat in its wake as it hurled itself through the hole in the cavern wall and out into the open air three hundred feet above the cove.

'Blessed Mother of Night,' Malus rasped, unable to tear his eyes from the burning puddles of human tallow stretching across the cavern floor. 'You stole a globe of *dragon's fire?*'

Hauclir grunted, wiping vile fluids from his face with the back of his hand as he drew one of Yasmir's needle-like daggers from his belt and began sawing at her bindings. 'You had me stealing from Bruglir's brandy cabinet. Taking a globe of dragon's fire was much less dangerous by comparison.' He shrugged. 'I thought it might come in handy somewhere down the road.'

Malus shook his head ruefully and turned to reply as the last of Yasmir's bindings fell away. He caught a glimpse of violet eyes and luminous skin as she moved with the soulless grace of a hunting cat, rising like smoke between the two men and plucking her knives from Hauclir as though he were a child. The highborn looked up at Yasmir with a mix of wonder and fear, black daggers glinting balefully in the green light. Her face was serene, her mind lost in dreams of slaughter as she faced Tanithra's smoking form.

The druchii corsair stood less than ten feet away, smoke rising from deep wounds burnt by drops of dragon's fire flung from the chieftain's writhing body. She swayed on her feet, the last foe still standing in the bloodstained chamber and her sword was pointed unerringly at Yasmir's throat. Urial lay nearby, knocked senseless by a glancing blow to the head. He'd been less than a heartbeat from death when Yasmir had risen, drawing Tanithra's undivided attention.

'Ah, how I've longed for this,' Tanithra hissed through scorched lips. She managed a halting, hateful smile. 'Bruglir escaped me, but we'll dance, you and I and I'll make you pay.'

Yasmir said not a word. She opened her arms like a lover and rushed at the battered corsair, her black hair flowing behind her like a cloak of raven's feathers. Tanithra made as if to shout, raising her sword, but Yasmir flowed effortlessly past her guard and wrapped her naked arms around her foe. Tanithra stiffened, drawing a single breath, her eyes going wide as she looked into depthless violet pools and felt twin daggers slide beneath the base of her skull and into her brain.

Malus watched his sister stare into the corsair's dying eyes, watching the light fade from them and feeling Tanithra's death tremors on her naked skin. At last, the corsair's body went limp and Yasmir stepped away, letting the corpse crumple to the ground. Then she turned her gaze upon Malus.

For the space of a single heartbeat they stared into one another's eyes. Slowly and deliberately, Malus set his sword upon the floor and then bowed deeply, until his forehead touched the rough stone.

When he rose from his bow she was gone.

It was several moments before Malus realised the melee was over. Bodies and pieces of bodies were scattered everywhere. One of Urial's surviving retainers was checking out each one and killing wounded Skinriders with a stroke of his sword. The other silver-masked warrior was helping Urial to his feet; his face was smeared with blood and his armour was pierced in a few places. Bruglir's man knelt by the body of his captain, his eyes hollow with shock.

Malus turned to Hauclir. 'Where… where did she go?'

The retainer pointed upwards. 'She went upstairs like a puff of smoke. Hunting for more raiders to kill, I reckon. Those eyes of hers were hungry.'

Urial groaned as he was pulled upright. 'You looked into those eyes,' he said, staring at Malus. 'What did you see?'

The highborn started to speak, then thought better of it. Finally, he just shrugged. 'Plains of brass and rivers of blood,' he said. 'I saw death. No more, no less.'

Hauclir raised his hand. 'Wait. What's that sound?'

Malus looked to his retainer and strained to hear what Hauclir was talking about. After a moment he heard it, too; a chorus of piping wails, riding the winds above the sheltered cove.

'Horns,' he said. 'Our fleet's arrived and they're sailing to their deaths.'

Chapter Twenty-Four
ACROSS THE RIVER OF TIME

BLACK SAILS STOOD out in sharp contrast to the misty horizon, rising like upswept raven's wings from the surface of the grey sea as the druchii fleet bore down on the Skinrider ships nestled in the small cove. Malus and Hauclir stood at the lip of the ragged opening in the cliff side and watched the frenetic movements on the decks of the anchored ships as the raiders prepared for action. The huge, broad-bellied ships were not meant for cut-and-thrust duels close to shore; for all their seagoing power and greater numbers they were almost helpless in their present position, sheep before a sleek pack of wolves. Except, that is, for the sea chain.

Malus ground a fist against the rock wall. 'Surely they can see that the damned chain is still up!'

The retainer nodded grimly. 'Most likely they do and are expecting us to drop it at the last minute, the better to surprise the raiders.'

But it was the druchii who were heading for a brutal surprise. With the wind at their backs they would be forced against the heavy iron chain and pinned there while the stone throwers in the sea wall citadels would smash them to bits.

Careful not to put any weight on his aching leg, Malus leaned out from the cliff opening. Hundreds of feet below, he could see the abandoned village near the shore, now seething with bands of Skinriders who had answered the call of the horns. The highborn studied the rock walls to either side and tested the strength of the wind. Far below, in the open field between the village and the abandoned stockade, he saw a smouldering shape still licked with the occasional tongue of emerald flame.

'No climbing down this,' he snarled. 'And even if we could, the chain towers are at least two or three miles away. We'd never reach them in time.'

'Pity we can't ride on green lighting like the Skinriders can,' Hauclir said ruefully. He peered down at the smoking remains of the chieftain. 'Not that it seemed to work so well for him, mind.'

Malus stiffened. 'Not lightning perhaps, but...' He turned to Urial. 'We need to get to the tower across the cove. What about that spell you used to get us to the *Harrier*?'

Urial leaned wearily on his axe. The blood and magic it had drank was all but gone now, leaving the wounded druchii pale and exhausted. He shook his head. 'What I did was build a bridge,' he said, his voice little more than a whisper. 'I need a resonance with the destination. Last time I used Yasmir's connection to Bruglir to bridge the distance...'

'You need a resonance? A connection?' Malus limped quickly across the chamber and scooped a small object from the floor. He held it up, revealing a broken chunk of glossy brick. 'All of these towers are made from the same scavenged brick. Would that be enough?'

Urial closed his eyes, concentrating on the problem. 'Perhaps,' he said at length. 'Yes, it's possible. But I would also need a frame – an enclosed circle that we could step through.'

Malus frowned, his gaze sweeping the room. Finally he pointed to the opening in the cliffside. 'Use that. And do it quickly – time is running out.'

Urial studied the irregular opening, his expression uncertain. 'The geometries are poor,' he said. 'I cannot guarantee the spell will work. If it fails, you will step through and plummet to your death.'

'The alternative is to be marooned here!' Malus snapped. 'The Skinriders will sink or capture every ship in the fleet – worse, they will kill every druchii the sharks don't get to first. We have no other choice.'

Faced with the alternatives, Urial nodded quickly and snapped orders to his surviving men, then limped to the opening. The retainers rooted through the bodies until they found the severed head of the Norscan warrior and brought it to their lord. Urial took the grisly trophy, inspected it like a servant buying a melon at market, then used his axe to split the skull in half and tossed the lower section aside. Then he passed the axe reverently to one of the retainers and went to work, dipping his fingers in the Norscan's brain pan and daubing crimson sigils around the rim of the opening. When he was done, he held out his hand for the piece of brick; Malus handed it over and surveyed his meagre force. Urial's two surviving men were unhurt and despite having to conceal himself in the stinking surcoat of a Skinrider, Hauclir seemed none the worse for wear. Bruglir's surviving retainer had spent several long minutes whispering over the body of his fallen captain before rising silently and taking his place with the rest of the party.

Six men to storm a citadel, he thought. It would have to be enough, somehow.

Bruglir held the segment of the Norscan's skull in both hands and began to chant. At first, nothing happened. Then a single, trembling tendril of steam rose from the brain pan, flowing towards the opening as though drawn by the wind. The tendril waxed and waned in strength, spreading blood and brains across the pane of sorcery until a thin red sheen gleamed across the rough opening.

Malus frowned. Something didn't look quite right. For one thing, he could still clearly see the grey sky beyond the faint membrane.

'Quickly now!' Urial hissed, his voice tight with strain. 'I cannot hold this for long!'

The highborn felt a touch of dread. It was one thing to speak boldly of a blind leap to death or glory and another thing entirely to come upon that last, momentous step. Then another thought struck him. What if the spell was only an illusion? What if Urial saw this as an opportunity to eliminate him? 'Are you certain the bridge is established?' Malus said.

'Of course I'm not sure!' Urial shot back. 'Hurry!'

No time for doubt, Malus thought, drawing his bloody sword. If the spell doesn't work we're likely dead anyway.

Taking a deep breath, the highborn ran forward, gritting his teeth against the pain in his leg and leapt through the opening.

HE STUMBLED ACROSS a heaving plain of blood, under a raging crimson sky. Howls of the damned filled his ears. Malus looked over his shoulder and saw a black tower rising in the distance just before a wave of searing cold washed over him...

Malus fell, rolling across a rough stone floor littered with refuse. Hoarse shouts echoed around him, sounding surprised and angry.

The highborn rolled onto his back. He lay on the floor of a circular room, its stone walls slick with slimy moss. A crumbling stone stairway rose along the outside of one of the walls, rising to a partially-collapsed ground floor and an open doorway that led somewhere outside. Just a few feet away he could see a faint crimson oval shining in the dimness, wavering and insubstantial. The spell had worked.

Then Malus heard shouts and heavy footfalls and remembered that he wasn't alone.

He rolled quickly to his feet, sword in hand and realised with a start that the Dark Mother had blessed his audacious plan – he stood only a few feet from an enormous capstan, not unlike the ones used to haul in ships' anchors except that it was far larger. Massive links of rusted chain were wound around the huge wooden drum. Urial's spell had taken him directly to the sea chain.

The rest of the chamber was heaped with bits of broken wood and piles of rubble from the collapsed floor above. When Malus had arrived there were Skinriders loading rubble into a large basket suspended from a rope and pulley system running through the gaping hole above – more ammunition for the stone throwers at the top of the tower, the highborn surmised. Now the raiders had recovered from the shock of his sudden arrival and rushed at him with everything from swords to chunks of broken brick.

There was an electrical crackle and the thud of a body behind Malus and the charging Skinriders pulled up short at the sudden flare of magic. The highborn took advantage of their hesitation and charged at them. His blade flashed, slicing though the skull of one raider and he stepped over the corpse's body and swung at the next man in a single, fluid motion. The Skinrider blocked the cut and fell back with a startled shout, piling into the men behind him. Malus pressed his advantage, hammering at the raider's guard until he was able to draw the man off-balance and bury his sword in the Skinrider's neck. The keen edge split the man's spine and left his head hanging by little more than a strip of flesh and diseased muscle.

Dismayed by the ferocity of the highborn's attack, the surviving Skinriders broke and ran for the stairs, shouting an alarm to other men somewhere above. Malus chased them all the way to the base of the stair, then turned at the sound of a sharp thunderclap to find Urial and the three surviving retainers staggering over to the capstan. 'Look for a lever to release the chain!' Malus cried.

'No need,' Urial said wearily, pushing the retainers aside. He raised his axe over his head and spoke a word of power, then brought the blade down on the taut chain. Iron links parted like soft cheese and the unwound links disappeared through the feed chute in the wall with a thunderous rattle, followed by a churning splash in the sea outside.

Ears ringing, the druchii looked at one another, unsure what to do next. Hauclir blinked like an owl. 'Well,' he said. 'That was easy.'

No sooner had he spoken then the entire tower shook beneath a tremendous blow. A section of wall just above ground level blew apart, showering the druchii below with jagged stones and enveloping them in a pall of gritty dust.

Malus whirled, coughing in the dust cloud and heard something large slither wetly through the opening. Peering into the haze, the highborn caught a glimpse of two pinpoints of greenish light rushing at him and leapt to one side barely in time as a seething mass of shifting flesh landed in the spot where he'd stood.

The daemon was a pulpy mass of melted bodies, welded together by magic and supernatural will. Arms and legs protruded haphazardly from the pulsating mass; some hands still clutched corroded weapons while others grasped spasmodically at the air. Distorted faces gaped and moaned across the yellow-brown mass. As the highborn watched in horror the shape contracted, producing a head on top of a thick neck of maggot-ridden flesh that rose above the amorphous body and vomited a stream of brown bile at Urial and his men. Urial brought up his axe in an instinctive move and the arcane weapon blazed with light, deflecting the spray away from its wielder. Urial's two men were not as fortunate as their master, however. They howled in agony as the acid splashed across them, melting armour, cloth and flesh with horrifying ease.

Without thinking, Malus threw himself at the daemon, slicing a deep cut into the fleshy mass that oozed steaming bile but otherwise seemed to have little effect. The long-necked head, still dripping bile from its malleable jaws, snapped around and regarded him with blazing eyes. The creature's body bulged and long tentacles studded with jagged bits of teeth burst from the mass, wrapping around Malus's waist and throat.

There was a wild scream of fury from the other side of the daemon and Bruglir's man clambered *onto* the creature, running up onto the monster's side and swinging his blade at the towering neck. The thick cord of foul muscle parted in a fountain of acidic bile and the head bounced wetly across the floor. At that, the creature's entire body seemed to recoil, hurling the frenzied retainer into the air, then it gave a huge spasm and lunged at the airborne druchii with a giant maw like a frog snapping at a fly. It swallowed the man whole and Malus grimaced at the sizzling sound as the monster's stomach juices dissolved the man in seconds.

The highborn slashed his sword through the tentacles around his throat, the blade slicing through them like they were pliable vines. The ropy tendrils around his wrist constricted, drawing him closer to the monster. Malus saw the skin near the tendrils bulge and a new head began to emerge from the depths of the creature, green eyes burning with hate.

Gangrenous skin stretched like a caul as the head pushed free of the daemonic mass. Its mouth opened – and uttered an agonised scream as Urial buried his enchanted blade in the monster's body.

Sensing his opportunity, Malus reached forward and grabbed the taut tendrils pulling at his waist and used them to haul himself even closer to the daemon, thrusting forward with his sword at the same time. He stabbed the creature right between his fiery green eyes and a jolt like lightning shot up his sword arm, throwing him back onto his back. There was a hideous crackling sound, like popping grease and the daemon's fleshy body lost its stability, melting into a spreading pool of bile and rotting flesh. Staring at the ceiling, the highborn saw a pall of greasy yellow mist rise from the body – and fly like a tattered wraith through the gaping hole in the wall above.

Moments later a pair of strong hands grabbed Malus by the arms and pulled him upright. Hauclir was breathing heavily, covered in brick dust and bleeding from a cut on his forehead. The highborn jerked loose of his retainer's grip. 'Your timing could have been better,' he snapped. 'That thing nearly turned me into paste!'

'An unforgivable breach of duty, my lord,' Hauclir muttered darkly. 'Part of the wall fell on me and I selfishly tried to free myself instead of immediately seeing to your safety.'

'Just help me up.'

Grunting painfully, Hauclir managed to drag Malus upright. Urial was already staggering up the splintered stairway, the ichor of the daemon still smoking from the edges of his axe. The highborn pushed away from his retainer's steadying hands and started after his half-brother.

'What was that image that flew up from the daemon's body?' Malus asked as he clambered up the stairs.

'Something that ought not to be,' Urial answered, his voice troubled. He reached the open doorway and looked out over the cove. Malus reached him a moment later and took in the scene unfolding before him.

The sea chain had fallen and the druchii wolves were in among the herd. Six nimble corsairs – a seventh was sinking at the mouth of the cove, holed through by stones from the towers – slipped past the huge Skinrider ships, loosing their heavy bolts at point-blank range into the hulls of the enemy ships. The heavy steel heads punched fist-sized holes at the waterline of the raiders, opening their lower decks to the sea. The Skinriders responded with showers of arrows and bolts of their own, but their heavy war engines could not be brought to bear on the corsairs at such close quarters. Already two of the enemy ships were sitting low in the water as their holds slowly flooded. Bodies and debris already littered the surface of the cove and here and there Malus saw churning splashes in the water as the sharks began to feed.

'The butcher's bill will be steep, but we've a good chance of winning,' Malus said grimly. 'The confines of the cove favour us and Bruglir's corsairs know their work well.'

'No,' Urial said bleakly. 'We are doomed. Each and every one of us.'

The fatigue and fear in Urial's voice brought Malus's head around. He pointed a bloodstained finger at the outskirts of the abandoned village on the far side of the cove.

Malus squinted, trying to make out details of what was happening at the shore. At first he could make nothing out beyond a huge crowd of Skinriders – and then he realised that none of them were moving. They were frozen in place, as though held in the grip of an unseen fist.

Then he saw a flash of greenish fire among the raiders and realised what was happening. 'The daemon,' he said. 'It's using the Skinriders to make another body.'

Urial nodded, his expression dark. 'It shouldn't be possible. The spirit should have been hurled back into the Outer Darkness when its first vessel was destroyed. But something is allowing it to remain here, rebuilding its strength and striking at us again.'

'There are just the three of us left and my power is nearly exhausted. It will keep coming until we are dead and then it will slaughter everyone in the fleet. They'll be helpless to stop it.'

'It's the island,' Malus realised. 'The tower of Eradorius—'

The words died in Malus's throat. Now he remembered why the bricks in the citadel – and here, in the sea wall tower – looked so familiar to him. Moving as if in a dream, he knelt, groping among the broken bricks lying on the floor. He found one that was mostly intact and turned it over in his hands until he found the symbol carved in its surface.

Urial watched the highborn with a bemused frown. 'What are you talking about?'

Malus traced the incised symbol with his thumb, feeling a fist of ice settle in his gut. 'You recall I told you that I sought the Isle of Morhaut to find an item hidden in a tower there. The tower was built by a sorcerer named Eradorius.' He held up the brick. 'And the Skinriders tore it down to build their damned citadels.' With a sudden burst of rage he hurled the stone across the chamber. 'Who knows? It might have been nothing more than ruins for hundreds of years before the raiders even arrived. We'll never know now.' Or what happened to the cursed idol, the highborn thought. For the first time since Tz'arkan stole his black soul Malus felt utterly lost.

'What does that have to do with the daemon?'

'The tower was built to escape *another* daemon. Eradorius used his sorcery to create a sanctum that was outside time and space. He created a place that was a realm unto itself, separate from all the others.' He pointed outside. 'That daemon hasn't been hurled back into the Outer Darkness because its pull cannot reach him here. No doubt that's why it picked this island in the first place.'

Urial looked at Malus as though he were mad. 'But you just said the tower was destroyed long ago.'

'The tower stood *outside time*! It was set apart…' the highborn's voice trailed off as his eyes widened in realisation. 'Outside time. Of course. It's on the shore of the river!'

Hauclir clambered up beside Malus and peered carefully into his eyes. 'I think you need to sit down, my lord,' he said warily. 'You may have taken a hard knock to your head.'

Malus pushed the retainer away. 'The tower was placed in a realm beyond the reach of time and space. It still exists in a sense – and the idol is still there.' He reached for Urial. 'When we crossed from the chieftain's citadel to here, you saw the red plain? The tower on the horizon?'

'You think that was the tower you speak of?'

'Yes!' He paced up and down, one finger tapping meditatively at his chin. 'It was all there, right in front of me all along! Why didn't I realise it before?' He turned back to Urial. 'You have to use your sorcery to send me there. Now.'

'But… but the resonance…'

Malus gestured at the scattered bricks. 'We have all the resonance we need!'

Urial shook his head. 'You don't understand. The… place you're speaking of is not of this world. It sits on a nether plane, if you will, rather than sitting at the other end.' He paused, his face suddenly weary. 'I can open a door and send you through, but it will have to be held open on this side for you to return through. And I don't know how long I can hold such a portal open. If it fails, you will be trapped there for all time.'

'And how is that any worse than being eaten alive by that vile thing?' Malus pointed to the distant village, where the daemon was still consuming the Skinriders. 'Open the gate! I'll take my chances on the other side. If I'm successful, the power binding the daemon here will fail and it will be drawn back into the Outer Darkness. It's our only chance!'

Urial seemed about to argue further, but one brief look at the chaos on the far shore convinced him. 'Very well,' he said hollowly and headed back down the stairs in search of blood.

'You mentioned an idol, my lord,' Hauclir said quietly. 'How will we know how to find it?'

'We? No, Hauclir. You're staying behind.'

The retainer squared his shoulders. 'Now see here, my lord–'

Malus cut him off with a curt wave of his hand. 'Be still and listen. You must stay behind to watch over Urial,' he said quietly. 'If he means some secret treachery I'll be helpless to stop him, so you must be the knife at his back. There's also the Skinriders.' He pointed to the upper floors of the tower. 'They may think us dead after the daemon's attack, but then again they may not. If they come down here you'll have to hold them off long enough for me to return.'

The retainer clearly didn't like what he was hearing, but there was little he could do about it. 'Very well, my lord,' he growled. 'And what if you don't return?'

'If it were me, I'd take my chances with the sharks.'

'You think I can swim to one of our ships?'

'No. I think you should jump in the water and hope the sharks get you before the daemon does.'

THERE WAS NO shock of icy cold or sense of dislocation. Malus stepped through the portal and it was as though he walked in the land of his nightmares.

The ground heaved beneath his feet and the sky churned overhead. The wind cried and moaned in his ears but he could not feel it against his skin. He looked back over his shoulder and saw the oval of pearlescent light floating in the air. Some kind of iridescent mist curled from its edges and somehow the highborn could sense how fragile it was, like a bubble that could burst at any moment. He could just make out the figures of Urial and Hauclir standing before the doorway; Malus raised his sword in salute and then turned his eyes to the dark horizon where the tower stood.

It was tall and square, its glossy black surface gleaming under the directionless light that permeated the nether realm. The tower seemed far more solid that the Chaotic landscape around it, like an island rising from an angry sea. From where Malus stood it seemed leagues distant. He took a deep breath and began to run.

The terrain flashed by beneath his feet. His weariness was gone and the pain in his wounded leg had vanished.

Then he realised with a start that Tz'arkan was no longer curled like a viper in his chest. The thought almost caused him to stumble. Was it possible, he thought? Could I have found a realm where he truly cannot reach, as Eradorius believed?

Laughter echoed like thunder through Malus's body, loud enough to send a tremor through his bones. 'Foolish little druchii,' the daemon said. 'Look at your hands.'

Malus stopped. With a growing sense of dread he held up his hand and saw the dark grey skin and pulsing black veins writhing like worms at his wrist. His nails, not quite talons, were black and sharp.

The strength he felt was Tz'arkan's. The daemon hadn't disappeared – only spread through every part of his body, rushing through him like blood.

'You see,' the daemon said. 'Here I am suspended between your pitiful world and the storms of Chaos that empower me.' Tz'arkan's awareness rumbled through him. 'I could never have reached this place from my prison – you were *my* bridge, in a sense.' The daemon chuckled. 'Yes. This place pleases me. I could remain here for a very long time.'

Malus fought to suppress a surge of terror. 'And trade one prison for another? Let's just get the damned idol and be done with it.'

'Why, Malus, if I didn't know any better I would think you were tiring of my company.'

The highborn ran on.

THE GHOSTS OF his dreams awaited him in the shadow of the tower.

They clawed their way free of the clotted, bloody earth, reaching for him with clawed, bony hands, flailing tentacles or barbed hooks. Some were human, some elven; many were twisted monstrosities from some sorcerer's nightmare. They crawled, leapt, flapped and slithered towards him as he ran across the plain.

A skeletal human with white parchment skin and a mane of snow-white hair reached for his throat; Malus swung his sword through the wraith's head and the figure wavered like smoke. An undulating mass of blue-veined flesh slithered across the ground and wrapped a thorny tentacle around his leg; the needle-like spikes pierced layers of leather and flesh with ease, leaving his flesh icy and numb. He snarled and slashed downwards and the blade passed harmlessly through the creature.

'What are these creatures, daemon?' he said.

'They are the lost,' Tz'arkan replied. 'Beings who found themselves thrown upon the shores of the island. When they died, their ghosts remained. Now they hunger for your life force, Darkblade. They haven't had such a sweet morsel in a very long time.'

The skeleton's hands closed around his throat. Malus aimed a cut at its head – only to have a withered elven prince grab his sword arm and trap it against its armoured body. Something locked its jaws on his leg, biting through armour and robes. The cold was seeping inexorably through his body now, sapping his strength. He could hear his heartbeat hammering in his chest. 'What can I do to stop them?' he cried as he struggled in their grasp.

'Why Malus, my beloved son,' the daemon whispered. 'You have but to ask for my help.'

The ghosts pulled him off his feet. He fell beneath a sea of grasping hands and snapping jaws. A creature like an octopus slithered onto his chest and wrapped its tentacles around his face. Its jade-green eyes glittered with malevolent intelligence.

'Help me, damn you!' Malus cried. Tentacles pushed past his lips and crawled over his tongue. 'Help me!'

'And so I shall.'

A new wave of cold roared through him – not the icy touch of the ghosts but a flood of black ice that surged from his chest and spread through the rest of his body. Dark steam rose from his pale skin and frost crept along the length of his blade. The ghosts recoiled – all save the octopus-creature, which could not unwind itself swiftly enough. Its skin blackened and its eyes turned pale blue and it let out a whistling shriek before Malus struck it with his hand and shattered it into pieces.

The white-haired skeleton recoiled from him, arms raised as if to shield itself from harm. Malus leapt to his feet with a roar and slashed his blade through the ghost's chest. The body blackened in an instant and shattered as it hit the ground. The highborn caught the elven prince in full flight; he laughed like a madman and slashed the prince across the back of his neck.

Everywhere the ghosts were in retreat, receding from him like ripples in a pond. He slew a one-eyed bear, stabbing deep into the creature's flank and then ran down two human sailors who cried for mercy with faint, piteous voices as his sword severed their heads.

Just beyond the sailors ran a druchii corsair. Drunk with slaughter, Malus leapt after him, smoking sword held high. The corsair looked over his shoulder at his pursuer, his dark eyes wide with terror. Malus recognised the scarred form at once, but the withered face was a cruel mockery of Tanithra's fierce visage.

The sight brought Malus up short, reminding him of the reason he'd come to this cursed place. He watched her stumble across the broken land for a moment more, then shook his head and resumed his journey to the tower, more determined to reach the idol than ever.

Chapter Twenty-Five
THE TOWER OF ERADORIUS

THERE WERE NO high walls or imposing gates guarding the Tower of Eradorius; the single dark portal at the base of the featureless structure beckoned almost welcomingly to Malus. Only the invisible currents of power coursing across his skin belied the illusion of safety. The closer the highborn came to the tower the more he felt the warping presence of the power contained therein.

'Tread carefully, Malus,' Tz'arkan warned. This close to the tower the daemon's presence seemed to pulse within him, waxing and waning to the beat of Malus's heart. 'The most difficult task is yet to come.'

The highborn frowned. 'The Tome of Ak'zhaal says that Eradorius is dead.'

'Perhaps, but his labyrinth still remains,' the daemon said. 'Eradorius built a maze so subtle that he himself was trapped within it. Think on that and be wary, Darkblade.'

'Spare me your feeble attempts at wisdom,' Malus sneered, crossing the last few yards between him and the tower and stepping through the open doorway. 'A maze is naught but an exercise of the mind. Eradorius was mad. But I...' He fell silent, feeling a pall of dread settle over him.

'Yes, Malus?'

'Nothing,' the highborn snapped. 'I grow weary of your taunts, daemon. Let's see what secrets this labyrinth holds.'

Past the doorway lay a short corridor that led to a space Malus first took to be an open-air gallery of some kind. Diffuse green light permeated the interior of the tower, seeming to come from every direction at once. Sword ready, the highborn stepped into the chamber.

The room's ceiling was lost in a luminous emerald haze. The highborn saw three doors of dark wood, one to the left, one to the right and one directly ahead of him. Door rings of polished silver gleamed in the light. Malus regarded each one in turn. As he did, he could not shake the sensation he was being watched, but he could not pinpoint its source.

'The doors are identical,' he said at last. 'No markings, no tell-tale footprints in the dust. Nothing to show the proper path.'

'All paths lead to the centre of the labyrinth,' the daemon whispered. 'As you said, it isn't a test of the feet, but of the mind. Are you certain you are ready to follow it to its conclusion? This maze is *aware*, Darkblade. It studies you even as you study it. And it will destroy you if you let it.'

The highborn laughed coldly. 'If I *let* it? What sort of devious trap is that?'

'Why, the very worst kind,' the daemon said, but Malus was no longer listening. Acting on impulse, he crossed the room in three quick strides and pulled open the door opposite the one he came in.

Beyond was nothing but utter blackness, an emptiness so deep it pulled at him, drawing him into its all-encompassing embrace. Malus felt a cold wind on his face and he plummeted into blackness.

A soft weight pressed against his side. Arms enclosed his chest, rising and falling with the rhythm of his breath. Malus started, sitting bolt upright amid a tangle of silken sheets.

The air was cool and fragrant with incense. The bed was low and broad, built for a druchii's tastes and surrounded by layers of drapes to trap body heat. Through the sheer drapes Malus could see an arch of pale light opposite the foot of the bed. All else was plunged into shadow; the woman by his side moaned softly in her sleep and rolled languidly onto her back. The faint light limned a bare shoulder and part of one alabaster cheek. Her lips were strikingly red, as though painted with fresh blood.

Malus reeled from the sight, stumbling awkwardly from the bed and landing naked on the dark slate floor. The icy shock of the cold tiles brought everything into sharp focus: he was in a richly-appointed bedroom somewhere in Naggaroth. How else to explain the furnishings, or the grey slate tiles, or the peculiar quality of the light streaming in through the drapes across the room?

The highborn's eye caught a hint of movement in one of the chamber's shadowy corners. He looked about hurriedly for a weapon and saw his swords draped across an expensive divan near the bed. The sword rasped icily from its scabbard as he launched himself across the room towards the source of the movement. For a fleeting instant he thought he saw the shape of a hooded figure, little more than a deeper shadow among the dark folds of the hanging drapes, but when he reached the corner there was no one there. Malus probed the heavy drapes with the point of his blade, but no one lurked within their depths.

Malus turned back to the bed dominating the large room, unable to shake a strange feeling of foreboding. Without thinking, he crossed to a nearby table and plucked a goblet of wine from a silver tray. He'd set the wine there just before bed; he could remember it clearly, as though he'd done it only moments before, but the very act of touching it felt wrong somehow.

'Come back to bed, you scoundrel,' the woman said, her voice sending a shiver down his spine. 'I'm cold.'

He could think of nothing he wanted more than to return to her side and breathe the scent of her creamy skin – but even that held an undercurrent of foreboding that he couldn't explain. 'I... I thought I saw something.'

To his surprise, she laughed at the thought. 'Are you jumping at shadows? Here in the Vaulkhar's tower? Even the Drachau is not so well protected as you now.'

Malus froze, the goblet half-raised to his lips. 'What did you say?'

He heard her turn onto her side, silk rippling across her bare skin. 'Not even the Drachau is as well protected as you are. Surely you realise this? No one else would dare move against you now. Isn't that what you've been working towards all these years?'

Malus carefully set the goblet on the tray, fearful that it would drop from his nerveless fingers. Moving as though in a dream, he walked to the window opposite the bed and pulled the heavy drapes aside.

Watery grey light flooded into the room. Beyond the narrow window Malus saw the blade-like central spire of the Drachau's citadel. It loomed only a few storeys taller than the tower the highborn watched from – a cluster of smaller spires rose in a black thicket below, comprising the towers of the Vaulkhar's household.

He stood in Lurhan's tower, not his own. Was this the Vaulkhar's very bedchamber? His heart went cold. This was wrong. Terribly, lethally wrong. 'I shouldn't be here,' Malus said to the woman on the bed.

The light from the open window shone against the hanging curtains surrounding the bed, rendering them opaque. He heard her body whispering against the sheets and imagined her sitting up, wrapping one arm around her knees. 'You didn't complain last night,' she said with a breathy chuckle. 'What difference does one day make? Tonight the Drachau will put the hadrilkar around your throat and then this will all be yours in truth.'

She moved again and this time Malus saw the silhouette of her body take shape as she crawled closer to the sheer curtains. 'I doubt anyone will gainsay your taking ownership of Lurhan's possessions a day early,' she said. The curtains parted and he saw her, outlined in pale sunlight. She reached for him with a slim hand.

Malus felt his mouth go dry. Terror and longing seized him with equal strength. Desire raced along his nerves like fire. 'My brothers will kill me for this,' was all he could manage to say.

Her violent eyes regarded him quizzically. 'Your brothers? They wouldn't dare,' she said with a laugh. 'You were the one Lurhan chose above all the rest.' She smiled, her red lips pouting wryly. 'And to the victor go the spoils.'

Malus's hands ached. He looked over to see his fist clutching the thick drapes in a white-knuckled grip. Terror washed through him in waves, even as a part of him reacted to her words with insatiable lust. He took a step, then another and then he was running across the room, reaching for the gleaming silver ring set into the dark-panelled door to the left of the bed. She called after him as he pulled the door wide, sending a spear of longing through him as he plunged into the darkness on the other side.

HE SMELLED BLOOD and the stink of ruptured bodies.

The chamber was close and hot with the presence of so many bodies, living and unliving. Sorcerous fire boiled from the broken vessel of a witchlight high on one wall of the hexagonal room. Broken by a flung missile in the furious battle, the wild flames set monstrous shadows capering across the smooth walls.

Uthlan Tyr lay on his back, his sightless eyes staring towards the ceiling as the last of his life blood pumped from the terrible wound in his chest. His sword dangled from one half-open hand. Malus looked down on the Drachau and felt a hot rush of triumph mingled with fear. The Drachau's servants and retainers lay scattered about the room; Malus's retainers had taken them entirely by surprise, hacking them apart in an explosion of carefully planned violence. Tyr and his men never stood a chance.

There was a sound permeating the thick walls of the chamber – it was the muffled voices of a thousand noble throats, rising and falling like the surf. In the centre of the room stood a suit of elaborate plate armour on a stand of blooded oak. Silar Thornblood and Arleth Vann waited by the harness, their faces splashed with gore and their eyes alight with the heady rush of battle.

Malus wore simple robes and an unadorned kheitan. There was no hadrilkar around his neck, nor was there the familiar weight of a pair of swords at his hip. Greenish light played on the razor-edge of the blade in the Drachau's stiffening hand. Without thinking he reached for it, but a voice cut through the thick air, bringing him up short.

'Do not touch the Drachau's sword,' the voice said. It was deep and even, surprisingly calm in a room that reeked of the battlefield. 'Take nothing from him nor let his blood stain your clothes, or the ancient armour will consume you.'

Malus turned at the voice. A hooded figure stood by his side, his form concealed beneath heavy black robes. An aura of icy power radiated from the man, taking the highborn aback. He began to ask the man who he was, but an all-too-familiar sense of foreboding made him pause. The figure turned to regard him, the cold voice washing over him from the blackness beneath the hood. 'Your triumph is not yet complete, Vaulkhar. The highborn of Hag Graef await. Don the armour and accept their fealty and then no one will be able to challenge your rule.'

The highborn turned back to the ornate harness. On a nearby stand rested the great enchanted draich that the Drachau carried during the ritual of the Hanil Khar. All at once he knew where he was – how many times had he dreamt of this very moment? How often had he languished in his tower and planned how he would seize the city for himself in the fullness of time?

Fear gripped him. He looked back at the hooded figure. 'Am I dreaming?'

'Ask the Drachau if this is a dream,' the figure replied. 'No doubt he wishes it were so.' The figure stepped closer. 'This is real. You have made it so, Malus. Do you doubt yourself now, on the verge of your greatest triumph?'

The highborn took a deep breath, trying to master the doubts that threatened to overwhelm him. What had the hooded man said that had frightened him so? Something about time?

He knew what awaited him. Once he donned the armour the highborn of the city would bow before him as their Drachau and offer their yearly fealty to him, thinking he was Uthlan Tyr. Once the oaths were sworn, they would belong to him and his usurpation would be complete. With dreamlike languor he stepped to the arming stand and let his retainers begin fitting the harness to his body. Each piece that locked into place sent a thrill of power tingling along his skin.

Malus longed to surrender himself to the feeling of that power, but part of his mind shrank from it. He tried to focus on what was wrong, but realisation eluded him, slipping like quicksilver through his grasp. As they fitted the ornate breastplate into place he turned and looked back at the way he'd come.

Just as he did so Malus caught sight of another hooded figure – this one wearing robes and an indigo-dyed kheitan – who stepped back into the darkness beyond the doorway. A frisson of pure terror struck him like a knife. 'There!' he said, pointing at the archway 'A man skulking at the threshold!'

Arleth Vann rushed silently to the doorway, knives glinting in his hands. He peered into the darkness. 'There's no one there, my lord,' he said, shaking his head.

'There was a man, damn you! I saw him with my own eyes!' Malus's hand clenched into a fist. 'He saw... he saw everything!' He *knows*, Malus thought fearfully. He knows I'm not who they think I am. The realisation made his blood run cold. 'We have to stop him.'

As he spoke he felt Silar slide the vambraces onto his arms and lock them in place. Then came the helm, settling like a crown of ice onto his brow. The hooded figure stepped forward, holding up a curved piece of silver steel. 'Put on the mask,' the figure said. 'Wear it and no one will know.'

Malus felt the mask lock into position over his face. His breath rumbled through the mask's vents and steam rose before his eyes. Heat suffused his limbs and the air around him took on a crimson sheen. Once again, he felt a surge of power so sweet his body ached in response, but at the same time he felt cruelly exposed.

The hooded figure turned, gesturing towards a narrow staircase that curved along the wall and rose into darkness. Malus moved to the steps, dimly aware of his retainers bowing their heads in supplication as he passed. High above waited the dais and the great throne where he would preside over the unknowing throng and accept their devotion. Unbidden, his feet began to climb the steps. The muted roar of the assembled throng called to him, promising him power and glory – everything he had craved for so long.

So long, he thought. So much time.

Malus stopped. 'Time,' he said to himself. He looked back at the hooded figure on the steps behind him. 'This is an illusion.'

'Time is an illusion, Malus,' the hooded figure replied. 'You have crossed the river and stand upon its shore, remember?'

The highborn shook his head, forcing himself to remember through sheer effort of will. 'This isn't real. This isn't really happening. I'm lost in the labyrinth.'

'You are wrong,' the hooded one said. 'This is entirely real. You made this happen, Malus. Is this not what you always wanted, deep in the darkest places of your heart?'

The highborn staggered, falling back against the hard-edged steps. 'Yes,' he said, the word rumbling from the mask. 'Is this my future?' he whispered. 'Does this glory await me in years to come?'

For a moment the figure regarded him in silence. 'All this and more.' The figure pointed past Malus, to an opening at the top of the stairs. Blackness lay beyond. 'Go forth and claim your destiny,' he said.

The roar of the throng washed over him, tugging at his soul. Malus let himself be pulled along, climbing the stairs into the darkness.

THE HEAVY FLAPS of the tent fell away from his armoured form and Malus stepped into the cool, salt air. Rising before him were the tall cliffs of Ulthuan and a forest of spikes rose from the sloping ground in between. More than five thousand elven warriors writhed on those gore-stained spikes, singing a chorus of agony to the fire-tinged sky. The sight staggered him; it was breathtaking in its glory. For a moment he was overwhelmed at the vista of torment spread before him, but then, bit by bit, he became aware of the great pavilion, bordered by tall banner-poles bearing the colours of the Six Cities and the armoured champions standing guard around the tent. He looked down and saw that he wore the rune-carved armour of the Drachau and a shock passed through him.

This was his army. Naggaroth had marched to war and as tradition demanded, the Drachau of Hag Graef marched at its head. This terrible victory belonged to *him*.

Malus strode from the tent, his stride clumsy on the fine, white sand. As far as he could see along the curving shore there stretched the largest druchii army he had ever seen. Thousands upon thousands of warriors, all busy at their tasks preparing for the next battle ahead – every one serving at his whim. 'Blessed Mother,' he breathed. 'Let this all be true.'

'It is,' a familiar voice said behind him.

Malus turned. The hooded figure stood some distance away. 'Why do you show me these things?' the highborn asked.

'I? No. This is your doing. These are the truths the labyrinth has revealed to you.'

The highborn took a step forward. 'So you admit it! I *am* still in the tower and this is all illusion.'

'You are in the tower of Eradorius *and* you are on the shore of Ulthuan,' a hint of impatience in its icy voice. 'Time and space have no power over you. You see what your mind wishes you to see. No more. No less.'

'And what are you? Are you the guardian of this place?'

The figure made no reply.

Malus sneered at the figure's silence. 'Is this how you guard the tower's secrets? By plying me with sweet visions of future success?'

'Success?' the figure echoed. 'Do you imagine your tale ends in triumph, Malus Darkblade?'

Malus's sneer faded. Cold fear gnawed at his guts. 'What do you mean?'

Before the figure could reply the flaps of the pavilion tent parted again and Malus saw a knot of armoured men issue forth, their expressions grim. He saw Silar and Dolthaic among them, their faces bearing the scars of war, but recognised no one else. They approached him swiftly, their eyes darting this way and that. They have the look of conspirators, he thought, one hand edging towards the knife hilt at his belt. Yet what would it gain them to conspire against me?

Then he realised. When the armies of Naggor marched, they did not do so alone.

Silar was the first to reach him. When the retainer spoke, his voice was strained. 'You cannot put off the Witch King's summons forever,' Silar hissed. 'You must act, now, or all is lost!'

'Act?' Malus frowned. 'What would you have me do, Silar?'

Before Silar could reply, Dolthaic stepped between them. 'Do nothing rash, my lord!' he said. 'You have given Malekith a great victory today! He can't suspect you!'

The highborn's mind whirled as he tried to grasp the events unfolding before him. Suspect him? Did Malekith have cause to suspect anything? Yet even as he asked the question, the answer rose unbidden.

Of course he does.

Silar pushed Dolthaic aside. 'What does it matter if he suspects or not? After what you have done today the entire camp is offering sacrifices to your name! Malekith won't countenance a threat to his rule, real or imagined. When you go to his tent, you must be prepared to strike! Now, while the army is behind you! Think of what you might achieve!'

A riot of emotions raged in Malus's breast. 'Shut up,' he said. 'Both of you just *shut up* and let me think.'

His mind reeled. It's an illusion, he thought. It doesn't matter, he tried to tell himself.

But what if it wasn't?

He tore his eyes away from the pleading looks of his men, his gaze wandering across the crowd of armoured retainers – and just as he did he caught sight of the hooded man slipping away from the rear of the group and stealing silently across the sands.

'A spy,' he said, his eyes widening with shock. He pointed at the man. 'Stop him!'

Silar and Dolthaic turned, following the panicked gesture. Dolthaic looked back at Malus, his brow furrowing with concern. 'What spy? There's no one there.'

'Are you mad? He's right there!' Malus raged, but the men were blind to the retreating figure. Some kind of foul sorcery, Malus thought. He's watched me from the beginning. He knows my secrets and he's going to betray everything to the Witch King!

The shock of his fear hit him like a physical blow and he realised at that moment how terrified he was of having the glories he'd seen taken from him. And then he thought he finally understood the peril of the sorcerer's labyrinth. The guardian had made his deepest desires come true – and it was going to use them to destroy him.

Malus shoved his way through the press of men, drawing the knife from his belt. He stumbled through the ankle-deep sand, eyes fixed on the back of the hooded man as he disappeared around the side of the pavilion. The highborn bent every iota of his will into forcing his legs to work, gaining speed to keep the guardian from reaching Malekith's tent.

The highborn rounded the corner of the pavilion and caught sight of the hooded man again, now just a few yards away. He moved calmly and quietly, unaware of Malus bearing down upon him like a hunting hawk. The highborn's face twisted into a vicious snarl. The fear he felt – and the ferocity it lent him – was almost exhilarating in its intensity. You're not going to expose me, he thought furiously. You're not going to show me for what I really am!

He leapt upon the figure, knocking him down. The man barely struggled, apparently stunned by the impact. Malus rolled him over, pressing his knife to the man's throat.

'You think me a coward?' Malus drove the knife downward, feeling the hooded man's throat begin to part beneath the blade. 'You think me weak, a flawed thing like the rest of my family? How strong are you, then, with my knife digging into your neck?' He laughed wildly at the thought. His face was inches from the darkness within the hood. The man lay still, offering no resistance. 'Just as I thought. It is *you* who are the weakling! *You* are the coward, skulking and scheming in the shadow of your betters! Let us see your face, guardian! Show me your real guise, or must I drag your guts across the sand in order to compel you?'

The hooded man did not move. Anger flared feverbright in Malus's breast. 'Do you hear me, weakling? Show yourself. *Show yourself!*'

He ground the knife deeper into the man's throat. The very air seemed to shimmer around the form, rippling like a disturbed pool.

The knife in his hand wavered, swimming in and out of focus. One moment it was pressed to the hooded man, the next it seemed to be aimed at his own neck, as though he were standing before a mirror. He roared in anger, pressing the knife deeper – and felt the point an inch deep in his own neck. Warm blood ran down his throat, soaking into the robe beneath his kheitan.

Malus's vision swam. A wave of disorientation swept over him, then suddenly he was kneeling in the square chamber within the tower of Eradorius, surrounded by three doors panelled in dark wood.

He was a heartbeat away from driving his own knife into his throat.

The highborn fell backwards, drawing the knife point from his neck. Pain bloomed beneath his chin and the sensation was almost exhilarating. 'An illusion...' he panted, 'all... an illusion.'

A shadow fell over him. Malus looked up and saw a hooded figure standing over him, his face lost in shadow. His breath felt like a cold wind against Malus's cheek.

'Who is the coward now, Malus Darkblade?' the figure said. 'Who skulks and schemes in the shadows of his betters?'

For a moment, Malus was startled into speechlessness by the figure. A lesser man might have broken beneath the shock of the revelation he'd been given, but the highborn was sustained by the fire of the hatred still burning in his heart.

'Do you think to break me with but a glance in the mirror?' Malus rose slowly to his feet. 'Did you think I would die from the shock of my own ugliness? If so, you are wrong. I am not broken. I am not defeated. My hate is strong and while I hate, I live.'

Malus rushed at the hooded figure, grabbing a handful of his robe with one hand. 'You've held a mirror up to my face – now let's have a look at yours, Eradorius!'

The highborn tore away the robe with a convulsive wrench of his hand, revealing a black-skinned figure whose muscular form swelled before him until it towered over him like a giant. A lantern-jawed face leered down at Malus, smiling a lunatic grin full of pointed fangs. Green eyes glowed eerily from the almost-human face and a long dragon's tongue licked from fleshless lips.

'Clever, clever little druchii,' Tz'arkan said. 'But yet so very wrong.'

Malus recoiled in shock – and the daemon struck like a viper, his mouth growing impossibly wide as it closed around the highborn's head and shoulders and swallowed him whole.

HE LAY IN blackness, coiled around a daemon's heart.

The darkness around him was empty, like the blackness between the stars. Malus had never known such cold could exist – it sank into his body and sucked the life from it, spilling his living essence into the blackness like a wound carved into his very soul. The cold spread like death itself – no, not death, because to Malus death was a force unto itself, like a storm or a raging fire. This was *nothingness*, utter and absolute and it filled him with fear.

There was heat in the heart of the daemon – heat nurtured from the lifeblood of worlds. Malus pressed himself against that horrid, unnatural organ, forcing his cold skin into the slime and feeling the souls squirming within. Hundreds of souls, *thousands* of them, all frozen in a single moment of pure, soul-shattering terror. He felt each and every one, like a shard of razor-edged glass and he crushed them against his flesh, savouring their brief warmth. He howled in agony and ecstasy, propelled by the mingled passions of entire civilisations as the Drinker of Worlds consumed them. For one titanic heartbeat Malus was pierced by the collective madness of an entire people – then they were gone.

Then came another beat of the daemon's heart and *another* multitude of souls shrieked in transcendent agony. Malus howled in absolute horror even as he forced these needles of crystalline passion deeper into his soul.

Tz'arkan had possessed him – now *he* was inside the daemon, feeling what it felt as it looked out upon the raging storms of purest Chaos. He saw with the daemon's eyes as universes span through the ether, each one trembling with the dew of countless souls. He could feel each soul on each world in each universe, taste a lifetime's passions in the space of a single breath.

Tz'arkan moved among worlds unnumbered and Malus realised how insignificant he was before such power. When the daemon spoke, all of Creation trembled.

'See the power of my will, mortal, and despair. Give yourself unto me, and all this will be yours in return.'

Malus felt himself fraying beneath the sheer pressure of Tz'arkan's awareness. He was dying. He could feel it. And with that realisation all his fear simply fell away.

Go on, he thought. Destroy me.

The storm of Chaos raged around him. Nothingness ate at his soul.

Yet he did not die.

Destroy me, Malus raged! I'm nothing but a speck to you – wipe me away!

He hung suspended over the maelstrom of Creation… but still he did not die.

Is this some kind of trick, Malus thought? And then, he realised: of course it was. It was just another turn in the labyrinth, another gambit to break his spirit.

All of it was in his mind. He knew this. And if it was in his mind, Malus thought, it was subject to his will.

You had your chance, Eradorius, he seethed, summoning his hate. Now you'll dance to my tune.

Malus bent his will to the raging storm around him. Show me your secrets, sorcerer! Open your mind to *me*!

The highborn's will blazed like a new-born star in the firmament of madness and Creation collapsed like a bursting bubble. Malus fell into darkness, but his descent was marked by laughter, wild and triumphant.

Chapter Twenty-Six
THE IDOL OF KOLKUTH

THERE WAS NO ceiling. He was standing in the centre of the square tower, surrounded by staircases reaching up to galleries that rose as far as his eyes could see. It was a vertical labyrinth that twisted and turned back upon itself and stretched upwards seemingly without end. The tower had looked simple and straightforward on the outside, but the reality was anything but, shaped by the insane sorceries of Eradorius and the Idol of Kolkuth.

The maze of the mad sorcerer was revealed at last, stripped of its illusions but no less daunting for all that.

Gritting his teeth, Malus chose a staircase at random and started upwards. It was a narrow, twisting stair, without rails or supporting walls to anchor it, but the stone was steady beneath his feet nonetheless. It carried him up to the second gallery, then turned right, leading into a small room. From there, four more staircases climbed upwards towards the top of the tower.

Stay consistent, he told himself. These things have a pattern to them. Make the same choice every time so you don't lose your place.

He went to the very same position that the first staircase occupied in the room below and started upwards. The stairway climbed up into the diffuse green light – and ended at a wall. There was a moment of vertigo – Malus's head swam and his feet seemed drawn to the wall as if by gravity. He took another step – and walked out onto the wall. Malus blinked, unable to orient himself for a moment.

The light was streaming down on him from above. He looked up to see the galleries of the tower stretching endlessly overhead.

He was back in the room where he had begun.

'Blessed Mother of Darkness,' Malus cursed. 'This is madness.'

'You have never spoken more truly in your life,' Tz'arkan replied. If the daemon had any awareness of the visions Malus saw within the labyrinth, it gave no sign. 'The labyrinth is a reflection of Eradorius's own tortured mind. You will wind up like one of those twisted ghosts on the plain before you come to fully understand the maze and its maddened paths.'

'I don't want to understand the damned place,' Malus seethed. 'I just want to reach the idol.' He tried to think of the resources he had at hand. 'We need some means of laying a trail.' Yet he had no chalk or string to hand. Malus bared his teeth. 'Is there something you could do to mark our path, daemon?' he asked reluctantly.

'Nothing could be simpler,' Tz'arkan said and pain bloomed from the back of Malus's right hand.

The highborn cried out, raising his sword arm – and saw the black veins on the back of his hand bulge and writhe like river eels. The skin of his hand distended as one of the veins took on a life of its own, extending itself as a pulsing tendril and burying itself in a crack between two paving stones. The line grew taut, but Malus guessed there was more length to be played out, as though his veins were just one long skein of twine he could unravel as he walked. He could feel the entire length of the living cord, like an extension of his own skin. It was the most revolting, unsettling sensation he had ever felt in his life.

'I bet you never thought you had such depths to draw upon,' the daemon chuckled. 'We can unravel you for miles before you spill your organs on the floor.'

Cursing quietly to himself, Malus picked the left-most stair and started upwards once more.

HE COULD NOT tell if he had been climbing for hours or days.

Malus had made quite a few wrong turns at first, ending up in places he'd been before and using the cord to retrace his steps. Over time he'd grown sensitive to the feeling in the vein stretching out behind him and was able to sense when he began to turn back towards it. So long as he kept it playing out behind him, he knew he was making progress and so he slowly but steadily climbed higher up the tower. Already, the floor of the tower was many hundreds of feet below. He was making progress, of that he was certain.

Unfortunately, he was equally certain something was stalking him in the sorcerer's great maze.

He'd begun to hear distant sounds – thumps and scrapes, like something heavy lurching across the stone floor. Once or twice when his path took him near the centre of the tower he would peer down at the galleries below and would catch a glimpse of shadowy movement. Was it one of the ghosts from the plain, or did the tower have its own guardian to keep interlopers away from its innermost secrets?

Whatever it was, Malus had few options. He wasn't about to retrace his steps and try to confront it – that could well be what the creature wanted in the first place. No, he decided, if it wanted to stop him then sooner or later it would have to confront him and when it did he would deal with it.

It wasn't long after making the decision that he began to hear the sound of deep grunts and long, snuffling breaths, as though some huge beast was sniffing the air for his scent and loping along his trail. The sound came from every direction it seemed – above, behind, left and right, as though the creature were circling him in the twisted maze. Fighting a growing sense of uneasiness, Malus pressed on. The closer it gets, the closer I must be to my goal, he thought.

Then, without warning, he came upon a door. It was a simple wooden affair, but it was the first one he'd seen since entering the tower. Malus laid a hand on the iron ring and pulled it open – and heard an enraged bellow echo from somewhere behind him. Now we're making progress, the highborn thought.

Beyond the door was a room with another set of stairs – the sight looked disturbingly familiar. Thinking quickly, he picked one staircase and started upwards. It led to another door and room virtually identical to the one he'd just left.

In the room just behind him, something huge smashed against the door with a thunderous crash and Malus remembered the dreams he'd had of this very moment. Without knowing why, he began to run. As if hearing his hurried footsteps, the guardian of the labyrinth bellowed in his wake and the door behind him banged against its frame as the creature burst through.

Malus ran on, focusing on the tendril playing out from his hand and using it to steer his course ever higher. Thunder followed after him as he ran, the beast smashing aside each door he left behind. Whatever it was sounded enormous and powerful and filled with mounting rage. He'd have tried to taunt it if he'd had any breath to spare.

Suddenly the highborn swept through another identical square room and up a flight of stairs – and found himself once more at the rail of a gallery overlooking the tower's centre. He was so high now that the floor was invisible in the greenish light. The highborn was further surprised to see that only one staircase lay available to him and it led up. Sensing he was near the end of the cursed maze, he sped on, only absently realising that the sounds of pursuit had stopped.

The staircase climbed without support into the open air above the gallery, winding around and around as it led upwards to a central point. It ended in a landing and a pair of rune-inscribed doors.

At last, Malus thought. Grinning triumphantly, he grabbed one of the iron rings and pulled the door open – and a huge creature leapt through the doorway with a thunderous roar, brandishing an enormous axe!

It was the guardian of the maze, Malus realised, hurling himself backwards barely in time to avoid a deadly sweep of the monster's blade.

The creature was huge, towering head and shoulders over Malus. Its powerfully-muscled body looked brutish and human, but its skin gleamed like brass and its head was that of an enraged bull. The creature swung its axe in broad, powerful strokes, but compared to the druchii it was clumsy and slow. Malus let out a savage cry and lunged beneath the monster's guard, swinging at its muscled belly. Just at the apex of his swing, however, his hand was pulled up short – the cord leading from his hand was binding him. The blade struck the monster but the blow was weak and the keen edge glanced harmlessly from the guardian's side. It advanced on him, swinging its axe at the highborn's neck and Malus was forced to retreat.

'What are you doing?' Tz'arkan raged. 'Kill it!'

Malus planted his feet and darted forward like a viper, lashing out at the monster's knee. This time there was enough slack in the cord that the blow struck with full force – and rebounded with a harsh clang. 'My blade can't penetrate its hide!' Malus cried in horror. 'It's as though it were solid brass! Can't you do something?'

'It's all I can do to keep the cord from breaking!' the daemon answered. '*You* think of something!'

The axe sliced at him in a short, backhanded blow and Malus saw it coming a fraction of a second too late. It struck a glancing blow across his breastplate, but the impact threw him off his feet. For a sickening instant he plummeted through the air, catching himself at the edge of one of the stairs at the last moment. His feet dangled over the tower's central chasm and Malus let go of his sword and fought for purchase on the smooth stones with his hands.

A shadow loomed over him. The guardian stepped ponderously towards him, his huge feet picking their way through loops of Malus's living cord. The highborn snarled fiercely, winding a length of the cord in his hand.

'I've seen how well you fight, beast,' he said, watching the creature's movements carefully. 'Let's see how well you keep your feet!'

Just as the guardian reached him it stepped through a loop of living cord. Malus hauled back on the black line with all his might, pulling it taut just as the monster moved forward. The huge creature stumbled, arms flailing for balance and then with a despairing bellow it pitched over and plummeted over Malus's head and into the central chasm. The highborn let go of the cord and listened as the monster's bellow receded into the distance. By the time Malus had climbed back onto the stair and rolled, panting, onto his back, it struck bottom with a sound like the tolling of an enormous bell.

BEYOND THE DOUBLE doors at the top of the stairs was a small, octagonal room. Inside lay a complicated set of sigils inscribed into the floor, surrounding a stone pedestal. At the feet of the pedestal lay a skeleton, contorted in a pose of agonising death. Upon the pedestal stood an idol worked from brass, barely a foot in height.

The Idol of Kolkuth. Malus saw it and expected to feel triumph, but instead felt only a sort of weary disgust.

'All this blood and intrigue for a piece of brass scrap?' he said.

'Can mere brass twist time and space to its master's whim?' Tz'arkan replied. 'Take it, Malus. The second relic is within your grasp.'

Powerful energies throbbed in the air of the small chamber. Malus studied the skeleton warily. 'Is that Eradorius?'

'Indeed,' the daemon said with some amusement. 'So much effort to build a tower where he thought I could not find him. The madman built a maze beyond the ken of mortal men and placed an implacable guardian to keep it safe – but in his paranoid zeal he gave the guardian too much power and it not only kept others out, but trapped Eradorius within. Wondrous irony, is it not?'

Malus stepped forward, the toes of his boots brushing the outer edge of the sigil – and a powerful wave of disorientation flooded through him. It was as though he was a piece of wood tossed on a stormy sea – and yet at the same time everything felt familiar, as though he'd been here many times before.

Time and space, twisted within the arcane loops of the sigil, the highborn realised. Malus took another step towards the idol and his mind filled with visions.

He hung from hooks in the Vaulkhar's tower, delirious with agony.

He stood on the deck of a heaving ship in the middle of a fight, ducking at the last minute to avoid a crossbow bolt fired from a would-be assassin.

He stood in the middle of a swirling melee and narrowly avoided a decapitating stroke from Bruglir's sword.

All points led to this moment. Malus took another step and the visions continued, stretching past him into the future.

He raised his arms in triumph over a swathe of blood-stained sand, holding a druchii's severed head in his hands.

He saw Yasmir striding towards him across a bridge made of skulls, naked and luminous, her daggers glinting in her hands.

He saw a tower backlit against a seething crimson sky, besieged by an army that blackened the snowy earth and cried out for his blood.

Malus staggered, stumbling forward and the visions came more quickly.

He saw himself upon a throne of red oak with a Vaulkhar's torc around his throat.

He saw himself at the head of a vast army of druchii, charging up a road towards a waiting elven army with the high cliffs of Ulthuan towering above him.

He stood in the great tower of Naggaroth, looking out over a landscape full of darkness and storms.

The highborn's questing hand closed on something cold and hard. He plucked the idol from its resting place and there was a flash of blinding white light.

MALUS STAGGERED FROM Urial's portal into the midst of a raging storm. Wind and rain lashed at the citadel, howling through the hole battered by the Skinrider daemon. The cold rain felt like a blessing from the Dark Mother as the highborn fell to his knees. Steam curled from the seams in his armour and he gasped greedily at the damp air.

Urial staggered, his strength all but spent, reaching out to prop himself against a nearby wall with a trembling hand. Hauclir stood at the foot of the tower stair, surrounded by the bodies of half-a-dozen Skinriders. Blood and bile pooled at the retainer's feet, thinned by the driving rain.

Hauclir rushed to Malus's side. 'Are you well, my lord?'

Malus nodded. 'Well enough for now,' he said. 'How long have I been gone?'

'Only a few minutes,' Hauclir said, shouting over the wind. 'One minute things were the way you left them and then all of a sudden we heard this terrible cry and the wind blew up.'

'It was the daemon,' Urial said wearily. 'The magic surrounding the island has failed and the spirit was drawn back into the Outer Darkness.'

'What about the storm?' Malus asked.

'The world is reclaiming the island,' Urial answered. 'It is a storm of time breaking over the isle and everything upon it.' As he said this there was a series of sharp noises and a huge spiderweb of cracks radiated through the bricks that comprised the nearby wall. 'We'd best be getting out of here!'

The druchii staggered into the wind and spray. Outside was a scene of terrible devastation. The Skinrider fleet was burning or in the throes of deadly boarding actions with the survivors of the druchii fleet. Of Bruglir's seven vessels, only three survived and of those two looked too damaged to return to sea. There were loud reports echoing from the cove as the sorcery that held the Skinrider ships together began to fail, causing rotting seams to burst apart and masts to break from their mountings. On the shore a pall of smoke rose from the abandoned village as building after building collapsed under the avalanche of years.

There was a terrible groan from high overhead. As one, the highborn scrambled down the slope of the sea wall and found an overhang to duck under just as the citadel behind them collapsed. Ancient bricks exploded into powder as they struck the sea wall. A stone thrower weighing as much as a dozen men arced overhead and landed in the cove with a tremendous splash. Across the water there was another grinding roar as the chieftain's tower collapsed as well, spilling its contents down the face of the cliff.

As the last of the bricks broke apart or splashed into the waters of the cove the wind and rain abated, dwindling almost to nothing. Out in the cove the Skinrider ships were settling into the water as their holds flooded. Shattered hulls blazed across the length of the harbour, sending plumes of smoke high into the sky. Distantly, Malus heard the war screams of the druchii corsairs as they recovered from the shock of the storm and hurled themselves upon their demoralised opponents. The battle was over; now the slaughter and celebration would begin.

WHEN THE WIND shifted in the right way Malus could hear the screams of the dying Skinriders.

They'd taken a few hundred prisoners in the wake of the battle and the survivors of Bruglir's shattered fleet had sated their lusts for pain upon their enemies' already tortured bodies. Despite the popular wisdom that the raiders were beyond suffering, the druchii found ways to make the Skinriders suffer for what they'd done.

The cavern beneath the ruined citadel still stank with the miasma of decay, but Malus barely noticed. He moved across the cavern floor, picking his way carefully among the twisted bodies. Every now and then he could faintly hear the cries of other druchii sailors as the corsairs searched for their living saint. Urial remained convinced that Yasmir had survived the battle and would be found unharmed. The crew certainly believed him and that was all that mattered. When the corsairs weren't looking for Yasmir they were breaking open the treasure vaults deeper beneath the citadel and hauling chests of gold out into the light of day. Hauclir had taken charge of the recovery efforts, which were proceeding apace.

Malus knelt beside the body of a druchii in corsair's armour. The corpse was stiff, but the body had yet to putrefy in the cool air. He rolled the dead figure on its back, frowning when he discovered that it wasn't the one he sought. The highborn sat on his haunches, surveying the carnage. His eyes lit on another figure, this one closer to the sacrificial crater. Nodding to himself, Malus made his way to the body.

It had been three days since the battle in the cove. Since he'd emerged from the portal Malus's sleep had been free of portents. Now it was his waking thoughts that filled him with unease.

He reached the corpse and knew at once that he'd found who he sought. With a grunt of effort Malus rolled the body onto its back and considered it thoughtfully. After a moment he drew a thin-bladed knife from his belt and bent over the ravaged face. The razor-edged blade sank effortlessly into the loose skin. The highborn smiled faintly as he worked, making cuts with long, smooth strokes.

There would be a reckoning when he returned to Hag Graef, Malus knew. Lurhan would be furious when he learned of the death of his firstborn son. Bruglir had been the Vaulkhar's chosen successor, his pride and joy, but he was also a pragmatic man. Another son would have to step forward and take Bruglir's place.

The highborn set the knife by his side and lifted his prize away with gentle fingers. In a few months he would return to the Hag as a conquering hero and both the Drachau and his father would have to treat him as such. From there, the possibilities were limitless.

Malus raised Bruglir's face to the light and carefully laid it over his own. 'Masks on top of masks...' he smirked. It suited him well.

ABOUT THE AUTHORS

Dan Abnett lives and works in Maidstone, Kent, in England. Well known for his comic work, he has written everything from the *Mr Men* to the *X-Men* in the last decade, and is currently scripting *Legion of Superheroes* and *Superman* for DC Comics, and *Sinister Dexter* and *The VCs* for 2000 AD. His work for the Black Library includes the popular strips *Lone Wolves*, *Titan* and *Darkblade*, the best-selling Gaunt's Ghosts novels, and the acclaimed Inquisitor Eisenhorn trilogy.

Mike Lee was the principal creator and developer for White Wolf Game Studio's *Demon: The Fallen*. Over the last eight years he has contributed to almost two dozen role-playing games and supplements, including the award-winning *Vampire: The Masquerade, Adventure!, Vampire: Dark Ages* and *Hunter: The Reckoning*. An avid wargamer, history buff and devoted fan of two-fisted pulp adventure, Mike lives with his family in the United States.